Dear My:

The unli⬛⬛⬛⬛⬛⬛⬛⬛⬛⬛ Lydia Chin returns i⬛⬛⬛⬛⬛⬛⬛⬛⬛⬛ourth in S.J. Rozan's popular series. Rozan, known for the effortless way she spins a clever tale, hasn't changed her trademark style here. And it's a style fans and critics love. She has received the highest of accolades, including winning the prestigious Shamus Award for Best First Novel for CONCOURSE, making her only the second woman to win the award (Sue Grafton being the first).

In NO COLDER PLACE, Bill Smith goes undercover to investigate the strange goings-on at a Manhattan construction site. When the foreman is killed under mysterious circumstances, suspicions arise. With the always energetic Lydia at his side, P.I. Smith is hot on a trail that may just lead . . . to murder.

Aptly hailed as "an engaging, quixotic pair" by *Booklist*, the adventures of Lydia and Bill are ones you won't soon forget.

Yours in crime,

Joe Veltre

Joe Veltre
Associate Editor
St. Martin's DEAD LETTER Paperback Mysteries

Other titles from St. Martin's
Dead Letter Mysteries

Also by s. j. rozan

No Colder Place

S.J. ROZAN

St. Martin's Paperbacks

NO COLDER PLACE

Copyright © 1997 by S. J. Rozan.

All rights reserved. Printed in the United States of America. No part of this book may be used or reproduced in any manner whatsoever without written permission except in the case of brief quotations embodied in critical articles or reviews. For information address St. Martin's Press, 175 Fifth Avenue, New York, N.Y. 10010.

Library of Congress Catalog Card Number 97-16636

ISBN: 0-312-96664-4

St. Martin's Press hardcover edition: September 1997
St. Martin's Paperbacks edition: October 1998

10 9 8 7 6 5 4 3 2 1

For Umberto, Alessandra, Jurek, Tom, and
Gary,
who should have been here,
and for Tommy, who was

acknowledgments

Steve Axelrod, my agent
Keith Kahla, my editor
perfect as always, and once again gentlemen

David Dubal
because architecture really is frozen music

T. Michael White
who can tell a hawk from a handsaw

Betsy Harding, Royal Huber, Jamie Scott, and Lawton Tootle
criticism is the highest form of flattery

Robert J. Randisi
the best of all

Deb Peters
at Brooklyn H.Q.
Steve Blier, Hillary Brown, Julia Moskin, and Max Rudin
and what's more, baby, they can cook

Nancy Ennis and Helen Hester
still reading, after all these years

and, at the site:
John Addonisio, Sr., John Addonisio, Jr., Vin Barone, Peter
Beltz, John Chester, Shahir Erfan, Eric Hahn, Joan Hill,
Mickey Kelly, Mark Kitchell, Carl Koch, Jay Kurtz, Dan
Lusterman, Steve Morhous, Kent Nash, Jerry Quinn, Rory
Ronan, Nazar Saif, Alma Shomo, Carl Stein, Blaise
Swiatkowski, and Bob Walsh, not one of whom
is in this book

No Colder Place

one

there's no place colder than a construction site.

An ironworker told me why once, explained the chill that pulls the warmth from your bones while you're working, the wind that blows through steel and concrete carrying the ancient dampness of echoing caves.

He was a welder, used to working the high steel—two hundred feet up and nothing between him and the air above the city but the girder he was on and the harness that, half the time, he didn't wear. He had a leather face and scarred, thick hands. We were sitting over a beer at Shorty's one evening in that time of year when the end of the workday and the start of the night push on each other, when everything feels like it's already too late.

A building going up doesn't live, he said. It grows, like that monster Frankenstein built—hammered, welded, bolted together out of things you bring from other places, things that had their own histories long before they were part of this. It looks like what you want it to be, but it's not. Not yet.

And while it grows, it pulls a little life from each of the men who work on it, making them leave something, something they are, behind.

Then one day, he said, when it's stolen enough life, stored up enough history, it starts to breathe. It begins to live, and living things are warm. You can feel that moment. The deep chill goes, replaced by a cold that's only temperature, no different

from anywhere else. It's not a construction site after that. It's
a building, the past of its bones and skin part of it, what they
are making it what it is, old things in a new place. And the
lives of the men who built it giving it life.

I don't know if he was right or not. I didn't know him well,
and I didn't run across him again. He was getting old, and I
was young then. I don't know how much longer he had, or
wanted, working the high steel.

But I know there's a bone-chilling cold, and a sense of
never being alone in an old and lonely place, on every building site I've ever been on.

I felt it the first hot July morning I walked through the gate
onto the Armstrong site, into the noise and the dust and the
mud behind the wooden fence that wrapped half the block.
Outside, on Broadway, traffic flowed with a purpose, most of
it heading south, commuters getting a jump on the day. Grilles
still blanked off storefronts and the sidewalks were largely
empty, square rough concrete expanses like ice floes support-
ing, here and there, a sleeping figure drifting each through his
own wilderness.

The site, though, was jumping. Seven-thirty was starting
time and, though I was early, I wasn't first. A guy in a leather
apron hefted a stack of two-by-fours up a wooden ramp and
disappeared into the first-floor darkness. A pickup backed
beeping toward a jury-rigged truck dock. I looked at its load:
pallets of bricks. I'd be seeing them later. The crane operator
lounged drinking coffee in his cab, one steel-toed boot
propped on the open window. Soon, some crew would need
steel studs, sacks of concrete, a half-ton of mechanical equipment up on the eighteenth floor, and this guy would swing
into action. The right switch, the right lever, a gentle touch,
and he'd do what Superman used to do in the contraband
comics I stole as a kid: one man moving the weight of the
world, making everyone else's work possible.

That's the job Lenny Pelligrini was doing when he disappeared.

The building was going to top out at forty stories. It was

half of that now, the core sticking up from the center, leading the skeleton by thirty feet. Rising from the lowest floor
and encircling the building, the brickwork was going in,
starting late and low because the other trades won't work
below a mason. I shielded my eyes, leaned my head back to
stare at the stark lines of the highest steel, black against the
ageless blue sky.

I headed for the wooden ramp, following the carpenter.
Half a dozen steps into the site, over the scrunch of gravel
under my own steel-tipped boots, I heard a yell.

"Hey, yo! Hard-hat site! What're you carrying it for, save
your jewels?"

I waved an acknowledgment to the guy with the two-way
radio and slipped my hard hat on. I'd worked construction in
high school and college, and some after, but I'd been away a
long time. Once, I wouldn't have stepped inside a fence with
my head bare, any more than, now, I'd grab my revolver to go
cover an assignment without checking the load. Safety
becomes instinct; it's easier that way. I wondered what else
used to be instinctive to me on a building site, what else I'd
forgotten.

The dry gritty heat of the yard halted suddenly at the top of
the ramp as though it had tried, failed, and by now given up
any attempt to confront the chill and the dimness inside.
Caged lightbulbs strung loosely along girders led toward a
warren of trailers in the back, and I headed that way, smelling
the sourness of long-unturned earth. As I heard my footsteps
echo on the bare concrete, I felt that chill against my skin, that
old coldness, and I knew I'd forgotten that too.

Thick black Magic Marker labeled the plywood doors to
the contractor's field offices. Mocking the corridor-and-
apartment setup the finished building would offer, the half-
dozen cheap trailers faced each other across a cramped,
ceilingless DMZ. I passed Crowell, first on the left and
biggest, because they were the general contractor, running the
job, in charge. Mandelstam was next—plumbing—and across
from him, the masonry sub, Lacertosa. That door was standing open.

I knocked and walked in.

The guy behind the desk raised his eyes without raising his head. He had a lined, shadowed face, pale blue eyes, a pencil stuck behind his ear, and a pencil in his hand. Papers piled the desk, but neatly. His greeting, not unfriendly, was, "Yeah?"

"Smith," I said. "Union sent me." I showed him my union card, legitimate but less than twenty-four hours old.

"Uh-huh. Mason or laborer?"

"Mason."

"Uh-huh. Fill these out."

While I did the paperwork, he went back to his own. When I was done, he glanced over what I gave him.

"Why'd you leave Houston?"

I'd never lived in Houston, but that was the story. That was because DeMattis, who'd sent me here, had people in Houston and could cover the paperwork there, in case anyone got interested enough to run a check. And though my accent was Kentucky, it was faded enough from years overseas and up North that it could pass for Texas to any ears but a Texan's.

"Hadn't worked in a year," I answered.

He grunted. Hard-luck Texas stories probably didn't even register on anyone in construction anymore.

"Hope you stayed in shape," he told me, shuffling my papers. "You ain't young."

"That's true."

He looked up with a slow, ironic smile. It softened his face, made him look both older and kinder. "Me neither. Got bumped up to sitting on my butt just in time. Okay, your crew's on six. Foreman's Joe Romeo. He'll tell you when to eat and where to piss." He handed me a paper to sign and I signed it. "We're up against a schedule, but do quality, okay? Joints even, struck clean—you know the drill." He sighed. "Crowell's a pain in the ass, both of them, father and son. Old man don't get up on the scaffold much anymore, but Junior comes around bustin' nuts, so watch out for him. At least the architect's rep don't give us no trouble. Owner's a lady, by the way, and she comes around sometimes too, so watch your mouth if you can. Use the south hoist, north one's materials

only. Got a problem, see Romeo, then me. John Lozano, by
the way." He half stood and offered me his hand. "Smith, huh?
You a paisan?"

"No," I said, "I'm a mick."

"You're on the wrong crew. How come you ain't driving
nails?"

"I'm a spy."

He grinned, I grinned, and I headed back through the maze
of naked steel columns and dangling wires to find the south
hoist. John Lozano went back to his paperwork, probably
thinking that what I'd just answered him wasn't true.

I exchanged morning nods with the mechanic running the
hoist. Boring, but not a bad job, seated and indoors. They put
the older guys there, the guys with seniority, not ready to retire but not productive on a crew anymore. The hoist creaked
and grumbled as it hauled me up.

Once past the second-floor level I could see outside the
fence. The old buildings up and down Broadway, brick and
worked limestone, copper cornices and, on the one on the
corner, a frieze of terra cotta suns and lions, stared down at
this rising, muscular, unliving frame I was moving through.
Looking at them, the early shadows lying across their
facades, the sun blanking their windows, I had an uncomfortable sense of being surrounded by the smugness of dis-
appointed hopes. You think you'll be different, those
buildings seemed to say to this one. Bigger, stronger, better.
Young. New. We thought so too, once. But look, look now.
And you're not made of anything different from what we're
made of. You'll be just like us.

I turned away, faced into the site, waited for the hoist to
stop. I thanked the guy running it, stepped onto the raw concrete of the sixth floor and went to find Joe Romeo, the guy
I'd been sent to see.

Chuck DeMattis had sent me. DeMattis was an ex-cop, off the
job about four years. He'd gotten a P.I. license the day he'd retired, but unlike most of us, who work from home or out of

someone else's back room, Chuck wasn't interested in running his new business from his Staten Island address. He'd rented a corner suite in a new tower in midtown and moved in before the paint was dry.

"You wanna attract ducks, you put out a decoy and sit in a duck blind," he'd explained. "I wanna attract lawyers."

The building was a steel-and-smoked-glass office tower in the East Fifties, a single sleek box that now stood where a dozen brick walk-ups had been for a century, since their developer knocked down the farmhouse, dug up the crops, and paved the fields for streets.

The marble lobby was hushed and cool. The silent elevator whisked me to Chuck DeMattis's twenty-eighth-floor office in less time than I usually take to climb the two slanted flights to my own place downtown.

Chuck and I knew each other professionally, had thrown each other cases once or twice over the years. We weren't friends, not really, but it was mostly a question of style. DeMattis was a team player who liked to party and see his name in the papers. I keep to the shadows, quiet places where there's good music and you can hear yourself talk, if anyone's there you want to talk to. DeMattis wore Hugo Boss suits and alligator shoes and claimed he could reach anybody in New York with two phone calls, but it was his connections that stopped him on this one.

"Made sense they came to me," he'd said, tapping coffee grounds into the stainless-steel bar sink in his private office, all sharp edges and glass surfaces and wide windows filled with great expanses of city and sky. In the outer room two secretaries juggled the phones while a bookkeeper probably juggled the books. On the other side of the suite, Chuck's full-time operatives spent most of their days staring at computer screens and talking on the phone, the men in shirts and ties, the women in heels and hose, and all visibly armed whether or not they ever hit the streets because agents ready for hard action at any moment impress the hell out of clients.

Chuck was clean-shaven, balding, and brimming with energy and good-natured street smarts, at least in front of the hired help. He brought me a cup of espresso, rich and steamy and bitter, and told me why I was here.

"They need somebody to put a net over a guinea, they come to a guinea P.I., right? How's the coffee?"

"It's good, Chuck."

He beamed. "Always. My girls, they can type and shit, but if I ever get one knows how to make a decent espresso, I'm gonna divorce Marie and marry her." Chuck had been married to Marie, a cheerful, hard-partying blonde, since the day after their high-school graduation. He gave her, every year, a present to celebrate their wedding anniversary, and another to celebrate the anniversary of the day she'd said yes.

"You really come in from the country just because I called?" Chuck asked me, rounding his desk to settle into a huge, soft leather chair.

"I drove in this morning," I told him.

He shook his head. "You're nuts, coming back to this furnace if you got somewhere else to be."

"I don't see you sitting around your pool on Staten Island."

"You would if you ever came out like I invited you. But I remember about you; you're the one don't like people."

"Not people, Chuck. Sitting around."

Chuck sighed. "Yeah. Whatever. You're ready to work, I got this thing."

"Tell me."

He sipped his own espresso, rested the tiny cup in its saucer on the king-size glass panel that served as his desk. "Crowell—you heard of them, right? Big outfit. General contractors."

"Sure," I said. "You see their logo around town. They have a few projects going."

"Two right now," Chuck agreed. "One wrapping up, one about six months in. Which is probably about half the construction business in New York, these days."

"Times are bad in that business?"

"Money's tight, I don't know. It happens that way in construction, they tell me. You buy property, plan to build, then you get caught with your pants down when the bank rethinks its investment strategy, or whatever they call it. Anyway, that's what's got Crowell's balls in an uproar."

"What has?"

"They got problems on the one site, the newer one. Upper Broadway, Ninety-ninth Street. Forty-story residential."

"I think I read about it. Commercial on the bottom, and mixed housing?"

Chuck nodded. "Low, middle, and high income. For poor people, normal people, and yuppies. Whaddaya suppose is the difference in the apartments?" He furrowed his brow. "I mean, you think they got marble bathrooms in the yuppie ones and tile in the regular ones, and maybe outhouses for the welfare ones?"

"Bidets," I said. "With a lifetime supply of Perrier."

He snickered. "Yeah. Anyway, the developer's some black lady named Armstrong. Otherwise they might be having trouble up there, putting up even half a yuppie building in that neighborhood."

"But they're not?"

"Nah, the neighborhood seems happy enough. Crowell says they went out of their way to hire locals. And the building's supposed to be pretty classy. Good-quality materials, all that shit. Armstrong lady wants it that way. What the hell, she owns it, she can do whatever she wants. 'Course, from the way old man Crowell's sitting here telling me what a great job it is, you'd think he owned it and designed it himself, besides building it with his own hands."

"Old man Crowell?"

"That's why they call it Crowell. Dan Crowells Senior and Junior. Family business. Senior's been doing this all his life, though he don't get up into the buildings much anymore. Truth is, he's sick. Leukemia, something like that. I mean, he looked okay when he came to see me, but nobody, but maybe him, seems to think he's gonna live more than another year or two."

"He told you that?"

"Not a chance. I checked them out between when they called me and when they got here."

"What made you do that?"

"I always do that. Clients never tell you the stuff you really need to know. You gotta find it out for yourself. You must have that same problem."

"All the time," I said. "So the old man's sick?"

"Seems that way. And whatever he's got, it keeps him moving kind of slow, so he stays in the office pretty much now. Between you and me, I think it drives him crazy that he can't get around the way he used to, up and down the scaffold, showing the guys how you stick a rebar in the concrete, how you hammer a nail. That he has to depend on the kid to do it."

"Crowell Junior's the hands-on guy?"

"Coupla years out of college, was working somewhere else. Now I guess he thinks he's taking over. Looks a little soft to me for that kind of work, but like everything else these days, construction's more filling out forms and less pounding nails than it used to be."

"And they both came to see you?"

"Yeah, sure. Though I got the idea Junior didn't think much of the plan. While the old man's talking, Junior sits here rolling his eyes, coming up with reasons not to hire me. I didn't like it."

"That he didn't want to hire you?"

"No, that he was disrespecting the old man like that, in front of me. I mean, it's not like I'm their old family friend."

"In that case, it would be worse."

"Yeah, true. Anyway, he ticked the old man off, too."

"But the old man did want to hire you," I said. "Which is why I'm here."

"You're here 'cause you ain't bright enough to stay away. But yeah, Crowell's got a problem. They been having trouble. Times this tight, they had to shave their bid pretty close to get this job. When you do that you don't wink at shit you might've let go if you had a little margin to throw away."

"What kind of trouble?"

"At the beginning, some small stuff—you get it on construction sites sometimes. Some tools walking, some deliveries shorted. Then early on, someone stole a frontloader."

"Stole it?"

"Just drove the damn thing off the site at four in the morning. Security guy was snoozing. They canned him, of course. Anyway, Crowell owns their own equipment, they don't lease, so they took the loss."

"But they must have been insured."

"Oh, yeah. It was more of a pain in the ass than anything else. But something like that, it takes planning. So it started the Crowells thinking, and maybe watching the site more carefully than most."

"And what happened?"

"Nothing like that again. Small stuff keeps going on, equipment and tools disappearing. Like anywhere; you almost can't stop it. But now that they're looking, they see a guy they don't like the looks of. Name of Joe Romeo. Masonry foreman. They got a feeling he's into some bad shit."

"Like what?"

"Shylocking, bookmaking. Also they think maybe drugs, nothing big, just some weed, but they don't want it around."

"The thefts?"

"Probably not. They don't put it past him, but his movements don't correlate."

"I love it when you talk dirty, Chuck."

He glanced at me over the rim of his espresso cup, but let it go. "Anyway, Crowell'd like to get rid of Romeo, but the union takes things like that personal, unless you got serious proof. And Crowell don't want no union trouble. A strike'd kill the schedule, Crowell loses a fortune, which on this job they don't particularly have. This Armstrong lady got no use for bad publicity either; it's her first big building, Crowell tells me, and being black and a lady, there's a lot of people out there just waiting for her to fall on her ass. So Crowell's been sort of lying low on the whole thing.

"Then about two weeks ago, this one crane operator don't show up for work. Don't call, nothing. They call him, can't find him. They lose half a day with the crane, everybody's behind, guys are sitting around with their thumbs up their asses while they wait for another operator to haul his butt in from Queens. Crowell's busting a gasket. Romeo and this operator, Pelligrini, been seen in each other's company. Someone up there says they weren't getting along so well, the last couple days. Now, maybe it's one thing, maybe it's another, but Crowell's fed up. They want Romeo out of there.

"So they come to me. Because, see, I met Crowell Senior at some testimonial dinner for some guy the other week. You know how it is, you gotta keep schmoozing, you wanna stay in business. At this thing, Crowell's already complaining about his equipment and shit walking. I ask him does he want someone to look into it, he says no, it ain't worth it. But I give him my card, just in case. He says yeah, he heard of me, I'm famous." Chuck spread his hands, palms up. Being famous is something that just happens to some guys.

"So this Pelligrini thing," he went on, "I guess that's the last straw. They come to me. They're telling me, start from Pelligrini, go undercover, see what I can dig up. But come on, I know every guinea in New York. Can you see me undercover in a room full of wops? Now, Crowell don't care how I work the case. The old man says he don't need to know. I get the feeling he don't want to know, in case I find a way to deal with Romeo that ain't exactly kosher. The kid don't like it. 'You got to have more control,' he tells the old man. 'You can't not know what's going on.' The old man tells him to put a sock in it, that Chuck DeMattis knows what he's doing. 'DeMattis'll take care of Romeo,' he tells him. 'You worry about getting the building built.' So I think about it for a while, and I figure as long as Crowell's letting me do this any way I want, I'll give you a call."

"What about your operatives?" I asked. "You have about two hundred guys who work for you."

"I got fourteen, and between you and me, buddy, they're the Stick-Up-the-Ass Squad. College boys. They're good investigators, make a good impression on clients, can follow a hell of a paper trail, but send 'em undercover to drink with a mason? Hah."

He stopped for some more espresso. "You, it's different,"

he said. "We could set you up, just some guy, nobody knows the difference. Whaddaya say?"

"I've been to college, Chuck."

"Yeah, me too, but on us it don't show." Chuck said this as though he were reassuring me that neither of us looked our age.

"Well," I said, "what's the gag?"

"Depends. I was thinking we find out where Romeo drinks, whatever, you move in on him, get to be his new best friend." He winked.

"And the point?"

"Get close, find out something Crowell can use to gently suggest to Romeo that he go away. Crowell's not looking to lock Romeo up, just to lose him."

"Will drinking with him get me close enough?"

"You could get closer?"

I sipped some more espresso, watched the city shimmer beneath the hot blue sky. "What are we really talking about here, Chuck? Guys walk away from their jobs for a lot of reasons. You really think this Pelligrini guy not showing up for work has something to do with Joe Romeo?"

"Me, it's nothing from nothing." Chuck shrugged. "But old man Crowell, he had a hunch."

"Just a hunch?"

"That's what he said. Between you and me, I think you're right: This Pelligrini thing's got nothing to do with anything. But that ain't really the point. It sort of lit a fire under them, Crowell, when Pelligrini disappeared, and now they decided they wanna take care of this Joe Romeo situation before it gets out of hand."

I finished my espresso, looked into the grounds coating the sides of the cup. "Lot of Italians in this conversation, Chuck," I said.

"Just two, besides me."

"Uh-huh. How many Italians do you need before you find one who's connected?"

"Is that one of those lightbulb jokes?"

"If it is it's probably not funny."

Chuck crossed one ankle over his knee, pushing back his

chair to give himself room. "This guy Romeo," he said. "His name came up before. He's not connected, because nobody'll have him. Oh, he's got guys behind him, especially for the shylocking operation, guys he goes to. And he works with some bookie out of Vegas, what I hear. But no one local wants him. That's a bad sign in a bad guy. I don't think Crowell knows this, at least they didn't say. But you might be doing the world a service if you could roust him."

And this was why I worked with Chuck, why I'd come here at all to this high-priced, high-profile place with the endlessly ringing phones and the framed *People* magazine article spotlighting "Ten Top Private Eye Firms for the Nineties." Behind the press releases and the late-night club-hopping and the winks and accommodating grins, the reasons Chuck had become a cop in the first place, so long ago, were still alive.

I lit a cigarette. Chuck shoved a slab of black marble across the desk for me to use as an ashtray.

"I used to work construction," I told him. "I can lay bricks."

"You're shitting me." Chuck's eyes opened wide. "You don't even *speak* Italian."

"Who do you think lays bricks in Dublin?"

"You been to Dublin?"

"No."

"They got a lot of crooked walls there, my fine Irish friend. Is that an offer?"

"Why not? I'd rather work with the guy than drink with him, I think. And it's easier. What if he drinks in some dive on Staten Island?"

"You're all gonna be sorry you said shit like that when we secede, you know." Chuck's tone was completely serious. A man's home is his castle.

"As long as you issue me a passport. So what about it?"

He steepled his fingers and tapped them to his lips, considering. "Well, okay. But I got a bad feeling about that site."

I grinned. "Aren't you going to back me up?"

"With everything I got, buddy. We'll do all your background shit from here, just call. You want me to send someone onto the site to babysit you?"

"No way. And do me a favor, let me do the background stuff myself. I don't want to have to get a sign-off from your bookkeeper every time I need a license run."

He frowned. "Just hand you off the case?"

"You and I don't do things the same way, Chuck."

I pulled on my cigarette, tapped gray ash onto the black marble. Framed in the window behind Chuck, a twin-engine plane made its way south over the East River. It was silent and the line of its flight was unvarying; it might have been pulled by a string.

"Now you put it that way," Chuck said slowly, "maybe it's a good idea. For the same reason Crowell don't want to know."

"You think I might do something you wouldn't approve of?"

Chuck raised his eyebrows. "You could think of something I wouldn't approve of? But anyway, maybe it's better. You're right, we do things differently. And I'm up to my ass in other things around here. Truth is I got no time for this, only I didn't want to turn Crowell down. Could be a good paying customer for the long term, you know what I mean? But this'll work out good. Your case, you work it. Only I don't know how Crowell's gonna feel about it."

"Don't tell them. I'll report to you, you report to them. I'll be working for you, Chuck. I have no problem with that. I just don't want to be part of the DeMattis team."

"If you're sure that's how you want it. But whatever, I got all these geeks back there, costing me overhead whether they're running licenses or reading the racing form. You could avail yourself."

"I have other things I'd rather avail myself of."

"Ah." Chuck smiled. "Your Chinese girl?"

"Woman," I corrected him. "Licensed P.I. Independent operator with a four-year apprenticeship, four years solo in the field, and a one-room office in Chinatown. And not mine."

"Whose fault is that?"

"Mine."

"You want my advice? As a happily married man?"

"No."

"Okay, here goes. You know that old joke, where the punchline is, 'Be patient, jackass'?"

"Uh-huh."

"That's my advice."

"Thanks, Chuck. Can we get back to work?"

"Sure. Where were we?"

"You were about to give me the case. Let's talk fee. When it's over, I'll send you a bill."

"If that's how you want it."

That was how I wanted it, and that's how we did it. Chuck handed me the file, told me I'd have a union card by tomorrow. We worked out a cover we thought would fit, and I went home to wait. On the way I stopped at a builder's-supply place on the Lower East Side and bought three different trowels, a hard hat, and a pair of heavy leather gloves. I sent Chuck the bill.

two

the scaffold I was on bounced slightly, its delicate bracing cutting the view across Broadway into triangular puzzle pieces as I made my way from the hoist and along the west side of the building to find my crew.

It was true, what I'd told Chuck: that I could get closer to Joe Romeo by being where he was eight hours a day than by trying to edge into his after-hours life; and that masonry work was something I could do. Being assigned to Romeo's crew seemed like a natural if Chuck could arrange it. It had taken him a few days, construction work being so slow in New York right now, but he'd arranged it, with a two-hundred-dollar-savings bond in the name of the newborn son of a mason on the crew, and a case of Glenfiddich for the guy at the union hall who sent that guy, this morning, to a garage foundation in Queens and me to upper Broadway.

It was true, and I could do it, and it might even be the best way to work the case. But there was something else, another reason I wanted to be here, where small dust clouds billowed six floors below me as men crossed the site and headed for the time clocks, where the deep-throated growl of an engine starting up was blanketed by the pounding screech of a jackhammer, where I felt a trickle of sweat wander down my back as I carried my gear and my lunchbox along the rough planks of the scaffolding in the early morning.

Restless. Not the right word, but the best I had. It didn't

cover the small, sad jolt—not fear but like it—of waking in the early morning; or the long, pointless hours not of sleep but of nothing else, in the night. Sometimes, playing the piano could ease the tightness in my back. Sometimes, I could feel myself calming as I sat on the porch of my upstate cabin at the end of the day, drinking Maker's Mark and watching the thick gold sunlight linger on the tops of the tallest trees and then gently slide away, leaving them in darkness. But I'd been at the cabin for a week when I checked in with my service in New York and found Chuck had called me. Usually I don't even call in from upstate; I did it because the shadows of the old trees around my cabin, the music, even the bourbon, none of it was helping, not this time.

I'd come in because Chuck had called, because I needed to work. And mason's work, hard and sweaty and resulting, at the end of each day, in something that hadn't been there before, something solid and undeniable, was the right kind of work.

The three other guys on the crew were already there when I got to where I was supposed to be. The one who wasn't was Joe Romeo.

"I'm Smith," I said to them as they lounged with their backs against the courses of brick they'd laid yesterday, one of them smoking, another finishing a cup of black coffee. "I'm new on this crew."

"Replacing Nicky, huh? I heard he got something closer to home. Mike DiMaio." The coffee drinker pushed himself to his feet, offered me his hand. I had my gloves on already; I didn't take them off to shake with him, didn't want him to know my hands weren't as roughed-up and scarred as the hands of a middle-aged mason were likely to be. DiMaio was young and stocky and short, maybe five-four. He had a thick pale mustache and bristling, brush-cut sandy hair. "You're with me," he said. "I guess that means we gotta get started. Shit." He grinned, picked up his gloves, crushed the empty cup. He pitched it over the unfinished wall back into the building. I heard it skid across the concrete floor. DiMaio pointed to the other men. "This is Sam Buck. He's gonna sit on his ass as long as he can 'cause that's the kind of work he likes. And this here's Angelo Lucca."

Buck, a shaggy-haired dark guy with narrow shoulders and thick muscles on his upper arms, said, "Fuck you, DiMaio," without particular interest. He stuck his cigarette in his mouth and shook my hand without rising. Lucca, also dark and bigger than either Buck or DiMaio, wrapped a wide hand around the scaffold steel and hauled himself up. "Good to meet you." He grinned, toed Buck with a mortar-stained boot. "Come on, Sam. Joe's gonna be around soon."

"Fuck you, Lucca," Buck muttered. Maybe it was his morning greeting. He added, "And fuck Joe. He don't scare me."

"We're down here," DiMaio told me. Buck got to his feet as Mike DiMaio and I started along the scaffold.

"Joe's the foreman?" I asked as I followed him. Like some other muscled short guys I've known, DiMaio walked with a bowlegged gait, like a sailor.

"Joe Romeo," DiMaio said over his shoulder. "Stay out of his way. You make your quota, do good work, Joe leaves you alone, which is what you want. He'll break your balls some, being you're new, but just ride it out and he'll find someone else."

We stopped two bays over, where the brick courses rose only to knee level, anchored with shiny steel tabs into the rough gray concrete-block backup. The backup was all in, dark rectangles sloppy with mortar enclosing the building top to bottom, barriers between in and out with voids at their centers where the window openings gaped.

"You seen the drawings?" DiMaio asked me.

"No."

"A lot of pain-in-the-ass stuff on this job, corbels, arches, setbacks like over here." He pointed at a dull steel column about sixteen inches in from the building's skin, standing in an unfinished collar of brickwork. "You'll get into it. Work slow when you start, ask questions if you got 'em."

He cupped his hands around his mouth, yelled through the window opening toward the center of the building. "Phillips! Yo, Betty Crocker! We're ready to go anytime, you wanna bring some of that batter over here! Make it chocolate," he added.

Staring hard into the dimness inside, I made out a small concrete mixer half hidden by stacks of blocks and pallets of bricks. A black man lifted a hand in response to DiMaio's shout. He pulled a lever and the mixer disgorged gray sludge into a wheelbarrow standing under it. Shoving the lever back to start the mixer up again, the man stuck a shovel in the wheelbarrow and headed in our direction.

"We got the plan up over there, you want to take a look at it," DiMaio told me, pointing to the other side of the wall. "You can get in two bays down, where Phillips is coming out. Or you can go over."

I went over, climbing the sides of the scaffold and swinging myself in through the window opening to land with a thud on the scuffed concrete inside the building. I felt a cool touch of air, the air from inside, on the back of my neck.

"What happens if the safety officer catches me doing that?" I asked DiMaio as we faced each other through the opening.

"Joe's the safety officer on this crew. Nothing happens."

I studied the plan, a tattered print of the architect's drawing, now marked with pencil and thumbprints and coffeestains. Another drawing was taped there too, the brickwork details, and I saw what DiMaio had meant. Arched windows with true keystones; projections at some columns, setbacks at others; patterns made by alternating the long and short sides of the brick, turning and stacking it, edging it forward and back, that would read on the face of the building. This wasn't a brick skin stretched taut, reading smooth and flawless as glass or steel, brick fighting for a place in the slick, modern machine world. Bricks are laid one by one, each measured weight held by a hand, each rough surface considered and handled and placed. When this building was complete you'd know that, see it in the movement and the patterns and the shadows cast by the bricks on each other.

DiMaio, with a smile, was watching me study the drawings. "What do you think?" he asked me. "Worked like this before?"

"Not for a long time."

"Since your apprentice program, I'll bet. Me neither. You'll get into it, like I said. Gives you a chance to show off."

"I'm not even sure my apprentice program covered stuff like this," I said doubtfully. "Did yours?"

DiMaio shrugged. "I started working with my old man when I was eight years old. My apprentice program was after school and weekends and summers."

"He taught you to do work like this? He was good, your old man?"

DiMaio grinned the ready grin. "He's still at it. Except for me, he's the best."

I went back to examining the drawings. "Must be expensive. I know it'll slow me down. Why are they doing it?"

"Hey, I'm just a bricklayer, what the hell do I know? Architect got a bug up his ass, sold it to the owner. Why not? Keeps you and me pulling down a paycheck, anyway. Hey, lookit, it's Phillips, dropping his morning load. Whaddaya say, Reg?"

"Move your butt, will ya?" Phillips answered cheerfully. DiMaio moved aside as Phillips maneuvered the wheelbarrow past him on the scaffold. "Reg Phillips," he said to me, and we shook hands as I gave him my name. He was young also, maybe twenty-five, a thin, dark-skinned man with a thicker mustache than DiMaio's. "Heard some poor sucker got— Jeez, I mean, I heard Mike here got a new partner. Listen, he gives you any trouble, you just come see me, okay?"

"Go back to your chemistry set and let the real guys get to work, Reg," DiMaio told him.

Reg Phillips threw a fake punch at DiMaio, who ducked, weaved, threw one back. The scaffold shook with their footwork. "I'm gonna have to report you for horsing around on the scaffold, DiMaio," Phillips said, dropping his arms. He turned, stuck the shovel into the mortar in the wheelbarrow, and loaded a couple of piles of it onto a board set on concrete blocks between me and DiMaio. "That good for you, Smith?" he asked.

I stuck a trowel into the mortar, worked it around. DiMaio watched as I did it. "Seems fine," I said.

"You want it up higher? Considering you're taller than some of these midget masons they got around here?" He jerked a thumb at DiMaio.

"What happens if I say yes?" I looked at my new partner.

"I throw you off the scaffold," DiMaio answered. "Just like I'm about to do to Mr. Nobel Prize here. Hey, smart guy, how much money you lose last night?"

Reg Phillips grinned. "*My* money, you sorry-ass white boy, was on the Yankees."

DiMaio raised his eyes to the sky. "Now I know you're crazy. You realize they only won to suck in guys like you, set you up for next time?"

"Hey, Mike," Phillips asked, "how come you never put your money where your mouth is?"

"I don't have to. I just watch you, it cures me of gambling forever. Smith, you want to raise this mortar up, it's okay with me."

"No, it's fine."

"Nah, go ahead if you want," DiMaio said. "If it'll slow you down . . ."

"Don't worry about it," I said. "Let's get to work."

I worked beside Mike DiMaio all morning, trying to keep up, to find my way back into the rhythm of the thing. I watched him, followed his moves as they flowed from one step to the next. It had been a long time since I'd worked as a mason, and I'd never done work this complicated. As I set the bricks forward and back, turned them on their sides or ends to run header courses or soldiers, I fell further and further behind. We were working on our knees, something I hadn't thought of; before we started DiMaio swung through the opening into the building and came back with a pair of knee pads for me.

"Thanks."

He shrugged. "Guy they belong to won't need 'em till tomorrow."

As we worked, the July sun mounted, and though our side of the building was in shadow and the chill from the inside escaped toward us in small breaths, after an hour my shirt was plastered to my back and a film of sweat covered my arms and neck. DiMaio didn't say much, just did his work, quick, clean, and efficient, and watched mine. Striking a sharp joint he wouldn't have to go back over, he nodded his head toward my trowels, my brick level, my hard hat. "All new?"

"I left everything," I said. "The hell with it. Came north with nothing. Change my luck."

He grunted as he tapped a brick into place. "Did it work?"

"I got this job."

We stopped for coffee at break time, nine-thirty, and it wasn't until then that I met Joe Romeo.

We were working higher by then, laying those hip-high courses that give you a choice of reaching up from your knees or bending as you stand. We were both standing—DiMaio, because at his height it made sense, and me, because my knees were beginning to wonder what the hell I was up to. A small bounce in the scaffolding let us know someone was headed our way.

"That's Joe," DiMaio said, snapping mortar off his trowel without looking around. "Always thinks he's sneaking up on you. Like being snuck up on by an elephant. Act surprised when he gets here, maybe you'll get points."

I looked over my shoulder, saw a big man, dark-haired and thick-necked, handsome in the way of football players, or soldiers. I straightened up, stood my trowel in the mortar. I lifted my hard hat and dragged the back of my glove across my forehead to blot up some sweat.

The big man reached us, stopped, looked at me to size me up and let me know he was doing it. My instinct was to do the same, give it back to him, set my place in his life where I wanted it; but that wasn't why I was here. I was the first to look away, out over the scaffold, where the buildings were watching our progress.

After a few moments Joe Romeo looked away too, down at the clipboard he carried. He peered at the brickwork Mike DiMaio and I had laid so far, then came back to me.

"You're Smith."

"Right," I said.

"From Houston?"

"Right."

"I'm Joe Romeo. Foreman. Lozano told you?"

I nodded.

"Just don't fuck with me, you'll be okay." He looked past me, to DiMaio. "Whaddaya say, Mikey? He any good?"

DiMaio shrugged. "Good as Nicky."

"Nicky? Nicky's a putz. Give us something better than that, you don't mind, Smith. Bring up the quality from this team."

"Fuck you, Joe," DiMaio said without a smile.

"Fuck you too, Mikey. That's my job, keeping up the quality around here. You got a problem with that, maybe you got a problem with quality. What the hell's that?" he suddenly said, pointing to my right forearm, to the snake-shaped scar there.

"Old mistake," I said.

"You make a lot of mistakes?"

"I try not to."

"Try harder. I wanna keep up the schedule here, keep Crowell and that asshole architect off our tail. Any team falls behind, that's a problem, you understand?"

"I understand."

"Good. You find the can, water cooler, all that shit?"

"Mike showed me."

"Mikey showed you." Romeo smiled at DiMaio, a slow, even smile. "Greatest partner a man could have, Mikey. Okay, just don't spend the whole day in the can, you got that, Smith?"

DiMaio said, "That thing don't get serviced more often, nobody's gonna be spending any time in it. Guys'll be pissing off the scaffold."

"Not my problem, Mikey."

"You're the foreman."

"And you know what that means?" Romeo said with mock delight. "It means I get to piss in the trailer! You got a problem with the facilities, Mikey, talk to Crowell. Little Dan Junior oughta be around this afternoon."

DiMaio's face didn't lose its belligerence but he didn't answer.

"All right, you two," Romeo said, smiling as he looked at

his clipboard, as though he'd won something. "Kenny's going for coffee. You want something, tell him, then get back to work. I want you at waist before you rest your butts."

He made a note on the clipboard, let his eyes move over me once more, then walked on, heading toward Buck and Lucca. I looked at DiMaio. It would take us another hour to get to the brick course at waist height, even DiMaio's waist.

"That's bullshit," DiMaio said. "He knows it when he says it. He knows we're gonna stop as soon as Kenny gets back."

"Then why does he bother?"

"So he told us to do something we didn't do. Gives him something to chew our asses about, later." As DiMaio reached for a brick I heard him give a snort. "Quality," he muttered. "Shit."

When the coffee came, brought around by a grinning Jamaican laborer whose hard hat sat high on his dreadlocks, DiMaio and I stripped off our gloves and dropped to the scaffold, resting our backs against the brick.

My throat felt coated with the same fine dust that dulled the sweat on my arms. I sipped my coffee, trying to wash the dryness away. Mike DiMaio bit into an apple turnover, said to me, "You're slow."

"Sorry," I said. "I'm rusty."

"Year's layoff?"

"Yeah."

"How much did you work before that?"

"Spotty. Only on and off since maybe 'ninety-three."

"'Ninety-three, huh?" He swallowed some coffee. Looking out over Broadway, toward the river, he said, "That thing on your arm don't look like a mistake to me."

"No?" I said, watching him.

"No. Looks like a fucking snake, one of them hooded ones. Looks like it was supposed to be just like that."

"It was," I answered. "The mistake was mine."

DiMaio was about to say something else, but sudden shouts from inside the building brought us both to our feet.

Someone's always shouting on a building site. It's usually the only way to be heard over the construction noise; you get used to it, and you block it out.

But there's another kind of shout, the kind that means trouble, that carries fear or pain or a boiling anger. You hear that differently, and when it happens, you jump.

Inside, framed in the square of the window opening, we saw men running, heading for the piles of brick and block around the small concrete mixer. Next to the mixer, someone crouched beside a dark figure motionless on the floor.

DiMaio was up the scaffold steel and through the opening while I was still taking in the scene. I swung through and followed. Someone inside called out, was answered by another call. Running footsteps slapped the concrete. At the mixer, I had to elbow through standing men to reach what I found: Reg Phillips, lying still, his blood soaking into the pile of sand he made his mortar from.

Still, but alive. His face was a glistening mess, covered with the blood pooling out of a deep gash in his scalp; but blood doesn't flow that fast if it's not being pushed by a heart that's still beating.

Two men, Mike DiMaio and a man I didn't know, were crouching next to Phillips, and others were standing, leaning in, but no one was moving. Everyone seemed frozen with the idea that it was too late to do anything, too late for anything to matter. I pushed away the man I didn't know, knelt, threw my hard hat aside. I tore off my T-shirt and pressed it to the wound. "Move! Give me some room!" I barked at the men surrounding us. Some did. "Find a blanket," I said to DiMaio. "Something to keep him warm. This much blood, he'll go into shock." DiMaio stared at me for a second; then he jumped up, pushed his way through. "Someone call 911," I yelled, looking at Phillips, not the men around me.

"I called," someone answered. "I called already."

"Don't bother," drawled a voice behind me, one of the men I had elbowed away. "He's gone."

"Like hell," I snapped. "What the hell happened?"

No answer from anyone; then, the same voice as before. "Must've tripped over his own fucking shovel, smashed his head against that pile of bricks."

That was Sam Buck's voice; now that I had time to think, I

knew it. I looked up, saw Sam Buck and Joe Romeo among the crowd of men.

It's a stupid mistake, and an old one, to trip over your own tools. My eyes searched the sandy concrete floor. Phillips's shovel was lying nearby, not standing up against something the way it should have been. Anyone could have tripped over it. A corner brick on an open pallet showed dark traces, maybe blood. Phillips's hard hat lay where it had rolled, down by his leather boot, against a pile of block.

Someone shoved through the forest of Levi-covered legs next to me; DiMaio, with a quilted gray fire blanket, the kind you toss over the flames to smother the whole thing. Heavy as lead, but we wrapped Phillips in it, never letting up on the pressure of my shirt on his skull. He groaned once as we moved him, a good sign.

"All right, you assholes," Joe Romeo called loudly, "move back. He ain't dead, so give him room to breathe."

Nothing happened. Another voice gave the order again: "All you men, move back!"

This voice didn't carry as well as Romeo's, but it was obeyed. The men moved back, but not far, the way a crowd will move. Someone came with a first-aid kit, and DiMaio rummaged through it for some gauze, which we folded thickly and pressed to Phillips's skull, throwing my shirt aside. I felt heavy with the weight of the stands of brick and block, the piles of sand and the crowd of men pressing in on this spot, and I wanted room, but I stayed where I was, kept the pressure steady, waited for the paramedics to arrive. They came soon, with something better than my shirt to bandage the wound, and something better than a fire blanket to cover Phillips, as they filled his arm with saline and rolled him away on a stretcher.

After that the men milled around for a while, looking at each other, drinking coffee that had gone cold.

"Dangerous fucking job, construction," I heard one of them say. "Can't let yourself get sloppy. You got to take it into account."

"I never known Reg to be sloppy before," another said.

"Always a first time."

They all agreed with that, that there was always a first time.

Some of them slapped me on the back, told me it was a good thing I thought fast; some of them didn't, and I knew they were the ones who hadn't thought fast themselves.

"Hey, hero." It was Joe Romeo, and he was talking to me. I was sitting on the concrete, my back against the raw steel of a column, away from the others. I'd just lit a cigarette. I looked up at him and waited.

"So, what, you were a fucking doctor before you decided to mix with the common man and lay bricks?"

I shrugged. "He was bleeding. I thought it might be a good idea to stop the blood."

"This kind of thing happen a lot in Texas?"

"Dangerous job, construction," I said.

"Christ!" he said suddenly, staring at my left arm. "You got a thing for snakes, or what?"

I glanced at the blue snake tattoo that winds from my elbow to my shoulder, a mark I've had for twenty-five years.

"No," I said. "Coincidence."

"Oh, *coincidence.*" He emphasized the word sarcastically, nodded. "You know, Smith, I'm starting to not like you, and I don't even know you. So now what? You gonna go back to work today, or I'm gonna have to give you time off for being a hero?"

I looked at him, his broad shoulders and sardonic grin. "I'll work," I said. "Let me finish my smoke, and clean up." I was sticky with Phillips's blood.

"Finish it fast, then. Your partner's back on the job already."

I looked across the floor to the bay where Mike DiMaio and I had been working that morning. DiMaio was on the scaffold, working on the complex brick pattern around one of the columns. His movements were sharp and hard, not smooth the way they'd been before. He had no flow, no rhythm, but the results were clean, and nothing he did, while I watched, had to be done over.

I stuck the cigarette in my mouth and went to rinse off in the icy stream from the hose near the mixer. Someone had picked up Phillips's shovel, taken it somewhere; someone else had moved his hard hat, rested it on his lunchbox next to his leather gloves. I picked up the hard hat, turned it over in my hands, looked at the plastic straps inside. There was nothing strange about it; it was just like mine.

"Smith!" It was Romeo again. I put the hard hat down, picked up the hose, ran water over my arms. I shivered with the suddenness of it as I splashed my face and the back of my neck. Romeo said, "What are you gonna do for clothes?"

"I can work like this," I said. Shirtless wasn't such a bad way to be, in this heat. "Until the sun comes around. I'll pick up a shirt at lunch." The one I'd come in, the one I'd bandaged Phillips with, lay in a puddle of water and blood and sand beside the mixer.

"Yeah," he said, "okay." I had the feeling there was something else he wanted to say to me, but he didn't try.

I walked back across the floor to where I'd worked all morning. I didn't go through right away. DiMaio turned when he saw me, straightened and stood, a brick in one hand, trowel in the other. He watched me. His jaw was tight and his pale eyes hard. He moved aside. I sat on the backup block and swung my legs through to the other side.

DiMaio kept his eyes on me while I picked up my trowel, worked the mortar around. Then, wordlessly, he turned back to his column, placed the brick he'd been holding.

I found my own spot, saw what there was to do. As I did it I said, "His pulse and his breathing were good, Mike. I think he'll be okay."

DiMaio straightened up fast. "You're a fucking expert? You know so fucking much about guys with their heads beat in? How is that, Smith?"

I turned to look at him. Color had risen in his face; tendons corded his muscular neck.

"Back off," I said quietly. "I worked on a rescue squad in Houston, while I was laid off. Volunteer, something to do. I've seen accidents before."

"Accidents. Yeah, you've fucking seen accidents." He picked a brick off his pile, laid it in where it needed to go, tapped it sharply. "Yeah, accidents."

I put my trowel down. "Mike, you have a problem with me?"

He looked over his shoulder. "Yeah, you might say that. You might say I got a problem."

"You want to tell me about it?"

He turned away from me, placed another brick while I stood and watched. That tied up a corner, finished a run in the pattern. His back still to me, he asked, "Why?"

"Why what?"

"What the hell is the point of talking to you? What the hell difference is it gonna make what I say?"

"It depends about what."

"About what." He turned around, glared. "About how you ain't touched a brick in years. About how you got glue in your pants, but the union sends you up here as a twenty-five-dollar-an-hour bricklayer. What you're good at, what you can do, is bandage guys' heads. Blood don't seem to bother you."

"I'm rusty," I said. "I told you that."

"Fuck that. Nobody ever done any serious bricklaying loses his moves like you."

"Then what?"

His jaw was tight; he didn't speak. I watched while he fought with himself, watched his eyes.

"What, Mike?" I repeated.

His eyes changed; he'd made his choice. "You're connected." He took a step forward, spoke louder, the way a man will speak to cover his fear. "You're some connected asshole, must've helped some Guido No-Brains lay a patio wall once, they thought they could pass you off as a mason."

"Why?"

"How the fuck do I know why? Somebody owes somebody money, somebody needs to be watched, somebody needs his head smashed in. That it, Smith? Reg needed to be pushed around a little, and you were supposed to make sure it all went okay? And then maybe it got a little out of hand, but thank God you were here, huh? You could fix it up, all nice, so he don't die, 'cause that wasn't the plan?"

DiMaio's fists were clenched, his weight forward. He spat his words at me, at the limits of his control. If I said the wrong thing he might rush me, I thought, right here on the scaffold.

"What happened to Phillips," I said carefully, letting the rest of it alone for a time, "the guys who were there said it was an accident."

"Nobody was there. Who the fuck you think was there? Sam said it was an accident 'cause Sam knows fucking everything. They all bought it, that's all."

"You don't?"

"Yeah, right. You ever seen that much blood from a guy tripping over his shovel?"

"I don't know."

"You don't know. You don't fucking know. Well, I don't know either, Smith, except I know that whatever the hell it is you're doing I don't want you doing it here, my scaffold, my bricks."

His left hand flew out, almost an involuntary move, pointed to his wall, the strength of it, the absolute solidity, the even lines of the brick and the delicate concavity of mortar. His pale eyes, hard and hot, stayed fixed on me. There wasn't anything he could do about Phillips, or about who he thought I was; but the walls he built were his.

I looked from DiMaio's work back to him.

"You're right," I said. "You're right but you're wrong. There's a reason I'm here. But I'm not connected. I'll tell you. But not now. Lunch break. Now I want to get back to work. Because I don't want to lose this job."

He stared at me, eyes narrow. I'd made my offer; I waited. Around us, the whine of a saw, jackhammers, the shouts of men. The graceful neck of the crane glided silently by overhead, carrying a steel beam that seemed to hang weightless, suspended on the thinnest of lines. Between us there was nothing but space and silence, and the mortar Reg Phillips had mixed that morning.

DiMaio made the move, but he didn't break the silence. He turned back to his work. I went back to mine. For the next two hours we didn't speak again.

three

I thought for the rest of the morning about what I was going to tell Mike DiMaio. Before the time for that came, though, another man came by, wanting me to tell him some other things.

"All right, you two. Knock off for a minute." Joe Romeo's voice was a little louder than it had to be to be heard from where he was, close to us, coming along the scaffold. I turned to look; he had another man with him.

DiMaio looked too, then turned his back on them to finish what he was doing with slow, deliberate motions. I was new; I put my trowel down and waited.

"This is Dan Crowell," Joe Romeo told me. "Junior," he added.

"How're you doing?" Crowell said to me. Round full cheeks gave his face a cheerful quality which his voice had also. The voice was familiar; I thought for a minute and remembered it, the order to move back and give Reg Phillips room to breathe that had been obeyed.

Dan Crowell, Jr. and I looked each other over. He was a medium-height man of maybe thirty-five, carrying a little too much weight for his build, not muscle weight and not beer, just softness.

"This is Smith," Romeo said to Crowell. "Bill Smith. New today. He was the one come up with the bandage, the shirt thing. You saw."

"I saw," Crowell agreed. "That was pretty good, Smith. You probably saved the man's life." Dan Crowell, Jr. smiled at me.

"He'll be all right?" I asked.

"Hard to say. I talked to the hospital. His skull's fractured. They're watching him close, waiting to do a CAT scan when the swelling goes down. All kinds of things can happen, they say. But they think he'll live."

"Yeah, but then what?" That was Mike DiMaio, behind me. "Will he be able to work anymore, or he's gonna be all fucked up?"

Crowell looked over to DiMaio. "I don't know, Mike. It's too soon for that. But he's got good medical coverage, and disability. He'll be okay if he's out of work."

"Oh, yeah. He'll be great. Sitting staring out a window for the rest of his life." DiMaio spat, spun around, and went back to his own work.

Crowell watched DiMaio for another minute, then came back to me. "I just have to ask you two some questions." He smiled, almost apologetic. "I'm Crowell Construction's safety officer. I have to investigate the accident. For the record."

"Sure," I said. "What about the union? They going to send somebody?"

"That's me," Joe Romeo said. "I'm doing it. Not a big deal. I mean, I was there."

"When it happened?" I put surprise in my voice. I knew what the answer would be; I just wanted to hear how he'd say it.

"Right after." Romeo gave me a cold look. "Same as Mr. Crowell and you."

Dan Crowell, Jr. asked his questions then, about what we'd seen, what we'd said, what we'd done. DiMaio never stopped work; he answered with grunts or with words of one syllable. I answered clearly and completely, watched Crowell write what I'd said on his yellow pad. Then I asked a question of my own.

"Did anybody see it happen?"

I could feel Mike DiMaio, behind me, stop for a second when I said that. He picked up his rhythm again right away; I wondered if anyone else had noticed.

"Haven't found anybody," Crowell said. "No reason why

anyone would, unless they happened to be passing by. Phillips has that mixer pretty well surrounded by piles of stuff."

DiMaio snorted.

"You got something to say, Mikey?" Joe Romeo asked loudly, addressing the question to DiMaio's back.

DiMaio straightened, threw down the trowel and the brick he was holding. "Yeah," he said, turning. "Yeah. It wasn't Reg's idea to pile all that shit around the mixer."

"What are you saying?"

"Unsafe condition, Joe. You're the foreman. You got the men working in unsafe conditions."

"Mike—" Dan Crowell, Jr. began.

"Look at it." DiMaio pointed through the opening toward the center of the floor. "Look at all that shit. A guy practically *has* to trip over something, working in there. And if he did, you might never know it." Looking at Joe Romeo, he added, "And if something else happened in there, you'd never know that either."

"Something else?" Joe Romeo said. "Something else like what?"

DiMaio shrugged, and smiled a hard smile. "Hell, I don't know, Joe. I'm just a bricklayer."

One good thing came out of the visit from Dan Crowell, Jr.: speaking into the walkie-talkie he lifted from his hip, he gave instructions, and, ten minutes after he left, a laborer stuck his head through the window opening and tossed me a T-shirt. It was green, good heavy cloth, with the skyline logo of the Crowell Construction Company across the front.

I left the shirt hanging over the scaffold until the lunch break got close. When I began to sense the change in tempo that meant crews were knocking off, I finished where I was, wiped my trowel, and looked over at DiMaio. He didn't look at me, so I swung inside and headed toward the mixer hose to clean up. I was slimy with sweat by then, and I figured the new shirt ought to start out with a clean field. At the mixer, the floor had been washed down, and Reg Phillips's things were gone. The new guy there didn't say anything, but he stood aside while I used his water, and even silently offered me the grimy towel he wiped his own mortar-coated hands on. I thanked him but turned it down.

Back outside, I looked down the scaffold. Most of the masons had gathered at the end, in the corner, where the work already done cast a cool shadow, to stretch out and eat. Instead of the usual talk, about last night's ballgame, about someone's anniversary and everyone's ideas for what he should get his wife, the talk down there today would be about the accident. Whether Reg Phillips would live. Other accidents on other sites they'd been on. About me, the new hotdog who could save guys' lives but was one slow bricklayer.

Mike DiMaio wasn't down there with them. He was sitting here, where I was, leaning on his wall, unwrapping a thick, drippy sandwich on a long Italian roll. I brought my lunchbox over to his side of the bay, sat down against the scaffold steel, not the bricks DiMaio had laid.

I pulled the Crowell shirt on, unwrapped my own sandwich. I was glad to be sitting for a while, not lifting anything heavier than salami.

For a time, neither of us spoke. Traffic rolled by on Broadway to the beat of the traffic lights. Over on the Hudson, a speedboat flew upriver, and a tug hauled a loaded barge patiently south.

DiMaio, looking beyond me to the river, said, "We had a big bet on the game tonight."

I twisted open a bottle of orange juice. "Who?"

"Me and Reg. Mets game."

"I thought you didn't gamble."

He shrugged. "Reg likes to lay odds, make a game interesting. Sometimes I'm in."

"How big?"

He paused before he answered. "Loser buys the beer."

"That's a big bet?"

"It is when I win."

I looked at him; he stared into the distance. "I'm sorry, Mike."

"Don't be." He brought his eyes back to me. "You had something to do with this, I'll kill you, I'm telling you that right now." His voice and his eyes were stony, and I didn't doubt that he meant it. "You didn't, you got nothing to be sorry about."

He waited, then, for me to tell him which it was.

I downed the juice, grateful for the liquid bite of it in my throat. I capped the empty bottle and looked at DiMaio. " 'Someone needs to be watched,' " I said. "You said that maybe that's what it was. I'm a private investigator. I've been hired to watch Joe Romeo." I fished in my back pocket for my wallet, showed him the copy of my license I keep under a hidden leather flap there.

DiMaio looked at it, both sides, turning it over and then over again in his hand. He handed it back to me. "Joe? Why?" Suspicion deepened his voice.

"My client thinks Romeo might be involved in things nobody wants going on on this site."

"What kind of things?"

"Loansharking, they told me. Bookmaking. Someone mentioned drugs too, but no one's sure."

He looked at me, measuring, not speaking. Finally he said, "Joe? Joe's a bookie? Joe's a shylock?"

"Maybe. I'm supposed to find out."

He watched me a little longer, asked, "Who's your client?"

I shook my head.

He tried another. "What are they gonna do about it if it's true?"

"I don't know."

"Slap his wrist and throw him off the site," he said with disgust. " 'Bad boy, Joe. Go home.' "

"Maybe."

"You know damn well. Nobody's gonna want trouble."

"You could be right. But if I don't do what I'm doing, they won't even get that far."

He nodded. "Or this whole thing could be bullshit. Private investigator. Joe Romeo. You could've just invented it to shut me up. Sounds like something a bricklayer might swallow."

"It's the truth," I said. "You don't have to believe it, but there's nothing else I can tell you."

"The name of the client."

"What if I did? What are you going to do, call and ask them? They'd pull me five minutes later."

"At least I'd know it was true. 'Cause that license, even if it's real, that don't mean you ain't connected. They got cops on the payroll, no reason they can't have guys like you, too."

"No," I said, "there's no reason. They might. But not me."

"And I'm just supposed to believe this? Just because you said it?"

"You're not even supposed to know about it."

"Then how come you're telling me?"

"I don't see that I have much choice."

"What are you talking about? You don't have to tell me squat. What am I gonna do, you say, 'For Chrissakes, Mikey, I'm just a bricklayer tryin' to make a living, get off my back'?"

"You already said you don't believe that."

"So what? I didn't hire you, I can't fire you."

"You could make me look bad."

He laughed sourly. "Man, you don't need me for that. And what's the difference? Whoever sent you up here, they got you a union card, they got you a job, who cares how you look?"

"I can't keep an eye on Joe Romeo if he's keeping an eye on me."

DiMaio gave me a long stare. Then he looked away, took a bite out of his sandwich, and didn't speak again until he'd finished it. I went back to mine, too, and gave him the time he wanted.

"What about Reg?" he finally said, balling up the paper his sandwich had come wrapped in. He ripped open a package of M & M's. "You come up here to keep an eye on Joe or whatever, and it just so happens someone clobbers Reg two hours after you get here?"

"That could still have been an accident."

DiMaio gave a cold laugh.

"Or maybe it wasn't," I said. "But I don't know anything about it."

"It wasn't, I'm telling you that. Reg's too careful, and too quick, to crack his head open tripping over his own damn shovel."

"Like I said, I don't know. But even if it wasn't, I don't know if it has anything to do with me."

"What the hell does that mean, 'I don't know'? Maybe you give a shit, maybe you don't?"

"I didn't say I didn't care, Mike. But it only involves me if it involves Romeo. And I don't know that."

He threw back a handful of M & M's. "But you think so."

I resettled myself against the scaffold, trying to find a more comfortable position. Stopping work may have been a mistake: my arms and back were beginning to ache.

I said, "I don't even know the guy. I expected to come up here and spend a couple of days just figuring out who everybody was."

DiMaio didn't say anything to that. He watched me closely. I guessed he had a right.

"I get suspicious when I see something like what happened to Phillips," I said. "Especially when I've already been told there's someone to be suspicious of. But that doesn't make it true."

I pulled my cigarettes from my back pocket, offered him one. He shook his head. I lit one and we watched each other. The sounds on the site began to change again, got a little louder, more urgent, as the lunch break ended.

"So you're telling me you're here to nail Joe," DiMaio said, collecting the debris that had come from his lunchbox, stuffing things back in.

"No. I'm here to see if there's anything to nail him on."

"Same thing."

I let that go.

"Joe's a bookie, huh?" DiMaio spoke softly. He looked along the scaffolding, squinting as though the light had changed. "And Reg is a betting man."

I watched him, asked, "Does he owe Romeo money?"

DiMaio shook his head. "I didn't even know Joe was a bookie till you told me. I don't know if Reg bets with him. But it would fit, wouldn't it?"

"It might. Or a million other things might."

DiMiao's look was sharp but he didn't answer. Six stories below, someone climbed into a truck, slammed the cab door.

"So what do you want from me?" DiMaio asked.

"Cover me."

"What?"

"If I'm that bad, make me look good. To where Romeo won't notice me, where he won't be thinking about me."

DiMaio stared upward, watched the boom of the crane swing slowly around. The empty hook on the end swayed against the hazy blue of the sky.

"Joe's bad news," he said. "Bookie or not, he's a mean son of a bitch. I seen him get guys fired at the start of a job just to show other guys he can. Just to keep everyone pissing in their pants."

"You don't seem afraid of him."

He shrugged. "It ain't worth it. This's a good job, but not good enough to kiss Joe's ass for. He gets me fired, I pick up something else." He fixed his eyes on mine. "I find out you're lying to me, Smith, I swear—"

"I'm not," I told him.

He pulled himself to his feet. "Yeah," he said. "Okay. But there's two things."

"What are they?"

"One: You find Joe had anything to do with what happened to Reg, you're gonna burn his ass, no matter what the client wants." He put quotes around "client," said the word as though he were talking about a mythical beast that I believed in and he didn't, whose behavior was therefore my problem, not his.

I stood up and joined him. "And the other thing?"

"It turns out he didn't, you're gonna keep looking until you find who did."

"That's not the job I was hired for."

"What the hell are you saying? You want to be paid? You need a fucking client before you give a shit about what happened to Reg?"

"No. I'm saying I already have a client, and something I'm

supposed to be doing here. I don't like to work two cases at once."

"And I don't like to bust my ass making some deadbeat look good."

Our eyes met and held each other. "I could say yes," I answered, "and then not do it."

"Yeah," he agreed. "But you won't. You make a deal, you'll follow through."

"How do you know that?"

He looked from me to my end of the wall, the place where I'd been working. "From your bricks."

four

I pushed through the swinging etched-glass doors into the familiar liquor-and-grill smell of Shorty's Bar. It was half past six, the day still so hot and close that Shorty's air-conditioning hit me like a dive in a mountain lake. I'd already been home, showered, worked for a while on a group of Scriabin études I was learning, and had the first beer of the evening.

I had also called Chuck. I got him at home in Staten Island; he was sitting on his couch, working on a cold beer, the way I was.

"Hey," he said in greeting. "So, how's the bricks?"

"Heavy as lead," I told him. "Heavier than they were last time I did this."

"Yeah, I heard that, that they're making bricks heavier these days," he sympathized. "You gonna manage?"

"I'll let you know. Listen, Chuck, something happened out there today. Did you hear about it?"

"I didn't hear anything. I'm up to my eyebrows on the cases I'm actually working, as opposed to the ones I farm out to suckers."

"I thought maybe someone from Crowell called you."

"Why would they? It have something to do with Joe Romeo?"

"I don't know."

"What was it?"

I told him.

"Shit. The guy gonna be okay?"

"I don't know that either. They might have a better idea by tomorrow. So Crowell didn't call you, huh?"

"Uh-uh. Unless they thought Romeo was involved, they got no reason to."

"I thought because I was in the middle of it."

"You? They never heard of you."

"Crowell?" I was surprised.

"Nuh-uh. I was gonna tell 'em. Then I thought, Why? You got better cover this way. Anybody happens to see something, phone message with my name on it, you know, it's still got nothing to do with you. Old man Crowell, he knows I'm on the case. I told you, he don't know how I'm working it, whether I got someone on the inside, or only outside guys digging, and he don't want to know." Chuck paused to drink some beer. "The kid, I told you, he don't like it, but he does things the way the old man tells him. So no one up there knows anything except you're an altacocker bricklayer who thinks bricks are getting heavier."

"I thought Crowell Junior was just being cute on the scaffold this morning."

"No, he really's got no idea it's you."

"Good," I said. "Thanks, Chuck. But here's something else I've been thinking. I think you'd have to let at least the old man in on this one." I told Chuck about an idea that had been growing in my mind since the middle of the day.

"Jeez, I don't know," Chuck said, when I was through. "You think we need to do this?"

"Yes, I do."

"Well," he said doubtfully, "you think she'll go for it?"

"Lydia? I'm having dinner with her. I'll ask her then. Can we do it?"

"I'll call old man Crowell now. I'll call you back."

I finished my beer while I waited. Twenty minutes later, Chuck was back to me. "He says yeah, but only if you're sure it'll help. He's worried about his bottom line."

"How sure does he mean by sure?"

"This is a guy spends his time putting buildings up. You

either got your steel or you don't. The thing either stands up or it falls down."

I thought about the études I'd been practicing, thought about searching for the right colors in an arpeggio, listening as the dominant voice shifts from one hand to the other, back and forth, a matter of trial, of interpretation.

"Tell him I'm never sure," I said. "But I think so."

After Chuck hung up I went back to the Scriabin. When it was time, I closed the piano, headed downstairs to Shorty's.

Home was the high-ceilinged apartment I'd built out of what had been an unfinished attic in the ancient brick building Shorty O'Donnell owned on Laight Street, the building his bar was in. On the second floor, between me and the bar, was Shorty's office, storage, and a place for him to crash on nights he couldn't make it home to Queens. I'd built those rooms, too, in return for a cheap lease on the apartment upstairs. That was eighteen years ago, after I was ready to admit to myself that my marriage wasn't going to make it to a third year and that camping in Shorty's attic wasn't just a temporary thing.

The bar was comfortably full, not crowded and not sparse. Dark wood and green glass lampshades soaked up the light, the same way the comfort of a familiar place kept talk low and easy. Shorty, busy behind the bar, managed to look up anyhow as the door opened, the way he always does, just to know who's coming and going from his place. I returned his nod as I surveyed the room from the door, spotted Lydia in a booth against the wall. Maneuvering between the tables, saying hi to the guys I knew, saw here most nights, I reached her and slid in across the booth.

"Hi, honey, I'm home."

She smiled as I leaned across the table to kiss her.

"You're early," I said. Lydia's glossy hair was black and short and scented with freesia. I settled myself on the leather bench across from her. It was farther away than I wanted to be, but it was where I was. "Why didn't you buzz me when you got here?"

"I didn't mind waiting. I didn't want to disturb you."

At the piano, she meant. She'd know that's where I was at the end of the day, where I try to be. She's asked me to play for her a few times, but I haven't, and she doesn't push it. I'm grateful for that, because I know how much she hates unsatisfied curiosity.

She also hates waiting.

I met her dark eyes briefly, then turned away to find someone to bring me a drink.

Lydia leaned back against the booth and sipped at her own drink—seltzer with three limes—through a straw. "How was work?" she asked.

Kay, a waitress who's been at Shorty's almost as long as I have, came to smile at me and take my order. When she was gone I turned back to Lydia. "What makes me think I can stand in the sun six floors above Broadway in July and lay bricks all day, just because I did this when I was twenty?"

"I asked you that last night when you called."

"Did I have a good answer?"

"No."

"I'm not surprised. Work was fine. If I can move in the morning, I'll go back." My beer came; I drank some of it down. "Actually, it wasn't fine. There's a problem on that site."

"Besides what you're there for?"

"I don't know. Something happened today. Could have been an accident, and I think that'll be the official word."

"But you don't think it was?"

I looked over my beer at her. "No."

I told Lydia about Mike DiMaio and Joe Romeo, and about the pile of sand soaked with Reg Phillips's blood.

She asked questions as I went, about the men I'd met, the way the place had looked, who had said what to whom. She asked if Reg Phillips would be all right.

"I don't know. I called the hospital before I came down here. They say 'serious but stable.' I don't know what that means."

She finished her drink. "Why don't you think it was an accident?"

I signaled for Kay. "You want dinner?" I asked Lydia. She did, so we ordered, and Kay brought Lydia another seltzer. When that business was over, I went back to the other. "His hard hat," I said. "When I got there, it was lying on the ground by his knee."

"Which means?"

"A hard hat fits pretty snugly. It's not going to fly off backwards when you stumble. If a guy trips hard and falls forward, his hat might fall off, but in the same direction he's going."

"So it should have been in front of him."

"Somewhere. Up around his head."

"Could it have rolled?"

"Not backward, if it's going forward."

She pursed her lips. "But if someone knocked it off, say in an argument, and then he fell . . ."

I nodded. "And then he fell. After someone slammed him over the head with a brick."

"You think that's what happened?"

"I don't know. I don't know enough about him, or anyone else up there, to know why anyone would."

"It's also not your job," she pointed out. "Unless Joe Romeo did it."

"Well, sort of." I told her about Mike DiMaio, what he'd said and what I'd promised.

"Is that a good idea?" she asked. "He's not your client. You already have a case."

"*We* already have a case. And this may be part of it. We have to look into it at least far enough to know that."

"Oh?" she said, slurping her seltzer. " 'We?' "

"Didn't I tell you when I called last night that I wanted you working with me on this?"

"No. You said you wanted to have dinner with me."

"You can't tell me you don't automatically suspect my motives when I say I want to have dinner."

"No, I do. But that you want me to work for you is not the first thing that springs to mind."

"Your problem. My motives, like my heart, are pure."

"Your problem. So what's my assignment, boss?"

I thought. "Well, I'd like to know a little about Reg Phillips. DiMaio says he gambles; maybe he's into Romeo—or someone—for more than he could handle. But I don't want to stick you with that; it's just boring paperwork, and I know how you hate that."

"Your concern is touching, and also suspicious."

"I'll do a background on Phillips. Chuck will spring for that, I think."

"Remind me again which one Chuck is. Have I met him?"

"Once, a couple of years ago at that barbecue at his old partner's place on Staten Island."

"Oh, God, I remember that. One of your worst ideas, to take me there."

"You wanted to go," I protested, wounded. "You *asked* to go."

"You should have stopped me. As a friend."

"At the time, you said if I were a friend I'd take you."

"You should have driven away and left me standing on the curb. An afternoon in the broiling hot sun inhaling charcoal smoke and lighter-fluid fumes and being leered at by drunken cops. Yuck. Which one was Chuck DeMattis?"

"Bald, a little chubby, handing out beers all around, knew everybody's name. You'd better remember him; he remembers you."

Lydia squeezed a lime into her seltzer. "Everybody there looked like that description," she pointed out. "I was the only person there who looked like me."

"True," I said. "Which is why you excited the admiration of all around you."

Lydia shot me a look; I returned an innocent smile.

"Okay," she said, choosing professionalism. "And you're working for Chuck on this?"

"More or less. I'll keep him filled in if anything happens, but it's my case now. He says he doesn't really want to know."

Lydia furrowed her brow as she finished her seltzer.

"What?" I said.

"I'm not sure. I just never met a cop before who didn't want to know."

"He's not a cop anymore. And he has a reputation to protect."

"And you don't?"

"Only with you and your mother, where it's already so low—"

At that moment Kay returned, bringing Lydia's spinach salad and my corned beef and cabbage.

"I don't believe you're eating that in this heat," Lydia said, pointing her knife at my steaming plate.

"What do you mean? This is very important food. Beef for protein. Salt to replace what you lose when you sweat, for those of us who do that. And cabbage, for your Vitamin Cabbage, a critical part of any diet." I speared some pink corned beef and a translucent cabbage leaf together on my fork. "And, of course, potatoes—"

"Don't go on. We have some metabolic differences and I'd like to keep it that way. So if you don't want me digging into Reg Phillips' background, what is it you do have in mind for me?"

I knew what sort of answer she was expecting, but I decided it was in my own best interests not to give it. I gazed at her thoughtfully. "You looking for a job?"

"I'm waiting for you to give me one."

"No, I mean a real job. Like, for example, as a secretary."

"*Me?*"

"None other."

"What are you, nuts?"

"Why? You can type. Answer the phone. Lick stamps. It's perfect."

"You're crazy."

"Chuck asked me if I wanted someone on the site. I told him no. I may have changed my mind."

She slowed down, gave me a strange look. "You want someone watching your back?"

"No. I'm not sure how anyone could, unless it was another bricklayer working right next to me, and that would mess up my chances of blending in with the scenery. I don't think I need that, anyway. No, here's what I'm thinking: Whatever's going on up there, what Joe Romeo's doing or whatever else, it'll be easier to pick it up if we come at it from two directions. The talk in the trailers is different from the talk on the scaffold. I'd like you to be in there, listening."

She gave me a long look. "I hate it," she said, "that you get to be up there in the middle of things and I have to be stuck behind some stupid desk typing somebody's stupid letters."

"I know," I said.

Her look went on for a while. Finally she said, "Are you sure you can get me in?"

"I already called Chuck and asked. Crowell Senior okayed it, as long as it gets results."

"You promised that?"

"No. But I said it had a better shot than anything else."

"All right," she said, after one more long look. "But I wouldn't do this for just anybody."

"I know," I said again. "I owe you big."

Lydia said, "You have no idea."

We finished dinner. I filled Lydia in on everything else I thought, had seen, had sensed about the site and the people there. I had coffee; she had tea and a slice of peach pie. I kissed her good night, put her in a cab for Chinatown, and went upstairs to bed. I was sound asleep a couple of hours before I usually turn in. I had to report to work at seven-thirty in the morning, and I wasn't twenty anymore.

five

through the dust and heat of the next morning, Mike DiMaio and I spoke very little. We had both called the hospital before work, so we both knew how Reg Phillips was doing: still serious but stable, still in a coma, swelling apparently going down. My back was sore and my shoulders ached, so I was slower than the day before, though I tried to find a rhythm I could stay with; and DiMaio, who didn't seem to be watching me, threw me a pointer every now and then that pulled me through some difficult spot.

At coffee break we stayed by ourselves, near our work, but didn't talk much. At lunch, we joined the other masons in the shade of the finished wall.

"Hey, look, it's Mikey and his hero partner," one of the guys called as we neared them on the scaffold. "We thought you was gonna keep him all to yourself now, Mikey, him being a hero and all."

"Nah, I just figured he had a tough enough day yesterday without having to deal with you jerks." DiMaio dropped himself onto the scaffold, opened his lunchbox. I put myself up against a pile of bricks near him. There were about a dozen guys there altogether, perched on mounds of brick or sprawled on scaffold planking. I introduced myself to the ones I hadn't met yet. The ones I had, Angelo Lucca and Sam Buck, sat together in the deepest shade. Buck was already halfway through his sandwich.

"That was quick thinking yesterday," a sandy-haired guy named Tommy told me as he shook my hand. "I'm sure Reg is gonna appreciate it."

That drew a moment of awkward silence as everyone's thoughts went to the unspoken "if." I took a bottle of juice from my lunchbox, uncapped it. "Not really thinking," I said. "While I was laid off I worked on an EMS team. Some things get to be instinct."

"I don't know," someone else volunteered. "I was a medic in the army, I never got used to it. Always had to think, 'What do I do now?' "

"Christ, Frankie, way you think, you probably killed more guys than the enemy," Angelo Lucca said.

Frankie grinned cheerfully. "Luckily, wasn't no war on. I never left San Francisco."

"Jesus, you did your service at the Presidio? Son of a bitch. I was bit to shit for three years by every mosquito at Fort Bragg."

That started a discussion about the military, a game of one-upmanship whose subject was the worst base to serve on, worst weather, worst drill sergeants, fewest girls. A couple of these guys, near my age, had been drafted; most were too young for that, but some of them had enlisted, looking for excitement, the American way.

"Hey," somebody said in the middle of it. "What about you, Smith? Your age, you must've been in Vietnam."

They all quieted, waited to hear what the veteran had to say.

I shook my head, taking in the last bite of roast beef on rye. "Navy," I said. "They kept moving us around the South China Sea, but we never got close."

"Too bad." Some guys made sympathetic noises. What good was a war if you didn't get to fight it?

"You was in the navy, isn't that right, Mike?" someone asked.

DiMaio nodded. "Lousiest years of my life," he said. "Tried to get away from bricklaying, look where it got me. You like the navy, Smith?"

"I hated the damn navy," I said. "Three years busting my butt doing work you can't see, then doing it over."

"Yeah. And now you're gone, some other dumb jerk is doing the same shit. Ship didn't care, didn't even know you was there."

"And what, you think this building cares?" That was Sam Buck, from the shadows. "You think it sees you coming in the morning, says, 'oh goody, Mikey's here'?" He cackled as he lifted a can of Coke.

"Shove it, Sam," said DiMaio, not looking at Buck. He crumpled the wrapping from his sandwich; his face was flushed with more than the heat.

"Hey, come on, don't get DiMaio started," the sandy-haired mason, Tommy, called out. "He comes over here to break your ass, Buck, I'm gonna have to get up and get out of the way, and I'm tired."

"I'm not breaking anybody's ass," DiMaio muttered. He popped the top on his own Coke can, took a long gulp. "I don't give a shit."

No one who says that ever means it, and it was too hot for a fight. I lit a cigarette, rubbed out the match on the scaffold boards. "There was one good thing about the Navy," I said, as though I'd been musing on the subject. Eyes turned to me. "There was always a poker game going, or if there wasn't, a crap game. You could always find action on shipboard. Only thing, in those days ship-to-shore was a bigger deal than now, especially halfway around the world. Three years I didn't bet on a horse." I shook my head in wonder. "I missed out on Secretariat. Can you believe that?"

The only black mason on the crew, a huge muscled man named Ray, grinned at me. "You troubled that way, Smith? Ponies your weakness?"

"Hey, I do all right. I have a system."

That brought an even bigger grin from Ray, and a few from some other guys too.

"Believe what you want," I said. "I have a natural-born sense for horses. Learned it from my grandmother."

"Yeah?" one of the younger guys asked. "Who do you like?" Men turned to look at him. Ray, still smiling, shook his head.

I ignored the doubters, looked at the kid as though weighing whether or not to let him in on a good thing. "Well," I finally said, "there's a filly running at Santa Anita tomorrow could pay your rent. You got any spare cash, I'd recommend Maribel, in the third. It's a beautiful horse." I felt Mike DiMaio's eyes on me, but I didn't look his way.

"Yeah?" Frankie said. "How much you got on Maribel yourself?"

With a disgusted toss I threw the wrappings from my sandwich in the general direction of the barrel inside the window opening. "Me? I've got a problem."

Frankie laughed. "Oh, I get it. You could spend Joey's rent, but you're not gonna crack open your own wallet for this great horse, huh?"

"I sure as hell would. I'd put the rent on her in a minute, if I could find anybody up here in your great state of New York who'd take my bets. You boys don't take easily to outsiders." Shaking my head over the unfairness of it all, I said, "I don't suppose . . . ?" I looked around, was met with smiles and shrugs.

I shrugged too, and sighed. "Well," I said, looking at DiMaio, "I guess there's nothing to do but get back to work. Right, Mikey?"

Without waiting for an answer, I picked up my lunchbox and gloves, threw my cigarette over the scaffold, and headed back to my bricks.

As I got to the other end of the building, to my side of our bay, I heard DiMaio come up behind me. "Santa Anita," he muttered, moving past to where his own work was. "So you're a handicapper, huh, Smith?"

"Every man has his vices, Mike. Some of us play the horses. Some of us are hot-tempered sons of bitches who'd start a fight on a six-story scaffold—"

"Hey—"

"Tell me something." I smiled as I buttered a brick, placed it carefully, laid a level on it.

"Yeah, what?"

"Am I really that bad?"

"What, as a bricklayer?"

"Uh-huh."

Pulling on his gloves, he looked over at my work. "Nah," he said. "Clean, neat, and straight. Just goddamn slow."

Slow or not, I'd laid what I thought were some pretty clean courses by the time afternoon coffee break rolled around. I went inside then, partly to use the can, partly just to be wandering around, to see who else was wandering around.

DiMaio was right about the portable john. It stank, but business was business, so I used it anyway. Gratefully stepping back out of it, I lit a cigarette and let my eyes wander over the wide horizontal spread of bare concrete and the tall steel columns moving across it in stately procession like trees in a formal garden. I watched the comings and goings of men, each focused on his own narrow task, the combination of all these small jobs somehow making a half-block-wide, forty-story building rise around us.

I remembered having the eerie feeling, on a construction job I'd worked years ago, that none of us were actually building this building: that the jobs we were doing were rituals to invoke the magic, to invite the gods, the way priests lit candles and burned incense. The building would grow and become what it was meant to be if we did these jobs, but the work wasn't making it happen. The building just needed to see the work, the way the gods needed to see the candles: as an expression of faith.

I'd said that to Phyllis when I'd gotten home that night, but the apartment was hot and the baby was crying and she'd said she had no patience for my bullshit. It surprised neither of us when we separated as that hot summer turned to fall. We were divorced by spring, but we tried for seven years after to be civil to each other, at least in front of Annie.

Then Annie died in a car crash. She was supposed to be spending the weekend with me, but I was in Chicago on a case. I'd promised to make it up to her, another weekend. She'd said it was okay. I didn't think much about faith after that.

* * *

I started heading back to my work through the cool of bare concrete and exposed steel. From across the floor the skinny figure of Sam Buck approached me, ambling just about as aimlessly as I was.

"Smith," he said in greeting, as our paths brought us face-to-face. "Hey, you got a cigarette?"

Why not? I thought. An opening's an opening. "Sure." I tapped a few up from the pack, he chose one, and I gave him a light from the tip of mine.

"So," he said, drawing in smoke, streaming it away, "you really looking for action?"

"I'm so desperate I'd bet on the goddamn Yankees," I said. "I'm just holding myself together till payday. I met this guy downtown, he'll take my bets, but he won't carry a stranger. To start, he wants to see cash."

"That's a pain."

"Tell me about it."

"Shame payday's not till Thursday. Because of your horse tomorrow, I mean."

I nodded. "Maribel. I'm telling you, that's some horse. It's you damn unfriendly northerners. Wouldn't be like this back home. A word and a handshake, there."

"I'm crying for you. But I might be able to help."

"Help how?"

"I know a guy who'll take your action."

"Before he sees my cash?"

"Anytime."

"No shit. Lead me to him."

"Just go back to work. I'll send him to you."

"Here?" I acted surprised.

"Yeah," he said. "Here."

So I went back to work, and Sam Buck went on his way, and twenty minutes later Joe Romeo was standing by my side.

"How you guys coming?" was his greeting as he stopped on the scaffold, hands in his pockets, and scanned our work.

"Need some more ties," DiMaio answered without turning around. He tossed one of the steel tabs he was talking about to the scaffold planking at Romeo's feet. "And what is this shit? Might as well be using rubber bands. Get me some decent ties, Joe."

"Other guys aren't having trouble with 'em," Romeo answered. "Other guys aren't falling behind, either."

DiMaio straightened up, turned. His face flushed; but after a glance at me, all he said was, "Christ, Joe, you gotta give us a day or two to get used to each other."

Romeo fixed DiMaio with a narrow stare. "This is day two. Be used to each other by tomorrow. I don't want you two fucking up my schedule."

"Shit!" DiMaio started, but Romeo cut him off.

"See you a minute, Smith?" He motioned with his head, started down the scaffold. I cut DiMaio a look, then followed.

Romeo stopped where no one was working. I stopped too. He turned to me, rocked back on his heels, hands in his pockets again. He said, "I hear you've been talking about finding some action."

I put suspicion on my face and in my voice. "Where'd you hear that?"

"I even hear you're trying to get the men to drop their paychecks on some glue factory out at Santa Anita."

I shrugged like a nervous man. "Subject of racetracks came up. We were just talking."

"Talking, huh?"

I didn't answer.

"Well," Romeo said, "could be I can help you."

I took a second, then said, "You?" .

"Yeah, asshole," he said. "Me."

I didn't say anything, as though I didn't know what to say. He went on. "Here's how it works. I'll take any action you want. I don't need to see the color of your money, because I know where to find you." He smiled, showing me a row of white, even teeth. "You want to lay odds on the number of cars coming through that red light, I don't care. But I don't carry you. You lose, you pay, or you don't work anymore. And I don't mean just on this site, pal. You understand?"

I nodded my understanding. I doubted Romeo had the muscle to back up a threat like that, but a bet-hungry mason just up from Texas wouldn't know that.

"And you don't tell anyone who's backing you," he said. "Anyone wants to know where your action comes from, you tell me, and I find him, if I want to. Sometimes I don't. My business, not yours. Got it?"

I let myself grin. "Jesus. This is great. The foreman. And here I thought you were going to ride my ass about my bad habit."

Romeo didn't smile back. "I love your bad habit, Smith. Guys like you lose more than they win. But remember this: I got a sweet thing going here. My crews don't produce, it ain't so sweet. First thing you are to me is a bricklayer. First time you call in sick on race day, you're fired, you're cut off, and you're unemployable. We understand each other?"

I agreed, as I put fifty dollars on Maribel—running at eight to one—that we did indeed understand each other. Or, I amended silently as I headed back to where I belonged, at least we understood each other as much as any two people, one of whom is being paid to lie to the other, can.

I found a reason to stop by the field office in the trailer on the first floor at quitting time. Something about my insurance, some paper I didn't know if the union needed, since I was from out of state. Something John Lozano didn't have the answer to.

"Crowell could tell us," he said, rising from his chair, slipping a pencil behind his ear. "They got a new girl over there, to keep the files straight. Come on, I'll go over with you."

"She'll still be there? It's after quitting time."

"Oh, yeah. Crowell's girls work eight-thirty to five-thirty. She'll be there."

And thrilled about it for sure, I thought. "I'll go," I said. "You don't have to come. They won't be able to tell me today anyway. Anything you want from anyone, you always have to come back tomorrow."

"Ain't that the truth," he sighed. "Okay, go ahead. Let me know if you need me."

Across the hall in the fluorescent-lit trailer, the new girl was standing behind a gray metal desk. She looked up, a file in each hand, as I opened the door. She was short and Chinese, wearing a green silk blouse and a set of flea-market glass beads with little painted fireworks on them that I'd bought for her last Christmas. She scowled evilly as I approached her.

"May I help you?" Completely contradicting her expression, her voice was well-modulated and ever so polite.

The other secretary, an older black woman, lifted her eyes from the computer screen in front of her, but must have decided to let Lydia handle this one. She went back to her work as I said, "I have some questions about insurance forms."

"Talk to your Allstate agent," Lydia muttered, not loud enough for the other woman to hear. Then she tossed her head and said, in a clear and syrupy sweet voice, "I'm not sure I can help you, but I'd be delighted to try."

With an uneasy feeling that I'd be paying for this for a long time, I started to explain what I wanted. Lydia put on a face of such earnest anxiousness to be helpful that I had to cough to keep from laughing.

We could have gone on for a while, parrying and thrusting, before the other secretary caught on, but our stride was broken by a loud voice coming from the conference room to Lydia's left.

"What the hell's the difference?" The voice, one I didn't know, was gravelly and annoyed. "Tell Lozano that Lacertosa has to put on two more crews, for chrissakes. Call Gilbert, get the steel here next week instead of August. If we have to do it, let's just do it, Daniel, come on!"

That was said in a way so dismissive and disgusted as to sound unarguable to me, but another voice answered.

"John's crews aren't producing now, Dad. He doesn't need more men, he needs men working harder." That was Dan Crowell, Jr., which told me who the other voice was.

Lydia gave me a little smirk, so I guessed she knew who was on John's crews.

"Then get on his case! That's your *job*, Daniel. You heard what the problem is." The gravelly voice softened; I sensed a reassuring smile in it. "Don't worry, Mrs. Armstrong. We'll give the bank what they need. Daniel, light a fire under Traco, maybe we can even have some windows in."

"You can't light a fire under those guys. They're too big and too far away to give a damn. If we were using someone local—"

"We're not, and there's reasons for it! Call them, or I will. And you know what else? Let me call O'Brien. I got an idea about that stone trim, maybe we could get it in fast and save a bundle besides. Hold on a minute."

I heard the sound of a chair scraping back. A large man, white-haired, fat in the gut where Dan Junior was still only soft, but with muscled arms, leaned through the conference-room door into the file cabinet–cluttered outer office. He looked me over and dismissed me, as though he'd already sized me up and knew he could handle whatever I was bringing, but later, after the more important work was done.

"Verna, get me the manloading chart for O'Brien. And see if you can find that new look-ahead schedule from Gilbert, the one for the next three, four weeks."

The secretary opened a drawer in her desk and began flipping through files. Crowell turned to Lydia. "Everything all right?"

"Yes," she said. "This is one of Lacertosa's masons. He just needs some paperwork."

Crowell nodded, eyed me again, then disappeared back into the conference room. A few seconds later Verna pushed back her chair and headed in there too, files in hand.

"Thanks," I heard Crowell say. "Okay, Mrs. Armstrong. By September, we're gonna have the dogs and ponies all in a row. You'll be able to give the bank their show."

"Thank you, Mr. Crowell." That was a woman's voice, deep and assured. She said something else, but I couldn't follow it. I wanted to edge closer to the conference-room door, but Verna walked back through it and fixed her eyes on me.

"Well?" I said to Lydia, my eyebrows raised, as though I'd been waiting for her to respond to something I'd asked. "Do you think you have it?"

"I'll have to look it up," she answered sweetly. "What did you say your name was?"

I told her what my name was.

"All right," she said, making a show of jotting down my name. The voices in the conference room had gotten back to normal, and I couldn't make out what was going on anymore, though I was still intrigued. I hoped Lydia would give me an opening to hang around, but she didn't.

All she said, smiling her helpful smile at me, was, "Come back tomorrow."

six

i'd arranged to meet Lydia for dinner at Pho Viet Hoang, a Vietnamese place in Chinatown we both liked. I had a nagging feeling as I left the site, trudged over the concrete floor, and down the wooden ramp into the brightness of the afternoon, that getting together on Lydia's turf might not be a great idea right now. I was trying to think of a way around it, some more neutral ground to suggest, but I couldn't come up with anything that she wouldn't see right through. I resigned myself to the summer storm clouds and occasional lightning flashes that I knew would be the weather at our table, and decided that, like weather, it was inevitable.

As it turned out, though, it wasn't. Dinner was at the Vietnamese place, all right. But Lydia and I were too busy to bother with issues like moral superiority and who owed what to whom. We spent the evening discussing the unearthing, in the elevator pit on the Armstrong site, of a body.

I wasn't there when they found him, but Lydia was. She called me twice from the site. The first time, just before six, was to tell me she wasn't sure she could make dinner, and to tell me why: The crew digging in the elevator pit seemed to have found a body; the cops were on their way.

"Jesus!" I said. "What?"

"What I said," she replied calmly and quietly. I could hear agitated men's voices in the background. "Mr. Crowell went out there with the workmen. He just came back. He told Verna to call the police. We're waiting for them."

"Whose?" I demanded. "Whose body? That crane operator—Pelligrini?"

"I don't know. I have to go. I'll see you later." She said that fast and hung up, the new secretary calling to cancel a dinner date, trying not to jeopardize her new job.

I spent the next half hour pacing, sitting with a bottle of beer, standing to light a cigarette, pacing some more. If I'd come up with a single half-plausible excuse to go back up there I would have, in a flash, but there wasn't one to be had, and I knew it. Having Lydia there in this sort of situation was the next best thing to being there myself—in some situations, a better thing—and I knew that, too. I thought about it the whole time I paced and smoked.

When the phone rang again, I yanked it up before the first ring was over.

"Smith," I barked into it.

"Wow. Relax. It's me. I'll meet you in half an hour."

"Who was it?"

"I'll see you later."

Dumb question, Smith. She can't answer that one with people around. Ask it the other way.

"Was it Pelligrini?"

"Yes."

"Jesus," I said, but she'd hung up by then.

I don't live too far from Chinatown; I was at Pho Viet Hoang inside of fifteen minutes. You can't smoke there, but you can eat pastel shrimp chips dipped in a blistering red sauce and drink Vietnamese beer, which has a thin, acid bite and is served very cold. The whole place was cold; they were giving their air-conditioning a workout. I breathed in the tang of fish sauce and cilantro and stared at the door, as though I could make Lydia materialize faster that way. Maybe I did. She was there twenty-five minutes after she'd called.

I stood when she came in; that annoys her but I can't help it. I touched her arm lightly and kissed her equally lightly. Her blouse was a stream of silk against the tips of my fingers.

"Give," I said.

"Did you call Mr. DeMattis?" she asked as she sat.

"He wasn't there. I left a message for him to beep me, before he talked to Crowell if he could."

"You're wearing that thing?" Her eyebrows shot up. "I thought you hated it."

"I do. That doesn't mean it isn't useful. Come on, give. What the hell happened?"

"The crew in the elevator pit, putting in the sump pump," she said. "Later you'll have to tell me what a sump pump is."

"It pumps out the sump," I said. "What the hell's the story?"

"I don't know. He was about half unearthed by the time they told us we could go. Actually they were ready for us to go earlier, but I bought some time by staying until Verna's husband came to get her. She was shaken up."

"Your basic human decency is humbling. They're sure it was Pelligrini?"

"Both Crowells identified him."

"And he was in the pit?"

"Buried. Under about two feet of dirt. Isn't there a floor at the bottom of the elevator pit, cement or something?"

"Concrete, you mean. No, it's just a hole. Once the elevator's in nobody ever goes there; it's just to make space for the cables. They were just digging and there he was?"

"Basically. One of the workmen saw these white things where he was about to stick his shovel next. He brushed the dirt off them and they turned out to be fingers. According to him that was all he wanted to know. He beat it out of there and got Mr. Crowell."

"Two feet of dirt," I mused. "I wonder why he was buried so shallowly. He was bound to be found when they put the pump in."

Lydia shook her head. "Mr. Crowell Senior said the pump was added to the job. He just authorized it the day before yesterday. There's a stream or a spring or something at the basement level, something that wasn't on the survey. Water was seeping into the pit. That's why they were working so late, so they could get it in and get it working before it rains tomorrow."

"So if the pump hadn't been added there wouldn't have been any more digging in the pit?" I asked.

She shrugged. "You're the one who knows about pits."

I sipped my beer. "So it was just bad luck for the guy who put him there. If they hadn't needed the pump, he'd never have been found."

We were quiet while the thought of that filled the space between us, the thought of a man deep in the moist, silent dirt below forty floors of stores and offices and apartments, below copy machines whirring and dinner cooking and people slow dancing as evening turned to night.

"How long had he been there?" I broke the silence.

Before Lydia could answer, a thin, sharp-faced waiter came to take our order. Without discussing it, with hardly a glance at the menu, I ordered us both shrimp grilled on sugar cane and lemongrass-and-coriander soup, and Lydia got us chicken with onions and hot peppers. Foods we'd had before; foods we knew we loved. We didn't discuss it afterward, either, how we'd thought alike, how easy it had been. We went straight back to business.

"I don't know," Lydia said. "Dan Junior thought of that right away, too. He didn't go out with Senior to see, but when Mr. Crowell came back and told Verna to call the police, Junior asked, 'My God, who is it? How long has he been there?' "

" 'I didn't dig him up, Daniel,' Mr. Crowell said. 'I didn't see his face.' Then we all waited."

"But the police did dig him up?"

"Partly. They've probably got him all out by now, but they were being careful about it. In case they can make something from the forensic evidence."

"And who ID'd him, both of them?"

"Yes. Although Junior, at first, didn't seem so sure. But after other people said it was Pelligrini, he said probably it was."

The waiter brought our soup. The clear yellow broth gave off pungent trails of steam from thick white bowls, leafy coriander and green stems of lemongrass floating on top, strips of beef and noodles swirling together as I sank my spoon down. I was hungry. To look at her, so was Lydia. Lydia can twirl noodles on chopsticks the way the rest of us can do spaghetti on a fork. I watched her clear everything solid out of her soup bowl in the time it took me to coax a couple of strips of beef onto my spoon and into my mouth. Then she picked up her bowl in both hands and sipped at the broth.

I asked her, "Why didn't Dan Junior go out to look the first time?"

Lydia put the soup bowl down. "Because Dan Senior said, 'Stay here, Daniel,' as he ran out the trailer door."

The chicken had just come, and with it fragrant bowls of steaming rice, when the beeper on my hip went off. The number the readout gave me was Chuck's, at home.

The phone at Pho Viet Hoang is up by the door, not a good place for the conversation I wanted to have with Chuck. I told Lydia who it was as I stood. "Don't eat all that," I said, pointing to the chicken as I headed out the door.

"You wish," she retorted to my back.

There was a phone booth a block away, at Canal. It's a busy corner, traffic and people coming and going, but it was better than being by the door at the restaurant, where everyone waiting for a takeout meal was looking around for something interesting to help pass the time.

Chuck picked up on the first ring.

"Couldn't you find a noisier phone?" he asked when he knew it was me. "Where the hell are you, Grand Central Station?"

"Worse. Canal and Mott."

"Great. What's up?"

"A lot," I said. "Did Crowell call you?"

"Yeah, as a matter of fact. Left a message to call forthwith. But since you called too, something told me to talk to you first, in case there's something going on I could get sandbagged with."

"There is. They found Lenny Pelligrini's body on the Armstrong site."

"What?"

A horn blared behind me, but it didn't mask Chuck's half-shout.

"That's what I said, too," I told him.

"What the hell are you talking about?"

"In the elevator pit." I told him about the sump pump, about the white fingers in the dirt. "Probably whoever put him there thought no one would ever be back there again."

"Jesus." Chuck's voice was low. "Who did the ID?"

"Both Crowells."

"Shit." He was silent for a moment, then said again, "Shit. Okay, what else?"

"Nothing else. Except the bad feeling you had about that site seems to have been accurate."

"I was a cop twenty years. My bad feelings, you could bet the ranch on. You think Joe Romeo had anything to do with it?"

"I don't know."

"But you got a bad feeling."

"I don't know." I paused, waited for a fire engine to race by, siren screaming. "I went in with a bad feeling about him, from you and Crowell. And I don't like the guy. But nothing else says he's connected to this."

"That could just be because you don't know anything else yet."

"That's true. Chuck, you looked into Pelligrini some, right? What do you have on him?"

"Not a thing. He's a choirboy, to hear everyone tell it. Ask me, to get dead, he must've seen something he shouldn't, been in the wrong place at the wrong time, something like that."

"Maybe he was into a loan shark—Joe Romeo, just for an example—and couldn't pay?"

"You got to be in really big before they write off your debt and do you. And if they do, they leave you around where other people could get the message, not in some pit where no one's going to find you. Look, I'll go back over that ground, just to be sure, but that kid's not the way to cut into this."

"Maybe you're right. And the cops will be working that angle, anyway."

"Uh-huh."

"I guess it's even possible that whatever happened to Pelligrini has nothing to do with anyone on that site except Pelligrini himself. Someone may have just found a convenient hole to shove a body in. How good is the security up there?"

"Average, I guess. Since the trouble they had early, they tightened up a little, but I still think they only got one, maybe two guys at night, and they probably coop half the night between rounds. Can't be that hard to get through that fence, either. Christ, I guess I better call Crowell."

"Listen, Chuck, there's a reason I wanted to talk to you first, too."

"Yeah? What's that?"

"Crowell's bound to wonder if Romeo was involved. They're going to tell the cops they've been looking at him, and the cops will pull him in. If they get something, great. If they don't, you'll still need me up there."

"Yeah," Chuck said thoughtfully. "Go on."

"Even if they do. There may be more going on. This Reg Phillips thing, Chuck. I want to see it through."

Chuck was silent while the light changed behind me and the roar of the traffic shifted from north-south to east-west. I waited for his answer, prepared to argue the point, to remind him that this was my case now, to be worked my way. But I didn't have to.

"So you don't want me to blow your cover to Crowell," Chuck's voice came back. "And you don't want Crowell blowing it to the cops. You want to show up for work tomorrow like usual."

"Right. If you can talk Crowell into it."

"What's to talk them into? They don't know about you. All I gotta do is make sure they want to keep *me* on the case. If I was them, I would, for the reasons you said. Crowell can send the cops to me if they want, I could lay it out for them. The kid might have a problem with it, but Senior'll tell him what to do and he'll do it."

"If you have to, tell them who I am. I just don't want them to pull me."

"I don't want to tell them. Especially if guys are getting whacked over the head and other guys are getting planted in the elevator pit. The more people know who you are, the more I got to worry your name is gonna be dropped where it don't belong and heard by somebody got no business hearing it."

"Well, I like it better that way too. So what do you say? Unless I hear from you, I'll just show up on the site tomorrow, as surprised as anybody when they tell me."

"Yeah, okay. We'll try it. What about your girl?"

"Hey, come on, Chuck—"

"Yeah, yeah, your Oriental female partner. How's that?"

"They don't say 'Oriental' anymore, Chuck."

"Oh, Jesus Christ up a Christmas tree. Listen, send me the instruction manual some other time, okay? What about her?"

"Does anyone except old man Crowell know who she is?"

"Maybe he told the kid, I don't know. I bet not. He's the type don't tell you anything except on a need-to-know basis, and he's the one decides if you got a need. At first, he wasn't even gonna bring the kid along to see me. Must be tough on the kid, always running around trying to figure out what he was supposed to know that the old man never told him."

"The old man doesn't trust him?"

"No, it ain't that. He just don't think anyone else can do anything as well as he can, so he don't see no reason to let anyone in on anything. I get the idea he wouldn't have nobody working for him at all if he had the time to do it all himself."

"I know the type."

"Drive you crazy. Anyhow, if he didn't think Junior had any reason to know about your—about Lydia—it wouldn't of occurred to him to say anything. And I don't think he'd of told anyone else."

"See if you can find out. If it's not common knowledge, then I want her to stay too."

"You sure? Until we know what—"

"Forget it. You're going to tell me it could be dangerous for her."

"It could."

"I count on that."

"On what? Its being dangerous for her?"

"Damn right. That's how I keep her working with me."

"What do you mean?"

"She lives for situations like this. I deliver."

Our table, I noticed as I re-entered Pho Viet Hoang, was clear of platter and rice bowls, nothing there but empty dinner plates and Lydia, both waiting for me. At least the dinner plates weren't bouncing their feet and drumming their fingers as they stared around the restaurant.

The sharp-faced waiter spotted me coming in and disappeared into the kitchen. The platter and the rice bowls made it back to the table just after I did.

"Oh, it's you," Lydia said in sarcastic surprise as I sat down. "Where did you go to make that phone call, Brooklyn?"

"We got to chatting about your good qualities," I said. "That always takes forever."

"I think I showed remarkable restraint in not coming after you."

"I think you showed remarkable restraint in not eating all the chicken."

I lifted the cover from the platter and spooned chicken chunks and hot peppers onto her plate. It turned out she hadn't eaten any of the chicken, just sent it and the rice back to the kitchen to keep warm as soon as I'd left. "You and I are both going to stay on the job, if that's all right with you," I told her.

"That's what Mr. Crowell wants?"

"Chuck hadn't spoken to him yet. But it's what I want, and Chuck agreed. Unless the cops find out by morning that Joe Romeo buried Pelligrini in the pit, so Crowell doesn't need us anymore."

"How likely is that?"

"Who knows?"

"And everyone will be working there as usual tomorrow morning? Even with a body dug up from the basement?"

"Nothing but nuclear war would stop work on a site like that. Delays are too expensive."

I lifted a sautéed onion from the platter to my plate. A thought occurred to me. "When I was in your office? That meeting in the conference room—was that the client?"

"The developer." Lydia nodded. "Mrs. Armstrong. Denise."

"Was she there when they found the body?"

"Yes. She went out with Mr. Crowell both times, to see the fingers and then to see if she could identify him once the cops had his face uncovered."

"She must have a strong stomach."

"You mean, for a woman?"

"Even if I did, I wouldn't admit it. No, I mean for a civilian, for someone who doesn't deal in bodies much."

"Well, I guess you're right. She didn't flinch. Which can't be said for Dan Junior, by the way."

"He flinched?"

"Turned green. I thought he was going to be sick."

"You were there?"

"Of course I was there. Not the first time, when Verna and I weren't sure what was going on and it would have looked weird if I'd gone running out there. But when they were looking for people to identify him."

"You must have a strong stomach too." Our eyes met. I touched her hand, just softly. She moved her eyes away, tossed her head, but left her hand where it was.

"For a woman," she said. "And right now I'm starving."

Lydia's appetite grows when she's angry or upset. I took my hand away. She shook out her napkin and laid it on her lap. We both started on the chicken.

It was perfect, something sharp in the sauce behind the heat of the peppers. I ate and asked Lydia, "Do you have any idea what that was about, that argument when I was there?"

"I'm not sure it was an argument."

"Senior seemed annoyed at Junior."

"I think that's just how he talks to him. He talks to Verna a little bit that way, too."

"If he talks to you like that I'll have to take him out behind the barn."

"Oh, he doesn't. He's very polite to me. It's the people he knows best he's like that with, I think. Maybe even the people he likes best."

"Nice guy."

"He can be. He's very nice to Mrs. Armstrong. And," she added, "to me."

"She's the client, he can't afford not to be. You, if your theory is correct, he probably doesn't like." I ignored her look, went on. "Which brings us back to what the argument was about, or whatever it was."

"Well," she said, with a sigh that seemed to have more to do with me than the Crowells, "I'm not sure. But it seems that Mrs. Armstrong is having money troubles. The bank that gave her the construction loan won't give her another one, or something. They seem to think the progress on the building isn't fast enough."

"So Crowell Senior is going to rush things along? That's what it sounded like."

"To meet some deadline. If the bank sees a certain percent complete by whenever it is, six weeks from now, I think, they'll give her the next loan."

"Crowell thinks he can do it?"

"He sounded like it." She paused for a piece of chicken. "Junior has a problem with it."

"Like what?"

" 'You can't get the steel here that fast. We don't have the crews, anyway, even if you could.' Stuff like that. He seems to think Senior's getting carried away."

"What was Senior's answer?"

" 'Then we'll put on more crews. Come on, Daniel, we've done this before.' "

"A can-do guy, huh?"

"I think he wants to be a hero. You know, save the day for

Mrs. Armstrong, that kind of thing. Junior, on the other hand, would just as soon never see her again."

"He said that?"

' "Not to me. But he dropped a passing remark to Verna that I happened to hear about how glad he'll be when this one is over and they don't have to deal with Mrs. Armstrong anymore. I asked Verna about it, as though I were just trying to figure out who's who on my new job. She said Mrs. Armstrong is a little bit difficult—more 'hands on' than most clients, is that the phrase?"

"You pick up jargon so beautifully. Even your accent is good. So she's around a lot, Mrs. Armstrong?"

" 'In their face' is how Verna put it. Probably making it even more imperative that Mr. Crowell perform like a hero for her."

"You make it sound as though that's a bad instinct in a man."

"Me? Don't be silly. You know I love it when big strong men rescue helpless damsels in distress. Hot sauce?" She smiled brightly.

"Absolutely not." I took the hot sauce out of her hand, placed it safely on the table. "There's other stuff that went on today," I said. "Not as dramatic as a body. But if we're going to keep working this case, or these cases, it's stuff you should know about." Not as dramatic; but easier to talk about. And it was better, always, to keep talking. I filled her in on my day as we finished dinner.

"So Joe Romeo *is* a bookie," Lydia said, while the waiter took away the empty platter and bowls and brought us another pot of tea. The tea, like the beer and the waiter, was thin and sharp. I wasn't crazy about it, but Lydia was. She claimed it was bracing and cleared the head.

"Looks that way. We'll see what happens when Maribel wins."

"Will she win?"

"Definitely. She's a great mudder and it's going to rain out there tonight."

" 'Mudder'? Is that like 'sump pump'?"

"Uh-huh. It's a guy thing."

She sipped her tea disdainfully. "So when he pays you tomorrow, or you pay him if this fabulous horse doesn't mud so well, you'll have what you need for Crowell."

"Not enough. I'll know it's there to be had. But they'll need more than my word if they want to be able to get rid of him without union trouble."

"Pictures? Tapes?"

"Maybe. At least a notebook full of times and places."

"This could cost you a lot of money, if you pick the wrong horses and teams and things."

"Expenses. Goes on the report."

"The client covers your bad bets?"

I nodded.

"And the winnings?"

"Well, now, I don't know. If Crowell profited from my gambling, that would be illegal, wouldn't it?"

"And if you do?"

"Also bad. But if I used the money for a good cause, like buying my partner a pair of emerald earrings—"

"It still wouldn't make up for the aching back she gets filing stupid paperwork all day, or the way her blood pressure goes up when those big macho construction men make kissy noises at her. Find a charity to give it to. It's better for your karma."

"My karma needs help?"

She smiled, got up from the table, and turned to leave without giving me an answer. I took that for a bad sign.

seven

As I came down from my place into Laight Street at seven the next morning, I could see dark clouds massing on the Jersey side of the Hudson, jostling each other in place, hungrily eyeing Manhattan. By the time I emerged from the subway a block from the Armstrong site, they were on the move. The hot air was weighty and damp, the kind of day when everything's heavy and you sweat just standing still. Not a good day for bricklaying.

I reported to the site, punched my time card in John Lozano's office, and was as speechless as anyone when he told me the lost crane operator, Pelligrini, had been found in the elevator pit.

I stared. "What?" I said.

"No, it's true." His tired blue eyes searched my face, prepared to deal with whatever he had to, whatever this brought up in me.

"Wait, I don't get it." I shook my head. "He used to work here, this guy? What the hell happened, he fell in there or something? How long has he been— Jesus. While we were working here, he was in there? What the hell happened?"

"I don't know. Mr. Crowell told me about it when I came in today. He didn't fall in there, Smith. Someone killed him and buried him there."

"Killed him?" My eyes widened. "Oh, Christ! Who? How?"

"The cops don't know who, Mr. Crowell says. I heard he

was shot, but I don't know, Mr. Crowell didn't say so. You okay with it?"

"Okay?" I echoed.

"I had one of the laborers quit on me already this morning. Says with what happened to Phillips day before yesterday, now this, it's a bad-luck site. If I'm gonna lose more men, I gotta know."

I shook my head slowly. "No, I need the job. I'll stay. The cops were here? What do they say happened?"

"They say Pelligrini was in the elevator pit," he said with a small smile. "They may be back later asking questions, showing around Pelligrini's picture, stuff like that. I want the men to cooperate, if they do."

"Me?" I put into my tone the mix of innocence and defensiveness I knew he'd be hearing all morning. "I don't know anything."

"No one's saying you do," he said patiently. That was an answer he'd be giving all morning. "Just answer their questions if they come around, okay?"

"Well, yeah," I agreed. "Sure."

He nodded, someone else came in to punch the clock and hear what I'd just heard, and I headed for the hoist, to start the day.

DiMaio wasn't there yet, at the bay where we were working. I pulled the plastic cover off of yesterday's bricks and swung inside to check the detail drawing to make sure I understood the pattern I was working on today.

When I had it set in my head, I climbed back through the window opening and started laying out my tools. DiMaio appeared behind me on the scaffold a minute later.

"Not sure it's worth it," he said.

"Why? You think it'll rain?" I glanced at the darkening sky. He nodded.

"What happens if it does?" I asked.

"If it looks like it'll pass, they'll keep us here. If it's gonna be all day they'll close down. And speaking of nice normal things like rain, they found a body here last night, Smith. What do you know about that?" We were standing facing each other on the scaffold; DiMaio hadn't moved around me to where his own work was. A gust of wind pushed between us.

"Just what you do, Mike," I told him evenly.

"And what's that?"

"What Lozano told me. It was some crane operator who used to work here. They don't know who killed him, how long he'd been there, or how he got there."

"And that's all you know about it?"

"That's all."

It wasn't all.

In the middle of the night, I'd spent some time on the phone with a detective friend of mine, Mike Doherty at the Ninth Precinct, who was working the graveyard shift this week. This case was way out of his territory, but cops don't have much trouble finding out what other cops are doing, if they have a reason to want to know. Or can offer a reason that the cop who supplies the information can pretend he believed, if anyone asks.

"I checked around on your boy Pelligrini," Doherty told me when he called at one in the morning, lunchtime for him. "Nobody ever heard of him."

"No?" I said groggily, trying to wake up. "He was clean?"

"Either that, or whatever he was into was so small or so new that no one was on to him yet."

"You don't know who'd want him gone?"

"No one I could find."

"Chuck DeMattis said Pelligrini and this Joe Romeo I'm after had bad blood between them. You know anything about that?"

"No."

"Can you find out?"

"Hey, Smith, you want a lot for a guy with nothing to trade."

"Come on, you're buying gratitude and goodwill."

"From a P.I.? Where's that gonna get me?"

"Okay, how about a first-round draft pick?"

"How about a date with your partner?"

"I love guys who can be funny at one in the morning."

"Hey, listen." The tenor of his voice changed. "How's DeMattis? He doing all right?"

"Seems fine." An undertone I heard in his question made me ask, "Why? Shouldn't he be?"

"No, it'd be good if he was. I like the guy. I never believed any of that shit anyway."

"What shit?"

"From when he retired."

"I don't know about this."

"Oh. Ah, crap. Well, forget I—"

"Hey, don't even try it. I'm working for the guy. Is there something I'm supposed to know?"

"No, not really." Doherty sighed. "He retired suddenly. Guy does that, there's talk, that's all. Doesn't mean anything."

"About?"

"It was all bullshit."

"About?"

"Ah, nothing. He'd just been assigned to some big investigation, drugs-and-guns task force kind of thing, and he up and quit. Looked bad, that's all."

"How close was he to retirement?"

"Eight months past his twenty years."

Twenty years is when a cop's pension starts, if he wants out.

"Then he was due."

"Oh, yeah, sure. But most guys plan, not just turn in their badge out of the blue. So guys with nothing else to do started wondering out loud. It was crap."

"Wondering about what?"

"Target of the case was this guy Louie Falco. Big shot from DeMattis's old neighborhood. Their mothers go to church together. You can imagine the shit that went on."

"I can. But you don't buy it?"

"DeMattis? Christ, no. Goddamn White Knight, clean as a whistle."

"Did I.A.D. do an investigation?"

"Never even considered it. I'm telling you, it never got past the gossip stage. Hey," he said. I heard a sheet of paper rattle through the phone.

"Hey what?"

"Shit. Maybe, probably nothing. But I'm looking here at Pelligrini's particulars."

"I thought you said he had none."

"Almost none. But he does have an address."

"Most guys do. What about it?"

"He's from the old neighborhood too."

"What, Chuck's?"

"Yeah."

"What neighborhood?"

"Howard Beach."

"Christ, Doherty, every Italian in New York's from Howard Beach."

"That's what I mean. It doesn't mean anything."

I propped the phone on my shoulder, lit a cigarette. "What came of that case?"

"The task-force thing? Nothing. Petered out, like most everything."

"You're full of good cheer."

"I'm a hardworking cop on the night shift, give me a break."

"And I'm a hardworking bricklayer. If you don't have anything else for me, get off the phone so I can get back to sleep."

"This from a guy who woke me this afternoon to ask for a favor?"

"Is it my fault you're on nights? If you had the brains to retire and get a private license—"

"I'd have it easy like you, getting up at six in the morning to lay bricks with guys half my age. No, thanks, I'll stick it out till my pension kicks in. Peace, buddy."

"The same. Thanks."

I hung up the phone, pulled on my cigarette. The faint glow from the streetlamp in the alley edged into the room around the lowered shade, as though if it were quiet enough about it I wouldn't notice.

I'd grown up in so many places there was no one left in my life from my past—no old neighborhood, no kids I'd played with now grown to adults, no one whose family knew my family. I thought about that, about what it might be like to have those connections. The connections Chuck had: guys you'd known all your life, young guys who grew up hearing your name. I thought about calling Chuck; then I pressed the cigarette out, turned over, shut my eyes. It was, after all, one in the morning.

And it was my case.

So I did know more than I told DiMaio I knew. But not in the way he meant, not in the way he was wondering about me. He gave me a long look, and I met it, and we both turned to our brickwork.

Work on the site lasted about an hour. The wind built up momentum, but it didn't bring any relief from the hot, heavy air. Stronger up here than at street level, it tugged at the orange safety netting hung along the scaffold, flapped the edges of the blue tarp I'd pulled off the bricks. Black-bottomed clouds skidded into place above us, circling like an army laying siege. A ballooning plastic bag tumbled through the air over Broadway. It took a free-fall dive, spun up again, and snagged on the boom of the crane before it shook itself free.

DiMaio and I, because we were behind, kept going as long as we dared, eyeing the sky as huge, round, single drops began pelting the dusty boards. I waited for the word from him; he kept on working right up until the rain swept out of the sky in sheets.

"Shit!" DiMaio yelled, striking off a joint as a slanted wall of water passed over us. "That's it. Get the tarp!" He dumped his tools into his bag.

I threw down my own tools, yanked the blue plastic from under the bricks I'd used to hold it down in the wind. We dropped it over the new work and fought to tie it down, weighted it with more bricks. Rain crashed down on us; I was soaked through by the time the tarp was ready to stay. I pulled

my tools together, heaved my bag through the window opening, and swung through after it, almost losing my grip on the
thin wet steel of the scaffold. DiMaio was right behind me.
We retreated into the building; rain chased us three or four
feet in, didn't bother to come farther.

The other masons were already inside, leaning against
columns or dropping their tool bags and themselves to the bare
concrete, to wait it out. Most of the other trades working on this
floor milled around idly also, unable to go on even if their work
was inside because almost everyone was using power tools and
you don't do that in a storm like this. A guy up on a ladder close
to the center of the building was tightening bolts with a hand
wrench and had no reason to stop, except the sight of the rest
of us was probably too much for him. He climbed down, sat on
the ladder's bottom rung, and lit a cigarette.

Thunder crashed, close and loud. I sat, lit a cigarette of my
own, settled my back against a column. The cold steel turned
my wet shirt clammy. DiMaio sat too, against a huge metal
lockbox beside me. He wiped water from his face with a wide
hand. I said to him, "Tell me about Phillips."

He turned his head to me, waited a moment. Then he said,
"Tell you what?"

"Whatever there is," I answered. "Something that could
give me a line on why someone would have tried to kill him,
if that's what happened."

He looked pointedly at me. "You mean, besides his gambling debts, money he owes Joe?"

"We don't know if he has debts," I said. "We don't know if
Romeo's his bookie and we don't know if he's behind. I'll
work that angle, but I want to look at other things too. Just in
case, Mike. Just in case."

"You're spinning your wheels."

"Maybe. But give me a chance."

He bent a strip of flat, corrugated steel, one of the brick ties
we'd been using, between his fingers. "I don't know. Shit."
The steel broke; he chucked it away. "Reg just comes in and
does his job, you know? Old-fashioned kind of guy; thinks
that's what he's being paid for. Started as a mason tender.

They put him mixing the mortar a few weeks later when they saw he was smart."

"Besides betting, does he owe any money that you know of? For tuition, old debts, something like that?"

"No. He lives cheap, small apartment, lousy neighborhood."

"An expensive woman friend?"

"He dates some, but I don't think he's seeing anyone steady. Why? You think maybe he's been sneaking around someone's back stair?"

I pulled on my cigarette, thinking. "Well, maybe, but I don't think that's it. If it didn't have to do with someone here, it wouldn't have happened here. A jealous boyfriend or something would hit him at home."

"Except if the boyfriend works here too."

"Possible," I conceded. "Seem likely to you?"

He shook his head. "Doesn't sound like Reg."

"Okay," I said. "You said he was smart. Is he a smart-ass? Could he have pissed anyone off?"

"You mean, like ratting on guys goofing off? No way. He's a straight-up guy. Does his work, don't really care if you do yours. Not like me, that way."

I took in his look. "I'm trying, Mike."

"Hey, I'm not talking about you. We got a deal. I'm just mouthing off. Sorry." He looked away.

I finished my cigarette and rubbed it out on the column. Rain sheeted in the window openings on the west, shoved through by a change in the wind. My eyes roved over the concrete and the groups of lounging men.

"Hey, Mike?" I said. "Who's that?"

DiMaio looked where I was looking, across the floor. John Lozano stood with Dan Crowell Junior and a young, skinny man who wore a short-sleeved white shirt and a tie, and a yellow hard hat.

"He with Crowell?" I asked.

"Nah. He's from the architect. What the hell's his name? Turner, Cutter, something like that. Carver? I don't remember."

"He's here for an inspection? Lousy day for it."

"Ah, he's here twice a week. But he don't make trouble, not like some of them."

"Some of who?"

He shot me a look. "Boy, it has been awhile for you, hasn't it? Architect's reps. Some of 'em are a real pain in the ass. I seen jobs where the super has a signal for the men when he's bringing the rep around. You hear it, like he whistles, 'When You Wish Upon a Star,' you're supposed to run over and stand in front of shit you don't want the guy to see, look like you're working on something real important over there and don't notice him coming."

I grinned at the thought of masons, carpenters, plumbers, all scattering, busily focusing on work they weren't doing as they shifted their bodies to cover imperfections in the work they had done. "That can't work on a site this noisy," I said.

"Nope. Good thing we don't need it. This guy never has anything to say."

"Maybe that's because the work is good."

"First off, I never known that to stop them. Second, yeah, the work's good, but really what the thing is, is the guy's a wuss."

"How do you mean?" I looked at Turner or Cutter or Carver. His tie and his smooth pale skin marked him as out of place here, and while I watched him he shifted his weight uncomfortably, as though he felt it too. He didn't have the easy sureness of the muscled men who lift block and weld steel, but that wasn't his job. "You mean because he looks like a strong wind could blow him away?"

"Nah, not just that. But it's probably not him. They're all wusses, I think."

"Architects?"

He shook his head. "I met some were okay. But this outfit, Melville."

"I don't get you."

"Well, look at it. That complicated brickwork they got us doing? That's all for the aesthetics. You know, art. Building would stand up if the bricks were a hell of a lot simpler, but it's the architecture part."

"I always thought architecture was the whole thing, not just the aesthetics."

"Yeah, they tell me it's supposed to be."

"But?"

"Well, you look at the drawings, you got all this fancy brickwork, someone put a lot of time into it. Colored mortar joints, I mean someone cared. But look at the shit they got us tying it back with." He leaned to pick up the brick tie he'd tossed. "This is two-story shit. Won't last ten years up here."

"Why not?"

"Building this tall, you need something heavier. Walls move, they got wind on them—I don't know, I'm not an engineer, I can't explain it. But you do this work enough, you don't need it explained, you could feel it."

"What happens if you use this stuff?"

"You use thin shit like this twenty stories up, your bricks shift. You get cracks a couple, three years from now. Place starts to leak. Someone's gonna have to come along and repoint, there goes your colored mortar. Not to mention you're gonna have water inside your fancy apartments. Maintenance headache all your goddamn life." He looked sideways at me. "Ladders are chintzy, too. Didn't you notice as you laid 'em?"

"Ladders" were the horizontal reinforcing in the brick coursing; I'd been handling them for three days. "So what are you saying?"

"I'm saying, the architect didn't give a shit about anything on this job except the fucking aesthetics. He don't understand what makes a building work. Wuss," he grunted. "Look around you. It's not just masonry. Down below, where the carpenters got the studs going in for the walls, you could see it. Everything here's too light gauge, too thin of a thickness. Cheap shit."

I looked around, at the steel, the rainwater puddling on the concrete, the plastic-covered brick beyond the window openings. "You think it's dangerous?"

He shook his head. "Steel's good, concrete's cured right. Those, you gotta file with the city, you got inspectors crawling all over you. This building won't fall down or nothing. It's just gonna leak. Sheetrock's gonna run cracks. Everything you do in your bedroom, your next-door neighbor's gonna hear it."

I picked up a brick tie, turned it over in my fingers.

"I don't know why I give a shit," DiMaio said. "I must be some kind of asshole bricklayer, likes things done right."

We sat around for half an hour, shooting the breeze with guys who wandered by. I smoked. The wind let up some but the rain didn't, and the clouds it fell from were so thick and low that the buildings on the other side of Broadway went out of focus, lost their solidity in the gray mist. The Hudson completely vanished. The traffic on the streets below could have vanished too, for all we knew; you couldn't hear anything from outside but pounding rain and an occasional thunder crash.

At nine-thirty Joe Romeo came around and told us to go home.

"Gonna rain like a son of a bitch all day, boys. I don't want to pay anyone to sit on their butts smoking. We'll make it up over the next week. Any crew behind already better be ready to bust it when you come in tomorrow." He gave me and DiMaio a sharp look, and then a smile. He moved on.

"When he says we'll make it up," I asked DiMaio as we stood, got our tool bags and lunchboxes together, "does he mean overtime?"

"You gotta be kidding. Lozano put out an order, no overtime on this job. Romeo loves it. It means he gets to ride our asses for more work in less time."

"Is that usual, no overtime?"

"Nah, but it happens. I been on jobs like this once or twice. Means they must be cutting the budget pretty close."

We walked together to the hoist, rode it to the ground floor with a group of other guys. Rain pounded the hoist's wood-board sides, dripped in around the edges of the plywood roof.

"I have to stop by the Crowell office," I said to DiMaio as we punched the time clock just inside Lozano's door. Lozano was there, scrawling figures on a Xeroxed sheet. He didn't look up. "Insurance forms," I explained. "I'll see you tomorrow."

"You met the new secretary over there?" DiMaio asked with a grin. "Cute Oriental girl."

"Oh? I'll look for her."

"Yeah, but watch yourself," Lozano put in, eyes still on his paperwork. "This one carpenter tried to pass the time of day over there yesterday, came out with icicles hanging off him."

"Sounds dangerous," I said.

"Yeah," said DiMiao. "Think safety first, Smith. Want me to pick up your forms for you?"

"Gee, no thanks. But I appreciate the offer."

Still grinning, he nodded, turned, and walked off. I crossed the corridor to the Crowell trailer.

The air-conditioning smacked me with a cold blast as I pulled open the door. My clothes were still damp, and the early-morning heat had drained out of me while I'd sat against the steel column on the bare concrete. I shivered, wondered if I could hit Dan Crowell, Jr. up for another T-shirt.

Lydia was sitting behind her gray desk, wearing a cream-colored linen shirt and three gold bracelets. She raised her head as I came in, wrinkled up her nose as she looked me over. She seemed about to say something, but the telephone rang. The other secretary, Verna, wasn't at her desk; Lydia was alone in the outer office.

She took the call, transferred it to Mr. Crowell—whether Senior or Junior I couldn't tell—and then gave me the sugary helpful smile. "Mr. Smith? Oh, look at you. You must have been caught in the rain."

"Uh-huh. Snuck up on me."

"Well, I suppose we can't all be lucky enough to be doing indoor work." She smiled brightly, glancing around the trailer. "I have the forms you were asking about." She handed me three meaningless pieces of paper.

"Thanks. And I'd like to talk to Mr. Crowell for a moment if I could."

She raised her eyebrows. "Mr. Crowell, Senior? Or Mr. Crowell, Junior?"

What the hell, I'd chatted with Junior already. "Senior, if he has a minute. It won't take much time."

Lydia stood and padded over to an open office door. She was wearing, I saw, a black linen skirt and a nice, new-looking pair of brown flats. I'd have to compliment her on them later.

From the open door Lydia came back, followed and over-shadowed by the bulk of Dan Crowell, Sr.

"You want to see me?" Crowell asked, eyeing me as Lydia slid behind her desk again. He was as tall as I was, wider in the shoulders. If Chuck hadn't told me he was sick, seriously ill, I'd never have guessed it. He looked to me like the kind of guy people moved aside for on the sidewalk without even thinking about it, the kind of guy whose opinion on Sunday's game was the only opinion that counted.

"Just for a minute, Mr. Crowell," I said. "I'm Smith. I'm a bricklayer, new on the job. Haven't done brickwork this complicated in years."

"Yeah," he grunted. "Pretty fancy stuff. Having trouble with it?"

"No, sir." In the office to Lydia's left I could see Dan Crowell, Jr. leaning back in his desk chair to where he could see us. I told Senior, "I was just wondering if I could take a look at the drawings and specs."

He frowned. "You oughta have drawings up there where you're working. Lozano didn't put 'em up?"

"We have the details. But what I want is a sense of the bigger picture."

"You do, huh?" He peered over the half-glasses perched on his nose. "How come?"

"Years ago—a lot of years ago," I grinned ruefully, "I did two years of technical college. Drafting and design. Didn't finish, joined the union. I'm not a desk man—I like outdoor work." Out of the corner of my eye I saw Lydia make a face. "But I kept an interest. When I'm on a job like this, different, I like to check it out, see the whole thing. The rain knocked out the rest of the day for us, so I thought this was my chance. If it's all right with you."

Crowell shook his head. "I'll be damned. Where does Lozano get you guys?"

Before I could answer, Dan Junior had lifted himself out of his chair and joined us at Lydia's desk.

"I don't think it's a good idea, Dad," he said. "The men hanging around in the trailer like that." He gave me a look of obvious distaste.

Senior looked over the glasses at Junior, then back to me. "You planning to make any trouble?" he asked. "Make a pass at my secretary, steal me blind?"

"No," I said.

"Didn't think so," he grunted. "Go on, help yourself. In there. Drawings are on the rack, spec book's on the shelf." Dan Junior turned, stalked back into his office as Senior spoke to me again. "Listen, son, you see anything that'll save me half a million bucks, you be sure to let me know."

"Sure, Mr. Crowell," I said. "I'll do that."

I spent close to an hour in Crowell's drafting room, sitting on a tall stool at a slanted table, listening to the aggressive rumble of the air conditioner in the trailer window. I flipped the drawings in the blueprinted set back and forth, scanned pages from the specification book. I made some notes on a yellow pad I found there. After I'd been at it about twenty minutes Lydia stuck her head in, saying Mr. Crowell had told her to ask me if I wanted coffee.

"Sure, thanks," I smiled. "Just black."

She went and got it, brought it to me. Standing close, she asked in a whisper, "What are you doing?"

"I don't know."

"Anything I can do to help?"

"You could wrap your arms around me to keep me warm. It's freezing in here."

She looked at me, cocked her head as though considering my request. Then she whispered, "I can't think of a single reason to wrap my arms around anything that looks and smells the way you do right now." She smiled, handed me the Styrofoam cup, and went back to her work. I stuck to mine.

* * *

When I was ready to leave, Mr. Crowell and Lydia were both on the phone. I rapped my knuckles on Lydia's desk, mouthed, "Thank you."

She looked up, nodded politely, and said into the phone, "No, I'm sorry. Mr. Crowell has instructed me not to put any more reporters through. No, he's said everything to the press that he's going to say. Well, you go ahead. Have a nice day."

She hung up, looked up at me. "Reporters," she said. "You'd think no one ever found a body before. Well, Mr. Smith, was it instructive, your session with the drawings?"

"Yes, I think so," I said. "Thank Mr. Crowell for me."

"Oh, I'd be glad to. Please feel free to come back anytime."

"Thanks. I will."

She gave me a totally phony smile and picked up the phone as it rang again.

When I left the site, the rain was still falling hard, pounding awnings and sidewalks, churning in the gutters. I had no umbrella, no raincoat, and no reason to really care: I'd already been about as wet today as I could get. I strolled to the subway, enjoying the warmth after Lydia's air-conditioning. I went home, to shower, change, and start the day over.

eight

An hour later, a new, dry, and reasonably well-dressed man, I stood in my own kitchen drinking a cup of coffee and eating a pastrami sandwich that had traveled to the other end of Manhattan and back with me. It was early for lunch, but six-thirty had been early for breakfast. When I was done I made a few phone calls. Then I called my service, to see if anyone had called me. No one had, so I pulled on my raincoat and headed out to see Joanie Wisnewski.

I turned up my collar, ducked through the wind as it whipped the rain around. Water pounded at my back, chasing me down the street; a moment later it spun and attacked me from the front, trying to manhandle me up against the corner of a building. A passing taxi sent up a tidal wave from the stream that raced in the gutter.

I sprinted the three blocks to the lot where I keep my car. I waved to the guy in the booth as I slid into the driver's seat, slammed the door on the wind and rain. The wind howled angrily at being shut out and the rain pelted the car harder. By the time I'd steered out the gate and nosed onto Varick, the windshield was steamed up and the rain I'd wiped from my face had been replaced by sweat. I turned the air-conditioning on to clear the glass. The rush of air and the metronome ticking of the windshield wipers laid down a steady background for the syncopated percussion of the rain as I drove through Manhattan and over the Williamsburg Bridge.

In the crowded chaos of the lot on Varick Street, my Acura's always up front, right by the gate, never parked in. I pay extra to the management for that, and more to each of the attendants to keep an eye on it. I need this car; like the phone, I'm out of business without it. I keep it in good shape, do whatever minor work it needs, but for big work, I don't mess with it.

I take it to Joanie.

The rain let up gradually as I crossed the bridge and merged onto the expressway heading for Queens. It had practically stopped by the time I pulled through the Middle Village intersection and onto the lot at Wisnewski's Foreign Auto.

I'd bought the car here, at Harry Wisnewski's dealership. Harry has two kids. His son Greg had never shown any interest in the business, and was now a middle manager with an electronics firm; but Harry's daughter Joanie was a natural with cars. She'd hung around her dad's place after school and on weekends, learning to set the timing on spark plugs, rotate tires, and fix electronic ignitions until, after she'd made it clear she wasn't going to college, Harry gave her a job in the service department. Now, ten years later, she headed it.

I maneuvered past a waiting Audi with a cracked rear window and edged the Acura up to the five-bay repair garage, parked there, and made my way through the fine falling mist to Joanie's office.

The office was empty, but I could hear Joanie through the open door connecting to the garage.

"Andy! Start it up again." The whine and roar of an engine; then, "Oh, shit! Okay, turn it off." Joanie had that broad Queens accent that made every *r* a *w*: "Stawt it up."

I came through the connecting door, leaned on the door frame, and was spotted by a mechanic, who waved me away. "No customers in the shop. Wait in the office, someone'll be with you."

That made the boss look over, shifting her eyes to me from the belly of the Mazda eight feet up on the lift she was standing under. Her thin face lit up in a smile, showing gleaming, even teeth Harry had paid a fortune for.

"Hey!" she greeted me. Then, to her mechanic, "He's okay. Unless you're working for insurance companies now?" she called to me. "Like investigating repair shops to see if they let customers near the cars?"

I held my hands up innocently. Joanie glanced up at the Mazda again. "Petey, see what you can do with this stupid thing. I swear, if it don't shut up I'm gonna shoot it." She wiped her hands on a greasy rag, tossed it onto a workbench, and sauntered over to me.

Her Mets T-shirt and her jeans were streaked with grease; her shoulder-length brown hair was streaked with blonde, and sprayed to stand out and frame her face the way shutters frame a window. Her nails were short, but they were crimson, and so were her lips. Filigreed gold earrings gleamed on each ear.

"New cars," she said to me as she approached. "Like the new ballplayers. Crybabies. Spoiled. This one goes *ping* every time it turns left before it's warmed up in the morning. Is that the stupidest thing you ever heard?"

"Must be good for business."

She grinned as she led the way into her office. "It's great for business. Buys me season tickets to the Mets so me and Larry and the kids can go watch the crybaby ballplayers. What are you doing here? Didn't I just check you out like a month ago?" She looked through the plate glass window for my car, as though she could diagnose its problem through the drizzle. "You having trouble with the ABS? I told you—"

"The car's fine," I said. "I have a great mechanic."

Joanie grinned again. She dropped into her desk chair and kicked the door to the garage shut. "You want to smoke, don't blow up my place." She didn't wait for me to say anything, took out her own Virginia Slims and a gold lighter with an enameled Mercedes insignia. "So what *are* you doing here, on a lousy day like this, if there's nothing wrong with the car?"

"I need your help."

"Really?" She seemed pleased at the thought. "What, you looking for a second car or something?"

"I'm looking for a frontloader."

Joanie raised her eyebrows. "What the hell do you need a frontloader for?"

"I don't need one. I just need to know where to get one."

"Why? Hey, is this like for a case?"

"Just like."

"Cool." She pursed her painted lips in thought. "Well, there's some heavy-equipment dealers on the Island I could get you in touch with."

"I need a used one. As a matter of fact," I added, pulling on my cigarette, "I need a hot one."

She stopped, her cigarette halfway to her mouth. "Oh, now, wait a minute. I'm just an honest mechanic."

"I know, Joanie, but I also know if it has wheels and an engine you'll know where to find it."

She smiled with pride, then covered it fast with another draw on her cigarette and a disapproving tone.

"You got that right. But only legit. I got a reputation to think of. My father's, too."

"My lips are sealed."

She looked through smoke at me. "Of course," she said, "Dad's a used-car salesman, so what kind of reputation has he got, anyway?"

"Good point."

"Well," she said, "construction equipment's not my specialty, you know."

I shrugged. "Wheels and an engine."

She took a long drag on her cigarette. I did the same with mine. Outside, even the drizzle had stopped. The cars and puddles in the lot gleamed silver as the sun tried to reach them from behind a thin veil of cloud.

"If it wasn't you, I wouldn't do this," she told me.

"Okay," I said. "For the record."

"Right," she grinned. "For the record. Okay, I can think of one guy." She squashed her filter into an ashtray with the BMW logo on the bottom. "Sometimes I get parts there for old models. He's got all kinds of weird stuff on the lot. He might know."

"Tell me who he is, I'll call him."

"I don't know," she said doubtfully. "He's kinda weird. He plays it real close, you know? And I'm not even asking for hot parts when I go. If he knows where to get hot equipment, why's he gonna tell you about it? He don't know you."

"I'll think of something."

"I gotta go over there in the next couple days anyway, to see if I could find a drive shaft for a 'seventy-two Triumph. I don't know why that guy don't just junk that car." She sighed. "Anyway, I'll ask him and I'll call you."

"No. I don't know what I'm looking at here, which means I don't know how dangerous it is. I don't want to get you messed up in it."

"Oh, you come out here to pick my brains but you don't want to get me messed up?" Her bright eyes sparkled. "Forget it, big boy. Here's a deal: We'll go over there right now." She stood. "What do you say?"

I thought about it. "You just introduce me and walk away. You don't even know what I want. You don't know what it's about."

She shrugged. "Sure. As long as you tell me what it's about on the way over."

"Deal." I stood too.

Joanie stuck her head into the garage, hollered over the growl and shudder of an engine. "Petey! I'm going to Sal Maggio's. Back in two hours!" She slammed the door shut again and we left the office to walk across the lot.

We took her car.

The visit to Sal Maggio's yard in industrial Greenpoint didn't produce anything, at least not that I could see. The clouds that had hovered weighty and dark in the morning settled now, thin and exhausted, to rest as fog and mist on the treeless streets. Long, low blocks of red brick or yellow stucco warehouses, punctuated by forlorn wood-frame two-families, shrank behind chain-link fence topped by razor wire along streets laid out without a grid. Joanie steered her Trans Am through the potholed asphalt with the confidence of a company commander taking a jeep through ground hard-fought-over but long since abandoned by any fighting force.

Maggio's Auto Salvage, I saw as she pulled over a broken sidewalk and through a wide gate, was wrapped with chain-link and razor wire too, but where other blocks were filled solid with buildings, this one was void, just gravel piled with the twisted steel skeletons and rusting hulks of cars that had once carried families to the shopping center or sat silently in lover's lane. A chained dog barked fiercely as we parked. We crunched between the puddles and across the gravel toward a broken-down trailer with crumbling concrete steps leading up to the door.

"That rain didn't cool anything off, did it?" Joanie said as we passed piles of hubcaps, stacks of hoods and trunks, and, on the right, a tower of stripped car frames and the crane that put them there.

I agreed with her as a bead of sweat trickled down my back. The door to the trailer opened and a man stepped out.

"Hey, Sal," Joanie called with a wave. We stopped just beyond the reach of the dog's chain. He lunged at us anyway.

"Joanie." The man nodded. Seeing him, the dog cut the barking and settled into a low growl.

Maggio was thin, and looked hard but worn, like the crooked steel frames and dented metal plates piled in his yard. His scraggly black hair was plastered to his neck by sweat. He had clear gray eyes. He might have smiled just a little, seeing Joanie, but I was looking at him through the mist, so maybe I was wrong.

"I came to find parts for a Triumph," Joanie said as Sal Maggio came down the stairs to join us.

He said to Joanie, "Same one, or a different one?"

"Same one. The guy's sentimental about it, he says."

"Guy's a jerk." Maggio dismissed Joanie's customer with the contempt of a man who spends his days among the remains of other people's sentimental attachments. He looked at me, waiting.

"This is Bill," Joanie said. "He wants to ask about something. He won't tell me what but he needs a salvage guy who knows the business. I was coming here anyway, so I brought him. You guys talk, let me go look."

"Yeah," said Maggio, still looking at me. "You know where?"

"Sure I do," Joanie said.

She rounded the trailer to the left, leaving me and Maggio and the growling dog. "Nice kid," Maggio said.

"Uh-huh."

"Knows her shit, too."

"Yes, she does." The salvage yard felt like a steam bath. "I'm looking for a frontloader," I told Maggio.

"Not my usual line," he said. "You need parts, or you need one that works?"

"One that works," I said. "A John Deere D4007."

"That's damn specific."

"I'm looking for a specific one."

His gaze didn't lift from me; his lips flattened into a thin line. "Oh," he said. "Yours?"

"No. A friend's."

"You think it's here?"

"No. I'm hoping you have some idea where I could look."

"Hot, right?" he said, not really a question. "That's why you didn't tell Joanie."

"It's not her problem."

"Mine either."

"But it's mine," I said.

"You want the thing back?"

I shook my head. "It was insured. I'm just curious where it went."

"Why?"

I told him the truth: "I'm not sure. I may be interested in the guy who took it there."

"Your interest professional?"

"I'm not a cop."

"That wasn't the question."

"Yes, it's professional."

"And this guy," he said. "The one you're interested in. He have a name?"

"Maybe. The one to try would be Joe Romeo."

He was silent, his stare hard and long. It was the same stare the dog was giving me. Finally he said, "I don't want trouble."

"No one does."

"Wrong. Some people love it. Not me. I like to drink cold beer and take cars apart."

"Okay," I said.

"I try to keep out of the way of people like you."

"I don't blame you. But this means a lot to me." I took my wallet out of my pocket, slipped five twenties out of it so he could see how much it meant.

He didn't reach for the money. Fixing his eyes on mine, he said, "Why did she bring you here?"

"Because," I said, "she said you can look in a lot of places, but if you really need to find something, go to Maggio's."

"She said that?" His eyes briefly flicked in the direction Joanie had gone. I almost thought I saw the ghost of a smile.

"Yes."

He was silent. "I don't know if I can find it," he said.

"You don't have to find it."

"I thought it meant a lot to you."

"Not to find it. Just to know where it went."

He and the dog watched me. Then he reached for the twenties. I let him have them.

There wasn't much more to that, only an exchange of phone numbers and the promise, from me, of more cash if there was a reason for it, although he hadn't asked. I wandered through the misty yard in the direction Joanie had gone. I found her on the top of a six-foot pile of junk, throwing clanking steel parts over her shoulder, looking for a drive shaft for a '72 Triumph. She didn't find one.

nine

by the time I nosed my car off of Joanie's lot it was pouring again. Like an excitable child, the rain carried on wildly to make sure it was noticed, pounding the roofs of cars for emphasis, throwing itself against windshields to get attention. I fumbled through the tapes in the glove compartment, found Britten's Cello Suites, good music for a dark day. With the slow, sad, single notes of the cello floating inside the car and the infinite rain whipping around outside it, I drove back into Manhattan.

I didn't head downtown, though; I didn't go home. I swung around on the FDR to the Battery, where it joins up with what's left of the West Side Highway, and headed north.

The rain had stopped again by the time I reached the neighborhood I was aiming for, just above 110th Street, a few blocks north of the construction site. Maybe it felt it had already pretty well covered everything there was for a good storm to do up here, earlier in the day.

I parked and walked a few blocks through shiny puddles and steaming air to the address I was looking for, an old two-story on Broadway. At the turn of the century, buildings like this were called "taxpayers": small shops on street level and offices above, built fast to be rented out to shoemakers and luncheonettes and dentists just to cover the property taxes, until the value of their lots rose enough to make it worthwhile to knock them down and build something serious. Ornate terra-cotta fronts vied with each other to attract tenants; the buildings' sides and backs were the simplest brickwork imaginable.

A lot of these taxpayers are gone now, replaced by their original builders, or by their sons and daughters. And a lot still stand, with OTB offices on street level and kung fu schools upstairs, a century older and shabbier. Investing in real estate, even in New York, has always been a gamble.

The Armstrong Properties building was beautiful. The glazed white terra-cotta had been carefully cleaned, the wooden window frames sanded smooth and painted a deep green. The Armstrong office was behind a wide storefront window; from the street I could see two secretaries answering phones and typing and, on a table between filing cabinets, a model of the building I'd been working in all week. The plant-filled office looked bright and cheerful in the wet, gray afternoon.

One of the secretaries, a light-skinned black woman with freckles scattered across her high cheekbones, looked up as I came in. She asked whether she could help me.

"Bill Smith, *Daily News*," I said. "Mrs. Armstrong's expecting me."

That she was was the result of one of my earlier phone calls, when I had concocted a story I thought would work.

The freckled secretary, cool and professional, picked up her phone and buzzed her boss. They exchanged a few words; then she stood, showed me to the private office in the back.

Denise Armstrong stayed seated behind her well-kept and well-organized old oak desk and watched me walk into her office and sit across from her. She was a tall, mahogany-skinned black woman, wearing navy slacks and a crisp white cotton shirt with thin red stripes. Her short, graying hair was shaped around her head like a cap.

"I appreciate your time, Mrs. Armstrong," I told her, as the secretary closed the door behind us. "You must be pretty well fed-up with reporters by now."

"I am." She leaned back in her desk chair, the old-fashioned, solid-looking kind that tilted back on its stem so southern lawyers in suspenders could put their feet on their desks. She held me with her gaze, direct and frosty.

I smiled. She didn't.

"Well," I said, "like I said on the phone, I'm not on the crime beat, though it was the body story that got my attention. It's your building I'm interested in. Good stories in a building going up. I'm thinking there may be a piece here I could do."

"I don't think there is, Mr. Smith."

Through the window in back of her, I could see the courtyard made by this building and the ones behind. It was a small, irregular, unloved space, only there because the law required it, a sacrificed concrete plain whose job it was to give the buildings around it some breathing room. In front of the window hung glass shelves filled with potted ivy, pale starshaped leaves and glossy plump ones trailing down the window, softening the view.

"You never know," I began. "If I could ask you a couple of questions—"

"You can't." She snapped her chair forward, folded her hands on the desktop. "There's no story in the building you can do because you don't do stories. You're not a reporter. I let you in because I want to know who you are and why you used that lie."

The heat of anger was in her voice, but her eyes stayed steady and cold. In the air stirred up by the air conditioner, the ivy moved gently. A sharp ray of sun broke through the clouds, found a cracked square of concrete in the empty courtyard.

"You called the *News*?" I asked.

"The real reporters all came swarming last night," she said. "I told them not to bother. I wasn't nice; I rarely am. I've found if I start strong, the word spreads. It saves trouble."

"You've been in this position with reporters before?"

"The technique works with anyone, Mr. Smith. When you didn't call until late this morning, I decided you were either very much out of touch with your colleagues, or lying. I called the *News* to find out which."

"Then why did you let me in?"

"I just told you: I want to know who you really are."

"If I don't tell you?"

She smiled a cold smile; I got the odd feeling she'd been hoping I'd ask that. "The door behind you," she said, "is locked."

I turned to look at the door, turned back to her. I didn't get up to try it. "Kidnapping?" I said.

"Hardly." Her voice was cool, even. "Dana locked it on her way out. In ten minutes, unless I tell her not to, she'll call the police. She'll unlock the door as they drive up. I sponsor the Twenty-fourth Precinct's PAL softball and basketball teams," she said conversationally. "They won't react well to a stranger lying his way in here and attacking me in my own office."

"Attacking you?"

She shrugged her shoulders. "It's a hard world, Mr. Smith. Who are you and what do you want?"

I looked again at the door. "I could break it down, I think."

"I think not. My grandfather built solid buildings. And if you use physical force—on the door or on me—that will just add to my story when the police get here."

"Your grandfather built this building?"

"I've been in real estate all my life, Mr. Smith or whatever your name is. Smith!" She curled her lip at the transparency of my alias. "My grandfather was burnt out of his house in Alabama by people with accents like yours. He came north, bought land, and began to build, solid buildings that would last. My father took over his business, and I took over my father's." Her eyes glinted like sunlight on polished stone. "I don't know what your game is, but I guarantee you I can play it better than you can. That's how a black woman in a white man's world gets through the day. You have eight minutes."

I shrugged. "This seems like a lot of trouble to go to just to find out who I am."

"You've gone to a lot of trouble to get in here and ask questions," she said. "Reporters have lied to me before, pretending to be other things. No one's ever pretended to be a reporter. There's never been a body buried under one of my buildings before, either. I don't like those two things happening so close together. Who are you and what do you want?"

"Maybe I'm a reporter for some supermarket scandal sheet I knew you wouldn't speak to."

"Maybe you'd better get started with the truth; you've got seven minutes left."

I met her eyes. Outside her plant-draped window, pools of rainwater sat on the broken and forgotten concrete.

"I'm a private investigator," I said. "In a way, I work for you."

I took out my license, handed it across the desk. She frowned at it, then frowned at me. "You don't work for me."

"I work for Crowell Construction," I said. "On a job involving your site."

"My site?" The frown deepened. "About the body?"

"I don't know."

She snapped my license down in front of her. "What does that mean? You don't know what you're working on?"

"The case I came in on was before that body was found. I don't know if they're connected. That's what I came here to find out."

"Here? From *me?*"

"Your building."

"I own it. I'm not the person digging regularly in the elevator pit. Why did Crowell hire you?"

"There've been losses on the site," I said. "Tools, equipment. They suspect someone, but he works for one of the subs, and they can't just fire him without proof. There'd be union trouble."

"Who?"

"A man named Joe Romeo," I said. "A masonry foreman."

"I've never heard of him."

"That doesn't mean he's not stealing from you."

"Not from me. From Crowell. I'm paying them to put this building up. If they run into trouble it's their problem."

"And they're handling it by hiring us."

She reached for the phone. "And I suppose if I call them they'll confirm who you are?"

"No," I said. "They don't know me. I'm just an operative at the agency they hired."

"Which is?"

I gave her Chuck's name, the name of the agency. "Call Crowell if you want," I said. "But I'd appreciate it if you'd talk to Dana first."

"Dana—? Oh. You mean you don't want to be arrested."

The answer to that seemed obvious, so I didn't give it.

She looked at her watch, smiled a frosty smile, and punched a single button on the phone. A few seconds; then, "Mr. Crowell, please. Senior."

She must, I realized, be talking to Lydia.

Mrs. Armstrong waited; then her tone changed, and I listened to her talk to Dan Crowell, Sr. "There's a man here in my office," she said without preamble. "He claims to work for a firm called DeMattis Security, and he says they work for you." She told Crowell Senior what else I'd said, about the trouble on the site, about Joe Romeo. She paused, listened.

"No, I understand that. But you did hire DeMattis Security, and for the reasons he claims?" Another pause, longer. Shadows moved across the courtyard, darkening puddles that would be there until morning. I began to reach for my cigarettes, thought better of it, put them back. "All right, but I wish you'd told me. No, of course it's your business, but if we're going to keep working together— All right, Mr. Crowell. We'll talk later." She hung up without saying goodbye.

She looked down at her watch, then at me, wordlessly. I could see the second hand sweeping around the dial; it seemed to me she was counting down the seconds, and although she didn't smile, I thought she must be enjoying it. I didn't move, met her gaze steadily. Finally, eyes still on me, she picked up the phone again, pressed a different button, and spoke. "Dana? No, it's fine. No, I'll let you know. Well, he is, but I can handle it. Thanks." She replaced the receiver.

"All right," she said. "Mr. Crowell confirms your agency's been hired. He confirms why. Now I want to know why you tried so hard to come see me."

"I was interested in the woman who didn't flinch when they dug a body up off her site."

" 'Didn't flinch'?"

"Mr. Crowell's new secretary was there. She told me that."

I mentioned Lydia mostly to see if Crowell Senior had blown her cover to Mrs. Armstrong, but if he had, she didn't tell me about it.

"And what did you expect?" she asked. "Should I have fainted? Averted my eyes? You're from the South, aren't you?"

"I was born in Kentucky."

"Then you know that that flower-of-femininity bull is for white women only. Black women are expected to get down on their hands and knees and clean up the stink that makes white women pass out from across the room. That man was dead. I didn't know him, I didn't kill him. He has nothing to do with me. He was buried in a property I happen to own, and just my owning it is enough to give some people fits."

"You think that's why he was there?"

"What do you mean?"

"Because someone doesn't want you owning that property?"

She gave me a scornful look. "Don't be silly. You mean as a warning, some kind of stupid melodrama? Of course not. These days, if you don't want a black woman owning a major property you just redline her loan application."

I remembered the raised voices in the conference room in the trailer, the argument Lydia had said was not an argument, just an excited discussion of Mrs. Armstrong's financial situation. "Has that happened to you?"

"Redlining?" she asked. "What if it has? There are other banks. Is that what you came here to find out? Whether I'm solvent?"

"I don't know what I came here to find out. I'm an investigator. I'm supposed to be looking into a guy who's supposed to be a crook. My second day on the job a body's dug up. I'm fishing."

"Have you caught anything yet?"

"Rumors. Stories. Are you going to help me?"

"Help you do what?"

"Figure it out. Whether there's a connection between Joe Romeo and the dead man, Pelligrini."

"No. I'm going to throw you out of my office."

"If there is a connection, your site could have a wiseguy problem."

"If there's a problem, I'll deal with it when it starts affecting me."

"A body in the basement doesn't affect you?"

"No. What affects me is anything that slows Crowell's schedule. That's it."

"What's the big deal?" I thought back, again, to the argument in the trailer. I went on, deliberately provocative. "A couple of days here or there. So the building opens a month later. You think that makes you look bad or something, like you're not Super Black Woman?"

"I don't give a damn when the building opens, and I don't give a damn how I look. But the bank does."

"One little building matters so much to them?"

Her eyes flashed. Gesturing around us, she said, "*This* is a little building. Ninety-ninth and Broadway is the start of something else. I'm looking at two other sites. I've already asked Mr. Crowell for preliminary construction budgets. Super Black Woman is going to be a force in this city, Mr. Smith. Now get out." She picked up the receiver, pressed a button on the phone. She didn't speak into it.

"Super Black Woman, and Crowell Construction?" I asked.

"Possibly. Why, is that too much for you to stomach, an upstart black woman working with a respected old Irish construction firm?"

"Hell, no. I'm half Irish myself. Black Irish," I added, as I heard the snick of the lock behind me. The door opened, with Dana in the doorway. I stood. "Thanks for your time, Mrs. Armstrong. I hope, for your sake, that things on that site aren't as bad as I think."

"I hope for yours that you stick to what Crowell hired you to do, and keep out of things that aren't your business."

The courtyard behind her was completely shadowed now.

Her eyes were still bright. I nodded good-bye and turned to where Dana held open the heavy door for me. I glanced at the door and the doorway as I moved through. She was right. I couldn't have broken it down.

It was late afternoon when I left the Armstrong Properties office, and the rain seemed to have quit for good. When I got to the corner I looked down the hill, west, to the river; the dark clouds above the Palisades were streaked with a bright glow. If the sun broke through before it dipped much lower, there would be hope of a rainbow.

I checked my watch, decided it was close enough to the end of the workday, and called Lydia.

"Crowell Construction," she told me pleasantly and professionally, answering the phone on the second ring.

"Hi, it's me. Can you take personal calls?"

"Not as personal as you have in mind."

"All I was going to offer you was a ride home."

"Really? That's totally different."

"Different from what?"

"Every other man on this site. Where are you?"

"About eight blocks north of you. What's wrong with the guys on the site?"

"I'm sure there's nothing wrong with them. I'm sure they're all red-blooded all-Americans and I'm supposed to find them boyishly charming. Should I come up there?"

"That would be good. So we aren't seen together on the site. I don't want the other guys getting jealous."

"Excuse me?"

"Just walk up Broadway, on the east side. You'll see the car. You get off at five-thirty?"

"Yes. What are you going to do between now and then?"

"Drink."

I did, too. I found a bar on the next corner with brick-patterned asphalt on the outside, and a floor so old that patches of marble tile broke the worn linoleum like an ancient mosaic surfacing under shifting desert sands. The decor was dark brown paint, the lighting too old and dispirited to give it a run for its money. The scent of stale smoke layered the air, but the air conditioner worked and the beer was cold and that was enough for me. I had a Bud there, listening with half an ear to the buzzing of the Coors sign and the subdued, sparse talk of the other patrons, guys who were lucky or unlucky enough to be able to pass a weekday afternoon in a bar.

I thought about how I'd spent my afternoon, and my morning too, and the other mornings this week, about the bricks in a north-facing window bay on the sixth floor of a building down the street that wouldn't be there if I hadn't put them in. Each one of them, lifted and turned and placed by my hands, each now in some way part of me, part of the memories my hands had, my arms and my back, memories that would stay part of who I was long after I'd forgotten about the building and the work I'd done there.

I drank my beer and thought about that, about what it meant, wondered whether what it meant to me was the same as it was to Mike, to the Crowells, to Reg Phillips. There was no way to know, so I wondered.

When the beer was almost gone and the accompanying cigarette just a memory, I looked at my watch, drained my glass, and went out to meet Lydia.

The sun had made it, splitting a heavy cloud over the Hudson and pouring out a deep yellow light that glowed triumphantly off every west-facing surface it found. It lit glossy terra-cotta, bounced off windows, sparkled on the chrome on parked cars, and gave a delicate golden outline to Lydia's head and shoulders as she leaned on my car reading a magazine.

"Hi," I said, coming up to her, kissing her cheek. She smelled of freesia, and faintly of sweat. I took up a position next to her against the car. "Come here often?"

"Depends what's parked here."

"Oh." I decided not to touch that. "What are you reading?"

"*American Builder*." She showed me the magazine. The cover was an aerial photograph of a deep pit excavation surrounded by a tall construction fence. Three tower cranes cut the hazy sky; the background was mountains. "I borrowed it from the office. I thought I should try to learn something about what it is you big tough construction guys do all day."

"You're including me in that? 'Big, tough'? I'm flattered, I think."

"Think again."

"Oh. Trouble?"

"Not that you'd notice. I love this job. I especially love the adorable way every man on that site has of hitting on me every time they open their mouths."

I looked into her narrowed eyes. "There's nothing I can say to that that would be right, is there?" I asked.

"No."

"Umm . . . Can I distract you by getting in the car?"

"You can try."

I tried it, unlocking the car, restraining myself from opening her door for her. She slid in and fastened her seat belt with a forceful click. I started to lower the windows and then changed my mind, switched the air-conditioning on.

We joined the traffic flowing up Broadway. "I'm sorry," she said aggressively. "I suppose I shouldn't take it out on you."

I shrugged. "I got you into this."

"Well, that's true. And you're a man."

"I can't help that."

"That's no excuse. Go ahead and open the windows."

"You'd rather that than air-conditioning?"

"No, but you would. You always do."

"Let me sacrifice my desires to yours this one time. It'll help me regain some of the moral high ground."

"No, it won't, but okay, leave it on. You're just lucky I'm such a professional."

"I'm sure I am," I agreed.

"Oh, I guarantee it. If I weren't, I wouldn't have been able to put my personal feelings aside to do the kind of serious snooping I did today."

I glanced across the car at her. "You did serious snooping?"

"Someone has to."

"Ouch."

"Well, maybe you are, too. How would I know? It's not like you keep me updated."

"How can I, during the day?"

"Another bad excuse. You haven't even asked me to have dinner with you tonight."

"Would you have?"

"No. I want to work out."

"After that?"

She sighed. "Not unless there's something we don't have time to go over now, okay? My mother's cousins are coming over after dinner and I ought to be there to be nice."

"Can you be nice, given the mood you're in?"

"Why not? They're not construction workers."

"Oh."

"Don't start getting monosyllabic on me. I'll tell you what I did today if you tell me."

"I would have anyway."

She suddenly grinned, and leaned back in the seat. "I know that. Do you know how hard it is to keep this up?"

I looked over at her again. "Keep what up?"

"The bad-tempered expression of righteous anger at my second-class status."

"It's a strain?" I asked. "Because if it is, you could stop. I wouldn't mind."

"And abandon the principles of militant feminism?"

"Just for twenty minutes?"

She gave the idea two seconds' thought. "Okay," she said, as I U-turned to head south. "But I get to come back to it at any time, without warning."

"Fair enough," I said. We rolled down Broadway. "So tell me about your snooping."

"You mean I get to go first?"

"Sure. But not out of chivalry," I added hastily. "Only because your report interests me deeply."

"It better."

I nodded, and she began.

"It's because Verna was out today," she said. "Because of the body yesterday; she was still shaken up, so Mr. Crowell gave her the day off. He offered it to me, too, but I thought that wouldn't look good for Mr. DeMattis, if his operative took the day off just because there was a body."

"Besides which wild horses couldn't have kept you from someplace where there was a body."

"Besides that. So I came to work, and two things happened: One, I got to answer all the phone calls, and two, I got to be alone with the files."

"That's good?"

"Sure it is. Files are wonderful things."

"And phone calls?"

"Even better. For example, a gentleman called for Mr. Crowell, Senior. When he wasn't there, he asked for Mr. Crowell, Junior."

" 'Asked for'?"

"More like demanded, actually. How did you know that?"

"It was the way you said 'gentleman.' "

"Oh. Well, Junior wasn't there either, so the guy got to yell at me."

"He yelled at you?"

"Of course he did. I'm a secretary. That's what secretaries are for. All men are entitled to yell at other men's secretaries."

"I don't— Go on," I said, swallowing the rest of that sentence.

"Smart move. Ask me why he yelled at me."

"Why did the gentleman yell at you?"

"Because he wanted to be paid."

"By you?"

"Don't be cute. By anyone. By the Crowells. He's some kind of supplier of something and he was tired of being jerked around, having his chain yanked, getting screwed over, being stuck behind the eight ball, and having all sorts of other unpleasant-sounding things done to him. He wants his money."

"Hmm," I said. I moved us onto West End Avenue. "Anything in that?"

"I wondered the same. So I headed for the files."

"And what did you find?"

"After a complicated and nowhere-near-exhaustive search, I can tell you it's crowded behind the eight ball."

"The gentleman's not alone?"

"The Crowells owe money all over town. Many people are demanding what's rightfully theirs."

"Interesting."

"You think so?"

"To the likes of you and me. But I wonder how unusual it is in the construction industry, to be behind in your bills."

"I have no idea," she said. "And how far behind?"

"What happened when the Crowells came in?"

"Junior was first. He saw the message slip on the board to call the guy and took it down. He called, and the whole thing didn't sound pleasant. Something about, 'You leave my father out of this, you deal with me.' I wasn't able to overhear anything else."

"But not from lack of trying."

"You bet not."

"And Senior didn't call him?"

"Not that I know."

"Who pays the bills?"

"You mean, between the Crowells? Junior actually writes the checks. I know that because he wrote two yesterday. But I think Senior looks at the invoices when they come in and tells him what he can pay."

"Not surprising. Where am I taking you, by the way?"

She looked over at me; by now we were on the West Side Drive, flowing smoothly with the river of traffic beside the real river, which shone bronze in the afternoon sun. "Where are you going?" she asked.

"Home. But you're not even invited, that's how much I want to prove I'm different from all those guys who hit on you."

She sighed. "It's probably just some very subtle kind of pass, but I'll ignore it. Take me to the dojo. Maybe if I punch a bag for an hour or two I'll feel better."

"Don't you have live men there you can punch?"

"I sure hope so."

The rest of the drive downtown was my turn, to tell Lydia about my day, where I'd been and what I'd done.

"Start from why you were in my office this morning, looking at drawings and things," she instructed.

"*Your* office?"

"I'm just trying to get fully into character."

"An approach I can only approve of."

"And your approval means so much to me."

"I'm grateful. I was trying to find out how the building's supposed to be made."

"Why?"

"There's some chintzy material, apparently, going into the construction of the place."

" 'Apparently'?"

"Mike told me. I'm not good enough at this to have picked up on it, but a lot of the things you won't see when the building's finished turn out to be pretty cheap items."

"Is that surprising?" she asked. "They do it that way in Chinatown all the time. Junk on the inside, marble on the outside. It's obnoxious but I don't think it's unusual."

"It might not be. But it started me thinking, and I just wanted to check it out."

"Did you find anything?"

"I'm not sure. But it seems to me the documents call for better materials than we're using."

" 'We'?"

"Just trying to get fully into character."

"But what do you mean, 'it seems the documents call for'? You learned that in my office? Didn't you tell me you have the drawings stuck up on a column up there so you can see what you're supposed to be doing? Don't the drawings say what the materials are?"

"No. They show you what the brick pattern is and where to put your brick ties but they don't say what they're made of, whether they're galvanized, what gauge they are, and so on. That's all in the spec book, and that's not something the bricklayers or carpenters or laborers use. They just take what's handed to them by their supervisors and build with it."

"So you mean you're supposed to be using good materials but someone's substituting cheap ones?"

"Looks that way."

"Who?"

"Well, most likely it's the subcontractors, like Lacertosa."

"That's who you work for?"

"Right. They and the carpentry sub, Emerald—they're the ones doing the gypboard walls—and some of the others could be putting one over on Crowell. That would have to mean both Crowell and the architect's rep are asleep, but it could happen."

Lydia pursed her lips in thought. "Crowell pays for materials?"

"Crowell has contracts with all the subs the same way the owner has with Crowell. They're paying them a fixed price to do their share of the work. If the subs can use cheaper materials, they make a bigger profit. Crowell and the architect are supposed to monitor that so it doesn't happen."

She asked, "What if the architect's rep were being paid off?"

I nodded. "That's possible. Then it just means Crowell isn't paying a lot of attention, and they're getting screwed. It was Dan Junior who was with the architect's rep today when he came around. Do you suppose that's the usual thing?"

"I'm sure it is," she said. "The guy—the architect's rep, that skinny guy, Hacker—just came into the trailer and asked for Dan Junior. I buzzed Junior, told him who it was, and he came out of his office with his hard hat and they left together. It was like they do it all the time."

"Did they have much to say to each other?"

"No. Dan Junior had his regular goofy smile, and he winked at me as they left. Hacker didn't say anything."

"I wonder how hard it would be," I said, "to put something over on Dan Junior."

"If you asked Dan Senior," she replied, repositioning the air-conditioning to point directly at her face, "I bet the answer would be, 'Not very.' "

The dojo where Lydia practices Tae Kwon Do isn't far from

where I live in Tribeca. As we headed there I told her about Joanie Wisnewski and Sal Maggio, about the mist and the dog's clanking chain and the chance that we might be able to connect Joe Romeo to the stolen frontloader.

"Or we might find out they have a whole other problem on that site," she said. "That Joe Romeo is a loan shark and a drug dealer, but someone else is stealing from the Crowells."

"We might," I said. I stopped at the light, waited for my chance to get off the highway. "The other thing I did today was to barely avoid getting arrested for assault and attempted rape."

"*What?*"

I glanced sideways at her. "At least I got your attention."

"Did you say that just to—"

"No. It really happened. But I didn't do it."

"That's what they all say. What are you talking about?"

I told her about Denise Armstrong.

"Boy," she said, when I was done. "It sounds like she had your number from the beginning."

"I underestimated her."

"Because she's black and she's a woman?"

"I don't like to think that," I said. "But it's probably true."

I could feel Lydia's eyes on me, but she was silent. I steered the car through the streets of Tribeca, near Lydia's dojo, near my apartment.

"What do you think of her now?" she said.

"There aren't many times I've been tempted to use the word 'ruthless,' " I answered.

"And really smart, she sounds like to me. I haven't known you to get outmaneuvered like that very often."

"At least I have the consolation of knowing that I deserved it."

"Why is that consoling?"

"It's a Catholic thing."

"You're only half Catholic."

"I'm only half consoled."

"What's the other half?"

"Mad."

"What are you going to do?"

"Nothing. I don't even know exactly why I went there; it was just an instinctive thing, to see what she was like. I'm going to go back to the cases we're supposed to be working on."

"Cases?"

"Joe Romeo, and Reg Phillips."

"And Pelligrini in the basement, and the frontloader? And the chintzy goods?"

"May all be part of the same thing. Maybe not. We've opened some doors. Now we just have to wait and see what comes through them."

I pulled to a stop in front of Lydia's dojo, a grimy-faced loft building that hasn't been gentrified yet and maybe now won't be, as the yuppie wave of the eighties recedes.

"Golly," she said as she got out, "you're philosophical, for a bricklayer."

"And you're gorgeous. For a secretary." I ducked as she whacked me with her rolled-up copy of *American Builder*, and I grinned as she stalked away from my car.

ten

i drove away from Lydia's dojo watching the lowering sun play off puddles and glint from windows. I took the car to the lot and left it there, walked home through damp, sparkling streets. As I reached the door to Shorty's, a couple was coming out, bringing with them a wave of cool air, the aroma of beer and grilling burgers, and the easy sounds of the kind of talk people use not so much to tell each other anything as to reassure each other they're still listening.

The place, as always, pulled at me, and I paused and thought about it. Then I went on a few steps farther and unlocked the door that led upstairs. I climbed the two slanted flights and let myself in. It wasn't as cool up here as in the bar downstairs, it wasn't as companionable, but I'd already had a beer, and up here was where the piano was.

I opened the windows at both ends of the apartment to get the air moving; there's no air-conditioning up here. I spent the first nine years of my life in the South, and some of the years right after that in tropical places, as my father was posted on short tours by the army. I have what Lydia calls a perverse liking for hot, damp weather. And this building doesn't get much sun; it's shadowed by the factories and warehouses around it. The only place the sun pours into is the back bedroom, the room I built for Annie, and no one uses that room anymore.

I sat down at the piano bench, set the timer. I lit a cigarette and studied the music. I'd practiced a little yesterday, late in the day, but not as much as I'd wanted, not as much as I'm used to. The Scriabin études I'd been working on for a while were just starting to connect for me, beginning to build on each other. A set of études is always interlocked, one to another and each to the whole set. Some of the relations, of key or meter, are clear from the start; a few come out gradually, as you play them; and always there are some that surprise, that reveal themselves suddenly, maybe after you've been playing the pieces for years. These Scriabin études were new to me, the links among them endless and encouraging, and I was impatient to get back to them.

I put the music up on the stand and played scales and exercises to get ready. The cool smooth keys gave almost imperceptibly under my fingers; my arms and my body moved with the notes ringing through the room. I began to focus, to lose the day that had just been and the evening coming up, to think of nothing except what to do now, this instant, how to play this note, this chord. When everything else was gone for me but the massive solidity of the piano and the whirling, vanishing, transitory sounds, I was ready for the piece.

Breathing deeply, hands resting, I ran my eyes over the music again. I concentrated on the opening notes, the few measures after; then I began. I searched for the rhythm, the tones, the timing, tried to keep the staccato notes as sharp as I wanted, the arpeggios as smooth. I went back over some passages a dozen times, played others straight through. I worked out some pedaling, changed it, went back to what I'd started with. Back and forth I flipped the pages, worked through the music, the sweet passages, the quick ones, the powerful ones, looking for what they were, and what they were to each other.

I'd been working awhile, I didn't know how long, when the phone rang.

It startled me; I'd pretty much forgotten it existed. I shook my head, to clear it, and cursed myself for not turning the phone off before I began. I got up and answered it.

"Smith."

A quiet, contained voice told me, "It's Maggio."

Joanie's guy. I reached for a cigarette, pulled myself back from the music. "This is fast," I told him.

"I like to take care of things fast. I don't like things hanging over me." Through the phone I heard the dog bark, heard its chain rattle.

"You found something?" I asked.

"Your frontloader."

I paused in my search for a match. "No shit."

"Isn't that what you wanted?"

"It's more than I wanted."

"Good, because you won't be getting it back."

"Why not?"

"Sold for parts already."

I lit up, shook out the match. "Why for parts?"

"You're lucky it was. That's the only reason it's okay for me to tell you about it. Guy who bought it off the guy who had it is pissed."

"About what?" I took a deep drag.

"Guy who had it promised he'd get the papers, too. Thing's a lot more valuable with the papers. You could sell it almost legit."

"But he didn't, this guy?"

"Nope. Never came back."

"And that's a problem?"

"Sure as hell. Without papers, you need a buyer not too particular. Or you got to sell it for parts. Parts, you could lose money. There's not that big of a market for these things."

"So the guy who bought it lost money?"

"No, he's not a guy loses money. But he didn't make as much as he wanted, and he's pissed."

"So he was willing to talk about it?"

"Yeah. He says if you could do him a favor and find this other guy, the one who sold it to him, he'd like to break his head."

"Who is this guy who doesn't lose money?"

"Uh-uh. He's not that pissed. And by the way, he wanted to know who you were, too. I told him no dice."

"I get your point."

"But I could tell you who's the guy who sold it to him. That's what you said you wanted to know."

"It is."

"That name you gave me. Romeo? No good. This guy never heard of him. Guy who brought the thing is called Pelligrini," Sal Maggio said. "I don't know him, but that's his name. Lenny Pelligrini."

I leaned back in the desk chair, pulled on the cigarette again. Lenny Pelligrini. "You don't know him," I said to Maggio. "Do you know anything about him?"

"Such as what?"

"Is he connected?"

"Fuck you," Maggio said. "You're asking that because he's Italian?"

"No. I'm asking that because he's an Italian crook."

"Shit." In Maggio's silence I heard the dog's chain clanking and jingling. I wondered if it was settling in for the night. "What the hell do you care?"

"I want to know what I'm up against."

"Yeah, well, if I was you, I'd drop it right here. You got your insurance money, right?"

"My friend's insurance money."

"Whatever. So walk away."

"Then he is connected."

"I don't know. I don't know much about Pelligrini himself. He sounds like a jerk, you ask me." Maggio paused. "You gonna drop it?"

"No. But I'll keep you out of it."

"Don't do me any big favors, Smith. I can take care of myself." I heard the pop of a beer-can top. He drank, I smoked, and we both said nothing.

"The law gonna get in on this?" Maggio finally asked.

"Not from my end. I said I'd keep you out of it."

"Not just me. This guy I called for you. Better not be trouble for him."

"I can't promise him that. But not from me."

"All I'm asking. Just keep your own mouth shut," Maggio

said. "This Pelligrini kid? He's just a punk. But he was talking like he knows a guy."

"Who's this guy?"

"Name of Falco. Louie Falco. You know him?"

I took a last drag on my cigarette, stubbed it out. Instantly I wanted another one. "No," I said. "But I know a guy who used to know him."

"Yeah? Then you don't have to know him, you know about him. He don't like people getting in his way."

"Yeah," I said. "Thanks, Maggio. Take care of yourself."

Maggio snorted. "Oh, yeah. Sure. You too."

"I'll be sending you a thank-you in the mail."

"Don't bother. Just tell Joanie I helped you out," Maggio said. "She's a good kid."

After I got off the phone with Sal Maggio I tried to go back to the Scriabin, but it was no good. I felt the ache of the past three days in my shoulders, heard the sound of a motorcycle in the street below. A couple of guys came out drunk from Shorty's, laughing and insulting each other. I turned to check the clock behind me on the desk, and decided as I was doing it that the answer didn't matter. I closed the piano, calculated the length of a karate class, and called Lydia.

"Chin Investigative Services, Lydia Chin speaking."

"I know."

"You think that makes you smart?"

"Don't be rude to me or I won't tell you what I just found out. Did you have a good class?"

"It was great. I worked so hard I sweated like a pig and forgot all about construction workers. Then I got to fight four bouts."

I glanced at the piano, thought about my hands moving over hard, flat keys, thought about forgetting everything in the timbre, tone, and length of sound. "Did you win?" I asked.

"It's not about winning."

"The need to win is a western white male hang-up?"

"If you say so. Did you call to discuss politics? Hold on a minute."

Lydia said something to someone else in the room with her, but I didn't catch it, because it was in Chinese. So was the answer. When she came back to the phone, Lydia said, "My mother thinks you're trying to give me pneumonia, calling when I've just come in from class and I'm all sweaty."

"How could I possibly have known?" I protested.

"You knew when class started, and how long it is, and how long it takes me to get home, and—"

"All right, never mind. But why would I do that?"

"So then you can save my life with some western drug that will at the same time put me under your spell."

"Aren't you already under my spell?"

"It's fading fast, unless you tell me what you called about."

"Lenny Pelligrini."

That stopped her. "Pelligrini," she said. "What about him?"

"He's the one who fenced the frontloader."

"No kidding!" She was quiet for a moment. "So Mr. DeMattis and the police were both wrong. He *was* into something. All those tools and other equipment disappearing from that site—do you think he did that too? That the police and Mr. DeMattis missed him being into something this big?"

"They could have, but only if he wasn't in it alone."

"What makes you say that?"

"You don't just jump into something this size as your first try on that side of the law. If he was some kid from the neighborhood who worked himself up to this, the cops would know him. He'd have priors, small stuff. I'll bet he wasn't running it."

"Who do you think was? Joe Romeo?"

"That would be handy, but I'd have to make the connection. And the guy who put me on to Pelligrini says he never heard of Romeo. He did say Pelligrini seems to be connected to some big-shot wiseguy by the name of Louie Falco."

"Do we know him?"

"No."

But Chuck does, a voice said inside my head. From the old neighborhood. I didn't tell Lydia that; I didn't know exactly what I'd be telling her, if I did.

"And how do you know all this?" she asked.

"Joanie's guy. The junk dealer I told you about."

"Is he what the cops will consider a reliable source?"

"The cops aren't going to consider him any kind of source. The one thing I promised him is that the cops wouldn't hear his name from me."

"Can you give this to the cops and go around him?"

"He wouldn't tell me the name of the guy he got it from, so I wouldn't be able to tell them where to go to check it out. No detective I know is going to thank me for that."

"Was it worth a lot, this frontloader?"

"It would have been. Eighty thousand, more or less, if Pelligrini had delivered on the paperwork, too."

"The registration and things? Didn't he?"

"No."

"So what does this mean, the thing wasn't worth anything in the end?"

"Something, but not much. The buyer says there's something in it for me if I find Pelligrini so he can do him some damage."

"So the buyer doesn't know Pelligrini's dead?"

"Looks that way. I didn't tell Maggio."

"What are you going to do now?"

"I don't know."

"Did you call Mr. DeMattis?"

"No."

"No, or not yet?"

I paused. "No."

"Bill, what's wrong?"

"I—" There was no point in pretending to Lydia that nothing was, but I didn't have an answer to her question. "It's my case," I said. "Our case. Chuck doesn't do things the way I do, and I'm not sure where he'd stand on this. I need to think about it for a while."

"Think about what?"

"I'm not sure," I said helplessly.

I knew that wasn't true, and so did she; but she'd known me for years, had worked a lot of cases with me. She backed off.

She said, "If you want to think out loud, or talk after you think . . ."

"Thanks," I answered, and we both knew it was for more than just that offer. "Now go take a shower and get out of your sweaty clothes, or you'll get pneumonia."

"That's all right, my mother just brought me a cup of preventative tea. It keeps you from getting all sorts of respiratory diseases. She looked very smugly at the phone when she gave it to me, by the way."

"Damn, outfoxed by your mother again."

"It will never be any other way."

"You know," I told her thoughtfully, "it occurs to me that you're a lot like your mother."

The morning dawned hot, hazy, and painfully early. I reached out blindly, mashed the alarm off, and stayed stretched out until I began to drift back off. Then I hauled myself out of bed and stumbled through the things I do in the morning with aching arms and a desperate wish for another hour's sleep.

I made it to the job site with my tool bag and hard hat but without my lunchbox: It was either stop for food or clock in on time. I could buy lunch at the break; as it was, I was a few minutes late, which bought me an inquiring look from John Lozano when I punched my time card in the Lacertosa field office.

"Sorry," I said. I didn't try to offer an excuse; whatever it was wouldn't have paid for the lost time my lateness caused, if my partner was sitting around up above, waiting for me.

Lozano's pale eyes rested on me. "Yeah," he said. "I don't like guys being late." He spoke mildly, just telling me how it was. "Not fair to the other guys, they managed to get here when they're supposed to. You're not going to make a habit out of it, are you?"

"No," I said. "I don't like it either."

He nodded. "Okay, go on up. I won't dock you this time, but I warned you, Smith."

That was fair, I thought as I headed for the hoist, stood together with the carpenters and plumbers waiting to go up.

Keeping an eye out for all the crew, making sure no one was taking advantage, seeing that every man held up his end. That was part of Lozano's job, to look after his men.

As much a part of his job as supplying the materials his men built with.

Mike DiMaio was up above, at our bay and ready to go, but he wasn't waiting. He'd peeled the blue tarp off the brickwork we'd covered yesterday, set out his tools, and run a string line from corner to corner for us to work to as we started.

"You must have had a good day off," he said as I slung my tool bag onto a pile of bricks, opened it to get at my tools. "You're late, you're moving slow, and you look like shit."

"Really?" I said. "I'm late?"

He snorted at that. "All right, let's get on it. Romeo's already been here, climbing all over my ass because we're behind."

I pulled on my gloves. It was a quarter to eight in the morning, and already a trickle of sweat crept from under my hard hat, slipped down my jawline. "Ah, Romeo," I said. "I've got to talk to Romeo." I stuck my trowel into the mortar brought over by the new mason tender, the one who'd replaced Reg Phillips. "Maribel won yesterday. Beat the field by half a length."

"Maribel?" For a moment DiMaio looked blank. "What, your horse out on the West Coast? No shit, she won?"

I grinned at DiMaio as I hefted a brick. "Paid eleven to two. Buy you a beer later, to celebrate?"

"Yeah," he said, looking at me for a minute, then turning back to his work. "Sure."

The work that morning was hard. We'd reached the bricks a few courses above waist, not high enough yet to set up a platform to work from; but every brick now had to be lifted a little farther, every pass of the trowel had to be made from a position more awkward than the ones I'd been getting used to over the past few days. The air had thickened back to the heavy dampness it had held before yesterday's rain, and DiMaio and I were pushing ourselves to try to make up some time. By coffee break I had streaks of fire between my shoulder blades; by lunchtime my shirt was soaked with sweat and my hands were getting clumsy.

Joe Romeo still hadn't come around by the time DiMaio and I knocked off for lunch.

"How do you like that?" I grumbled. I wiped my trowel clean, put it down on the board where my other tools lay. I wiped my face, too, and reset my hard hat. "The one day I'd actually be glad to see that smiling S.O.B., and he doesn't show up once."

"He showed up once," DiMaio pointed out. "Before you did."

"Yeah, okay," I said. "Anyway, I'm not worried. I know where to find him. I'm going down to get lunch. You want anything?"

"No, I brought."

We ambled along the scaffold together, DiMaio settling himself in the shade with the other masons, me exchanging hellos with them but not stopping. I went on past, into the hoist and back down to the street.

On a construction site nearly everyone brings lunch. The standard lunch break is only half an hour, and getting down to the street from wherever you're working, finding someplace to make you a sandwich, and getting back up, can chew up twenty minutes. That's time you'd rather spend sitting, resting, trying to get your back, arms, shoulders, ready for the afternoon.

Only two other guys rode down in the hoist with me, wandered off to the pizza place or the deli across the street. Most everybody was on the site, sitting in the shade, lunchboxes open and, against regulations, hard hats off, when the buses drove up.

There were two: rickety yellow ex-schoolbuses, one of them coughing dull black smoke from its tailpipe into the still, hot air. Black paint covered the bus-company names; nothing identified them, nothing gave me an idea, crossing the street back toward the site as the buses pulled off Broadway and rolled through the gate, what they were there for.

I heard the security guy shouting, though, saw him wave

his arms, jump aside when the buses didn't stop. I quickened my pace as the bus doors opened, the second bus just half inside the gate, straddling the sidewalk. I heard the first guy off a bus, a tall, muscled black man, yelling back at the guard, saw them standing toe-to-toe in the dirt still puddled in places from the rain.

"Get these men the fuck out of here!" The guard, red-faced, jabbed his nightstick at the buses. "I called the fucking cops already! Get outta here before they come!"

"Fuck you and fuck the cops!" was the answer. "If we don't put it up it's comin' down!" Men clambered down the bus steps into the dirt.

Heads turned on the site. Guys saw the action, dropped what they were doing, started to circle toward the shouting men.

"Fuck!" someone yelled. "Coalition!"

More men poured off both buses, black men, most big, all clench-fisted and tight-jawed. They spread, but not far. Some carried baseball bats, some tire irons. The security guard faltered, backed off; the yelling ended.

I reached the site, squeezed through the gate past the second bus, stopped in back of the men who'd come off it. Behind me, on Broadway, traffic hissed by. Horns honked. A car with a loud radio went past, broadcasting music for the whole neighborhood.

In front of me, inside the gate, sound and movement had almost stopped. The men from the site and the men from the buses stood, two knotted crescents, spilling waves of anger back and forth over an invisible line no one seemed to want to cross.

For a long moment, time didn't move. Possibilities were endless. Anything could have happened; nothing did.

Then someone shouted something. More shouting, and more; someone was shoved.

Someone threw a punch.

Everything broke.

Men charged at each other. Some from the buses streamed toward the building. A tall carpenter tackled the driver of the first bus as he raced for the ramp. Groups fought, two men, four, rolling in the mud. Men from the buses swarmed up the scaffolding.

From inside the building Dan Crowell, Sr. came running, red-faced, pounding down the ramp, chest heaving as he drew panting breaths. Dan Junior followed, and Lydia was behind them. The Crowells were yelling too, at their own men, the workers from the site.

"Stop it!" I heard Crowell Senior bellow. "Leave it! Get out of here! The cops are coming, let them deal with it!" He grabbed hold of the ramp railing with both hands, supported himself there, shouted orders in a hoarse but powerful voice.

Dan Junior grabbed his arm. "Dad, you can't! Get back inside, I'll deal with it!" Senior snarled at him with disgust, shook off his hand. Still leaning on the railing, he shouted again at the brawling men.

Junior threw a look at Senior, then charged down the ramp and waded into a fight, yanked apart a mason and a man off the buses, yelled at the mason again to get out. He got an elbow in the eye, but kept at it.

Lydia's eye caught mine. She was hanging back, at the top of the ramp. She snapped at the air with her hand, trying to push me away, back out the gate. I looked a question at her; she pushed again.

More of the men from the buses ran toward the scaffolding, shoved aside construction workers in their paths, but didn't stop to brawl. On the scaffold planks, up against the building, men took their tire irons and baseball bats to the walls. The air rang with the clang of steel on brick. Someone's tools were tossed from the scaffold, raining down into the dirt below.

I looked up. Men were staring from above, leaning over the scaffolding. I saw Mike DiMaio, six stories up. He spun around, charged toward the scaffold stairway.

"No!" I yelled, though I knew he couldn't hear me. "Mike! They're on the stairs!"

"You!" Dan Crowell, Sr. roared, pointing at me. His rasping words jerked with the shortness of his breath. "Get the hell out of here! All you men, get out! Let the cops handle it!"

I ignored him, started for DiMaio's stairway. Then, from

behind, from a place I didn't see, something hard and heavy caught my shoulder. I stumbled forward, twisted around. The steel rebar that had pounded me was lifted, sliced the air again. I jumped back; it missed my arm by inches. The man swinging it grinned and raised it once more.

My eyes raked the ground, looking for an equalizer. I yanked at a length of two-by-four half buried in the mud; but when I hefted it I saw the man with the rebar had looked away, found something else he was interested in. He swung the bar up over his head two-handed, and down again, grinning as though it were the sledgehammer in the carnival game where you test your strength. He wasn't aiming at me. His target was Dan Crowell, Jr.

Junior's back was to the guy; he was struggling to hold two fighters apart. I flung the two-by-four, threw myself after it across the space between the rebar man and me. I tackled him around shoulders like sacks of concrete. We crashed to the mud, tangled together, steel, wood, arms and legs. I tried to get a purchase in the mud, slipped wildly. He did better. He hefted his bulk, twisted, and half pinned me in the dirt.

Voices shouted everywhere, sounds I couldn't make out, the slap of running feet. Dirt clogged my eyes and my throat. I tried, failed, to wrench myself from under the weight of the guy. I blinked, couldn't see, but didn't need to. His breath reeked of beer and it was blasting my face.

My right arm was under me, under the weight of him, but my left was free. I sent a fist flying up toward the smell and the grunting, felt pain all the way back to my shoulder as I met his jaw.

He softened for a second, started to deflate. I pushed hard against his chest, tried to shove him away, but his groping hand found my jaw, my throat. He closed his fingers like a vise, forced my head back, back. My hand scrabbled over his, trying to pry a finger up, just one, to peel it back so the pain would loosen his grip, but I couldn't do it. I choked, couldn't breathe, couldn't pull away from him, from the load of him and the crush of his hand.

Then suddenly his squeezing fingers went slack. Another

moment, two, and he was just deadweight on me, like lying under a mattress. I shoved him off. He slid away and I lay in the dirt swallowing air, coughing and choking.

Sirens approached; I heard them faintly, then louder, over the yelling and the pounding of feet and my own coughing. I opened my eyes. Dark against the brightness of the sky, Lydia, my abandoned two-by-four tight in her hands, stood over the man who'd been crushing me. Mud crusted her new brown shoes. As I turned my head to look at the man she'd clobbered, he stirred, blinked blankly. He didn't try to rise.

A thick, rough hand closed on my arm, dragged me up. I helped, clumsily finding my feet, staggering against my bene-factor, who stumbled but stood his ground. The sirens came closer. Mike DiMaio, his nose bloody, the side of his face scraped and bruised, pulled me a few steps away, up against a load of plywood, out of the action. He loosened his grip on my arm as I focused my dirt-filmed eyes.

"What happened to you?" I asked him hoarsely.

He shrugged. "Some bastard was breaking up my wall. But Jesus, Smith. You saved Junior's ass." He pointed at Dan Crowell, Jr., who was pulling himself unsteadily up from the dirt, holding his hand to a gash on the side of his head. Then he pointed to Lydia. "And she saved yours."

"The one I was trying to save was yours," I pointed out. "You could've been killed protecting your goddamn bricks."

He gave me a scornful look. "I could take any three of these fuckers," he answered.

"How many were there?"

He wiped blood from under his nose. "Four."

DiMaio turned to Lydia, who held the two-by-four lightly in one hand now, looking sharply around as if she were ready for more action. "You did good work with that stick," he said.

Lydia flashed him a smile that competed with the July sun. "Thank you," she answered graciously.

"Thanks," I said to her myself.

Her eyes met mine. "Mr. Smith, isn't it? From yesterday in my office?" she asked. "Are you all right?"

"Uh-huh," I answered. "Fine."

The sirens could be heard everywhere now. Heads snapped around. Shouts started, different ones. Everything began to happen in reverse.

Men from above charged down the scaffold stairs, leapt to the dirt, didn't bother with the ramp. Fights ended abruptly as the men off the buses shoved their opponents away, turned, made for the street. Panting construction workers stood, empty-handed, as the chaos the men had brought with them swirled toward the gate.

"Leave them!" Dan Crowell, Sr. bellowed as some masons started to chase after the running men. "Let them go!" The chasing stopped, and everyone watched as men poured from the building, sped from the site, disappeared up, down, across Broadway.

That's where people's eyes were, on the fights ending, the men racing away. That's why, until the scream, no one looked up. No one saw Joe Romeo thrown over the rail, off the scaffold, no one knew until we all saw him, arms waving frantically and uselessly, as he hurtled toward the dirt. He slammed into the ground, bounced, hit again, and settled sickeningly still, lying in the dirt too limp, too given over to it, like a doll or a rag or an old stick of wood, not like something that lived.

eleven

joe Romeo was dead. Fallen or pushed from the fourth-floor scaffolding, the police wouldn't commit, investigation ongoing, findings preliminary at this time. But any of the men who'd been working on the scaffolding knew. All the scaffold platforms wrapping this building had midrails and safety netting, all secure, all checked weekly by Crowell and daily by the safety officer for any subs with crews on the platforms. The cops couldn't find anyone who'd been there, no one who could say he'd seen what happened, but Joe Romeo had worked on scaffolds all his life, summer, winter, rain, ice. No one had seen it, but everyone knew.

It wasn't long after the scream, not long after Romeo's body had settled in the dirt, that the police cars reached the site. The buses were still there, parked where they'd stopped, but the men who'd come off them were all gone, or almost all. Dotting the site were some who'd picked the wrong fight, like the guy Lydia had hit with the two-by-four, guys who'd been too dazed or hurt to run when they had the chance. The cops rounded them up, looked over Romeo's body, called for the ambulances.

The men from the crews milled around, not knowing what to do, not knowing what they wanted to do. Everyone waited, for instructions, for something. Cops spoke to the site supers and the supers to the men, telling everyone to stay until the cops had taken their stories. Then they could go; there wouldn't be any more work on this site today.

Paramedics arrived, looked at the injured men, piled some of them on stretchers, but mostly not. Dan Crowell, Jr., with the gash on his head, was one of the ones bandaged and taken to St. Luke's, for observation.

Once the cops arrived I faded away, blended back in with the milling men, waited my turn to be interviewed. Out of the way, I squatted against the fence, rubbed my shoulder, sore and getting stiff. I felt the sun beat on my face and hands, saw it pushing its way to the ground through dust-thickened air. I scanned the faces of the cops, looking for any that were familiar; if any of these guys knew me, it would require a little conversation on the side to head off trouble. But there was no one. Beeping, Dan Junior's ambulance backed out the gate. I watched as Lydia walked up the ramp toward the field office with two detectives and Dan Crowell, Sr.

Senior was sure to blow her cover now, sure to tell the cops about hiring Chuck—it would be foolish not to, now that Joe Romeo was dead and his death a police matter. But Lydia wouldn't mention me, and Crowell didn't know about me, so I stayed where I was. It might be time to give all this up, get me off this site, with Romeo dead and the trouble here being what it was, but that was Chuck's call. Until he made that decision, I was just another mason here, just another guy who'd been in a fight.

And before he made that decision, I wanted to talk to him.

And maybe to a couple of other people.

A shadow fell across me; I squinted up, saw Mike DiMaio between me and the sun.

"Hey," I asked him, "how's your bricks?"

"Fine, no thanks to you," he answered. He lowered himself to the patch of dirt beside me.

I checked my back pocket for cigarettes. The pack was crushed but still there. I found a couple that were intact, offered him one and he took it; we smoked together in the sunlight and dust, watched cops and paramedics and construction workers move around. A blue tarp, the same as the one DiMaio and I had been using to cover the day's work, draped Joe Romeo's body. I could see the edge of it from where I sat.

"You really on your way up the scaffold to save my ass?" DiMaio finally asked, inspecting the burning tip of his cigarette as though it were something new.

"Uh-huh," I said.

He nodded at that. "Well, do me a favor?"

"What's that?"

"Next time, get there in time to do me some good."

I considered this request. "What'll I do about Crowell Junior, next time?"

"Let that little Chinese girl take care of him. You're lucky she was looking out for you." DiMaio's tone was casual, his words nothing extraordinary; but he was drawing deeply on the cigarette, and his eyes, moving here and there, kept away from the blue tarp.

"She was just looking for a fight," I said. "I think she's that type."

"I don't know," he said. "I thought she swung that two-by-four pretty good. Think she plays softball?"

"Shortstop," I said. In answer to his questioning look I asked, "What else is she going to play, at her size? Did you really get your face messed up like that fighting over bricks?"

He touched his swollen nose gingerly. "Yeah."

"Why?"

"Why?" He looked at me incredulously. "Because I'm a big fan of yours, Smith, and I wanted to be like you, only I figured I'd never be big, but if I worked on it I could get to be ugly. What the hell do you mean, why?"

I pulled on my cigarette. "Never mind." A carpenter slung his tool belt over his shoulder, trudged across the site as the cop who'd been with him wandered off to find somebody else. "Mike, tell me something: what the hell just happened here?"

"You got nothing to do today but ask dumb questions, Smith? Coalition came and broke up the joint. You never saw this before?" He shook his head, answering his own question. "I forgot, this isn't really what you do. Well, that's what happened."

" 'Coalition'?"

"Full-employment coalition."

"Looking for . . . ?"

"Ah, shit. What they say, they're looking for local hires on the job, get some black and Spanish guys into the trades, into the unions." He spat on the dirt. "It's bullshit."

"It is? What are they really looking for?"

"They're looking to get paid off. You grease the coordinators before you start work, they don't come."

"Coordinators? That's what they're called?"

DiMaio nodded.

"And that's all you have to do? Pay them off?"

"Well," he said, shifting, looking away, across the site, "well, it's better if you hire a few local guys, too. That way you could point to them, when the coordinators come around. You say, 'I already got some, so fuck off.' "

"So they *are* looking to get men hired."

"No!" He sighed. "Look, it ain't like I don't see their point. Yeah, it's hard for those guys to get into the unions; yeah, maybe they're not gonna get a job this good somewheres else. But you saw those guys here."

I rubbed my shoulder. I'd more than only seen them.

"Those bastards," he went on, "the ones who come here, they don't want to work. They get twenty bucks each and all the cheap shit they can drink to pump them up. This is a goddamn shakedown. The men out there really looking for work, this isn't doing them any goddamn good."

"But men do get hired out of it."

"Yeah," he admitted. "Yeah, okay. They lose any edge they might have, if you hire and pay 'em off, both. Then you can be pretty sure you'll never see 'em."

"And Crowell didn't do that?" I asked. "At the beginning?"

"Well," he said, "that's what don't figure. I heard they did."

"Heard from where?"

"It goes around. Guys like to know this isn't gonna happen, when they sign on. Word was Crowell'd already dealt with the coordinators and taken on men. Ray, you know, the big black bricklayer? And some other guys."

"Sort of an unofficial quota, to keep the peace on your site?"

"I guess."

I asked, "What about Reg Phillips?"

DiMaio bristled. "What, just because he's black?"

"Is it a stupid question?"

He knocked some crusted dirt off the leg of his pants. "Nah, I guess not. But you're wrong. Reg's been a mason tender for years. Maybe he started from some shit like this, I don't know. But he was one of the first guys Lozano hired for this job, because he knew him. Knew he did good work."

I mashed the end of my cigarette out against the sole of my boot. "I wonder where you find them," I said. "These coordinators."

He gave me a long look. "What are you thinking?"

I stared across the site, didn't answer.

"Let me put that another way," he said. "How come since you come here investigating Joe Romeo, Reg Phillips is in the hospital, some crane operator is dug up from the elevator pit, and now Joe Romeo's dead?"

"Mike," I said, "I wish I knew."

He was silent for a long time, staring across the site. "You think this was an accident, what happened to Joe?" he finally asked.

"You mean an accident, like he slipped and fell?"

He shook his head impatiently. "No, that's bullshit. You know how hard it is to fall off shit like this?" He waved his hand at the back rails and the orange netting of the scaffolding that wrapped the building. "No, I mean an accident like he got into a fight with one of them drunk fuckers and he heaved him over. Someone from one of those buses that he didn't know from Adam. You think it was like that?"

"You think it wasn't?"

"You're the fucking detective!"

Surprised by the force of his words, I didn't answer.

DiMaio stared up at the building, the steel skeleton rising inside the new brick skin. "I want to know what happened to Reg," he said. "I want to know why he's lying up there in St. Luke's with a tube up his nose. But I've never been in the middle of shit like this before. Christ, I'm just a fucking bricklayer. A fucking body buried in here, and now Joe—" He stopped.

I looked at him curiously. "Mike, are you trying to tell me to be careful?"

"Shit. I don't know. Maybe. Maybe I'm trying to tell you that if you get your fucking self killed, I don't want it to be my fucking fault."

"Okay," I said, "fair enough."

He looked at me suspiciously.

"Look, Mike," I said. "This is what I do for a living. It's what I've always done. I don't have to do it, but I do. That makes it my choice and it makes whatever happens my fault."

He asked, "You had that kind of choice?"

The question threw me. "What?"

"You feel like you had a choice?" he asked again. "I didn't. I was born to lay bricks. I tried other shit, didn't do me any good. You done other things besides what you do now?"

"Yes."

He nodded. "Like the navy, right? But here you are. Your old man do what you do?"

"No. Not even close."

"Mine does, and his old man did too. It's in the genes or something, I don't know. It ain't like I asked to be doing it. But anything else I tried, it's like the work don't stay, you know what I mean? You do it, so what? But bricklaying, forget about it. You go home at the end of the day, there's something *there*. You *did* something. You die, or you get too old to remember, doesn't matter, what you did is still there." He shook his head. "But the rest of this shit . . ." He looked at me again. "You had a choice?"

I looked up at the building too, at the bricks I had worked on, next to DiMaio's. "I don't know," I told him. "I don't know."

Chuck didn't blow my cover, not that day.

His BMW wheeled screeching around the corner and double-parked on Broadway about half an hour after I'd seen Lydia, the detectives, and Crowell Senior disappear into the dimness of the building. Suit jacket open, Chuck rounded the car, quick-walked across the dust and mud through the gate. He stopped for a minute to peer at the buses, at the painted-out names and the silent interiors; then he trotted up the ramp and inside.

I saw all this from above, from the sixth-floor scaffolding where I had gone to collect my tools. The cops had come, finally, for DiMaio and me, one for each. The one who'd talked to me, as far as he knew, was just talking to a mason who'd tried to tackle a big guy, was put out of commission by the big guy, and was saved by Crowell's Chinese secretary.

"You gotta be kidding," the cop said, when I told him that. Beads of sweat cut gleaming paths through the fine layer of dust coating his pudgy cheeks, came to rest in his mustache. "That cute little piece, with the short hair? Nice ass on her. She give you her number?"

"Not even her name."

"Maybe I oughta go see her next," he said, leering, guy to guy. "Make sure your story checks out."

"You'd better do that," I agreed. "I could be lying."

"Yeah," he said. The tip of his tongue moistened his heat-chapped lips at the prospect. Then, quickly turning cop-tough, he demanded, "So, what, you see anything when this guy fell off from up there, or what?"

"No."

He seemed not to know what to make of the shortness of my answer. He considered for a moment whether it was a challenge, an affront to his authority or to the dignity of the NYPD, but he didn't take it up.

"Yeah. Well, okay," he said gruffly. "I got your name, I'll call you if I need anything else." He spoke as though the investigation of Joe Romeo's death were under his personal supervision. "You can go now."

"Thanks."

"I'm gonna go to the office. See if I can find that girl." He smiled a wolf's smile.

"Do that," I said. I stood, headed for the hoist. "But stop by the paramedics on the way."

"Why?"

"For a sling," I told him. "For your ass. You're going to need it."

Chuck's car was still double-parked where he'd left it when I walked out the gate. I gazed at it for a few moments, then headed south on Broadway.

Chuck was probably carrying his cellular phone. If I called him from the corner, he'd be cool enough not to give me away even if he was in the middle of discussing Lydia and Joe Romeo with the police. We could set up something for later; he'd know I was available, know what I was planning.

I came to the pay phone on the corner, looked at it, passed it by.

At home I showered, pulled on clean clothes, made a few phone calls. I left the mason's bag behind, headed for the subway, to go talk to some people.

My first stop was not my first choice, but it was the way things played out. It was something that needed to be done, a piece to be followed up, and now was even a good time. Now Joe Romeo's death would be distracting everyone, would be the biggest thing on everyone's mind. It would have shaken people up. That could be good for me.

The architectural office of Bernard Melville Associates was on Nineteenth Street in Chelsea, in a neighborhood where the large, bright loft spaces that used to hold button factories and handbag assembly lines had been subdivided for architects, graphic designers, photographers, as the manufacturers had moved south or overseas or just folded up their tents over the course of the last fifteen years.

I hadn't been invited up to the office. I was meeting the man I'd called around the corner, in a coffee shop on Sixth Avenue. The air smelled stale when I walked in, the floor was dirty, and the food didn't look any better. Maybe that's why he'd chosen this place: maybe we could be sure of not being seen here, because no one who worked in the neighborhood, no one who was likely to know him, would be coming here.

I looked around from the door, spotted him already there

at a table against the mirrored wall, as edgy and out of place as when I'd last seen him, on the Armstrong site. Donald Hacker. The architect's rep, the young, skinny guy who walked around twice a week with Dan Crowell, Jr. and didn't have much to say. He was hunched over a bowl of greasy soup, looking miserable. His eyes swept up to meet mine quickly, as they probably had met the eyes of every man who'd walked in here in the last ten minutes. I nodded. Now he could stop looking up nervously every time the door opened. I was the one.

I moved to his table, sat across from him. He twitched as I pulled my chair in, as though he were about to jump up and run away, but he didn't. He didn't say anything, either.

Well, I could start us off. "I'm Smith," I said.

He nodded. "I figured that." His words came out weak and gravelly, caught in his throat. He coughed, said in a voice he tried to make stronger, "What do you want?"

"I just want to talk," I said. "Relax."

A waitress came over, asked me pretty much the same question Hacker had just asked, though the subject was different and the answer didn't matter to her one way or the other.

"Just coffee," I told her. Nothing else seemed like a good idea here. Coffee might not be, either, but chances were I'd survive it, and Hacker seemed to need some sense that the universe was not about to end, that things were close to normal. Coffee was a normal thing to order in a coffee shop.

"Talk about what?" Hacker said, staring into his soup after the waitress was gone. "What do you want to talk about?"

"What I said on the phone. The Armstrong site. The construction inspections."

"Who are you, anyway?"

"I told you that, too. I'm a private investigator."

"Can you prove that?" he suddenly demanded, looking up, fear creating courage. He was trying to catch me out, to find a way to stop what was about to happen.

I was tempted to ask him what he'd do if I couldn't, but instead I reached for my wallet, showed him what I'd shown Mike DiMaio when he'd asked the same question. I decided they were close in age, these two men, a year on either side of thirty; I wondered how Hacker felt about the work he did.

The waitress brought my coffee as Hacker was looking over my license. He handed it back to me fast, glanced around the room as though he was worried someone else might see it also, might know why I was there.

"Tell me about it," I said. "Let's get it over quickly. It'll be easier that way."

"About what?" he tried. "I don't know what you mean."

"If that were true you wouldn't have agreed to meet me. You want me to start?"

He shrugged, stared back into his soup, so I started.

"Your office," I said. "I mean, Bernard Melville's office. How long have you worked there?"

"Six years," he muttered without looking up.

"Well, you landed a good job. I checked around; you people have a good reputation. Clients come to you looking for a quality job. That's what I understand Denise Armstrong wanted, on the Ninety-ninth Street site. Quality."

Hacker's pale face, it seemed, was getting paler, but he still didn't speak.

"I've been around a little," I went on. "I can read architectural documents. I've read yours."

I tried my coffee. It was terrible: weak and bitter.

"And it's true," I said. "Everything Mrs. Armstrong could have asked for in terms of quality, especially in materials. Sound insulation in the interior partitions. And heavy-gauge brick ties, for example. They're in the documents."

Hacker swallowed, sipped water from a scratched plastic glass. He didn't look at me.

"But they're not on the job," I said. "Are they?"

"Sure," he said, too quickly. "Everything the specs call for."

"I've seen the job, Hacker."

"Well . . ." he said. "Well, of course, there've been field changes. You're not in construction, you don't know how we do it." I heard a touch of contempt in his voice, but he still didn't look at me. "A lot of times we make changes during construction. It's normal."

"It's normal," I agreed. "And it's documented."

He flushed red, neck to forehead, like a container filling up.

"So if I went to your office," I said, "if I looked in the files, I'd find the memos where the architect agreed to the substitution of this for that? Agreed to leave something out of the job entirely? I'd find those, if I looked?"

"Of course," he insisted. "All that stuff. It's all in the . . ." He didn't even finish. That little burst of lying energy was all he had in him. He slumped back in his chair. "Oh, God," he said, in a voice so soft I barely heard him.

I sipped some more of the rotten coffee and put the cup down. "When I came here," I said, "I didn't know if you were crooked, or stupid. The cheater or the cheated. Now I know. Are they paying you? Or is it blackmail?"

He sat motionless, his eyes on the water glass. He was silent so long I began to think he hadn't heard me. I was about to speak again, to demand an answer, when he said, in a quiet but clear voice, "Both."

He still wasn't looking at me, but that was all right. He sounded as though something had shifted in him, like a machine that grinds its gears until it suddenly coughs itself back into running order. "They paid me," he said quietly. "At first. At first it wasn't anything important, either. The brick ties; common nails instead of galvanized ones. Never anything big, anything structural." He looked up suddenly, met my eyes for the first time. "Not even now, I mean. Not the concrete or the steel. Not the rebar. Nothing that mattered." He looked away again. "Just this little shit. Small, picky stuff. What the hell difference would it have made?"

"It seems to me those things are the difference between quality and mediocrity."

"Oh, come on," he snapped. "You sound as pompous as my boss. You really think those nails will rust through before someone knocks that damn building down in thirty years? You think heavy-duty ties will keep the walls from moving when the subway goes by? It's expensive stuff, that's all. It makes guys like my boss look like they know what they're talking about. Or think they do."

He drank some more water, this time looking as though he wanted it. "No contractor in his right mind would use half the stuff we spec."

"Who told you that?"

"It's obvious."

"Not to me."

"Well, they said so," he said smugly.

"Who?"

He hesitated. "They did."

"Who's 'they,' Hacker?"

He looked up at me. "Do I have to?"

"Why the hell do you think I'm here, Hacker? You think I'm interested in you, come to track you down? You think if I lock away a punk like you, that'll be enough to make me happy?"

"Lock me—" His face lost all the belligerence, all the smugness, sagged into the miserable look it had had when I'd first walked in.

I didn't think I actually could lock him away based on what he'd done; taking a bribe to ignore deviations from the documents might be something you could get fired for, maybe even sued, but it didn't sound like a crime to me. That was speculation, though, and I didn't see any reason to share my speculating with him.

"What'll happen to me?" he asked quietly.

"That depends on how well you cooperate." Clichéd question, clichéd answer; but it worked.

"Well, shit, how hard can it be to figure out?" he muttered, then said, "The contractors. It was their idea."

"Crowell, you mean?"

He looked at me contemptuously. "Of course not. The subs, the subcontractors. Old man Crowell's a real straight-arrow type. He'd never go for this shit."

"What about Junior?"

Hacker shook his head. "*He's* the one who's stupid. That's the only reason the whole thing worked."

"What do you mean?"

"He comes around with me, twice a week, up on the scaffold, through the building, but he doesn't see a damn thing. He's an accountant."

"What's that, some sort of architect's insult?"

His look was uncomprehending; then he caught on. "No, no, that's what he does. That's what he went to college for. He doesn't even like construction. He just came into the business because his father needed someone."

"He told you that?"

"Sure. The old man looks like a brick shithouse, but he's sick. Someone said he's got leukemia or something, but I don't know. I do know he can't keep going on the way he's been. He needs help."

I thought of Crowell Senior, red-faced, clinging to the ramp railing, breathing hard but yelling orders.

"So he brought Junior in?" I asked.

"Well, he didn't put it that way. The old man didn't. Not that *he* needed help. That Junior needed a good job with a future. Security. That the business would take care of Junior for the rest of his life."

"So Senior was doing Junior a favor, taking him into the business?"

"Says Senior. But that's not why Junior did it. He did it because the old man needed help, whether he'd admit it or not." Hacker gave a sour laugh. "The pair of them, doing each other favors. What a joke."

"What's the joke?"

"The joke is, Junior probably *is* set up now for the rest of his life."

"Why is that funny?"

"Because a geek like Little Danny Junior can make eighty thousand a year and be fixed for life as a contractor even though he's so dumb he can't see what's happening right under his nose. But I'm six years out of architecture school, with a master's and a license, and I'm barely making thirty thousand a year, and if we don't get another project into the office soon I'm going to get laid off."

"I see. So you're poorly paid, and that makes it okay to do what you're doing?"

"I'm telling you, it wouldn't have mattered! It *won't* matter! No one living in the building will ever have any idea, and the contractors are saving a fortune."

"Tell me about the scheme."

"What the hell is there to tell? The contractors buy and use cheaper stuff than we specified. I don't see it. I sign off the requisitions and I collect my payoff. That's what it's called, isn't it, a payoff?" He said that with a sneer, maybe at me for knowing what to call it, maybe at himself for collecting it.

"Anyone else in your office involved?"

He stared at me. "What are you, crazy? This isn't exactly the kind of thing you discuss over the lunch table."

"Not even your boss?"

"Especially not the boss."

"When I asked you if it was blackmail or bribery, you said 'both,' " I said. "Why?"

He rolled the empty water glass between his hands. "I wanted to stop. In the beginning, not long after we started."

"Why?"

"I was nervous! I could lose my job, and it's a bad time. Jobs aren't that easy to get."

Especially, I thought, with the reference you'd get from your boss. "But?"

"I was told that might not be such a hot idea. That I had a good thing going and I should keep it going."

"Who told you?" I asked. "Which contractors are involved?"

"I think they all are."

"All?" I asked. "Emerald? Mandelstam? Lacertosa?"

He nodded. "I never talked to any of the supers, or anything. But I'm approving cheap crap in all the trades."

I thought about the Lacertosa field trailer, about John Lozano's kind blue eyes. I reached for a cigarette, was about to light it when the waitress caught my eye. She shook her head, pointed to the No Smoking sign. She brought me more coffee, with a sad smile.

"Who did you talk to, Hacker? And who was it who told you not to stop?"

"The same guy who came to me with the idea in the first place. A masonry foreman. I'm up on the scaffold one day, Dan Junior's wandered off someplace, and next thing I know this masonry foreman's buddying up to me. He said this was what they wanted me to do, this was how it was going to work. He had a hundred-dollar bill right there for me. Right there." Hacker stared emptily through the room, seeing something else, another day in another place. He brought his eyes suddenly back to me. "To tell you the truth, I was a little afraid of him. That's one of the reasons I did it."

He looked at me hopefully: Maybe fear would excuse what greed hadn't.

I didn't soften. "Who was this guy, Hacker?"

Hope faded, replaced by resignation. "His name is Joe Romeo."

So I was the one who got to tell Donald Hacker about Joe Romeo. I watched him grow rigid, watched the color, which had returned to his face, drain out again.

"Oh my God," he whispered. "Oh my God. Off the scaffold? Just right off the scaffold?"

I nodded.

"What's going to happen now?" he breathed. "Oh, God, it'll all come out. Oh, shit, oh God, I'm screwed. Now I'm really screwed."

"And another man's dead," I said. I tried to keep the disgust out of my voice, but I could hear its echoes. "Jesus, get ahold of yourself, Hacker. Why would your little scam come out because some drunk threw Joe Romeo off the scaffold?"

"Because . . . because—" He blinked, looked around him as though trying to remember where he was. "I don't know," he finished lamely. "Because . . . Won't you tell them?"

"Tell who? The cops?"

He flinched. That obviously was even worse than what he'd had in mind.

"Or your boss? No, not right away, Hacker. I have to think about this. Just make sure you don't leave town. That would piss me off." I checked his face, to make sure my threat had registered; in his condition, I didn't think it needed to be any more specific. "I'm working on something else," I told him. "I want to fit it all together. Meanwhile, go back to work. Keep your head down."

"Something else?"

"You didn't kill Joe Romeo, did you, Hacker?"

"Me?" He barely choked the word out.

"Well, somebody did. Maybe somebody connected with your little scheme, maybe not. Watch your back." I stood to go.

"Oh my God," he whispered. "Do you really think—?"

"No," I said. "But you ought to choose your playmates more carefully next time, Hacker. You're not ready to be in the game with the big boys."

I turned from his table, turned back when I heard his whispered "Thanks."

"For what?"

"For not . . . not . . ."

"Don't think I'm doing you any favors. If I blow the whistle on you now it could mess up the other thing I'm working on, which, believe it or not, is more important. Try to stay cool, Hacker."

I left the greasy-smelling but air-conditioned coffee shop, stood on the sidewalk in the blazing sun. Heat radiated up from the concrete as I lit a cigarette. It was true, what I'd told Hacker: that I needed to know how his scam fit in with the case I was working on.

But more than that, I thought, eyeing the traffic as it streamed uptown, I needed to know, exactly, what the case I was working on was.

twelve

My next goal was back uptown. I headed for the subway, a block over and a block down; but first I stopped at a pay phone, to call Lydia.

I dialed the construction trailer number. A voice answered that could only be a cop's.

"Who wants her?" he demanded, as though any call to anyone in the trailer might be a major break in the case.

"The plumber," I said. "I'm in her house. I got the leak stopped, but I gotta know what she wants me to do about the valve."

"Well, she's gone," he told me. "Left about half an hour ago. Probably on her way there now."

"Yeah," I said. "Okay." Hell, I thought as I dialed Lydia's office. I would have been interested to know what had gone on in the trailer this morning, what the cops and Lydia and Chuck and Dan Crowell, Sr. had found to pass the time with. I left a message on her machine and took the subway back to upper Broadway.

The two-story white Armstrong Properties building looked just as handsome in the gleaming afternoon sunlight as it had yesterday in the deep overcast after the rain. The freckled secretary, Dana, looked at me just as coolly and professionally as yesterday, too, when I walked in.

"I want to see Mrs. Armstrong," I said.

"No, I don't think so," Dana said calmly. "Yesterday she

threw you out of here. I don't think she's expecting you back."
She made no move toward the phone.

"Yesterday I pretended to be a reporter. Today I called one
who's a friend of mine. He was interested in this whole
setup." I let that linger, vague and unpleasant.

Hesitation blinked in her eyes; that was enough. "Buzz the
boss," I suggested. "Ask if she'll see me."

She did that, in a brief, low conversation. She rose, frostily,
and showed me into the office in the back.

Denise Armstrong stood in the center of the room, lips in a
tight line. The sunlight picking out a square of courtyard in
the window behind her was warmer, more golden, than yesterday, but my reception was the same.

Dana, with an angry look at me, left us, and the door closed
behind me.

"Why are you back?" Mrs. Armstrong asked icily as the
door clicked shut. "Didn't I make my point yesterday?"

I turned to look at the door. "Did she lock that?"

"Not this time. I have no reason to keep you here today. In
fact, I had no reason to let you in at all, except to ask why you
keep trying to lie your way in."

"I told her the truth: I wanted to see you."

"You told her you'd spoken to a reporter. That was a lie."

I shrugged. The movement made my shoulder ache, sore
where the rebar had caught it. "I thought it was better than
pushing past her and charging in here."

Her eyes flashed. "Are you telling me I should be grateful
you didn't use force? You're out of your league, Mr. Smith.
Get out of here."

"I'm trying to help you."

"I doubt that. Or else you're not very good at it."

I took a breath. When I spoke, it was in calm, reasoned
tones. "Can we start over, Mrs. Armstrong? Give me five minutes. You know what happened on your site this morning?"

Her mouth curled contemptuously. "Of course I know! I
just got back from there. I talked for a long time with the
police and Dan Crowell, Sr. And your employer, as a matter
of fact."

"Chuck DeMattis?"

"I told him you'd come to see me." She added, with a cold smile, "He said that behind your manner, you were actually one of his best men."

Leaving as a matter between me and Chuck just whose man I was, I asked, "My manner? I came here with a polite lie. You were the one who locked me up. Did you tell him that?"

"No. Believe it or not, we didn't talk much about you. Everybody was more interested in the dead man."

Maybe that meant my cover, on the site, hadn't been blown. I'd have to find that out, later.

"You wanted five minutes," she said. "I'll give you three. What for?"

"I'm trying to help you," I repeated. "To do that, I need you to help me."

A joyless smile bent the corners of her mouth. "If I had a nickel for every man who said he was trying to help me when he was trying to screw me, I'd be a very rich woman. What do you want *me* to do for *you*?"

All right, I thought. We'll do it your way. "I want to talk to the coordinator who brought those men to your site this morning."

"And why did you come to me?"

Her eyes told me she knew, and told me that if I tried to sweeten it I'd end up thrown out of this office again.

"Because you're black."

The hard mask of her face seemed to soften just a fraction, with something like the relief you feel when an anticipated pain has come and gone. But nothing showed in her voice. "Am I the only black person you know?"

"The only black person I know in this business, in this neighborhood. The only one whose building site this coordinator's men rioted at."

"That alone could make him not interested in talking to me. And I think they call that a job action."

"They can call it whatever they want."

"The police are looking for him. Why not just wait?"

"I'm betting they won't find him."

"Why not? They've arrested five of the men he brought."

"Those men won't talk. They'll never be charged with anything. There's no way you could prove they were on those buses. I'll bet they all had a story set before they got there, in case of trouble: 'Gee, officer, I was just there looking for a job. What buses?' "

"Is that what you would say?"

"In their shoes, I probably would."

"Well, you may be right. So the police won't find him."

"But I still want to talk to him."

"Then find him if you can. Why should I get involved?"

"I would have thought," I said, "that finding out what's going on on your site would be important to you."

"You would have been wrong. What's important to me is that we get that job back on schedule."

"More important than finding out who killed a man there and why another man was buried there?"

"Yes!" She perched against the edge of her desk, regarded me levelly. "A lot of people's jobs—*living* people—depend on that project. As does my future in this business. Those things are what's important to me. Neither of those dead men is anything to me one way or the other."

"That may be true. But someone killed them."

"And that's supposed to upset me? Get me all riled up in the name of justice? You must be joking."

"Share the joke with me."

She smiled a cold, slow smile. "It's the one about how a white bully wants a black woman to forget her own interests and help him find out what happened to two other trashy white men. What's behind it is the idea that whatever happens to white men is more important than anything else. It's pretty funny; it always gets a good laugh around here."

"Lenny Pelligrini and Joe Romeo aren't laughing."

"I'm sure when they were alive they found plenty to laugh about that I wouldn't have thought funny."

"So they deserved to die?"

"A lot of people die who don't deserve it. Lenny Pelligrini, from what I'm told, was a heavy-metal punk who occasionally came to work stoned. Joe Romeo was probably one of your white macho types who just *had* to stand up to a mob of black drunks instead of having the sense to run. That was stupid, they responded as you'd expect, and it's his problem."

"Not anymore."

"So it's no one's problem. It's certainly not mine."

The ivy on the shelves behind her trailed gracefully down the window. It was well tended; carefully watered and fed, all the brown leaves picked off. These were all plants that would do well in the kind of light she had here; she clearly hadn't given in to the gardener's urge to try to grow something the conditions were wrong for, just because she loved it.

I asked, "Hasn't it occurred to you that this all might be aimed at you?"

"No."

"Why not?"

Her words were clipped and contemptuous. "If things had worked out for whoever killed Pelligrini, his body wouldn't have been found. Joe Romeo's death couldn't look any less related to my building unless he'd been killed off the site. If someone wanted to compromise me, there are much more direct ways."

"So you don't care if these murders are ever solved?"

"I didn't say that."

"A minute ago—"

"What I said was, I didn't care who killed those men. I don't. But I would prefer it if the media and police attention these things have brought, were to end. It's not the kind of publicity I want for this project."

"Then will you help me find this guy, this coordinator?"

She sat silent, watched me. She rubbed a finger back and forth on the wood of the old oak desk. Maybe it had been her grandfather's desk.

"I don't know," she finally said. "Maybe I will. If I find him, I'll call you."

"How will I know whether you've decided to try?"

"If I call you, it will be because I have the answer. If I don't call you, I didn't try."

* * *

As I left Mrs. Armstrong's office, the beeper on my hip beeped.

I flicked the switch but kept walking, didn't lift it off for a look at the readout until I was out of range of the Armstrong Properties windows. I didn't want anyone in there thinking someone was checking on my progress with them.

The digital red phone number the beeper gave me was Lydia's, at her office. I found a pay phone and called.

"Oh, good!" she said when she answered. "I was wondering how long I should wait."

"Gee, I don't know," I said. "I'd wait forever for you."

"For a phone call?"

"Well, maybe not. Buy you a drink?"

"Sure," she said. "Even though I just had one."

"You did?"

"Uh-huh. With the nicest guy."

"There's such a thing as a nice guy?"

"I may have to reconsider. A construction worker, too. Who'd have known?"

"You're kidding. Who?"

"Your buddy Mike DiMaio."

That stopped me. "You've been drinking with Mike DiMaio?"

"Isn't that what construction workers do when they get off work—drink?"

"Come on. Really?"

"Of course, really. It wasn't like a big deal. He asked me."

"Asked you what?"

"*Out*, you birdbrain. For a drink."

"I thought you didn't like construction workers."

"I wanted to see what one of these guys is like when he's trying to show a woman his good side."

"And what was he like?"

"He was very nice, but that's what you've been saying about him. We talked for a while and then I came down here, where I've been sitting in my office doing my paperwork and taking very calmly the fact that you haven't called to keep me informed—"

"Haven't called? I spent my last quarter to hear some cop tell me you'd left the trailer, and then my last dimes to hear your machine babble in Chinese, and now—"

As though I'd paid it and given it a cue, an electronic voice interrupted to demand more cash for more phone time.

"Come down here," Lydia said.

I answered, "I'm on my way," and the phone cut us off.

I caught an express train to Canal Street, to reach Lydia's office on the fringes of Chinatown. The downtown streets were glazed with heat as I came out of the subway, but somehow it didn't seem as warm as it had just a few minutes ago.

Lydia buzzed me in and stood waiting at the door at the end of the hall. She still wore the blue-and-tan blouse and pale linen skirt she'd had on at the site, but she'd traded in the mud-caked shoes for white sneakers.

"You're all sweaty," she said. She kissed my cheek anyway, and I felt a little warmer.

"It's hot out there," I said as we entered her office. "You haven't noticed?"

Lydia's small office is tucked away in the shadowed back of the building, on the ground floor. The window's pebbled glass cast a muted light on the deep-green walls while an ancient air conditioner gurgled in the corner like the rush of a mountain stream. It was the urban equivalent of a cool, secluded forest grove, where a man and a woman could be alone at the slow finish of a hot summer's day.

Either that, or it was a one-room low-rent rear office in Chinatown.

"It's not as bad as yesterday," Lydia said, closing the office door.

"We're not really going to talk about the weather, are we?"

"Hmmm." She appeared to consider that. "Well, you could fill me in on the case."

"I don't know," I said, reaching into the tiny office fridge. "When a man's partner is out drinking with his partner, he kind of wants to know—"

"Whatever he wants to know is none of his business. And

his partner wants to know where we stand on a case where our subject was murdered in front of us eight hours ago."

A cold breeze swept from distant mountaintops into the forest grove. I took a bottle of grapefruit juice from the fridge, clinked some ice into a glass, settled on the junior-sized sofa. I stretched my feet onto the coffee table.

"You probably know more about where we stand than I do," I told her. "You and Chuck and Mrs. Armstrong talked to the cops together, am I right?"

"Is that just a logical guess, or do you know all about it?"

"It's not a guess, but I don't know anything about it except that it happened."

"You haven't called Mr. DeMattis?"

"No. I've been busy."

"Doing what?"

"I saw two people. I'll tell you about it in a minute. First tell me about Chuck and the client and the cops."

She nodded; that was a reasonable request, since what I was asking about had happened first.

"Well, it wasn't so very interesting," she said. "Mr. DeMattis and Mr. Crowell Senior explained to the cops about Crowell's interest in Joe Romeo, and what I was there for. Mr. DeMattis said he'd been looking into things from the office end, too, and hadn't found much. I think the word he used was '*bupkes*'; is that Italian?"

"Yiddish. Literally, it means 'chickpeas'; figuratively, it means 'nothing.' " I took a swig of juice, tried to ignore the image that rose in my mind of Lydia and Mike DiMaio in a cool and quiet bar.

"Anyway," Lydia said, "he offered to share what little he had with the police."

"Including me?"

"Not Mr. DeMattis. Mrs. Armstrong asked him about you, and Mr. DeMattis admitted you work for him, but he made it sound like you were just one of a bunch of people doing backgrounds. She said you should work on your approach. He agreed and apologized."

"Oh, great. But he didn't say I was on the site?"

"No. I was a little worried that Mr. Crowell would remember your name from the time in the trailer."

"Not likely, and especially a dull name like mine. A GC wouldn't know the names of the guys who work for the subs unless they make a real strong impression. I just have to be careful Mrs. Armstrong doesn't see me there."

"Mr. DeMattis," Lydia said, "now I remember him, from the picnic. He's kind of obnoxious, isn't he?"

"Besides apologizing for me to a woman who almost had me arrested, what did he do that was obnoxious?"

"He was pushy, fast, and loud, offering to do this and that for everybody. The cops' best buddy."

"Did he know them?"

"The cops? Yes. Bzomowski and Mackey. Homicide detectives from the Twenty-fourth Precinct. The same ones who came about Pelligrini. They seemed like okay guys, but they're not happy."

"Why would they be? Two open homicides in three days."

"Anyway, Mr. DeMattis wants me to stay on the case."

"Chuck? But there isn't any case anymore. Joe Romeo's dead."

"Yes, and it seemed to me Bzomowski and Mackey really want it to be what it looked like, something that just happened as a result of a fight."

"That's what they want it to be. What do they really think it was?"

"Right now, that's what they say they think. Do you think something else?"

My shoulder was stiffening up; I moved it around, trying to loosen it. "I think it's a hell of a coincidence that one of fifty drunks randomly picked one of fifty guys to toss off the scaffold, and it happened to be Joe Romeo." I took another swig of grapefruit juice. "On the other hand, Romeo seems like he might be the type of guy to go right up in their faces, get them so pissed off they'd do something like that."

Lydia tilted her head. " 'Seems like.' You knew him. Do you think he *was*?"

I rested my eyes on a framed Chinese brush painting of mountains and pine trees and mist. "No. He was a bully. Bullies are cowards. He pushed the masons around because he was a foreman, so he had authority. I don't think he'd have gone up alone against a bunch of wild drunks like the ones off those buses."

"So you think this was deliberate? Someone taking advantage of the situation?"

"I don't know," I said. "I wonder what Chuck thinks."

"He must think the same; that must be why he wants me to stay."

"How did the cops feel about that?"

"They liked the idea."

"What about Crowell?"

"Mr. Crowell doesn't mind, either, for now."

"He doesn't?" I considered that, swirling my grapefruit juice around in my glass. "His Joe Romeo problem is solved; why would he come across for this?"

"I think Mr. DeMattis made some sort of arrangement."

"Arrangement? Chuck's picking up the tab?"

"I think so."

"So how can you think he's obnoxious? He's paying your salary."

"When I work for you, you pay my salary. That doesn't stop me."

She had me there.

"Anyway," she said, "you might want to call him. I'll bet he wants you to stay, too."

I'll bet he does, I mused. And he's picking up the tab.

"How about the rest of your afternoon?" I prompted as Lydia went back to her club soda.

"How about yours?" she countered.

"You go first."

"I already went first," she pointed out.

It was easier to give in than to argue. I pushed the dark, cool bar of my imagination away, told her about Hacker.

"My God," was her response. "Do you think it's true, that there's nothing structurally wrong with the building now?"

"I don't know," I said. "But probably. With concrete and steel, there are all sorts of other checks: testing labs and sign-offs, papers at the Building Department. And big liability if anything goes wrong. I think this is probably just about what Hacker says it is, materials substitutions that make a good building into a chintzy one."

"Still, it's pretty serious, isn't it?"

"It is if you're the person paying for the quality materials. I felt guilty talking to Mrs. Armstrong, knowing this."

Lydia's eyes widened, and I thought I heard the rumble of thunder over the mountaintop. "You talked to her, too? You're holding out on me."

"On the contrary," I said innocently, "you're holding out on me."

"I've told you everything I know."

"Well, I don't know," I said. I felt the air growing thick and sticky as I heard myself say, "You were out drinking with a bricklayer. Italian, too. I mean, what would your mother say?"

Her eyes flashed. "You're kidding. You can't possibly—"

I held up my hand for her to stop. "Wait," I said wearily. She was right, and she was right about why I'd dropped the news about my chat with Mrs. Armstrong the way I had. I lit a cigarette, reached onto the windowsill for the ashtray she keeps there in case smokers come by.

"Don't start," I said. "It's been a long day. I'm a deeply flawed human being. You knew that." I drew in a lungful of smoke, wondered why the things that comfort us are the things that kill us.

"I'll tell," I said. And I told her, almost word for word, about my talk with Mrs. Armstrong, who didn't like me very much.

She asked a few questions, all of them good ones. When I was done, she said, staring into space, "I wonder if she'll look, and I wonder if she'll find him."

"I don't know. I can't read her. She hates me, but I don't know if it's personal, or because I'm just another piece of low-class, ham-fisted white trash trying to push her around."

"You're not so bad," Lydia said softly.

I looked at her in surprise. "I'm not? I thought you were about to throw me out of here a minute ago."

"I was. And you can't do that, Bill. You know you can't."

I ground the end of my cigarette around in the ashtray. "I just . . ."

"I know. But you can't." She fixed her obsidian eyes on me. "I'm an investigator. You put me on that site to see if I could learn anything. If every time I'm alone with a guy—"

"It's not like that."

"It's close."

"I can't help how I feel," I said.

"Neither can I," she said, her voice quiet. "But you can help how you act."

I looked at her, and away, to the framed prints on her walls, and back to her again. I wanted to say something, though I didn't know what; then, inexplicably, she smiled.

"So do you want to hear about it?"

"About what?"

"My afternoon."

"Don't play games."

"I'm not. There's no reason not to tell you about it. It's just that it wasn't a big deal, and you were making it into one."

"Okay," I said, after a moment. I leaned back on the sofa. "Tell me about this little deal."

She recrossed her legs, settled more comfortably in her chair, too. "We went for a drink," she said. "And he is a nice guy."

I couldn't argue with that, and a part of me felt bad about wanting to. "What did you talk about?"

"The trouble on the site. It was a natural. And softball. That was why I went out with him in the first place."

"What was?"

"He had an opening line I couldn't resist." In the hard consonants of Mike DiMaio's Brooklyn accent, she said, " 'You swing a bat the way you swung that two-by-four, I'll bet you hit three-fifty.' "

Lydia's lifetime average in the Central Park pickup league where we play is .296; she's very proud of that. Mine's .270.

"I can see how that would make a man attractive. What was on his mind?"

"Nothing different from what you'd expect, I don't think. But he was a perfect gentleman. We went to a bar called the Liffy, on Ninety-sixth Street. We talked."

"About what?"

"He wanted to know who taught me to swing like that."

"Did you tell him?"

"And blow your cover?"

"Yours. He already knows about me."

"Oh, right. No, I didn't. I told him I learned from my brother."

"Which of your brothers could possibly have taught you to swing a bat?"

"He doesn't know that. And we talked about his work. And he brought up Reg Phillips. He's really upset about that."

"I know he is," I said. "They're close friends."

"I asked him why."

"Why what?"

"Why they're friends. What they like about each other. I thought if he talked about his friend it might make him feel better." She caught my look, cocked her head to one side. "Why, is that a peculiar thing to do?"

"It's just not something men think about much," I said. "Why they're friends."

"But you must have reasons, even if you don't say them out loud."

"Assuming men have reasons for anything. Generally I believe we're thought to respond only to primitive Neanderthal-like urges—"

"Completely true, I'm sure. Shall I go on?"

"Please do. What did he say?"

"He said, Reg cares about his work. Not because he's paid to, but because he's made that way. That's important to Mike, that people care about what they do. It frustrates him about most people he works with, and meets. It's why he likes you."

"You talked about me?" The air began to grow close and

confining, as though the heavy thunderclouds from the mountaintop were rolling our way.

"He mentioned you. His new partner, one of the few guys up there, he says, who deep-down cares. He's impressed because, he says, as rusty as you are—"

"And at my age, probably. Forget it; I don't want to know. Anything else about Phillips?"

"No. Just how impressed Mike is, how he doesn't think *he'd* have the energy to go back to school, and he's sure he's not smart enough anyway. . . ."

"Phillips is in school?"

"Night school. An engineering program. Didn't Mike tell you that?"

"I think we've established that men don't tell each other the same things they tell women. Where?"

"City College, I think. Why?"

"I'm not sure," I said slowly. "Except that a guy who gambles *and* goes to school could rack up a big debt, it seems to me. I wonder how he's paying for school."

"It's cheap up there, City College."

"But it's not free."

"You want me to talk to Mike again?"

"Is that a straight question?"

"What else?"

"Well, the real answer is no, I'd be happier if you were never even on the same continent with him again. But I can't say that, can I?"

"No."

"Well, then, the other answer is yes, it might be useful, but not yet. Let's save it for later. For now, are you interested in dinner?"

She shook her head. "I can't. My brother Ted is making one of his rare Chinatown appearances, with his kids. Unless you really need me, I should go home."

Unless I really needed her. Well, there wasn't much chance of that.

No more than there ever was.

Our eyes met, almost by accident. The air was suddenly and very briefly charged, as though a lightning storm had broken over the mountaintop far above, close enough to be felt, but not close enough to change things in our forest grove.

"No," I said. "I'm not going to do anything tonight except sleep. I'll see you on the site in the morning."

That was it, then. We couldn't think of any reason why we shouldn't lock up Lydia's office, leave the forest grove for the heat and bustle of the street outside. A light kiss before she headed east, to the noisy chaos of family in the walk-up apartment on Mosco Street, and I went west. A few parting words in the gold of early evening, and each of us going in the direction we'd chosen, finding our own way to deal with the lingering sound of Joe Romeo's scream and the image of the blue tarp.

thirteen

i did start walking across town, west on Canal Street, but I didn't go home. The subway stop came up first, the stop for the IRT that would take me uptown, to the Village, the West Side, the Armstrong site, and beyond, if I wanted to go.

As the subway flew north, the car I was riding in collected young people, mostly black and Latino, some Asian, some white. They wore baggy pants and big, unlaced sneakers, the boys in fade haircuts and the girls in gold earrings and dark lipstick. At 137th Street we all got off together. They streamed west through the park and up the steep hill, toward City College. They walked with more purpose than I: They had classes to get to. The sun's horizontal rays haloed them from behind as they headed for the hilltop campus gate.

I reached the hilltop in my own time, took in the area as I waited for the light to change. The streets surrounding the City College campus were lined with run-down apartment buildings punctuated by a graffiti-walled grade school, bodegas, and a Chinese take-out place broadcasting waves of garlic and old sesame oil. To the beat of salsa music, five guys worked on two double-parked cars. This late in the day the grade-school yard was empty except for a flock of pigeons and a dozen dazed-looking seagulls, who stood on the wide expanse of asphalt facing west as though they expected a distant surf to roll in.

Directly across the street, a wrought-iron gate stood open.

Beside it, on the right, zoomed a huge, slick, white-brick structure, stretched skin and sharp angles, deep shadows under four-story overhangs. The sun lit up its entire taut, western face. Left of the gate, a massive old building of rough gray stone and white terra-cotta hunkered into the sloping ground, and beyond it another one, similar. On them, the light picked out gargoyle faces and flower petals and the faceted edges of dressed stone.

Separating the buildings was a hundred years and a wide tiled path, and at the bottom of the path stood a campus map. I reached it, located the Engineering Department, and headed over.

Engineering was in a new building just outside the north campus gate. I walked under the gate's wrought-iron arch, watching some crows in the tall old trees settle on one branch, give it up, try another. A hundred years ago, these gates enclosed a few stone buildings and a broad green field at the top of the bluff. That was all the college you needed then, everything you had to have to impart all the critical knowledge of the Western world. Today, buildings in every style that's come and gone in the last century squat where the field used to be, and beyond it; the gates are only ornamental now, just reminders of a time when we were confident knowledge was finite, achievable, and benign.

The Engineering security guard wanted to know who I was and I told him. I asked who the head of the Engineering evening program was and he told me. He pointed me to the elevator, but I climbed the two flights to the faculty offices.

The man the guard said I wanted, Dr. Donald Cannon, turned out to be a round-faced, balding black man, and he was in, sitting behind a paper-covered desk in an office a secretary told me to go on into. The office was crowded with shelves of books, tables of papers and balsa-wood models, walls of thumbtacked posters for design competitions and grant deadlines. Although the building's air-conditioning was on, the unit in Dr. Cannon's office wasn't. Both windows were thrown open, and the room was filled with soft evening air and the trilling of birds in the park behind the campus.

Cannon's desk was set so that he could look up and see trees and sky in one direction, or, in the other, the corridors and classroom doors of the program he ran. Through his window I could see my crows lined up on a tree branch; I wondered what that branch had that the others didn't, and who decided.

Cannon wore gold-rimmed glasses and a guarded smile. He dropped his pen onto a pile of papers and asked what he could do for me.

"I'm interested in one of your students," I told him. "Reg Phillips."

"Reg," he said. The smile faded a little; he gestured me to a chair. "You are . . . ?"

I told him as I sat.

"Private investigator?" What was left of the smile vanished entirely. "What's your interest in Phillips?"

"Reg Phillips had an accident," I said as, outside the window, a pair of sparrows darted behind some thick green leaves. Sitting where I was, I could see nothing of the dry, hot concrete and heat-softened asphalt of the Harlem neighborhood that surrounded us; the trees and the birds and the golden evening light could have been the Kentucky of my childhood.

Cannon nodded. "It's a shame. He's a promising student. Is there some question about it?"

"I don't know," I said. "Maybe not. I'd like to ask you a few questions; I won't take up much of your time."

"There won't be any problem, will there? With his medical coverage?" Now I heard a controlled note of belligerence in Cannon's voice. One of the crows inched over closer to the one next to it; the other one eyed him but didn't shift away. "That was why he'd kept that job," Cannon said. "For the insurance. He hasn't got anything else."

"How do you know that?"

"People don't come to school here, especially in a night program, if they have anything else." His glittering eyes challenged me to contradict him, to say something polite but untrue. I didn't take him up on it; he knew who his students were and what their options had been.

"Then what choice did he have about keeping his job?" I asked. "How else would he have lived, school or not?"

The combative moment passed, but Cannon didn't warm up. "We have other students here who work construction jobs in the spring and summer. They save up, quit, and take full semesters in the day program. They stay until the money runs out, then go out and look for another job. Phillips could have done that, but he isn't that type."

"What type is he?"

"He's methodical. He's taking two, sometimes three, courses a semester, year-round, while he's working. It'll take him longer to get through the program, but he's not one to quit a job if he's got one."

"I heard he has another source of income," I said. "I heard he gambles." I wasn't sure whether I should have led up to that a little better; but if I was looking for a reaction, I didn't get one.

"He's an adult," Cannon said coldly. "He works hard all day and spends his evenings in a classroom instead of in a bar with his friends. If he enjoys putting a few dollars on a horse, why shouldn't he?"

"A guy who has nothing?"

"A man," he placed the barest emphasis on the word, "who seems pretty good, so far, at deciding what to do with what he has. Look, is this part of your investigation? What exactly did you come here to find out?"

I looked out the window at the honey-colored light on the leaves, tried to phrase it in a way that would tell Dr. Cannon we were on the same side. "I'm looking for a picture of the kind of man Reg Phillips is."

He shook his head. "Actually," he said, "what you're looking for is a way to prove that what happened to him was his fault, so the insurance company won't have to pay."

His gaze was direct and unwavering, his face hard, like a soldier preparing to fight a battle he's fought and lost many times before.

"No," I said. "I'm not from the insurance company."

"Then where are you from?"

I chose my words carefully. "What happened to Phillips may be part of another case I'm working on. Or it may not. I need to know, but I'm not here to take anything away from Phillips."

"Good," he said emphatically, responding to what I'd said, though clearly he hadn't decided yet whether to believe it. "Because these students—men like Reg Phillips—work harder than you or I have ever worked, just to catch up to where we started from. They don't need anyone—insurance companies, whoever—trying to block their way."

Behind him a breeze made the branches nod. As they moved I caught a glimpse of the rooftops of Harlem and the Bronx stretching down and away, until they were lost in the smoggy July haze.

"Will he be a good engineer?" I asked.

My change of direction, my refusal to argue with his politics or his protectiveness, seemed to throw Cannon off balance.

"Yes," he said. "Yes, he will."

"Tell me why."

His look remained suspicious, but he said, "I told you he's methodical. He doesn't make decisions before he's examined all the available data. But he's creative, too. He can come up with solutions that work once there's nothing more that can be known."

"That's what makes an engineer good?"

"Yes. He's also resourceful. One of the concepts we try to teach—and some of the students never get it—is that, all other things being equal, the more problems a single solution can solve, the better solution it is. It's what we mean by 'elegance.' "

"And Phillips got it?"

"He not only understood it, he applied the idea to his course projects."

"How do you mean?"

Cannon allowed himself a small smile. "Last semester, for a statistics class, he analyzed a decade's worth of race results from five different tracks to see if he could come up with a system."

"For doping out races?"

"Yes."

"Did he?"

"No. He claimed that what he'd proven was that picking horses named after your maiden aunt was as useful a system as any other. Everyone got a pretty good laugh out of it. But it was as solid a project, in terms of methodology and presentation, as we've seen in that class."

"And that was an example of—elegance?—because he was using something in his course work that he'd be doing anyway?"

Cannon nodded. "This semester he took a similar approach to a structures class. He's doing an analysis of the building he's working in. He's going to see if he can work out the basis of the design from the results. Backwards, I mean; from what he can see on the site and find in the documents. Then he'll check his assumptions with the building's design engineer."

"Interesting project," I said. "How far had he gotten?"

"Pretty far, I think. He's got the dead load figured; that's straightforward. He's making some live load assumptions, and checking them; then seismic. He's moving along."

"I'm sorry, I don't know those terms. Except seismic— that's earthquake, right?"

"Earth movement, that's correct. Live load is essentially anything that moves or can be removed—people, furniture, wind, rain, snow."

"And dead load?"

"The weight of the structure on itself: the concrete, the steel, the brick. It's what the building can't escape, the loads it imposes on itself by what it is."

I thought about that, about loads from the outside; loads from the ground, supposedly solid and still, that you stand on; loads from within. .

I asked, "How was Phillips doing this analysis?"

"Mostly from the documents. The size of the steel beams, for example, is shown on the drawings. Beams of a given size have a weight that can be calculated, and a capacity for doing certain kinds of work—carrying walls, acting as stiffeners, whatever it is. Phillips' project is to decide on what basis the engineer sized the beams in the southeast corner differently from the ones in the northwest corner; that sort of thing. It's a pretty ambitious attempt."

The scent of honeysuckle rode in on the breeze as I considered the project Reg Phillips was working on. "Professor," I said, "could he have found something? Some flaw in the building design, something that suggested maybe it wasn't safe?"

Cannon pursed his lips, furrowed his brow. "No," he said at last. "I don't think so. For one thing, there are so many checks on a building like that, here in the city: The Building Department has to review the drawings; there are inspectors at many points; and there's nothing special about the design of that building. It's not unusually complicated or innovative. If there were design errors, they'd have been spotted long before construction started."

I nodded. "Is there anything else you can tell me about Phillips?" I asked. "Does he have any enemies that you know of?"

Cannon's mouth turned down. He took off the gold-wire glasses and dropped them on his desk. "Are you telling me you think what happened to Phillips wasn't an accident?"

"I don't think anything. I'm just gathering information. To see if what happened to him could be connected to the other thing I'm working on."

"Can you tell me what that is?"

"No."

He nodded, as though he'd expected that. The golden light began to disappear from the branches of the old trees, cut off by the sharp-edged shadow of the building. "Well, there isn't much more I can tell you, either," he said. "Phillips seems to be well liked, but I don't follow the students' social lives closely. He doesn't cut classes and he gets his work in on time. He's a good student and I'd like to see him succeed."

"All right," I said. "I appreciate your time. If you think of anything that might help, will you give me a call?"

I stood to go, handed him a card.

"Listen." The tenor of his voice changed, softened. "You don't know how he's doing, do you? The hospital won't tell me much, because I'm not family. Do you know if he'll be all right?"

"I don't know," I said. "My job is just to find out about him. He sounds like a good guy to me. I'm hoping he makes it."

"I am too," Cannon said.

The crows on their branch shifted position a final time, settled in for the night. Cannon and I nodded to each other, and I turned and left.

I was almost at the subway when the beeper on my hip went off again. I lifted it and checked the readout; the glowing red phone number was Chuck's, still at the office. I backtracked half a block to a phone booth and called him.

"Hey," he said in greeting. "Hell of a day, huh?" Chuck's words were as hearty as ever, though I thought I could hear a soft layer of weariness behind them.

"You're telling me."

"I heard you were a hero again, though," he said. "Old man Crowell'd probably give you a medal for saving Junior's ass, if he knew it was you."

"He doesn't?"

"Nope. Your girlfriend told me about it when we had a minute alone, but she didn't say anything to the old man. She didn't want him to start noticing you. She's pretty smart. I'd keep her if I were you."

"I'll remember that if it ever comes up," I said, not willing, right now, to get onto the subject of Lydia. "Chuck, what's going on?"

A guy with a beeper on his hip, too, and a pit bull on a leash, glared impatiently at the phone I was on. I nodded at him, keeping my face wooden. Chuck said, "What do you mean?"

"Well, I could mean, we have two men dead and another cracked over the head—doesn't that mean something's going on? Or I could mean, since one of the dead men is the one we were watching, maybe we don't care anymore even if there *is* something going on, so why are you willing to pay for Lydia to stay on the job?"

The guy with the pit bull, hearing me say "dead" so much, backed off a little.

"You too," Chuck said.

"Stay on the job? Why?"

"Ah," Chuck said. "Well, because we got a situation. You busy, or you got time for a drink?"

"I have time."

"Good. Where are you?"

"Way the hell uptown."

"At the site?"

"No." I didn't elaborate.

"Oh. Well, can you get down here? There's a bar in the building, the Vault. Okay with you?"

I told Chuck the Vault was just fine with me, and hung up the phone. I briefly thought about calling Lydia, but the guy with the pit bull had been just about as patient and polite as his type of guy is likely to be, and I was too tired to fight with him over a pay phone.

It would have been good to talk to Lydia, because some things were beginning to build on each other in my head, things that seemed to fit where I was trying to put them, but there were still some parts that didn't have places, and some places that didn't have parts. I wanted to go over it with her, to see if she could help me get at what I wasn't seeing, what I was seeing that I wasn't understanding. But I could call her later, when Chuck and I were through.

The subway going downtown was emptier than the ride up. I had room to stretch my legs and think. I mostly thought about Reg Phillips, and Joe Romeo; and about the Crowells, Senior and Junior, and Donald Hacker, and John Lozano. And Chuck.

It was dark when I came out of the subway. I walked east across midtown, through streets that didn't seem to have cooled down much just because the sun was gone. The cars and the buses moved sluggishly, dispiritedly, as though the air were harder than usual to push through and they just didn't have the heart for it.

I reached Chuck's building and found the Vault, called that because someone, in the grip of inspiration, had set a nine-foot, case-hardened bank-vault door into the black-glass sheathing. I spun the wheel and the door swung aside. Cold air and loud conversation spilled out into the street, was gathered up and swept back inside with me, as the door closed again.

I stood just inside, let my eyes wander the place, let my ears get used to the swirling chatter of talk and the pounding beat of music I couldn't really hear, just feel. The sharp cold air sidled up close around me, tried to erase the memory of the hot July streets like a one-night stand offering to help me forget the woman who'd broken my heart. It never works, but I was willing to try.

I didn't see Chuck, so I headed for the bar. The crowd, well dressed and young, cheery and on the make, parted for me, closed up again behind me. Some of the women glanced my way: new material, worth inspecting. Older than they, weary, and never handsome, even when I was young, I didn't pass inspection, and they turned their backs and let me through.

Chuck was at the bar, gin-and-tonic in hand, talking animatedly with two other guys while the bartender racked glasses and occasionally chimed in. The subject was the Yankees and nobody was saying anything that wasn't being said in every other bar in New York at the same moment.

I inserted myself between one of Chuck's companions and the guy behind him, a three-piece suit who was forced by my presence to move a step closer to the silk-bloused young woman he was trying to get to know. I thought he owed me for that. I ordered a Brooklyn Lager; Chuck spotted me as I did.

"Hey," he said, waving his drink, climbing down off his bar stool. "See you later, fellas." The other Yankee fans dismissed him from the discussion and turned to argue with each other.

Chuck waited while I collected my beer, and he paid for it before I could. He steered me to an empty table by the black-glass window. The tabletops were also black glass.

"Crowded in here," I said as I dropped myself into a chair.

"Always," Chuck said. "That's why I like it. Crowded and noisy. Bad place to try to listen in."

"This conversation we're about to have is one you don't want anyone listening in on?"

He nodded. "You got it. It's maybe a little delicate."

I watched a car roll by in the street outside. The black glass obscured everything, but sharpened things, too, took the softness off headlights, made strolling people into hard-edged shadows. "Go ahead," I said.

Chuck crossed one leg over the other, got comfortable in his chair. "Well, what you said before, about Romeo, you're right," he told me. "He was our subject, now he's dead. You might expect we'd be through with this case."

"I might."

He smiled ruefully. "But I turned up something. The kind of thing, when I was on the Job, it would've burned my tail if some private cop had something like this, didn't turn it over. But now I'm the private cop, I got a client . . ." Chuck frowned into his drink. "Seems someone was shaking down Crowell Construction."

I took that first swallow of beer, always the best, and put the bottle back onto the table. "How do you know that?"

"Source I got. Street scum, and he don't know no more than that. But you can see it's a problem."

"Maybe," I said. "You have any idea who?"

He shook his head. "This guy, he's telling me it could be someone Pelligrini knew about. But that could be just an idea of his."

"Shaking them down over what?"

"I don't know. Could be some labor scam, could be something else. If I knew, I'd know more what to do; maybe we wouldn't have a problem."

"And our problem is, if this comes out it could implicate the Crowells in Pelligrini's death?"

"And Romeo's," Chuck said. "He's the type, it could have been him."

"I'm not sure I see why it's a problem. Just because they're the client? We didn't marry them—love, honor, and obey for better or worse. Sounds to me like they should be checked out, and soon."

"Yeah," he said. "But lookit. They came to me, right? To start this whole thing?"

"And?"

"Well, it don't seem likely they'd bring a P.I. into a situation where they'd already killed one guy and were thinking about doing another."

"Not likely, no," I conceded.

"Right. So the fact that they come to me makes it look like maybe it wasn't them, right? But you think a homicide cop would buy that?"

"Buy the idea that someone was shaking these guys down, two guys turn up dead on their site, and they had nothing to do with it?"

"Yeah."

"No."

"Right. So that's the problem."

I pulled a cigarette from my jacket pocket, looked around. "Can I smoke in here?"

"I don't know. Something about near the bar, not near the bar. Go ahead, try it."

I lit up. No one reacted.

"It's circumstantial," I said. "If they didn't do it, there won't be anything else. They probably won't even get arrested, and they'd never get convicted."

"Yeah," he agreed. "Assuming there's not a whole pile of other circumstantial shit, and you don't get some judge and jury in a bad mood." He poured back some gin-and-tonic. "But here's what I'm thinking. Suppose they didn't do it, but suppose I give what I got to the cops. The cops poke around, maybe the Crowells get cleared. But that project's down the toilet. The Crowells will be so busy with cops and lawyers they won't have time to run it, and no bank'll touch it as long as they're on the job. You've seen construction projects go belly-up before. A lot of rusting steel, a lot of guys out of work in a bad time. Not to mention that Armstrong lady all messed up. I don't like it. Not if I'm not sure."

"So you want me and Lydia to stay, and make sure?"

"One way or the other. That they did it, or that some other guy did."

No one had yet objected to the cigarette, so I kept smoking it.

"And you're paying for this?"

Chuck opened his hands. "What's it gonna cost me? A few hundred bucks? Another day or two. Don't bother with the Pelligrini end, there's nothing there, I did that before. But somebody up there must have seen something, even if he don't know it. I'm not saying you gotta be able to prove anything, just see what the odds are, whether it's worth wrecking something this big for this."

I dropped my cigarette to the floor and pressed it out under my foot. "Did you talk to the Crowells?" I asked. Outside, two sharp shadows stopped on the clouded street, gestured at each other, waved their arms. Maybe in joy, maybe anger; I couldn't tell.

"About this?" Chuck sounded surprised. "No. In case they did do it, I don't want them knowing we're on to them."

"But they know Lydia's still on the case, even though their Joe Romeo problem is solved?"

"Sure."

"What do they think she's doing there?"

"Doing the cops a favor."

"And what do the cops think?"

"Same thing."

"And they're not surprised you're paying for it?"

"The Crowells? Hell, no. They know I used to be on the Job. They think this is a chit I could call in later. Could be that, too. And like I said, how much could it cost me? Seems like a good investment."

I finished my beer, wanted another cigarette, but didn't light one. The shadows outside, arms around each other's shoulders, moved on.

"Okay," I said.

"Great," said Chuck, with a relieved smile. He drained his drink. "Keep me filled in, okay? The minute you got something you think could lead to a yes or a no, that's all I want."

"Okay."

"Great," he said again. "Hey, I gotta get home. You want a ride? I got the car in the garage."

"No thanks. I think I'll stay and have another beer, try to cool down a little before I head out."

"Yeah," he said, "good idea. Just remember, you're the one's got to get up early in the morning and go lay bricks."

"I don't see how I could forget."

Chuck, standing, caught the bartender's eye, pointed at me. "It's on my tab," Chuck said. "Business expense. Drink whatever you want, buddy, as long as it's deductible."

He clapped me on the shoulder, turned, and left. I watched him shove open the huge steel door, watched him move, sharply outlined but obscured, down the dark street. The heavy sound of the door closing was lost in the noise of the crowd.

fourteen

i sat at the black-glass table by the black-glass window, finishing my third cigarette and my second beer. The crowd was as lively and predatory as when I'd first gotten here, circling each other, smiling and talking and glancing over each other's shoulders to make sure someone better hadn't just come in. The chilled air smelled faintly of cigarette smoke, liquor, and sweat. The crashing-surf roar of ten dozen cruising people almost drowned out the electronic call from my beeper, when it came.

I cursed the thing indifferently, lifted it from my hip, and checked it. I didn't recognize the number, but the need to find a phone was a good excuse to get away from the hammering chatter and ricochet of appraising glances around me. I slipped a few dollars under my beer bottle for a tip, and left, almost welcoming the damp-laden heat rising from the sidewalk because of the sudden quiet that came with it.

From the street-corner phone, I called the number from my beeper. The phone was answered, after the fourth ring, by Denise Armstrong.

"I thought this might be you," she said.

"I didn't think it would be you," I told her. "I had the feeling you wouldn't be calling me."

"I wasn't sure, either. But I thought I'd see if I could find the answer to your question first and then decide whether to share it with you."

"And?"

"I found it—found who that coordinator was—and it makes me think you might have been right. There might be more to what happened than it looks like. If you want the address I have it."

"What do you mean, 'more to what happened'?"

"I'm not sure. This man has a certain reputation."

"Reputation?"

"For being involved in things. Do you want his name or not?"

"What kinds of things?"

"I'm not sure," she said again, sounding impatient. "Crimes for hire, I was told, and that's all I know. Are you willing to talk to him?"

"That was the idea."

"Then . . . ?"

"Go ahead."

"Chester Hamilton is his name. He lives at 157 West 142nd Street, in the rear of the storefront where his office is. I understand he's usually found there about this time of the evening."

"His office?"

" 'Strength Through Jobs/Jobs Through Strength.' That's the name of his organization."

"Catchy."

"In my experience," she told me, "a catchy name usually means energy is being wasted on trivial things."

"You don't cut anybody any slack, do you?" I asked, leaning against the cool steel of the phone enclosure.

"Is there a reason I should?"

"Not one I'm up to explaining. Did you give this information to the police?"

"No."

"Why not? You know they're looking."

"You," she said, "are working for people who work for me. That gives my interests at least a chance of being weighed before any action is taken. The police are only interested in clearing cases, not necessarily in a good outcome."

"What's a good outcome?"

"That would depend on what the problem is and what solutions are available. I've done what you asked and now this is what I ask: I want you to go see Chester Hamilton and I want you to report back to me before the police get involved."

"I don't work for you."

"And I don't work for you! But you asked me to do something for you and I've done it."

That was true. "I'll go see him," I said. "I'll decide from there."

"I'll be waiting to hear from you," she said pointedly, and hung up.

I replaced the receiver and watched the cars rolling up the avenue, watched the light change, some cars stop and others go. I reached for the phone again, almost called Lydia, put the receiver back. I wasn't sure what I would say, wasn't sure what I had that needed to be talked over right now instead of tomorrow. I wasn't sure what I was thinking.

No, that wasn't true. I knew what I was thinking, but I didn't know where it would lead. I was tired of trying to fit the puzzle together, taking the same pieces, the ones that looked right, and pushing them over and over into the same places, where they wouldn't go. I didn't like the pieces spread out in front of me, and I didn't think I was going to like the picture they made when I finally saw it.

But I had a new piece now: Chester Hamilton, coordinator of the Strength Through Jobs/Jobs Through Strength full-employment coalition. I lit a cigarette, hailed a cab, and headed for Harlem.

I had the cab drop me a block south of the address I was looking for. The Pakistani cabbie had argued with the idea of coming up here in the first place, but I wouldn't get out of his cab. He burned rubber leaving, racing by a man and woman trying to flag him to a stop.

I stood on the corner, looking up Broadway, where the fire escape–draped fronts of five-story brick apartment buildings stared each other down across the dry brown dirt of the traffic islands in the center of the street. Here and there, a wizened

bush or tree or patch of ivy too cussed to die stood defiantly
in one of those islands, waving in the slipstream of the passing cars.

The aroma of frying fish from a Jamaican fast-food place
reminded me of how long it had been since I'd eaten. I
stopped at the sidewalk window, bought a fried-haddock
sandwich and a ginger beer, ate and drank leaning on the
counter. Then I walked north, threading my way along the hot,
crowded sidewalk.

Everyone in the neighborhood seemed to be on the street,
talking, playing cards, trying to find some relief from the heat.
Women in cotton housedresses fanned themselves with folded
newspapers as they sat on stoops, watching little boys race by
on bicycles and little girls skip rope. Three middle-aged men
in sweat-soaked T-shirts smoked cigars and played a slow
game of dominoes to a Latin beat from a tinny radio. On the
corner, as I turned down 142nd Street, a bigger, booming
radio was surrounded by five young men and a red-lipped
young woman. She was giving one of the young men hell in
rapid-fire Spanish, poking him in the chest with a crimson fin-
gernail while he pretended he didn't care and his buddies
smirked.

Not many stoop-sitters seemed to have chosen 142nd Street
over the avenues that crossed it, and it was easy to see why.
The block was dotted with abandoned buildings, dented tin
covering their windows, front steps crumbling. In the center
of the block, four tenements had been knocked down. The
empty lot was knee-deep with garbage I could smell from
across the street, outside the storefront at number 157.

The storefront glass was painted with a red, black, and
green flag below an arch of gold letters reading, STRENGTH
THROUGH JOBS/JOBS THROUGH STRENGTH. I still thought it was
catchy. The pale streetlight in front of the empty lot across the
street wasn't close enough to illuminate the storefront, only to
help whatever was inside cast deeper shadows into the darkness. I couldn't see anything; I knocked anyway.

I waited; nothing happened; I knocked harder.

A light came on as I lifted my fist to pound again. It glowed grudgingly, uninterested, like the man who emerged through a door in the shadowed rear wall and ambled unhurriedly toward me.

The door swung open, but not far. A black man about my own height, with a sharp nose and a short beard, held it open about a foot, stared at me. "Who the hell you?"

"You're Chester Hamilton?" I asked.

"Yeah, and I already knew that. Who the hell you?"

"I'd like to ask you some questions."

"Well, seeing as I already asked you the same one twice and I ain't heard no answer, you can take yours and shove 'em." He started to close the door.

I planted my foot on his side of the threshhold, said, "Bill Smith."

Hamilton looked down at my foot, then up at my face again. "Well, whoop-dee-damn-doo. What you want with me?"

"I have a situation I think you can help me with."

He made a show of looking behind me, up and down the street. "Hmmm," he said. "You was a cop, you'd come here in a car. With another cop. I mean, this bein' a bad neighborhood and all. So whatever your problem be, it ain't on behalf of the NYPD."

"That's true."

"So why the fuck I'm supposed to care?"

"I have a proposition for you."

He paused, tilted his head a fraction of an inch, as though to see me differently. "What kind of proposition?"

"One that could make you some money. But I don't want to discuss it out here on the street."

He stared at me in silence for a few moments, greed battling wariness in his eyes.

Greed won.

Hamilton stepped back, pulled the door half open, just enough for me to move past him into the room.

The Strength Through Jobs/Jobs Through Strength office consisted of a battered desk, a phone, and six mismatched chairs around a card table, an arrangement that suggested strategy sessions, or poker. The peeling paint on the walls was partly obscured by posters: a large tattered one of Malcolm X and a faded four-color glossy proclaiming a Pan-Africa Day Rally on a Sunday in 1993. Bugs had laid down and died inside the globe of the weak overhead light, and the soft, heavy smell of years of grime and take-out food was so thick it was almost visible.

"Okay." Hamilton closed the door behind me. He moved to the card table, sprawled himself in a chair. I sat across from him as he said, "Now tell me what the hell you talking about."

"I want you to do for me what you did this morning," I said.

"This morning," he said with a smirk, "I got a haircut. Got my beard trimmed all nice, nice hot towels, too. That what you interested in?"

"I'm interested in fifty men rioting on a construction site."

He shook his head. "Sound like a terrible thing."

"Depends who you are. Could be a useful thing."

"How's that?"

"In the same way it was this morning."

"You keep talking in riddles, we gonna get nowhere."

"You keep pretending you don't know what I'm talking about, it's not going to be much better."

"What the hell you want? You from some union, got a deal to make?"

"I want to make you the same deal you had this morning."

"I can't recall no deal I had this morning. You want to lay it out for me?"

All right, I thought. We'll play Let's Pretend. "I want a couple of busloads of men to shut down a construction site."

His eyes widened theatrically. "You shittin' me."

"That idea never occurred to you before?"

"Well . . ." he said, with oratorical emphasis. "Well, naturally, a lot of peoples round here, they filled with righteous anger about the way they been treated, about the discrimination they suffered in they lives. Peoples got to have a outlet for expressin' that anger. Sometime, when the system just ain't respondin' to peaceful means—"

"Yeah," I said. "That's what I want."

"Exactly what?"

"Exactly what you did this morning."

"Man, you keep singing the same song, 'this morning, this morning.' Maybe—"

"Two thousand dollars."

He stopped. "Say what?"

"That's what he said he paid you."

I had no idea who I was talking about, or even if I was right. I waited to see Hamilton's response.

He waited too. Finally, he slowly said, "Who?"

"The man who hired you to come to the Armstrong site this morning. I don't know his name; we met in a bar. I only know him as Lefty."

A grin spread itself across Hamilton's face. "Lefty?" He snorted with amused derision. "He callin' hisself Lefty?"

Sure, I thought. And he was drinking with Sleepy and Dopey.

"Can we make a deal, then?" I said. "Like you had with him?"

Hamilton paused, then nodded. "I'ma tell you what: 'Cause you a friend of Lefty's, here's a idea—"

I never got to know what that idea might be.

The explosive rattle of the first round of shots was lost in the crash as glass from the storefront window blew across the room. I hit the ground. Shards rained down around me like razor-sharp rain. Plaster dust filled the air as bullets smashed into walls. The hammering roar of the second round came as I yanked my .38 from my side. I fired through the gaping, jagged hole where the window had been, the report jarring my elbow into the hard floor; but by then no one was there, no answering shots, just a screech of tires as a car tore down the street, away from here.

I rolled over, crawled to the door, yanked it open from a crouching position. Nothing. I looked up and down the street, across, then stood. Empty, everywhere. I stuck my gun into my shoulder rig and turned back into the room.

Chester Hamilton lay on his back on the grimy floor, a circle of blood on his chest, a spreading dark pool under him.

His folding chair was tangled with his legs. I looked at him, his wide eyes and open mouth. I crouched and felt the artery at his neck. His body, the table, the floor, were covered with glittering splinters of broken glass. They crunched under my feet as I turned and left.

fifteen

I called 911 anonymously from a subway pay phone, in case no one else had done that yet. I called Lydia from my apartment after I'd poured a flood of Maker's Mark over ice and gone through about half of it.

"Is everything okay?" she asked when she knew it was me. Behind her I heard the electronic chatter of the living-room TV fade as she closed her door. "It's late for you to be calling."

"No," I said. "Just talk to me a little."

"What's wrong?"

"Give me a minute." I took another drink.

"Bill?" When I didn't answer, her words quickened. "Are you all right? Where are you?"

"I'm home," I said. "I'm okay. I just . . . I'll tell you in a minute." I lit a cigarette, listened to her breathing softly on the other end of the phone, felt bourbon and the presence of Lydia slowing my racing blood. I drew in smoke, told her, "I went to see a guy. Someone shot him."

"*Shot* him? When? Who?"

"When I was there. I don't know who." I told her about Hamilton, about how I'd gotten to him, about the deal we'd almost made, and the shards of glass.

"Oh my God," she said softly. "Are you okay? Do you want me to come over?"

I lit another cigarette off the end of the first. Yes, I thought.

"No," I said. "No, it's late. Talking about it is good. That's what I wanted."

"Bill?" Her voice was tentative. "The police . . ."

"I didn't see the guy," I said. "What I know about Hamilton might help them figure out who killed him, but not because I was there."

"But you're not telling them what you know."

"No," I said. "Not yet."

"Why?"

It was time to tell her now. "Because of Chuck."

"Mr. DeMattis?" she said. She hesitated, then asked, "Why? What about him?"

She sounded as though she wanted to hear what I had in mind; but she didn't sound surprised.

"I don't know," I said. "But something's not right. Something hasn't been right from the beginning. I saw him tonight, too."

"You saw Mr. DeMattis? When?"

Through another cigarette and another bourbon, I told Lydia about the Vault.

"But you don't believe him," she said softly, when I'd gotten to the end. "You don't believe his reason for keeping us there is in case we can turn up something that will protect that project and the jobs of all those men."

"Honest to God," I said, turning off the lamp I was sitting near, "I don't know." The light still on, the one by the piano, cast long shadows down the room, crossing the shadows the streetlights threw in. "That would be like Chuck, something he'd do. But from the beginning, there's been something strange . . . or maybe not. I don't know." I reached for the cigarettes, made myself pull my hand back. I rubbed my eyes. "I don't know," I said again, my words cloudy with liquor, smoke, and uncertainty. I thought about Chuck, about the plane cutting through the clear sky above the river out his office window, about watching through the Vault's black glass as he walked away, just a few hours ago.

"Tell me why," Lydia said calmly.

I was almost startled when she spoke; exhaustion and bourbon had been carrying me elsewhere, into a place where shapes moved in the darkness and the cool wind brought echoes of sounds that were not words.

I took another swallow, brought myself back. "From the beginning," I repeated, trying to make the shapes take form for her, reaching for something solid in the darkness; "and you saw it too. He turned the case over to us too fast. Remember, you said you never met a cop who didn't want to know? And I said he wasn't a cop anymore."

"He said he had other cases he was working on."

"Then why take this one and then farm it out, give it to us and say he didn't want to know? Why not just send Crowell to someone else? Me—if he thought I was the right guy for the job—or someone else?"

"He said he saw them as a repeat client he didn't want to lose just because he's too busy to deal with them now."

I nodded, even though she couldn't see it, appreciating what she was doing. She probably didn't believe a word she was saying, but she was forcing me to look past whatever theory I had going. When we worked together, it was what we always did.

"Maybe," I said. "But there's the Pelligrini thing."

"Pelligrini?" she asked. "What about him?"

"Sal Maggio told me Pelligrini was involved with some mob guy. Louie Falco. Falco's connected to Chuck somehow. From the old neighborhood."

"He is? How do you know that?"

"Doherty told me."

Lydia was silent for a few moments. "This is what you haven't been telling me."

I pried off my shoes, lay back on the couch, eyes closed, phone to my ear. I didn't ask how she'd known there was something, didn't try to pretend there wasn't. "I'm sorry," I said. I expected an outburst, anger, a jabbing reminder that this wasn't the way our partnership worked. I deserved it, but that's not what happened.

"Not telling me," she said softly; "that was a way to make it not true, right?"

I moved on the couch, felt my back and shoulders relax into the comfort of the cushions.

"If I didn't talk about it," I said, "I didn't have to think about it."

"But now you do."

"Leaving Hamilton," I said, "being there when he was killed, and leaving . . . I had to be sure I wanted to do that."

"It could make a big problem for you," she said. "If the police find out you were there."

"And it could be dangerous for other people, if what I know could help them find his killer and I'm keeping it back."

"But you're doing that," she said, "for the same reason Mr. DeMattis says he wants us to stay on the site. You want to protect him, unless you're sure, the same way he wants to protect Crowell."

"Yes," I said into the warm, dim room, grateful for a partner whose thoughts moved along with mine, who understood. "Because the question is the same. If he's mixed up through this guy Falco in whatever the hell is going on on that site, why did he bring us in in the first place?"

She waited, then asked, "What are you going to do?"

The next question, the next step. I didn't know the answer.

"Jesus," I said. "I'm exhausted. I can't think. But I want to go back to work tomorrow, up there. At least one more day. Are you with me?"

"You know I am." In the darkness, her voice smiled.

"Thanks," I said, and we said good night.

I turned over on the couch, settled in, too tired to try for the bedroom. As the night sounds moved in the room around me and the colors began to float behind my eyes, I thought I sensed the freesia scent of Lydia's hair. I started to reach for the phone, to call her again, to tell her something important; but my arm was heavy, too heavy to lift. I felt as though I were piled with weight, much more than my own body, too much weight to carry, even to move under. I couldn't pick up the phone; the weight kept me from Lydia. It kept me here, in the place where I'd lived for years, the place where I'd come, almost by accident, when things went bad, the place where I'd been so long that the place and I were part of each other now. From the darkness outside me, where the weight was, I heard the sounds, traffic and my own breathing and the ticking of a clock, that I knew I'd hear. I smelled the bourbon and sweat and cigarettes I'd put in the air. From the darkness inside me, I heard, softly, other sounds: dim voices, some I knew and some I didn't; a long, thin scream, that could have been from years ago, or from this morning; and the crunch of broken glass under my own feet as I turned and walked away.

sixteen

I was stiff in the morning, hurting all over, from the fight and the bourbon and the night on the couch. My dreams had been troubled but not clear, and I woke with the Scriabin études in my head, phrases from one piece calling up another, nothing finishing; the connections that would make the pieces make sense for me, elusive and ahead.

I put up coffee and I showered. Dry, shaved, and half dressed, I threw back the first cup standing at the counter. Before I could pour myself more, the phone rang.

It stopped immediately; that meant my service had gotten it, which is what they'll do unless I check in with them and tell them to go off duty for a while. Lydia scoffs at me for using the service instead of a machine, but I started with them eighteen years ago, in the days when people—clients—didn't believe an investigator wasn't just a fly-by-night operation if he didn't have a secretary. As soon as a human voice answers the phone, people conjure up images of waiting rooms, inner offices, file cabinets, carpeting, and conference tables. It's never been more than my apartment, me, and whomever I take on to work a particular case with me, but I've gotten used to hearing a human voice at the other end of my phone, too.

I let them take it, finished the coffee. Then I called in.

"Good morning," a cheerful young man wished me. This was Tommy, one of the underemployed actors who irregularly staffed the place. "You're up early. Phone wake you?"

"Just about," I told him. "I was mainlining my coffee."

"You really should turn off the ringer before you go to bed," he scolded me. "That's what I'm here for."

"I forgot. Anyway, who the hell was that, at this hour?"

"Please. This is the third time she's called. Twice late last night, and then now. What did you do, stand her up?"

"Who?"

"A lady named Denise Armstrong. And I mean a lady, too."

Denise Armstrong. Oh, Jesus. *Go see Chester Hamilton,* she'd said. *Report back to me before the police get involved. I'll be waiting to hear from you.*

"Yeah," I said. "I guess I did, in a way."

"Well, she left a phone number. She certainly sounds awake and alert. I'd recommend another hit of coffee before you call her."

"Thanks, Tommy," I said, but I didn't have the time to act on his recommendation, and it probably wouldn't have helped anyway.

I dialed the number he gave me, Denise Armstrong's office. She answered herself; I was glad, though a little surprised, to see that she didn't demand that her office staff come in at six A.M. just because she did.

"Mr. Smith!" she snapped into the phone when I told her who it was. "What in the hell did you do?"

"Slept? Made coffee? It depends what you mean."

"Don't even try to be cute with me. Chester Hamilton is dead. Don't tell me you didn't know that."

"No, I did. How do you?"

"The police called me, just after midnight last night. They wanted to tell me they're pretty sure he was the one who brought those men to my building."

"Did you tell them you knew that already?"

"Don't be ridiculous. Did you shoot him?" The question sounded as cold and direct as any she might ask in a business negotiation.

"No," I said. I didn't know how convincing a denial that single word was, or how convinced she was by it, but she went on without missing a beat.

"Did you speak with him?"

"Yes."

"And?"

"Not much," I said. "We didn't get far."

"How far?"

"Only one thing: He just about admitted he and his men were hired to come wreck your site."

A short silence was the only evidence that she was digesting what I'd said. "It wasn't a true job action?"

"Looks that way."

"Did he tell you who hired him? Did he say why?"

"No. Do you have any ideas?"

"Of course not. Why would I?"

"Well," I said, "it seems to me, one reason to do a thing like that would be to send a message. If that's what happened, most likely the message would be for you. So what did it say?"

"I have no idea." Her voice was icy, her words stiff.

"Someone's unhappy," I said. "I suggest you think about who, and why."

"And I suggest," she said, "that you tread very carefully, especially where my affairs are involved. Have you spoken to the police?"

"Why would I?"

"Because you saw him. You might have gone to them, running scared, thinking about your license and your reputation."

"And my neck," I said, "as possibly"—definitely—"the last person to see Hamilton alive. Which is a more and more risky position to be in, the longer I wait to come in."

"So you haven't spoken to them." Under the cold control, I thought I heard relief. "If you do, how will you explain how you found him?"

"You don't give a damn, as long as I don't tell them it was you."

"I'd like to point out that in the discussions I had with them last night, I didn't mention you."

"As a favor to me, no doubt. Let me ask you something."

"What is it?"

"What would you have done if I'd said I'd shot him?"

"I hadn't decided," she said. "But you can be sure I would have found a way to handle it."

I was sure.

After we hung up, I looked at the time and the piano, tried to tell myself that fifteen minutes' practicing, ten, would be worth it, but I knew it wasn't true. Sore as I was, it would take me a half hour just to loosen up enough to feel comfortable reaching for the notes. The Scriabin was still there, in my head, and I sensed—heard—that it was almost at the point of understanding I'd been reaching for; but it needed focus, complete attention, the kind that only comes when time is meaningless, when five minutes or five hours or whatever you need is what you can have. If I wanted to get to Broadway and Ninety-ninth to start my shift, I didn't have that now.

I was on the site before Mike DiMaio this morning, so I was the one to pull off the tarp and wave over the guy with the mortar. The sky was clear and the sun, even this early, was direct and hot. I'd checked the detail drawing on the column inside and was laying out my tools when DiMaio came up.

"Hey," he said, stopped on the scaffold, studied me. "You're back."

"Shouldn't I be?" I asked, maybe more sharply than I meant to.

His response was a half-second slow, surprised about something in me, reacting to that. "I don't know." He moved past me, slung his bag onto the board between us, spread his own tools out. "I thought you was here because of Joe."

"I was."

"Then what now? He's dead, your client is gonna keep paying your bill to be here? Or that was bullshit from day one?" He grinned, showing me he thought it probably wasn't bullshit; we knew each other better now than when I'd started a few days ago.

"No," I said, reining it in, my tone more reasonable. "But I'm not finished."

"Not finished doing what?"

"Building this wall."

DiMaio glanced at the brickwork, seemed not sure how to take what I'd said. "I'm the bricklayer," he told me, pulling on his gloves. "You're the guy I cover for."

"That's true," I said. It hit me how tired I was, though the day was new. "I'm the guy who came here to do one thing and got caught up in other things, so many I don't know what the hell is going on. But I don't think I'm finished."

He picked up a trowel, turned over some mortar on the board between us.

"Reg?" he asked.

"I said I'd do it."

DiMaio's steady gaze held me for a few moments; then he nodded, turned, picked a brick from the pile the mason tender had placed, the pile we hadn't used yesterday. He balanced it in his hand as if taking its measure.

"If it was Joe," he said, "how are we gonna find out now?"

"Not 'we,' " I said. "You're the bricklayer. I'm the guy you cover for."

I didn't like it as soon as I'd said it, but I didn't apologize. DiMaio's eyes flashed, but he said nothing.

"Listen," I said, working at it, "how is he? Phillips."

He looked at me, considering. "I was over there yesterday," he said. "They say he's doing better. He seems to wake up some, tries to talk. Not while I was there, though."

"But that's good," I said. "I'm glad to hear it. Listen, Mike, I hear he's in school."

"Yeah, nights at City College. I didn't tell you that?"

"No."

"I must not've thought of it. Sorry."

"You should have."

He bristled. "Hey, you wanna know something, you gotta ask. My mind don't work like a detective's. I'm a bricklayer. I only think to answer questions if someone asks them."

"It could be important."

"Well, you know about it now. Shit, Smith. What the hell is your problem today?"

I met his eyes, clear and blue, and had the sudden, uncomfortable feeling that I could see right through them, see right into who he really was. Solid and real. Like a brick wall, made from things you could see, nothing hidden, nothing fake, nothing weak and buried inside that could bring the whole thing crashing down one unexpected day.

He was looking into my eyes too.

I lifted my hard hat, wiped my face, settled the hat again.

"I'm sorry, Mike," I said. "Bad day yesterday. Let's get to work, okay?"

I picked a brick off the pile, felt the morning heat loosening my shoulders.

"What are you thinking?" DiMaio asked, a little less belligerent, backing off too. "You think someone up there, City College, could have something to do with what happened?"

"I don't know," I said. "I'm not thinking anything. I just want to get through the day without thinking much at all. Maybe something I already know will float to the top that way."

"Yeah." DiMaio nodded. He crouched, sorted through a bucket of plastic weeps until he found one he wanted. "I know what you mean. Just do your bricks, then, when you go home, the problem you had that morning's all figured out. Like you had nothing to do with it."

He straightened up and we got to work. I hefted bricks, spread mortar, sweated and drank coffee and struck clean joints. The sounds on the site—shouts, growling engines, the whine of a diamond-blade saw—were punctuated by the syncopated tap of DiMaio's brick hammer and the creaking of the scaffold boards as men came and went. The July sun moved slowly through the morning, wrapped us in heat like a blanket. My arms were tired but they didn't ache, not like when I'd first come here, and my movements had more rhythm now, more flow. I focused on what I was doing, this brick here, set like this, reach for the mortar, straighten, another brick. There were connections here too, movements and objects that went together, were related in ways you couldn't see at first. The Scriabin études ran in my mind, first this piece, then that. They and the bricks and the bright dusty heat became my day.

John Lozano came around that morning, up on the scaffold to look at our work. "We'll be bringing on a new foreman in a day or two," he told us. "Until then it'll be me."

"Good," DiMaio said, grinning at Lozano, speaking to me. "Softy like Lozano, you and me can kick back, relax a little."

"Don't even think about it," Lozano said. "I was a masonry foreman eleven years." His blue eyes and his mouth smiled the same kind smile. He made notes on his clipboard, moved on.

"It'll take him a few days to find a new foreman?" I asked as DiMaio and I went back to work. "With jobs being so scarce?"

"Nah. He could have someone here by afternoon, if he wanted. Most likely he thinks by him coming up here for a few days himself it'll calm the men down."

"The men like him?"

"Lozano?" He seemed surprised at the question. "Yeah, sure. Nice guy. Fair."

"You've worked with him before?"·

"Couple of times. Wants the work done good, but always cuts you a break if he can. You gotta work for somebody, you want to work for a guy like him."

By eleven, when we broke for lunch, the site was busy with rumors—the murder of a coalition leader last night, maybe the one whose men had torn our work apart. No one knew, but that didn't stop the speculating, the muttering, the diatribes against a city going straight to hell. There were a few dissenting voices, DiMaio's among them, about the meaning of it all, but no one disagreed with the general assessment of the murdered man.

"Fucking bastard," Angelo Lucca said, and everyone nodded, offered expletives of their own. "If that was him, I'm glad he got it. Screw the son of a bitch."

"I don't know why the city can't do nothing about bastards like that," the sandy-haired mason, Tommy, said. "What the hell is wrong with this place?"

"Shit, Tommy," said DiMaio, through the remains of his sandwich. "They don't hold up the city. They hold up guys like Crowell. The city probably don't even know where to find 'em."

"City don't know shit. Asshole place, this city."

DiMaio shrugged. "I don't know. There's always work, even in times like this. And pretty girls. What else do you need?"

Someone snorted. Tommy said, "Yeah, I seen you yesterday, DiMaio, with that new girl of Crowell's. You living dangerously, or what?"

"DiMaio likes that," Lucca said. "Girls as likely to brain him as the other way around."

"Hey, fuck off." DiMaio reddened. "I never hit a girl in my life."

"Yeah, well, you keep seeing that Chinese girl, you're gonna have to start. In self-defense."

"That true?" I asked DiMaio, sipping my coffee. "You like dangerous women?"

DiMaio shook his head. "I just like ones who know what they're doing, that's all." He added, "Maybe if you guys didn't act like assholes they wouldn't treat you like you were."

"Oh, shit, look at this!" Sam Buck cackled. "You a women's libber now, DiMaio? You gonna demand equal rights, girls on the scaffold?"

"Might be better company than some of you jerks." DiMaio stood. I stood with him, and lunch break was over.

I made it to the end of the workday, moving slowly in the afternoon, and by then I'd had it. I punched out, sank onto a subway seat, felt the rumble of the tracks and the sharp chill of the air-conditioning, and wished that the trip were longer. All I wanted was to go home, shower, sleep.

I managed the first two, then left my place again before the desire for the third wiped out any other plans I had.

Because I did have plans.

I called Lydia at the Crowell office, told her where I was going.

"Good idea," she said. "Anything special you want me to do?"

"Everything you do is special," I told her.

"If you're counting on the fact that I have to be polite to you on the phone because I'm in the office—"

"Absolutely not. It's light-headedness from lack of sleep. I'm not responsible for my actions."

"Call me later if you have anything worth saying."

"I'll call you even if I don't."

"That, I'm sure of," she said, and hung up.

I went to get the car and drive out to Queens, wondering whether Lydia would be in when I called her later, and if she wasn't, where she would be.

Howard Beach is a neighborhood of low-rise brick apartment buildings and small, close-set one-family houses with ground-floor garages and handkerchief lawns, of aging strip malls and new giant discount superstores. People here know their butchers and their dry cleaners; kids work at the supermarket or the McDonald's after school and often grow up to go into the family business. Sometimes, in Howard Beach, the family business is organized crime.

I drove slowly down a street whose aluminum-sided houses with their iron-railed front porches had been part of New York's exuberant expansion in the fifties and sixties—baby-booming optimism rolling acres of neighborhood over field and swamp. The streets and the buildings and the early residents were all older now, exuberance muted, optimism turned a little grim, but kids still played in the streets and some of the first-planted trees spread broad limbs across the sidewalk.

The house I was looking for stood at an intersection in a residential area, a short section of sunlit white picket fence and a rosebush barricading the lawn at the corner so neighborhood kids wouldn't cut across it on their way from here to there. I parked, straightened my tie, headed up the walk. In my dark blue suit, I wasn't likely to raise any eyebrows coming here today; and even if it hadn't been necessary, it seemed only right.

A boy, maybe fifteen, answered my knock. A cousin maybe, or a younger brother. Awkwardly, not sure what his duties were, he tried to reach open the screen door for me, still holding the knob of the other one.

"I'm a friend of Lenny's," I said, to make it easier for him. "From work."

"Oh," he said, exhaling gratefully. "Yeah. C'mon in."

The living room was carpeted in dark gold, its brocaded curtains drawn, light provided by end-table lamps. On a burnt-orange-and-gold sofa, a plump woman sat, dressed all in black, as was the thinner woman beside her. They looked up as I entered, the heavy one seeming dazed and uncertain, the other determinedly, protectively, in control.

"This's a friend of Lenny's," the boy told them. He looked to me as if for further instructions.

"Bill Smith," I said. "I'm a bricklayer, on the Broadway job. I'm really sorry about Lenny."

"Thank you," the heavy woman said. Her voice was husky. She held out a hand to me; I took it in both of mine, gave it a squeeze. "Please," she said, "sit. Anna, please get Mr. Smith a coffee. You'll stay and have coffee? Or whiskey. Tony—"

"Coffee's fine, thanks."

She nodded and stopped speaking when I spoke, watched me as I sat on an armchair upholstered in nubbly, burnt-orange fabric.

"I'm Lenny's mother," she suddenly said, as though it had just occurred to her I might not know that. "This is my sister, Anna Mannucci. And Tony, my nephew."

Anna Mannucci rose and smiled at me, her eyes fierce, silently warning me not to upset her sister. "I'll get the coffee." She left the room. Tony stood, looking uncomfortable but willing to do his duty, if he only understood it.

"Did you know my Lenny well?" Mrs. Pelligrini asked the question sadly, as if the answer couldn't possibly matter now.

"No. Just from the job. But when you work with a guy . . . well, you know," I finished. "I just wanted to pay my respects."

"That's very kind," she said.

"Actually," I said, "I know a couple of other guys who knew him. Chuck DeMattis, for one."

I'd thrown Chuck's name out the way you throw stones in a pond, just wanting to see what the ripples would be. I wasn't really expecting any; the name I thought I'd get a reaction from was Louie Falco's, and I was planning to try that next. I wasn't prepared for Mrs. Pelligrini's eyes to open wide, for her to lean forward, to say, "Chuckie? You're from Chuckie?"

"I work for him, on and off," I said, hoping she didn't notice I'd been thrown off my stride. "Things he needs, if I can." I wondered if that made sense, would keep things moving.

"Is he going to help me? Chuckie's going to help?"

The rattle of cups and saucers made us both turn. Anna entered the room with a tray; Tony, looking grateful for something to do, rushed to clear off the coffee table so she could put it down.

"Mr. Smith is from Chuckie," Mrs. Pelligrini told her sister. She seemed to sit up a little straighter, to try a little harder at pulling herself together. I realized with a small pang of guilt that that was out of respect for who she thought I was. "He's going to help."

Anna, bending over the coffeepot, looked at me. Her distrust was obvious.

"Chuck hasn't helped much yet, Elena," she said. She streamed black coffee into a white porcelain cup, handed it to me. She lifted the creamer and sugar bowl in manicured hands; I thanked her, turned them down.

Elena Pelligrini waved her hand, as if shooing her sister's remark away. "He tried. It's not his fault. My Lenny . . ." She cut herself off just as I heard a catch come into her throat. Leaning her short form forward, she poured a cup of coffee for herself, added cream and sugar. Looking away, she sipped at it. Her sister offered me biscotti, and we drank our coffee in silence for a while, until Mrs. Pelligrini was ready to start again.

"My Lenny," she said, her voice clear but damped-down, "I couldn't tell him anything. A mother can't. I thought Chuckie could, that's why I called him, but it isn't his fault that Lenny wouldn't listen. It isn't his fault, what happened."

"What did you want Chuck to tell him, Mrs. Pelligrini?" I asked quietly, sipping coffee.

"Chuckie didn't tell you about it?" She sounded surprised.

"I'd rather you told me," I said apologetically. "Otherwise I feel like I'm playing telephone."

She nodded; that seemed to make sense to her. She finished off her coffee, placed the cup carefully on the tray, put her hands, folded, in her lap. "About Louie Falco," she said. She muttered something under her breath, in Italian, looking down; then she lifted her eyes back to mine and went on. "I asked Chuckie to talk to Lenny. Lenny, he's—he was . . . was a wild boy. Not a bad boy. But he wanted to be like them."

"Like Falco?"

"But to a boy . . . it's like cowboys and Indians. You can see, even a mother can see why. They have money, cars, beautiful women. Respect. They can walk in a room, everybody looks at them. What they do to get it, what that's like, what it makes them into, you can't expect a boy to see that."

From the corner of my eye, I caught Anna Mannucci looking at Tony, an expression on her face something like fear. And I saw Tony pretending he didn't know.

"And you wanted Chuck to help?"

"Just to talk to him. Because Chuckie and Louie, everyone knows. So Lenny might listen, because he knows Chuckie don't make it up, he really knows."

"What is it everyone knows?" I asked. "About Chuck and Louie?"

"I don't mean it's some special *thing,* like something that happened," she said, almost apologetically, trying to make clear for me that she was talking about something she obviously thought I already knew. "Just what friends they used to be, when they were kids. Growing up, before one went one way and one went the other. How Chuckie could have been like Louie, if he wanted to. All the money and everything."

"And you wanted him to talk to Lenny about that?"

"Because everyone respects Chuckie, looks up to him. Even my Lenny did. A man of honor, the old-fashioned kind of man."

"And Lenny knew that about him?"

"Everyone knew. He'd just made lieutenant, when he quit. And he loved being a cop. He's almost like a legend in this neighborhood. You could tell him that. I told him, but I don't think it sank in."

"When he quit?" I said. "Four years ago?"

She nodded, gave me a confused look. Anna Mannucci gave me one too, more suspicious.

"You don't know about it?" Mrs. Pelligrini asked.

"I just work for him," I said. "His personal life . . ." I shrugged, let that hang there, hoped it was enough.

"Well, that's like Chuckie," Mrs. Pelligrini said. "Not to brag." It didn't sound to me like the Chuck DeMattis I knew, but I waited for the rest. She said, "They put him on a task force, at the police. They didn't know where it would lead, but Chuckie did. Right back to Louie. They hate each other now, you know."

I nodded, as though I knew.

"Louie . . . his poor mother, she acts like she don't know, but she knows. He's bad. He kills people. Now I guess he's big enough, he gets other people to kill for him. Chuckie hates him, because of what he's like now, and he hates Chuckie because Chuckie's not like him. Chuckie could have done it. He was a cop, it was his job. But he quit."

"Quit being a cop?" I said. I repeated it to her as I understood it, to see whether I had it right. "So he wouldn't have to take a spot on the task force that was going to bring Louie down?"

"Well, he couldn't, could he? It's not right. With what friends they used to be. With his mother still right here on the next block, his sisters and their children. He couldn't do that."

"So he quit. So he wouldn't have to."

She nodded. "And that's why I wanted him to talk to my Lenny. I thought it would help. And I suppose Chuckie felt responsible, I suppose that's why he wanted to help."

"Responsible for what?"

"If he stayed on the task force, maybe they could have done it. Arrested Louie and sent him to jail. But they didn't. After a while they just gave up. And kids like my Lenny, that made them think Louie was even tougher, better than the cops."

"And so you thought if Chuck talked to Lenny, it would help?"

She nodded. "But it didn't. I suppose it was too late already."

Her eyes suddenly moistened, and she looked down at her hands, at the carpet. She pulled a white handkerchief from her sleeve, wiped at her eyes, tucked it away again.

"But he sent you now," she said huskily. "He wants to help now. That's so good. That's so much like Chuckie."

"Can I help?" I asked. "Now?"

"Of course," she said. "That's why he sent you and didn't come himself. That's why he didn't say anything when he came to the funeral home, why he left so fast. He still can't do anything to hurt Louie, not himself. That's not different. But he must know that what happened to my boy had something to do with Louie."

"How would he know that?"

"He keeps track of Louie. He always has. He can't hurt him, but sometimes he can stop him from hurting other people. He must know. See, he sent you. And that's your job, isn't it?"

"My job?"

"To stop Louie. To be the one. Chuckie can't. So that must be your job."

s e v e n t e e n

my job. I drove along the quiet streets of Howard Beach, thinking about my job. At the tree-shaded park on the corner, little kids played in sandboxes while bigger ones jumped their skateboards on the sidewalk. The windows in the car were open, the way they usually are, and I could hear the bravado of teenage boys shouting to each other, young skinny boys who owned the world but sometimes, in the middle of the night, wished they still believed their teddy bears could talk. Kids who were scared of being scared. Kids who could easily fall for the swagger of a gangster like Louie Falco, if they believed he wasn't scared of anything.

I pulled into a one-story shopping center where the paint was peeling off the slender steel columns at the covered walkway. I found a pay phone and called Lydia. Her workday was over by now too, and I caught up with her in her office.

"Do you think it's true?" she asked when I'd told her about Lenny Pelligrini and Chuck DeMattis, about Lenny's mother and my job.

"I don't know," I said. "It could be. If Chuck can't bring down Louie Falco himself but wants him brought down, maybe that's what this is all about."

"What does Joe Romeo have to do with it? That's where we started."

"Mrs. Pelligrini said Chuck keeps track of Louie. Maybe he knew Romeo was involved with him somehow. Maybe he knew following Romeo's trail would lead us back to Falco, back to something we could prove."

"Then," she said, "you're right that something was strange about Mr. DeMattis, but it's not what you were worried about. It's the opposite."

"If it's true," I said.

"What are you going to do now?"

"Call Chuck."

Chuck was in his office too, getting ready to go home for the day. I told him where I was.

He hesitated. "Shit," he said. "What are you . . . ?"

I didn't answer.

"Shit," he said again.

"Meet me," I said.

"Yeah." I heard him sigh. "There's a bakery, not far from you." He told me where. "They make good coffee, have a couple of tables. Sometimes they got the opera on."

"However you want it," I said.

It would take Chuck half an hour to get here. That gave me time to walk around a little and think, to find the bakery, and to set up something else. I did the thinking first, leaving the car at the shopping center, walking along the concrete sidewalk that took me past an auto-body shop, a bridal-gown store, a couple of bars. I lit a cigarette at the corner, turned off the commercial street into a residential area, walked past white-painted houses and houses of red brick, houses where the small yards were wrapped with chain-link fence to keep in barking, bounding dogs, houses where the yards were open and full of sweet-smelling roses. I wondered where in this neighborhood Chuck had grown up, on what street, in what kind of house, then decided I didn't want to know.

I finished a second cigarette as I approached the shopping center again, from the other direction. I made another phone call, then got back in the car, headed toward Santoro's bakery the way Chuck had told me.

At Santoro's the air was scented with brewing coffee, with yeast and cinnamon. Three marble-topped tables hugged the wall opposite the glass cases filled with pies and cakes. Two heavy women, beaming, talking, eating cannoli, sat at one; a young mother and her spoon-banging three-year-old took up another. At the far end of the kitchen I could see a screen door.

"You have tables outside?" I asked the spectacled, skinny kid behind the counter.

He wiped his hands on his apron and led me through the kitchen, where the rich sugary smell of cookies baking followed us out through the screen door into the garden. The garden was tiny, a high-fenced, stone-paved yard barely big enough for the four white metal tables and eight folding chairs it held. But it was private, and it was empty.

The kid brought me an espresso; I'd barely started it when Chuck arrived.

He smiled, stepping down from the kitchen onto the paving stones. The smile seemed real, but tentative; it wasn't hearty, hail-fellow, the way Chuck's smiles usually are.

"Hey," he said.

I didn't smile back, said nothing. Chuck sat on the folding chair across from me while the kid set an espresso down on the table for him. When the kid left, Chuck looked around the tiny garden.

"I practically grew up here," he told me. "Worked at Santoro's all through high school. That's when Santoro owned the place. Now it's his son-in-law. Santoro sold it to him, retired to Florida."

"I went to see Elena Pelligrini," I said.

"I didn't want you to do that." Chuck's answer was direct and calm, matching my own tone.

"I know that now. I wasn't bright enough to figure it out before, when you said not to bother with the Pelligrini kid, that there was nothing there. I thought you were just trying to save me trouble. Did you know he was dead?"

Chuck picked up his espresso, sipped it, put the thick cup carefully down. "No. I didn't know that until they pulled his body out of the basement."

"But you suspected."

"No. If I'd thought something had happened to the kid, I wouldn't have told you to forget about him, not for nothing."

"You told me to forget about him again last night."

Chuck's eyes moved across the stone floor, along the whitewashed fence, as though he were looking for something, something he'd left here. "That's true," he said softly. "The kid was dead by then. You couldn't help him."

"What did you think had happened to him, Chuck?"

"I thought he was smart enough to have disappeared, gotten the hell away, where that son of a bitch Falco couldn't get to him."

"Why would he do that?"

"I don't know. Sometimes they do."

I drank some more espresso; so did Chuck. "Not bad," he said, with a soft smile. "Almost as good as mine."

"What did happen to him?" I said quietly.

"I don't know. I don't know what he was into. But he was in way over his head, whatever it was."

"How do you know that?"

Chuck looked at me, not smiling now. "Lenny Pelligrini was twenty-two. All he wanted was to be somebody, get out, see the world. To have the maître d' rush over whenever he walked into a restaurant. Louie Falco eats kids like that for breakfast."

"You think Falco killed him?"

"Whatever he was messed up in with Falco, got him killed. You ask me, that means the same as Louie killed him." He brought his espresso to his lips again, drained the cup. He lifted it, gestured with it to someone in the kitchen, put it down.

"What you said about someone shaking down the Crowells," I said. "That was bullshit, right?"

He nodded, without words.

"Just to keep us on the case?"

"I don't know what Louie's doing up there, on that site," Chuck said. "But whatever it is got the kid killed. I needed you to stay up there."

"Pelligrini's mother thinks my job is to bring down Louie

Falco for you," I told him. "That I'm supposed to do what you can't do."

Chuck's eyes wandered the garden again. Pots of red geraniums shone against the whitewashed fence, some in sunlight, some in shadow. He turned back to me. "I'm sorry."

"Why the hell didn't you tell me?" I stood suddenly, stalked a few paces, stopped, my back to Chuck. There was no place to go in this tiny garden. I turned. "Who the hell are you to use me as a cat's-paw?"

Chuck stayed seated, shook his head. All the heartiness was gone now; he looked weary, sad. "I couldn't tell you," he said. "I couldn't set it up like that. If I could do that, I could do it myself. Son of a bitch . . ." He looked around, at the geraniums, the tables and chairs, as though trying to find something to help him explain it to me. A neighboring tree hung over the fence, sharing its shade with us.

"When we were kids, Louie and me, I had a dog," Chuck said. "Butch, his name was. Louie's mom didn't like dogs, so he never had one. Me and Louie and Butch, it was like the Three Musketeers. Everywhere we went it was together." He looked at me, made a hopeless gesture with his hands, as though he knew that whatever he had wouldn't be enough. But he went on. "One time, when Louie and me were about nine, dumb dog ran out into the street. Car was coming fast. I was scared shitless, I couldn't move. Louie, he charges out there, pushes the stupid dog away. Dog ended up without a scratch. Car hit Louie."

"And?"

"Couple of weeks in the hospital, all summer in a cast. Nine years old. Leg healed crooked. He still walks a little funny, limps. You wouldn't see it unless you know, but I know."

The screen door creaked open, and the skinny kid came out with two fresh espressos. He looked at Chuck, at me standing, and stopped, lost. Chuck gave the kid a small smile, tapped on the table for the espressos. The kid put them down and left.

"He going to listen through the door?" I asked Chuck.

Chuck shook his head. "Santoro's son-in-law won't let

him." He pushed one of the new espressos to my side of the table. "Come on, sit down."

"What are you saying, Chuck?" I asked, still standing. "Louie Falco saved your dog, so now he gets to kill whoever he wants, and you just stand there?"

"For Christ's sake!" Chuck leaned toward me. "I grew up with the guy. I dated his sister. My mother and his mother, they still pick each other up for church. My old man was a pallbearer when his old man died."

He kept his eyes on mine. My face must not have changed. "Don't you have anyone like that?" he asked, part incredulous, part pleading. "Someone you go back so far with that it don't matter anymore what it's about? That you got to do them favors and get them out of trouble even though you can't stand them anymore?"

I shook my head. "No. There's no one like that." I came back to the table, sat, lit a cigarette. I smoked about half of it; Chuck said nothing. The wind rustled the tree's branches, moving the shade around. I asked, "You do Falco favors, Chuck?"

He was silent a long moment. "I guess maybe," he finally said, quietly. "I could have taken him up once or twice, but I didn't. If that's a favor, I guess I did."

"You warn him?"

"Christ, no. I even tried to set it up so someone else would see it, so someone else could follow it back to him, but no one picked up on it. That was all I could do. You gotta believe me. That was all I could do."

"And now?" I lifted the new espresso, tried it. It was as good as the first, bitter and strong, still hot. "That's what you're doing now, too?"

"Yeah," he said. "Now, too."

"Romeo? That was bullshit?"

"No, that was the beginning. For you to follow it back."

"Romeo was tied into Falco? You know that for a fact?" The sun had slipped out from behind the roof of a house. Delicately, it picked out one red geranium in its pot as though it were somehow special, different from the others.

"Got to be. Falco's involved in something on that site. If Romeo was too, dope, thefts, whatever, it's gotta lead to Falco."

"What is it he's involved in?"

"I don't know."

"I don't believe you."

I expected anger, defensiveness; all I got was a shake of the head. "No, it's true. When I heard they were having problems, the thefts and shit, and I knew he's got something going up there, I figured that's got to be Louie. That's everything I got. I was looking for you to follow it back."

"How do you know he's involved?"

"Word on the street. I keep track of him."

"That's what Elena Pelligrini said."

"What?"

"That you keep an eye on him. That you sometimes get in his way."

He nodded. "In small ways. Not much, but the best I can do. Like talking to the Pelligrini kid. That was supposed to be one of those times."

"She's grateful that you tried."

"She shouldn't be. Her son's dead."

"Not your fault, she says."

He picked up his espresso cup. I rubbed out my cigarette, lit another. We had suddenly run out of things to say to each other, Chuck and I.

"I'm sorry," he said again, as he had at the beginning. "You and Lydia . . . Thanks, anyway. I appreciate everything you did."

I looked at my watch. "I have to meet someone," I said. "I set something up."

Chuck frowned, confusion showing. "On this?"

"It's my case. We said that at the beginning. My case, to be handled my way."

"But now . . . ? With this . . . ?"

I stood. "My case," I said. "I'll call you."

I pulled open the screen door, took in the aromas of vanilla, sugar, anise, as I moved through the kitchen and the bakery, out to the street. I left Chuck sitting with an espresso at the metal table, in the shade of the neighbor's tree, in the tiny garden where he'd grown up.

eighteen

I'd left early to get to the next place I had to be, but the drive from Howard Beach to the far end of Brooklyn was long and frustratingly slow, a jerky procession of stuck traffic and honking horns. I made it to my destination just about on time. The air was full of dry dust diffusing the low sunlight as I rolled the car slowly down the pitted streets between the walls of razor wire and chain-link fence. I pulled into Sal Maggio's auto salvage yard and parked out of range of the snarling dog on his heavy, clanking chain. The slowly swirling clouds of dust hovered over the piles of rusting iron and steel the way the mist and fog had, the first time I'd been here.

Sal Maggio must have heard the dog barking, or maybe he just had a sixth sense for when people drove into his yard. He came out of the trailer, waited at the top of the concrete steps as I left the car and made my way over there. The dog snapped at me from the end of his taut chain.

Maggio didn't say anything to discourage the dog, just watched me approach. When I reached the bottom step I stopped.

He looked at me silently for a few moments. Then he said, "C'mon inside." He pulled open the trailer door as I climbed the steps. "Want a beer?"

The inside of the trailer was one long musty-smelling room, bed unmade on one end, a ratty old recliner and a TV in the middle, kitchen where we came in. The floor in the kitchen was grimy vinyl tile; everywhere else was grimy carpet. A T-shirt draped the back of one of the two kitchen chairs. Maggio lifted it off and tossed it in the direction of the TV. He pointed to the chair for me and I sat as he pulled open the fridge and took out two cans of Bud.

"Thanks." I popped the top, took a long drink. All the windows in Maggio's trailer were open, and the heat and dust moved as easily through here as among the mounds of car parts in the yard.

"So what is it?" Maggio asked, sitting in the other chair, taking a pull from his own beer. He squinted at me as though I were something unusual. Maybe, a stranger in his trailer, I was.

"That kid," I said. "The one whose name you found me, Pelligrini. Who fenced the frontloader."

"What about him?"

"He's dead."

Maggio took another pull on his Bud. "Shit. And?"

"You said he was tied in to Louie Falco somehow."

"I said the guy I talked to said that."

"Okay, the guy you talked to. I want to talk to Falco."

"Why?"

"You want to know?"

Maggio drank more beer, squinted at me again. "No," he said.

"Can you set it up?"

"What makes you think I can?"

"I don't. I'm asking."

"If I could," he said, "why would I?"

"Because the kid was twenty-two, and now he's dead."

Maggio asked, "This have anything to do with Joanie?"

"No."

"She brought you here, the first time."

"She didn't know why."

"Kid was dead then?"

"I don't know."

I took out a cigarette, lit it. The smoke joined the dust drifting gently through the air.

"You could've told me 'Yeah, Joanie wants you to set this up for me,' " Maggio said. "More than likely I'd have done it."

"It would have been a lie."

"You telling me you never lie?"

"Didn't seem like the right way to play you, Maggio."

His eyes still on me, he pulled a pack of Camels from his shirt pocket, reached behind him onto the drainboard of the sink. Between the crusted dishes and the dirty coffee cups he put his hand precisely on a book of matches, blind. He lit his cigarette.

"Anything going to happen to him? Falco?" he asked.

I shook my head. "I just want to talk."

Maggio streamed smoke. "Know why I live here?"

"No."

"Instead of some apartment, where I could spread out a little?"

I waited for the answer.

"Trailer's made of steel," he said. "Rivets and welds. No bullshit. Wait there."

Maggio got up, moved past me and through the trailer, sat on the unmade bed. He put the phone on his lap, dialed a number, had a low-voiced conversation I couldn't overhear. He hung up, dialed a different number, had another. He waited a long time, receiver to his ear, then spoke again, and hung up. Coming back to the kitchen, he pulled another pair of Buds from the fridge. He sat again at the table, said, "It's set up."

I opened my can of beer, cold and wet in my hand. "He coming here?"

Maggio took a long gulp of his Bud, lowered it. "You crazy?"

"Where, then?"

"The Staten Island Ferry."

"What?"

"Someplace public, nobody's territory. He don't know you, you don't know him, right? This way nobody needs to get nervous."

"Thanks, Maggio."

"For Joanie," he said.

"I told you, she has nothing to do with this."

"Yeah. But you tell her I helped you out. Maybe next time that jerk smashes up his Triumph, maybe she'll come here for parts."

"I bet she will."

He nodded. "She's a good kid."

I drove through the tunnel to Battery Park to catch the nine o'clock ferry, but, before the ferry, there was an argument with Lydia.

"Absolutely not," she said when I called her from the ferry terminal to tell her what I'd found and what I was going to do. She was home by now, in Chinatown, answering the phone that rings through from her office. "Absolutely not alone."

"You'd kill me if I said that to you."

"But you'd be right, even so. And—"

"And," I drowned her out, "I probably wouldn't even get the chance to say it because you probably wouldn't even call me to tell me where you were going."

"Because you'd tell me absolutely not." She dismissed that argument. "Anyway, I can be there in ten minutes. I—"

"Besides," I rode right over that, "you probably have other plans."

"Me? Like what?"

"Like drinking with construction workers."

"Hey," she said warningly.

"You know I had to say it."

"Okay, you said it. What time is the ferry?"

"No. It has to be alone."

"No," she said. "It only has to *look* like you're alone. I'll lean on the rail with a camera, like a Japanese tourist. He'll never know I'm there. But someone has to watch your back."

"I don't want to spook him, Lydia."

"Bill? You're going to accuse a Mafioso of murder and you don't want to spook him?" She sighed at the illogic of the human mind, or maybe just mine. "Besides," she said, "do you really think *he's* going to be alone?"

She won the argument, but not on logic. She won on the basis that it's a free country and she, Lydia Chin, born and raised here, had a right to take a ferry to Staten Island any hour of the day or night with or without my permission.

I hung the phone up, walked back across the vast, echoing terminal. Red sunset gleamed in the arched western windows; a pigeon swooped through the air up to a steel joist, where it shuffled its wings and settled in for the night. I bought two hot dogs from the guy at the stand, smothered them with peppery fried onions, and watched the late commuters drifting toward the turnstiles while I ate. I wondered which one of these men, in their tie-loosened business suits or their overalls or their bermuda shorts, was Louie Falco, and which were the guys who worked for him, who would be sure to be with him, as Lydia had said.

I was the one who was supposed to be alone.

I didn't see Lydia, but I knew she'd make it, and I knew she'd be invisible, even to the men whose job it was to watch Louie Falco's back.

I pushed through the turnstile, to the glassed-in waiting room upstairs. A minute later, they let us on the boat, the commuters and the tourists and me.

The ferry creaked and swayed in the water, holding its berth patiently as the passengers boarded. I crossed the metal-plate gangway, went through the bad-weather room with its long wooden benches and scratched plastic windows. Outside, I took up a position at the center of the rail on the west, the way Maggio had set it up.

The salt smell of the ocean was all around me, the screech of seagulls and the wind moving over the water. Ships crowded the harbor, cut through the silvery water on their own errands. The sky, already dark in the east, was streaked with fading red and orange in the west. On my right, a young Latino had his arm around his girl, rubbed her shoulder as they gazed dreamily across the river. On my left, a large, immaculately dressed family of Japanese tourists took turns snapping each other's picture with the lower-Manhattan skyline in the background.

A change in the rumbling beneath the deck and a loud clanking told me the ferry was ready to go; a minute later it did, pulling regally out of its slip and into open water. I looked back toward Manhattan, taking in the sights, and spotted Lydia in baseball cap and dark glasses, sitting cross-legged on a bench with a good view of the Statue of Liberty and me.

As the ferry plowed across the water, Manhattan dwindled and the dark mass of Staten Island rose through the haze. Lights twinkled on its distant shore. The cool, water-flecked wind the ferry kicked up reminded my skin it had once known weather beyond the damp heat of New York's July. I stayed where I was, leaning on the rail, waiting. I smoked a cigarette, cupping it in my hand to keep the wind from burning it down to the filter before I could.

I'd just finished the smoke when I spotted a man of average height, and considerably more than average girth, making his unhurried way among the people walking up and down the deck. He was balding, like Chuck, and clean-shaven, and tan. His walk was uneven, but only slightly; it could have been the rolling of the boat, or the result of his weight.

He reached the place where I was, sauntered over and leaned next to me against the rail, not so different from the ferry settling into its berth. He wore a tan summer suit over a white polo shirt, not cotton knit, but silk. The suit was spectacularly well cut; it fit his bulk perfectly, even managing to hide the gun in the shoulder holster, unless you were looking for it.

He turned to peer into my face, then looked away.

"Smith?" His grainy voice was casual, unconcerned.

"That's right."

"Talk."

"You're Louie Falco?"

"Isn't that what you wanted?"

"I don't always get what I want."

He looked at me again, small brown eyes in a pudgy, well-kept face. "I'm Louie Falco. So talk."

"I want to ask you about Lenny Pelligrini."

Falco's eyes followed a seagull gliding alongside the boat,

a white shape across the striped sky. Reaching into his breast pocket, Falco slid two cigars out, offered one to me. I shook my head.

"Cuban," he said.

"Thanks anyway."

"Legit," he added. "I got a damn import license. Through Switzerland."

When that didn't change my mind, he replaced one cigar and lit the other, watched its tip glow brightly in the salt breeze.

"I heard about Pelligrini," he said. "It's a shame. Young kid."

"What happened to him?"

He shrugged. "I don't know."

"You know anyone who does?"

The seagull took a dive into the churning water in our wake, rose with a frantic beating of wings. Falco said, "Who're you?"

"Friend of the family."

He nodded. "His mother send you to me?"

I missed a beat. "What?"

"His mother. She looking for me to help? To find the guy?"

Another seagull came flapping up beside the first. They squawked at each other for a moment, then both banked and wheeled away, back toward the distant towers of Manhattan.

"His mother thinks you killed him, Falco," I said.

Falco turned his head to me and stared. "You're shitting me."

"Or had something to do with it. Something the kid was involved in with you."

"Christ. I barely knew the bastard." He shook his head, stared back over the darkening water. "He come to me all the time, Louie this, Louie that, but I got no use for him. Not real bright, you follow me?"

"What if he'd been real bright?"

"Maybe then I coulda used him. But he had no future, what I used to do, or what I do now."

"Those things are different?"

He turned his face to mine, then back to the harbor. "None of your damn business, but I don't care who knows. I'm getting out of the game. Strictly legit Louie, from now on. Import, export, investments, shit like that. Got tired," he added by way of explanation, though I hadn't asked. "Legit, I got even less use for a guy like him." He gave a short, low laugh; it made his huge sides shift, like the movement of earth. "Guess he had no future anyway, huh? She don't really think I killed him?"

"Yes, she does."

He was quiet for a minute. "Guess I better talk to her."

"I wouldn't do that."

"No?" He turned his head sharply. I felt, more than saw, two men at the edges of my vision snap to attention. "So just what the hell would you do?" Falco asked.

I ignored the two men, said evenly, "Pelligrini was stealing things off the construction site he worked at."

Falco raised his eyebrows. He turned back to the water. The electric anger that had pulsed from him a moment ago faded as though a dial had been turned; but I didn't get the feeling it had shut off entirely.

"No shit," he said. "Maybe the kid had more going on than I gave him credit for. What kind of things?"

"All kinds, I think. I have him fencing a frontloader."

"A frontloader? Jesus Christ. That's good."

"He wasn't working alone."

"So?"

"Who was he working with?"

"What the hell you asking me for?"

"Because I thought it might be you."

"Me? Why the hell would it be me?"

I took a breath. "Because you have something going on at that site, Falco. If it's not the kid's scam, what is it?"

"Me?" Falco's face darkened, like the sky behind him. I felt the electric current increase again. "Who says I got anything going on there?"

The two men watching us began to move.

"Chuck DeMattis," I said.

Falco stared. "Fucking Chuckie," he said slowly. "That what this is, you're working with Chuckie?"

"Just trying to find out what happened to the kid, Falco."

"You said you were a friend of the family, Smith." His voice was soft, like the sound of the distant ocean. "You shouldn't have said that if it wasn't true." Falco kept his eyes on me another few moments. Then he nodded. "Now all this makes sense. Musta been Chuckie put it in the Pelligrini lady's head I did her boy."

"I don't know whether he told her that. But I know he thinks it, too."

The two men circled toward us, slowly, casually.

"Fucking Chuckie," Falco repeated, shaking his head. "Squirrel dies in Central Park, Chuckie thinks it was me."

"What do you have going on up on that site, Falco?"

By now the two men who were on the move had reached us. One, tall and mournful, with a turquoise stud in his ear, maneuvered his way onto the rail at my right. The other, shorter, but with the wide shoulders of a bodybuilder, came to a stop behind me, crowding close.

"What makes it your business what I got going anywhere?" Falco asked.

"Someone killed that kid, Falco. Chuck thinks it was you, because of whatever you have going up there. If he's wrong, show me."

"Screw you," Falco shrugged. "This what you got me here for, accuse me of killing the kid? I thought you was looking for help."

"I am."

Falco regarded me evenly. Over his shoulder I could make out the wide mouth of the Staten Island ferry slip and the aging buildings around it, growing closer. "I didn't have no reason to kill that kid," he said. "But I got nothing to prove to you, or to fucking Chuckie. You and Chuckie better keep out of my way, Smith. I don't want you jamming me up."

"Not my intention. But someone killed that kid."

"And I don't give a shit who! That clear enough for you? So help me, if you get me messed up in this—" He broke off, gave me a long, flat look. "That's the point, ain't it?" he said. "Ah, shit, Louie, you're slowing down. Chuckie *wants* me messed up in this, this Pelligrini thing, don't he? Fucking Chuckie, he knows everything about me, every damn time I scratch my ass. He knows I'm getting out of the business, and it burns him, don't it? So he's gonna get me. He won't stop till they stick it to me over this, if he has to build the frame himself. Am I right?"

"No."

"Yes. Fucking Chuckie." His eyes caught the eyes of each of the other two men in turn, the bodybuilder and the sad man with the turquoise stud. The guy with the stud put a gentle hand on my arm.

"How well did you know Joe Romeo?" I said to Falco.

The bodybuilder stepped forward, a hopeful glint in his eye. The soft hand on my arm closed its grip, still gentle.

"Another loser," Falco answered. "Maybe he was working with the kid."

"Another dead man on that site," I said. "Don't you think someone besides Chuck is going to put this together soon?"

"Jesus." Falco took a step toward me. So did the bodybuilder, smiling now. "What the hell is that, a threat?" Falco asked in wonderment.

"No," I said. "But it might be useful to you if I could lay this whole thing to rest."

"What whole thing?" Falco said. "The kid, and that loser Romeo, and whatever, it's got nothing to do with me. You bring me into it, Smith, I'm telling you, it's really gonna piss me off."

"You're already part of it."

"No, and I don't want to be." He looked at me thoughtfully. "You want to be useful to me? Okay. What would be useful to me is you take a message to Chuckie, that he better leave me the hell alone. You feel like doing that?"

"I'd want something in return, before I tell Chuck anything from you."

"Tell? Who said anything about tell? You're just gonna take a message." He nodded at the bodybuilder and the tall, sad man. "Bring him along, fellas. We're gonna put this message in a way so Chuckie gets it."

The sad man's grip on my arm became an iron band. Something in his other hand pushed softly but unmistakably against my ribs. The bodybuilder, doing his best to keep a grin of gleeful anticipation from his face, pressed close on my other side. The sad man's voice came softly in my ear.

"The gun has a silencer," he said sorrowfully. He sounded like a man apologizing for bad weather, something he couldn't do anything about but which he knew would inconvenience me. "I got a bullet in it would shred your liver. If I had to shoot you now and you went down, me and Mr. Falco and Shrimp here, we'd be gone before anyone noticed. Believe me, you're better off coming with us."

I didn't believe him. I glanced around, saw the ferry slip yawning to receive us, saw the white water of our wake spreading and relaxing as it receded. I heard the screech of the gulls, diving and calling. In my ribs, the hard nose of the gun pressed a little closer.

Then I heard a shout, my name.

"Bill Smith! Hey! Bill!"

I turned, and the men with me turned too. In fact, the shout was so loud that half the deck turned. Lydia stood about twenty feet away, wildly waving her baseball cap, Coke can in her other hand. As I watched, a wave of Coke slopped up and out, splashing a couple of unvigilant and unappreciative tourists. "Stay there!" she called—as if I had a choice—and started plowing her way through the crowd. She spilled more Coke, and must have stepped on toes, too; she left a path of scowls and evil-eyed stares in her wake. Stumbling over a man trying to rise from a bench, probably to get out of her way, she reached us, still in sunglasses, a wide smile plastered all over her face. "My God, it's you, isn't it?"

"Mishika?" I asked. "Mishika Yamamoto?"

"What a hoot!" she exclaimed, throwing her arms wide, losing the rest of her Coke. By now half the travelers on deck were glaring and muttering in our direction. A man in a Cokestained white suit yelled something at her. She ignored them all.

"I haven't seen you since Max's martini party!" she beamed. "How are you? 'Scuse me." She smiled winningly around her, rose on tiptoe and kissed my cheek. "How've you been?" she chattered on, resetting her baseball cap. "Have you seen Max lately? I don't see him much in the summer, he goes out of town, to this place he has. Have you been up there? Me neither. Hey, come over here. This'll just take a minute," she said to the three men who stood near me, momentarily dumbfounded, as the rumble of the ferry's engine changed and the slip approached. "He'll be right back," she assured them. "But you have to meet my family." She tugged at my left arm; the iron grip on my right became uncertain, loosened as I moved toward her, under the scowling, watchful eyes of dozens of other passengers. "Right over here. They came from Japan, like just last night. I'm showing them around. We went to the Empire State Building today, and Chinatown. Boy, do they have some weird people there! Be back in a minute," she promised Falco and the others, smiling at them once more, and hurried me down the deck, blundering through the still-glaring crowd toward the cheerfully indulgent Japanese parents herding their well-dressed, excited children down the exit ramp and off the boat.

"Do you know," Lydia said, "I don't think I've actually been in Staten Island in *years*. I mean, gotten off the ferry."

She buttered a half-moon of toasted english muffin, looked with interest out the diner window. Nothing was happening out there except a denim-dressed biker holding his Harley steady while a girl in a thin pink top climbed on behind.

We'd hoped for a cab at the ferry terminal as we issued down the ramp, keeping tight to the center of the crowd of commuters and the few stray tourists who had crossed the water with the idea of Staten Island as an actual destination. The tourists, including Lydia's once and future Japanese relatives, stood looking befuddled in the gaping terminal, took a few tentative steps onto the streets outside, and spun around to take the next boat back to Manhattan. The commuters, meanwhile, snapped up the few waiting cabs. That meant we couldn't get one, but it meant the same for Louie Falco and his pals. So Lydia and I jumped on the nearest bus and sat in the back, peering out the window until we were pretty sure we weren't being followed. We got off at the Island Diner—an electric-blue neon palm tree blinking on the sign—and sat, now waiting to be picked up by the cab company we'd called.

"Go ahead," I said, as she bit into her dripping english muffin. "Gloat."

"Oh, no," she answered. She put the english muffin down, sipped delicately at her Lemon Mist tea. "It was such a lovely night for a boat ride. I just want to thank you for the opportunity to come along."

"Maybe they only wanted to talk some more," I said. "Maybe Falco just wasn't sure how to phrase the message for Chuck, and he wanted to think about it."

"Mm-hmm," she said. "Maybe they wanted to beat your brains out."

I drank some coffee that had been on the burner much too long. "Maybe it would have served me right," I said.

She answered thoughtfully, "It might even have helped."

I wanted a cigarette, but the diner's attitude on that was clear, so I drank some coffee instead. "I thought you didn't like Coke," I pointed out.

"I wasn't planning on drinking it, just spilling it, so what's the difference?"

"I just wanted to make sure you know I keep track of things like that."

"You'd better."

"I do," I said. "And thanks."

"For saving your life? Oh, you're welcome. Anytime."

"And," I said, "for not listening when I said not to come."

"Ah," she said, "that. You know, maybe I shouldn't ever listen to you. It might save us both a lot of trouble."

"I'm never right?"

"Occasionally," she admitted. "Often enough that, when you get these really demented ideas, I wonder about you."

"Demented how?"

"Oh, like you think Louie Falco killed Lenny Pelligrini so you're going to just ask him about it. 'Oh, sure, Smith, yeah, I did that.' Honestly, what did you expect him to say?"

"I expected him to tell me he hadn't done it."

"Well, and there you go."

"But that's because I don't think he did."

She looked at me over her teacup, then put the teacup down. "You don't?"

"No." The waitress came along with more hot water for Lydia and a refill on the foul coffee for me. "Look," I said. "Falco knew the Pelligrini kid back in the neighborhood. He'd have known where to find him outside the jobsite. If he wanted to kill him, why kill him there? Why bury him there?"

She tilted her head in thought. The blue neon from the palm tree outside the window glinted in her hair. "To make some kind of point of him, some example when he was found?"

"But he wasn't supposed to be found. All the digging in that pit was supposed to be over."

"Well, then, it was a good place to hide him."

"But an inconvenient place to come kill him, if you don't work there. And you'd have to be sure he'd be there late, or get there early, or something, so you have time to bury the body when no one's around."

"Hmmm." She sliced the other half of her english muffin into two more perfect half-moons, munched on one. "You think it has to be someone connected to that site who killed him."

"That's the only way it makes sense."

"But Mr. DeMattis said Falco *is* connected up there."

"But we don't know to what. And Falco's a pro at this. If he wanted a body found, he'd put it somewhere it'd be sure to be found. If he wanted it not found, it wouldn't be found."

"So why did you even start with him?" she asked, frowning at me.

"*Because* I didn't think he did it. Because I thought he might point me toward who did."

"Why would he?"

"To get me out of his face? To get himself a little more elbow room for whatever it is he's got going up there?" I shrugged. "To do a widow a favor?"

Lydia's look suggested what I could do with that last one.

The waitress, a perky blonde high-school girl, quit flirting with a guy at the counter, came and refilled my coffee cup again.

Lydia said, "Bill? What is it Falco's likely to be doing on that site, if he's not involved in stealing the things Pelligrini was fencing?"

"I don't know. But there are endless scams you can run at a construction site. Extortion. Racketeering. Money laundering. It could be that whatever Pelligrini had going was totally independent of what Falco's into. Falco didn't even seem to know about it."

"Then," she said, "we need to find whoever Pelligrini was working with, don't we? I mean, they would be up there, on the site. They would know when he was coming and going. Isn't that what we need to do?"

"Yes."

She nodded. "What are you going to do about Falco?"

"I need to do something about him?"

"Well, he *was* about to beat you to a bloody pulp. He might consider he has unfinished business with you."

I stared out the window, watched a cat wash its face on the porch of a house across the street. "No, I don't think so," I said. "He thinks I'm going to report back to Chuck. The threat will be as good as the reality would have been, to deliver the message. If I were him I'd keep an ear to the ground and see what happens. If his name doesn't come up again connected to Pelligrini, I think he'll back off."

"And if it does?"

"You mean, if Chuck was right?" I swallowed the last of my coffee. "Like I said, I don't think he is. But that's the job, isn't it? To find out."

She gave me a long, quiet look, then went back to her tea. Just as she finished, a short chubby guy stuck his head in the diner door. He bellowed, "Anybody call a cab?" I left a few bucks on the table, Lydia slipped on her sunglasses and adjusted her baseball cap again, and we headed over the bridge and back toward the sparkling lights of Manhattan.

nineteen

the next morning I got to the site early. At a quarter to seven, the sky above New York was a pure, bright blue, not yet dimmed by the haze of daily living. The subway on the way up was cool and close to empty. The site was quiet, no dust raised yet, no trucks rumbling, no spilled coffee or running hoses to make new muddy puddles in yesterday's dirt. Inside the fence, the steel and concrete, the bricks and conduit and sheet metal that would become a building, waited, silent.

I crossed to the ramp and headed for the Lacertosa trailer, to clock in and have a talk with John Lozano.

He was there; I'd expected him to be. Site super, and now foreman too: a lot of responsibility, a lot of paperwork. Long hours. He looked up from his desk as I came in, raised his eyebrows.

"You're early," he said. "Clock in if you want, but I don't pay overtime on this job."

"I know. That's something I want to talk about."

Lozano shook his head. "Can't do it, Smith. Budget's too tight. A lot of the men are unhappy about it. I'm sorry, but nothing I can do."

"I'm not looking for overtime. I heard about the budget." I pulled up a molded plastic chair that looked as though it had seen more than a few construction sites itself. "I want to talk."

Lozano watched me sit. "You having trouble up there? You

started slow, but I thought you were doing better. You and Mike are producing okay."

"Mike is," I said. "I'm not half as good as he is. But laying bricks is only half the reason I'm here."

He cocked his head. "I don't get you."

"I'm an investigator," I told him, watched his face. "Private. Not a cop, and I'm not working with them. But I have to ask you some questions."

"Investigator?" Lozano's forehead creased. He put down his pencil. "What do you mean? Working here? You're supposed to be a bricklayer."

"You've had trouble on this site," I said. "You had it before I came here and you've had more, a lot more serious, since. My client wants to know what's going on."

"What, so he sends you here to lay bricks?" His frown deepened. He had known who I was when I'd walked into his office; now he didn't know, found the ground shifting.

"No. That was my idea. The client doesn't want to know how I'm handling it. They don't know I'm here, on site."

"What client? Who is it? What the hell are you supposed to be 'handling'?"

"I can't tell you who the client is, and I'm not sure about the rest. But I have some ideas. That's why I came to talk to you."

"Me? What the hell do I know? About what?"

"I'd like to ask you some questions."

"What questions? Hey, listen, how do I even know this shit is true?"

"What's the difference?" I asked.

He glared. The masonry foreman in him, the guy whose decisions were fast and final, kicked in. "You're a damn brick-layer, is all I know. You're here in my office, want to ask questions, I don't even know about what, and you wanna know what difference it is if you're telling the truth?"

I took out my wallet, showed him what I'd showed Mike DiMaio. "That help?" I asked.

"No. I still wanna know who you're working for."

"I'm not going to tell you. And to save you the trouble of

asking, I don't know if what I'm working on has anything to do with Lenny Pelligrini or Joe Romeo, either." I didn't mention Chester Hamilton; I didn't see any reason to let Lozano know that that connection was, for sure, more than a rumor. "But at least one of those men had a scam going on this site: Pelligrini. And there's at least one scam I know about on this site, and you're part of it, Lozano."

"What are you—?"

"Save it," I said. "I already talked to Donald Hacker."

For a moment Lozano didn't react. Then the masonry foreman, the one sure of himself and in charge, faded away. Lozano seemed to grow older as I watched. His shoulders drooped. He leaned back in his chair, ran his hand across his lined face. "Oh, God," he said. His blue eyes stared bleakly at me.

"Don't fight me on this," I said quietly. "I can get it other places. I came to you to give you a chance."

"A chance," he repeated softly. "It's over, huh?"

"I think it is," I answered. "I want you to tell me about it."

He kept his eyes quietly on me for a long moment, and neither of us moved. Then he got up and walked around me, closed the office door, came back to his battered desk chair. It creaked as he sat. "I didn't mean for it to go on," he said with a sigh. "Not even this long. It wasn't supposed to. But the money . . . It didn't seem like there was anything else I could do."

"The money was that good?"

"Good?" He stared. "Hell, no. It's because there wasn't any money."

"You lost me."

"I don't like it," he said. "Using shit like we're using here. I don't like it on any job I'm on. Old days, even if the architect *called* for shit, I used to try to talk the boss into letting me do the right thing. Sometimes they'd go for it. At least I tried." He gave a small, bitter smile. "Look at me now."

"What do you mean, there wasn't any money? Hacker says he's getting paid."

"He hadda get paid. If he didn't, he'd of blown the whole thing as soon as we started."

"And you weren't?"

"Not me personally. Jesus, you think I'd do shit like this for money? When I'm gone from here people are gonna be wondering what asshole built this shitpile of a building. How much money you think that's worth?"

"If you're not doing it for money, then what?"

Rapping knuckles shook the plywood door. Lozano threw me a look, got up and answered it. It was a Teamster with a truckful of concrete block in the lot. Lozano signed his manifest, told him where to pull the truck. "I got two guys out there waiting," he said. "Joey and Paolo. See them." Then the Teamster was gone and Lozano turned back to me.

"You got a job here, Smith."

I looked up at him where he stood by the door. "You telling me to get to work?"

"No. I'm telling you you got a job. And so do about a hundred and fifty other guys, thirty-two of 'em mine. You lose this job, where are you gonna go?" He shook his head impatiently. "Well, not you, you're a fucking detective, I guess you don't need this shit, no matter what. But Mike. Where's he gonna go?"

"He'll pick up something else."

"What the hell is he gonna pick up, now, the way things are?"

"He'll find something," I said, though I knew as I said it that finding something, if things were as bad as everyone was telling me, would be hard.

"All of them? All thirty-two masons? The carpenters? The ironworkers? The tin-knockers? Where the hell are these guys gonna go, Smith, if this building goes under?"

"This happens in construction," I said. "Fat periods and tight ones. Guys who work these jobs know that."

"Yeah. In the fat periods, they put money down on houses and take the kids to Disney World. When it gets tight, their wives take on night jobs at McDonald's and the bank takes the house back."

"Lozano—"

"What I'm telling you is, it was the only way to keep paying the men."

He stood for a moment, silently; I was silent too. Then he circled back to his desk, wary, his eyes still on mine, waiting for my reaction, prepared to meet it.

"I don't get it," I said, although I thought I did.

Lozano sighed, rubbed his face again. "Not in here," he said. "The men are going to start coming in soon, clocking in. Come in the back."

The trailer's back room was a storeroom, half the size of the one Lozano used for an office, piled with boxes of caulk tubes, ten-pound bags of fine colored sand to tint the mortar, metal cans of dry and wet chemicals you could add to the mortar so work could continue in the heat, in the cold, chemicals to retard curing, to hasten it, to give high early strength, to control shrinkage, to adjust the job to the conditions you had.

Lozano flicked on a buzzing overhead fluorescent, and we each chose a box to sit on. Once we were settled, I said nothing, let him tell me as he was ready.

He looked at me, said evenly, "Crowell's in debt up to their eyebrows. My second requisition, I find out they're already in the hole. They got plenty of nothing."

"They can't pay you?"

"Every month it's a scramble," he said. "Anyway, that's what they're telling me. I don't know, but they're telling me it's true."

In my head I heard Lydia's voice. *The gentleman yelled at me,* she'd said. *The Crowells owe money all over town.*

"I think it's probably true," I told Lozano. "I've heard that too. But what about the owner? Can't they go to her?"

"She's having trouble too, what I hear. Bank problems. Not so easy for a black lady to get a construction loan, especially in times everyone else thinks is bad. Bank probably figures she don't know what the hell she's doing."

"You think that's true?"

"How the hell should I know? All's I know is, she's hanging on by her fingernails. She's paying her requisitions and bills as they come in, but she can't come up with more. I hear she already chewed her way through the first construction loan, and she can't get the next till the building's fifty percent closed in. Crowell's pushing for that to be October."

"What's she using for money in the meantime?"

"I got no idea."

"But if she's paying, out of whatever, what do you need this scam for?"

"She pays Crowell, but everything she gives them don't go to us. Crowell's trying to keep their head above water here. One month they pay this guy, next month that guy. They lowballed this job, big time. They got no slack, no float, nothing." He rubbed the back of his neck. "Junior, he thinks Senior lost it. Got his damn pencil too sharp, came in with numbers they couldn't meet, just to get the job. Junior thinks the old man don't have it no more."

"Is that true?"

Lozano moved his shoulders helplessly. "Seems smart as he ever was, to me. But this money thing's a real bad problem. Payroll's only partial, almost since the job started."

"Only partial? And you stayed on this job?"

"What the hell am I gonna do?" His eyes pleaded with me. "Good times, I take my men and walk. But times like these? Some of my men left other jobs to come here. Because I called 'em, said this was solid, good for a year. Me, Smith. What am I gonna do, tell 'em, 'Sorry, my mistake'?"

"So you came up with this scheme? Substitute cheap materials, put the difference into payroll? Is that how it works?"

"That's how it works. Some trades are cutting corners on work, too, less layers of Sheetrock, that kind of thing. More work in less time, payroll's smaller overall. Mandelstam even let three guys go. Not me, I'm not letting that happen, not with the bricks." Understand, his look said. "Just until Crowell gets on their feet. Wasn't even supposed to be this long. We're still working low on the bricks, stuff like this matters less, the lower the floor. I thought it would be over by now."

"It's not," I said.

"No, it's not. Shit." He shook his head, let his hands drop between his knees. "I'm sorry I ever bought in."

"It wasn't your idea?"

"Me? You gotta be kidding. I don't have the brains for this kind of shit."

"Hacker told me all the subs were in on it."

He nodded.

"And they're all doing what you're doing? Paying their men from the difference?"

"I don't know about that. O'Malley, at Emerald, I got a feeling he's taking some home. Emerald's got deeper pockets than Lacertosa, I think, so he's got something to pay his men out of until his requisitions are met. But what the hell's the difference what he's doing? His men are working. So are mine."

I pulled my cigarettes out of my pocket, silently offered the pack to him. He shook his head, kept his eyes on me. I lit up, breathed the smoke. "So you guys all got together and worked this out? Brought Hacker into it because he's got to sign off on all the materials you're using? And it's true, what Hacker said: that Dan Crowell Junior's so dumb he doesn't suspect a thing?"

Lozano stared at me. "You don't get it."

"I don't?"

He shook his head. "Hacker, yeah," he said. "He hadda sign off, and there's nothing in it for him but money, so he's getting paid off. But us all get together? Dan Junior don't suspect? Hell, Smith." He snorted. "Whose idea do you think this was?"

I clocked in, as it turned out, a little late that day, after Lozano and I were done. He shook his head with a sad smile and said my late time card should be his biggest problem. I told him I didn't know what his biggest problem was going to be, and that it might come from me, but not right away.

"I don't get it," he said. "You're investigating. You turn over a rock and find a pile of shit. You ain't gonna do anything about it?"

"I don't know what I'm going to do," I said. "It depends on the answers I find. I have some other questions."

"Go ahead." He sighed. "This's been killing me for months, Smith. It's almost good to talk about it."

"What was Joe Romeo's role?"

"Nothing much. He was a nosy bastard, so I brought him in, otherwise he'd have figured it out for himself and made trouble. He was kinda useful, too. He was the one approached Hacker, got a few bucks for that."

"Why him?"

"Why Joe, go to Hacker? In case Hacker said no, he still wouldn't know about anyone else. And we figured, a guy like Joe, Hacker might be too scared to buy in but he's not gonna have the guts to drop a dime on Joe."

"And Lenny Pelligrini?"

Lozano shook his head. "Far as I know, nothing. He was a crane operator. Didn't have nothing to do with materials. That was a bad night, when they found him. I almost . . ." He trailed off, looked into space, maybe thinking about what he'd almost done.

"But you didn't."

"No." He seemed about to say something else, then changed his mind. He asked, "Smith? What were you talking about, about him—he had a scam going on?"

I regarded him, considered whether to tell him, and how much. "A lot of things went walking from this site early on," I said. "Tools and equipment, right?"

He shrugged. "Yeah, sure. Always happens, more or less."

"But it was particularly bad here."

"I guess, for a while. Till Crowell Senior beefed up security. Junior told him it would cost more for guards than they were losing, maybe they should just let it go, but Senior, he said that wasn't the way to do things, it wasn't right. He brought on another night guard, more lockboxes. Made Junior chase the men down, make sure they were following lockup procedures. Things got normal again. Wait a minute." Lozano frowned at me. "Are you telling me Pelligrini? He had something to do with that?"

"Seems to be."

"That skinny kid? He was stealing all that shit? Jesus."

"Yeah, he was. But I don't think alone, Lozano."

"No? Who—? Oh, hold on," he demanded, as it dawned. "Whoa. You think it was *me*?" His tone was incredulous, as though being thought of as a criminal was a new idea for him.

"It had crossed my mind."

"You gotta be—" He started strong, then deflated. His eyes looked into mine; he even gave me a rueful half-smile. "I guess I could see why. But it wasn't me, Smith. Not that kind of shit. This's bad enough."

"You have any idea who it might have been?"

He shook his head. "Unless it was Joe? He had that kind of balls."

"I don't think it was. The guy who gave me Pelligrini's name, the guy who bought the frontloader, hadn't heard of Joe Romeo. I tried his name out on Pelligrini's family, too. Nothing."

"Then I got no idea."

"What about Louie Falco?"

"Who?"

"Falco. What was his role?"

"I don't know him. Who's he?"

I'd asked it that way, same tone of voice, no big deal, to sandbag him, see what reaction I'd get. I wanted to know if Lozano's eyes would widen, his voice miss a beat, to hear that I knew how far back this thing went; but if he was acting, he was far better than I thought.

"Who's he?" he asked again.

"He's a guy who's part of something," I said. "A guy you don't want part of anything you do."

"Well, if he's got something to do with this site, I never heard of him."

"Maybe I have it wrong," I said.

"Yeah, maybe. Or maybe there's shit I don't know about. Jesus, I'm sure there is."

I had only one more question, more about the man himself than about what he'd done. More because I wanted to know than because I needed to.

"Lozano?"

He looked up.

"How far was this going to go?"

He sighed. "Believe me, I been thinking about it. You hadn't come, I might've blown the whistle myself, after Joe. Only Crowell Junior says don't worry, John, it's all gonna come okay. He says these things, they got nothing to do with each other. What you're doing is right, John, to be paying your men. Soon we'll be past this, it'll be over. That's what he said."

"And you believed that."

"I wanted to. Christ, wouldn't you?"

His voice almost broke on that one.

I didn't have an answer to it.

"What about Crowell Senior?" I asked.

"I didn't talk to him. I don't talk about this stuff much, Smith, not to the other supers, not to anyone. Partly, it's safer that way. Partly, I can sometimes forget it's happening, that way."

Lozano and I left the storeroom, back to his office, he to his paperwork, me to punch my time card and head up above.

"What now?" he asked.

"I don't know. I'm going to sit on this for a while," I said. "There's something else I need to know, another piece, before I'm done."

That wasn't completely accurate. It was true I didn't have the whole picture, not even close. There *was* one more thing I wanted to know, to be able to show, and my plan was to try for it at the end of the day.

But whether I was satisfied or not, whether I got what I wanted or got a handful of air, I was ready to come in. One more try; then I'd call Bzomowski and Mackey, go down to the precinct, give them everything I had, no matter if I had everything I wanted or not. I'd waited too long already, and what I had might be enough. Three murders, one attempt. At least two scams that needed to be protected. If all this was connected, as it had to be, this was way beyond me now, and the end that would be best for Chuck, for Denise Armstrong, and for all the men on this site, wasn't something I could control anymore.

But I didn't tell that to Lozano. I didn't want him afraid, knowing how close I was to blowing the whole thing. Not that I was worried about Lozano. He wasn't dangerous. But frightened men are unpredictable: they act in strange ways, and they talk. If Lozano felt safe, at least for now, my chances were better of coming up with something when I took my last shot.

"Sit tight," I said. And for some reason, looking into his eyes, I said, "I'm sorry, Lozano." He nodded, and half smiled.

I left the office, felt Lozano staring after me as I went. I didn't close the door behind me; all the men knew Lozano's door was always open.

I crossed the raw concrete from the trailer offices to the hoist, ready to head for the sixth floor, ready to start the day. Mike, I knew, would be up there by now, laying out our work, wondering where I was, wondering about me. I stood at the barrier with three other guys, watched the hoist creak down from above. I was ready to step on, but when it opened, it wasn't empty.

Dan Crowell, Jr. and Denise Armstrong, both in green Crowell hard hats and deep in conversation, moved aside as they came out, to let us enter.

I almost made it, almost walked right past her behind a tall pipefitter I thought might shield me. But it didn't happen. Still talking to Dan Junior, she glanced around her, it seemed automatically, to get the lay of the place. An instinct, maybe, so nothing would take her by surprise.

I did.

She stopped in the middle of her sentence. "Mr. Smith!" She stared into my eyes.

"Mrs. Armstrong," I answered smoothly, stepping back out of the hoist I'd gotten halfway into. The operator closed it and it started up without me. "How are you?" I asked before she had a chance to say anything else.

Crowell Junior looked from her to me. "Smith," he said. "You two know each other?"

"I worked for Mrs. Armstrong on another job," I answered.

"That little terra-cotta renovation up Broadway. Your office?" I said to her, making it a question, though not the one I was asking out loud. "Nice building. Well built, when it started. Easy to repair, because of that."

"Yes," Denise Armstrong said. She'd skipped half a beat, but maybe no one noticed that but me. When she spoke, her tone was deliberate, her smile impersonal. "My office. Quite a good job, that renovation. You're working here now?"

"Yes. I'd heard you owned this building, too."

"I do. I trust the work you do here will be up to the standard your employers have come to expect from you, Mr. Smith." She smiled again, a smile that was borderline frosty, and turned away. "Dan, I need to ask you about the windows." She started across the concrete without looking back. Dan Junior trotted after her.

I lit a cigarette, watched them on the other end of the building, Dan Junior pointing out details at an opening in the masonry, Denise Armstrong nodding her head. The groan of wood and the creak of gears announced that the hoist guy had come back for me. He made some crack about buddying up to the big boss; I made some crack about using it if you've got it. He took me up to the sixth floor and I headed along the scaffold to find Mike DiMaio, and my work.

DiMaio was laying a reinforcing ladder in a bed of mortar when I came up. "Christ," I said, "you got that far already?" We were working high by now, above his shoulders, almost to mine, and yesterday we'd rigged a plank platform on the scaffolding to work from, to bring our work back to waist height. A few more brick courses and we'd have to take the planks out from the scaffolding above, to stick our heads through as we finished out the bay.

DiMaio looked down at me. From the platform he was taller than I was, though not by much. "Someone's gotta do some work around here, Smith," he said. "I got here early."

"So did I." I slung my tool bag onto the platform next to where I'd be, stepped up there myself. I looked at his work, found my place in it.

For a while I worked silently, following DiMaio's lead, placing the bricks and the mortar and the ladders, laying in the ties. The sun from the east was hot and steady, throwing criss-cross shadows from the safety netting onto our work, and us.

DiMaio didn't have much to say either, just tips to help me out. Lozano came around once, with his clipboard, greeted us both as though it were the first time that day. Kenny, the Jamaican laborer who was low-ranking man on the crew, and, on that account, stuck with the daily coffee run, came by to ask what we wanted. We gave him our orders and a few bucks, and went back to work.

I started a shift in the pattern, headers that would mark a line around the building at the level of the center of the windows. DiMaio's line was done, and he'd begun the bricks between the window openings, something we were both supposed to be responsible for.

I placed a brick, tapped it back, moved it forward, to line it up with the one beside it. "Mike?" I said.

"Yeah?"

"I have a line on what happened to Reg."

DiMaio froze in his movements. Then he reversed them, put the brick he'd just lifted back down on the pile he'd gotten it from, straightened up. He turned to face me.

"You been standing here all goddamn morning and you waited till now to tell me?"

"I'm not sure," I said. "But it fits. But I don't want you to do anything about it, Mike."

"What the hell does that mean?"

"If I'm right, it's part of the whole thing. But I don't know how and I can't prove it. I want to work it out, so I know; then I want to go to the cops. They'll take care of it."

"I can't believe you fucking know what happened and you're just standing there like that."

"I told you, I don't know. I have an idea. I want to tell you. But I want *you* to tell *me* you won't go off half-cocked."

He regarded me silently, motionless on the scaffold. The sun had moved around by now; we were both in shadow.

"What you're saying," he spoke slowly, "is that it wasn't

Joe. Because if it was, you wouldn't give a shit what I do, being he's gone."

"I think it was Joe," I said. "But it goes deeper than that."

"Then what the fuck—?"

Steps on the scaffold made us both turn; it was Kenny, carrying a cardboard box from the deli on one palm, like a tray. "Great," DiMaio said. "Coffee break. You can tell me about it on our own time, not Lozano's." We took our coffee and doughnuts from the box. Kenny grinned, wandered on past us, whistling a reggae tune.

DiMaio and I sat in the shadow of our work. I peeled the plastic top off my coffee.

"I went up to City College."

DiMaio ripped open two sugar packets, gave me a questioning look. "You really think that has something to do with it?"

"Not directly. But Reg had a project going that involved studying the drawings for this building."

"Yeah, he told me. See if he could figure out what the engineer was thinking, or something."

I nodded, swallowed. The coffee was only lukewarm, but my cinnamon doughnut was fresh.

"You think there's something wrong with the drawings? With the design of this thing?" DiMaio asked.

"Not what he was looking at. Not the structure, the important stuff. But there is something wrong, and I think he saw it."

"What are you talking about?"

I reached up, picked a reinforcing ladder off the platform. "This stuff," I said. "You were the one who clued me in. All the cheap materials going into this building. It wasn't what Reg was looking for in the drawings, but I think he saw it."

"Saw what? That the place was made out of cheap shit?"

"No. Saw that it wasn't supposed to be. This isn't what's in the drawings, Mike, or the spec. The building was designed to be quality, inside and out."

"That's bullshit. How can it? Lozano buys us what the specs say to buy. The architect must have called for this shit."

I shook my head. "I had a look at the spec. The stuff I saw was higher quality than this. If I could see that, Reg must have seen it, too."

"But the architect's rep that comes around, that skinny guy—"

"Hacker. He's in on it."

"In on it? In on what?"

I told him about the scam, how it worked, Hacker and all the subs, but I didn't take it all the way back. The telling didn't take long. His face reddened as I talked.

"Shit!" he exploded when I was through. His voice was hoarse. "Son of a fucking bitch! Lozano, that son of a bitch—"

"No," I said. "Mike, I can't say it was right, what he did. But he did it for the men who work for him."

"Don't tell me he was doing me a fucking favor! I don't need to be part of shit like this! I can get work—"

"Maybe. And maybe if you don't, it won't matter for a while, you can ride it out. But Frankie has a kid going to college in the fall, first in his family, ever. And Ray's wife is sick."

He shook his head, face hard. "Don't make me part of this, Smith. Don't make the guys part of it."

"I'm just asking you to calm down. Not to do anything. There's more, Mike."

"What the hell do you mean, there's more?" He stopped. "Jesus Christ, what are you telling me? You're saying Reg found out what was going on, and Lozano had Joe try to whack him?" He stared at me. "I'll kill that bastard—"

"Not Lozano, Mike. I don't think so."

"Who, then?"

"Crowell."

That silenced him. In the quiet that fell between us, I realized the sounds on the site had changed, the rhythms of work replacing the rhythms of rest. Coffee break was long over; DiMaio and I were lucky the foreman was also the site super, that he had so much more to do than come around and check on us.

We climbed to our feet without exchanging a word, took

our places on the platform, and began work again. Once we were established, our pattern and our moves, DiMaio spoke without looking at me. His words were deliberate, timed with his movements as he used his hammer to snap a brick in half. "What the hell do you mean, Smith? What do you mean, it was Crowell?"

I said, "I thought this was a scam the subs had going, something they were putting over on Dan Junior. That's what Hacker thinks. But Lozano says it was Dan Junior who put the idea to him."

"Dan Junior? Dan fucking Junior?" DiMaio's voice was sharp with scorn. "He never in his life came up with something like this. Too soft. Too chicken."

"Then who?"

"Christ! The old man, of course. If it's really Crowell. Jesus, that's fucking hard to believe. But that's what Lozano says?"

"Yes."

"Well, then, I guess that's it."

I nodded, thinking that even now, even though he knew what Lozano had been doing, DiMaio was ready to believe something was true if Lozano said it.

"What gets me is, why?" DiMaio went on. "Big company like them, what do they need this kind of penny-ante shit for?"

"They're in debt, Mike. It was supposed to be a stop-gap thing, just a couple of months until they were on solid ground again. According to Lozano the price they gave Mrs. Armstrong for this job was much too low."

"Why'd they do that? Why not just give her a price she could live with, and do the job right?"

"Junior thinks the reason is the old man's losing it."

"Oh, right. And Junior'd know. You seen the old man lately? He seem to you like a guy losing it?"

"No. But look, Mike. Senior's sick, times are bad, it's a big job, a great opportunity. He must have wanted it a lot. And Mrs. Armstrong's a pretty tough cookie; I'll bet she had the contractors bidding hard against each other."

"You mean he might have just blown it, come in too low

because he wasn't thinking right, had so much on his mind and all?"

"Could have happened. And now he's got to make good on it."

"That would be like him. 'I goddamn said it, now I'm gonna do it, no matter what.' Or," he swung his hammer, cracked another brick, "more likely the old man decided he'd been a sucker all his life, that he could make a lot more money this way than the old way."

"He could also ruin a lifetime's worth of reputation."

"What the hell does he care? He's not gonna last much longer."

"Then what's the point of making all that money?"

DiMaio snorted. "To leave something for Dan Junior. He probably figures he's gotta give Junior the biggest head start he can come up with, because Junior's gonna run through every penny as soon as the old man's not around anymore to tell him what to do."

"You think it'll happen that way?"

"Sure. Junior's got no nose for this business, and he don't seem to like it much. He's only here because his father's handing it to him on a silver platter."

"That's what Hacker said. But he also said that Junior claims the old man needs help, that's why he's here."

"Help!" DiMaio snorted. "What a pair. They're helping each other, you and me are busting our butts, and the people gonna move into this dump are gonna get leaks at their windows and short out their wires every time they plug in the damn coffeepot while the TV's on. Help. Jesus," he said. "I hope nobody ever tries to help me."

It took me the rest of the morning to get a promise out of DiMaio that he wasn't going to go straight to the Crowell trailer with a crowbar.

"The police will handle it," I said, not for the first time. I jumped down off the platform, stepped to the edge of the scaffold to peer critically at the course of bricks I'd just completed. It was a good, sharp line, the joints not as perfectly identical to each other as the joints DiMaio had done, but overall, starting and ending at the right spots, level and clean and pleasing to look at. "When it's laid out for them, as far as I have it, they'll be able to fill it in. If what happened to Reg is connected up, they'll find it."

"If that's true, then what the fuck are you crapping around up here laying bricks for? Why haven't you gone to them already?"

"Because there's one more piece," I said. "One more thing I don't understand."

"Who the hell gives a shit what you understand? With all due respect, Smith."

"You're right," I said, climbing back onto the planks of the platform. "But there's someone else involved, Mike. A guy who's connected, and bad enough on his own that that almost doesn't matter. He's slipped out from under enough raps already. I want to make sure he doesn't slip out from under this one."

DiMaio turned to look at me. "Connected? Who? And what's he got to do with this, any of it?"

"I don't know the answer to that, but it's what I want to be able to hand to the cops, all tied up and wrapped in blinking neon. Because the cops have missed him before, when they should have had him." And if they hadn't, Lenny Pelligrini's mother might not be sitting dressed in black in her darkened living room. And her sister might not be looking at her own son with fear in her eyes. And Chuck DeMattis might still be a cop, might not have run out of words to say to me in a tiny back garden in Howard Beach.

"Who is this guy?" DiMaio wanted to know.

I looked at him over my shoulder. "Mike, you were ready to take me on right here on the scaffold a few days ago, when you thought *I* was connected. I was dumb enough to go up against this guy myself yesterday, and lucky enough to have a friend there who saved my sorry butt. You're probably smarter than I am, but I'm not sure you're as lucky."

"All of which means what?"

"Means I'm not going to tell you who the hell he is."

"Oh, because you're being a big hero and saving *my* sorry butt?"

"No," I said. "Because I don't think I'm enough of a hero to do that, so I don't want to have to try."

DiMaio went back to his bricks, and I to mine. A few minutes later as he laid a level along the windowsill he said to me, "So what are you going to do about it?"

"About what?"

"About this guy who's connected."

"I'm going to try one more time to see if I can tie him in."

"How?"

"You don't need to know."

"Yeah," he said. "Yeah, I do."

I looked over to where he was.

"I do," he said, "because I want to go down there and knock Crowell's fucking head off. Both of those bastards, and Lozano too. If I'm not gonna do that, I want to know exactly why. What is it you're gonna do and how long is it gonna take you?"

"One more night," I said. "Tonight."

"Doing what?"

"Mike—"

"You tell me, or God help me, Smith, all bets are off."

He was facing me now, on the platform. He'd put down his tools, the brick he'd been about to place; his hands were empty.

I watched him there, standing without movement, not advancing or retreating; sure of what he wanted, sure of what he could do.

"I'm going to break into the Crowell trailer and go through the files," I said.

For a moment, no reaction; then a grin broke onto his face. "Shit," he said. "You are?"

"Why not?"

"You can do shit like that?"

"I can't lay bricks," I said. "I've got to be able to do something."

He shook his head. Then he said, "Looking for what?"

"I don't know. That connection. The thing to tie this guy to them."

"And if you find it, you'll go to the cops?"

"Either way, Mike. I'm going to take this one last shot. But either way."

At lunch break I took a quick trip to the pay phone on the corner and called Lydia.

"Crowell Construction."

"It's me."

"Oh, are you still alive?"

"Not funny."

"Depends."

"I need you to do something for me."

"Anything."

"You mean that?"

"No."

"Well, see if I care. I want the code for the trailer alarm."

"Here?"

"Where else?"

"Well, not right now."

"No," I said. "When you can. Call my service. I'll call in. Will you be able to?"

"I think so. Today?"

"Yes. For tonight."

"Want help?"

"No."

"Damn."

"Sorry."

"Got to go," she said. "Good-bye."

Lydia was as good as her word; but she always is. At afternoon coffee break, I went back to the corner phone, called my service, and had a smoky-voiced young woman tell me, " 'Outside, three, five, one and four together, seven. Inside, one, two, eight, four, four. On the wall behind the door. File key, Verna's desk, top drawer.' I hope that makes sense to you."

"Completely," I said. "Run it by me again?"

She did, and I made sure I had it. I stuck the flat mason's pencil and the scrap of paper I'd scratched the numbers on into my back pocket, thanked her and hung up.

I finished out the day on the scaffold, cleaned my tools, rode the hoist down with the other men. DiMaio was edgy, staring into the sun still high over the river as the hoist lowered toward the mud and dust of the end of the day.

"Tonight?" he said to me as we crossed the bare concrete, made our way between the steel columns, under the exposed ductwork and piping and conduit that would be the lungs and arteries of this building, when it was ready.

"What?"

"Whatever you're doing. Your next big move, whatever. Then you go to the cops?"

"Yes."

"No matter what?"

"No matter what, Mike."

"You get what you want, you don't get it, it don't make no difference? You're not gonna wait?"

"No."

He nodded. "Good. Because I'm going on up to see Reg, now. I'm gonna tell him you got it figured out and you're gonna get those SOBs."

I looked at him in surprise. "Is he conscious? Will he understand? Will he respond?"

He shrugged. "I haven't seen him respond to nothing I said, yet. But I think he'll understand."

twenty

We clocked out with three or four other masons, got a nod and a grunt from Lozano, deep in his paperwork. He raised his eyes to us; the look that fell on me might have been a little longer, more uncertain, than the one DiMaio got, but I didn't react, punched my time card like a guy with nothing more on his mind than a beer at the end of the day. DiMaio cut Lozano a look of his own, but Lozano didn't catch it, and DiMaio, after a moment, turned and left. He headed for the ramp, for the street and the heat and the traffic of a city afternoon.

I didn't.

I wandered away from the field office trailers, away from the ramp, away from the other men, the guys wiping sweat from the backs of their necks, lighting cigarettes, jiggling pockets full of subway change. No one saw me go.

On the south side, where our building butted up against the buildings that sat on the other half of the block, the walls were up already for the places that would hold janitor's sinks, telephone switchgear, electrical boards. Much later, other trades would come and put their equipment into these rooms the masons had built. Right now, small and windowless, their concrete block rough and their floors unfinished, these dim, square caves smelled dank, echoed with the silence of things begun and abandoned.

I settled into one of them, decided it was made for phone equipment, imagined in my head the endless clicking as con-

tacts and wires shuttled future conversations into this building
and out of it, back and forth from this place to the wide world,
in the day when this place we were building would be full of
life.

I lit a cigarette, listened to the tiny sizzle of the match as I
dropped it into a puddle on the concrete beside me. In the dark
I opened my lunchbox, took out the thermos I'd filled at the
afternoon coffee break. I smoked, I drank black coffee, and I
waited.

Construction workers left the site at four-thirty. The
Crowell office closed for the day an hour later. I'd give Dans
Senior and Junior another half hour after that, then go over
and see if the coast was clear. If the trailer wasn't empty, I'd
reoccupy my switchgear room, give them more time. I wanted
to get into that trailer tonight.

Probably I was being a fool, probably there was no percentage in this. What I wanted to find in the trailer was something, anything, that would tie Louie Falco into the Crowells,
into the substitute-materials scam and the deaths that I was
sure, somehow, grew out of it, so that, when I turned the
Crowells over to the cops, I could give them Falco too. Falco
all knitted in, Falco in a way no one could overlook, Falco
wrapped up in the way Chuck had wanted him wrapped up,
when Chuck brought me into this with hearty fellowship and
half-truths.

Maybe there was no percentage, but there shouldn't be
much of a problem, either. I had the office codes. I could get
the file keys. I had a feeling the night security guard had a lot
to do and didn't do it particularly avidly. I could avoid his
rounds, see if I got lucky. If I did, good. If not, I was on my
way to the cops, to give Bzomowski and Mackey the
Crowells. It would be up to them, then, to see what the
Crowells would give them.

I sat with my back against the cool unpainted block, took
up the time by letting the Scriabin études play in my head. I
went over the parts I didn't understand, back through what
wasn't clear to me. Nothing resolved itself, none of the reasons for the unexpected transitions, or the harmonies that to

me were discordant, were revealed as I let the notes and meters drift through my mind. But sometimes it happens that way, that as I work on a piece the only way I know, the piece is working itself out in a place in me I can't reach, don't even really understand. Then one day I'll sit down to play it and know things I never knew before, things I couldn't tell you when I learned.

The guard's footsteps came, went, came back, went again. I timed his round, figured when in the cycle of yard–north side–south side he most likely checked the trailers. I gave Dan Senior and Dan Junior that extra half hour to clean up their paperwork, finish the last phone call, and lock up. I gave the guard the time beyond that to be just far enough away from the trailers that he wouldn't see me coming, but close enough that he wouldn't be on his way back for a while.

Then I started.

It was still early on a July evening. Outside, on Ninety-ninth Street, the drivers heading west would be wearing sunglasses, putting up their hands to shield their eyes from the piercing brightness of the setting sun. Here in the brick-wrapped depths of a construction site, scaffolding shadowing the window openings and just a few caged lightbulbs glowing feebly, it was twilight. The trades that were working indoors had worklights, but those were off now, and in the dimness, the sweep of bare wires and the odd shapes of columns and ducts did not announce their functions, gave no clue to their value or their place.

I made my way quietly between the dark bulks that were the field office trailers, along the way I had walked my first day here, until I came to the biggest, the general contractor's, Crowell's. Usually near the trailers the growl of air conditioners could be heard through every other sound; some of the field offices had two or three, stuck haphazardly out windows or on roofs. Their constant rumble was the underlying sound of work as the day went on. Inside the raw building, the air was cool, as always; but in the trailers, with their scuffed vinyl tile, their fluorescent lights and Formica tabletops, it would be as stuffy as in any small room anywhere.

That first day the air conditioners had been rumbling and the other noises on the site had started before I'd arrived, had built up as I talked to Lozano, had been going full blast by the time I'd stepped back out of his office with my assignment. Now, with the workday long over, the stillness was almost total. My own soft footsteps were sounds I could hear; a honking horn on Broadway and the gentle flap of a piece of loose scaffold netting caught by a breeze reached me here, deep inside the center, deep under the rising skeleton and skin that would be the building above me.

At the Crowell office door, I stopped to listen, for voices, for other footsteps than my own. I heard nothing. The steel-meshed trailer windows showed no lights; the guard seemed to be far away. I pressed the numbers I'd gotten from Lydia into the keypad lock on the door. I knew it would open and it did. Behind the door, on the left, was the alarm keypad, as Lydia had said, and I pressed the numbers there too. The red light turned to green in plenty of time, and I crossed the room to Verna's desk, to find the key to the files.

It was where it should have been, in a little tray in the top drawer. A tiny silver key; I took it, but didn't use it yet. All I wanted was one connection, one link; Falco's phone number in Crowell's Rolodex, his address in their book, would be enough. I took out my penlight, paged through the appointment calendar on Verna's desktop, but I didn't find anything.

Crowells Senior and Junior each had an office, and probably each had card files and appointment books. Senior's office was closer, so why not start there? I moved silently across the outer office and through Senior's door, found his desk, his card file.

I had just begun flipping through it when a soft sound behind me made me whip around, but too late.

A black crash of pain exploded at the back of my head. Thrown forward, I grasped for the edge of the desk, but my hands couldn't grip. I slipped, landed hard on the floor. The last thing I saw before the blackness engulfed me was my own hand dropping the tiny silver key.

* * *

Pain smacked me slowly, rhythmically, in the face, but the real bursting, blinding pain pounded inside my head with each blow. Half-aware, I tried to lift my hand, keep the blows from landing, but my arms wouldn't move. I turned clumsily on my side, to move away. A hand pushed me onto my back again, and I heard myself groan as my head hit the floor. Another smack. A voice said, "Wake up, you son of a bitch."

I started to open my eyes, but the bright light above me was a stabbing pain as bad as the pounding. I squinted, trying to find the voice. Another blow; with the pain, a wave of nausea.

"The light," I said, my lips thick, my words a harsh croak. More awake now, I tried to move my arms again, but my wrists were bound tight together behind my back.

There were no more blows; I lay still, heard someone move around the room, then come back.

"It's off," the voice said. "Open your eyes and talk to me, Smith, or I'll blow your fucking head off."

I opened my eyes again then, and found myself looking into the shadowed, soft face of Dan Crowell, Jr. "What the fuck are you doing in my trailer?" he said.

He was standing over me as I lay on the floor of his father's office. The light in the outer office, Lydia's office, was on, spilling in through the door. I opened my mouth to make some sort of answer, but before I did he lifted his right hand, showed me the silenced revolver there, pointed it at my head.

"I'm not much of a shot," he said. "But you're a hell of a target. You yell, make any kind of noise, no one'll hear you, but I'll shoot you anyway. Got that?"

Behind his words I could hear the churning of the air conditioners; cold air fell on me in waves from the one in the window above me.

I didn't think I had the strength to make a noise you could hear from the next room; forget about outside the trailer over the air conditioners, as far away as wherever the guard might be now.

"Yeah," I managed.

"Good. Now answer the question. What the hell are you doing in here?"

"I was trying to rob you, for Chrissakes. Could you move that gun?"

The gun went nowhere. "What do you mean, rob me?"

"Jesus, what do you think I mean?" I rasped. "I had a run of bad luck at the track. Two guys named Guido are out to break my legs. Every GC I ever worked with keeps cash in the office. I was looking to score."

"How'd you get in?"

"Happens to be something I can do, beat an alarm system. I learned it in Houston."

Dan Junior didn't move fast, but he didn't have to. There wasn't anyplace I could go. He stooped, swept the gun butt into the side of my head. Pain crashed like cymbals, burst like fireworks. Over it, I heard him speaking.

"Bullshit, Smith. You're not from Houston, you're not a fucking mason. You're a goddamn private eye, you work for DeMattis, and I want to know what the fuck you're doing in my trailer."

He stepped over me, perched on the edge of his father's desk; the movement was dizzying for me to follow. He tossed something toward me; it fluttered down and landed on my chest. The copy of my license, from under the flap in my wallet.

"If you're thinking about stalling until the guard comes around," he said, "don't bother. He knows I'm in here. What the hell, it's my trailer. I'm working late, so what? He won't come looking over here. He won't hear you, Smith, he'll never see you. If I shoot you, he'll never know. Talk. That's your only choice."

"Shit," I said, so weakly I could barely hear myself. I asked him, "You knew all along?"

"What, that you weren't a mason? If I had, you'd have been out on your can the day you started."

"Mrs. Armstrong told you."

"Nah. It was your little sweet-talk with her before that tipped me off, but she just blew right by it. But I started thinking: you just came up from Houston, how did you work for her five years ago when she did her office? You didn't work for her, how do you know her? So I got your social security number from the records, did some looking into it. Looks like you and that little Chinese girl aren't the only investigators around here."

He smiled smugly. "So, what, Smith? She put you here? Tell me about it."

So Mrs. Armstrong hadn't blown my cover. Well, I could return the favor. "No. I work for DeMattis. I met her a couple of years ago, on a whole other case. She was probably as surprised as anyone to see me here. Remember, DeMattis doesn't work for her. We work for you."

Crowell Junior nodded; then the smile faded. His soft face grew dark. "So now talk to me, Smith. Tell me what the hell you're doing here. Because here's the deal. You don't talk to me, I shoot you and stuff you in the hole Pelligrini left. You do talk, maybe you and I can make a deal."

I didn't believe that. One way or another, he was going to kill me, even if only because I'd seen him with a gun, threatening to kill me. Because now he'd shown me, if I hadn't known it before, that he had something to hide.

"So what the fuck were you doing in here?"

I was still dizzy, beginning to feel sick. Concussion, the part of my mind that could still think told me. You're going to fade out on your own soon, Smith. When you do, it's over. You have to set him up before that. I put as much strength into my words as I could. "Looking for something."

"What?"

"I don't know. Something concrete."

"What the hell does that mean?"

"You and the subs," I said. "Substituting crappy materials for what you were supposed to use. I know about it; I wanted solid proof."

He frowned, said, "To take to DeMattis?"

I tried to give him a laugh. The sound I made didn't convince me, but maybe he was an easier mark. "Screw DeMattis. I was going to bring it to you."

"What the hell—"

"Blackmail, you asshole. I didn't tell Chuck or that Chinese girl about it. Why would I? I thought it might be worth a couple of bucks to you and your father to shut me up."

I struggled to keep my eyes focused on him, fought to stay away from the edge of the black pit that yawned for me. Come on, Junior, I thought. Fall for it. Either way, I'm gone. But this way, maybe not Lydia, maybe not Chuck.

He appeared to be considering. "DeMattis doesn't know?"

"No."

"And that Chinese chick he insisted on sticking in the office—her either?"

"She doesn't know a damn thing. She was only there to get me the alarm code, that's all. She's not really an investigator, anyway."

Then: "I ought to shoot you myself for that."

My heart leaped, my blood raced, and Junior swung around at the sound of that voice. He wasn't fast enough to get ahead of Lydia. She was through the door and had her gun jammed into his back before he saw her move.

"Jesus," I breathed. "Where did you come from?"

"You told me you didn't need help," she said, from behind Dan Junior. "But remember, we decided I was going to stop listening when you said that?" Then she spoke quietly to Junior. "I'm going to take this gun out of your hand now. If your heart even starts to beat faster I'll shoot you. Thank you very much. Now go stand over there. Spread your legs and put your hands on the wall. Try not to move, I promise you'll like it better that way."

She stood motionless, waited for Junior to set himself up as instructed. I didn't move either, until he'd stopped; I didn't want to distract her. Then I sat up, slowly, carefully, closing my eyes against the flood of sickness that came with movement. Lydia, without taking her eyes off of Junior, rummaged around on Senior's desk, found a scissor, knelt behind me, and cut the tape from my wrists.

"What happened?" she said.

"I got cocky. I never heard him coming."

"Dumb."

"That's true," I agreed.

"You're bleeding," she said, her voice softer than before.

"I'm all right," I told her, as the room spun and the darkness gathered at the edges of my sight. I leaned my back against a file cabinet, tried to take some even breaths.

"Macho knee-jerk answer. You need a doctor." She stood, reached for the phone on the desk. "I'll call—"

"No," a man's voice came from the doorway, a voice used to being obeyed. "Don't do that."

The bulk of Dan Crowell, Sr. loomed in the light from the outer office. Standing in the doorway, he switched on the overhead lights in here, the ones Junior had shut off so I would talk to him. The sudden bright flood revealed Senior's angry face and the gun in his hand. My eyes squeezed shut, trying to block out the stabbing pain; I forced them open.

Looking up, I saw Lydia and Dan Senior facing each other, each with a revolver raised; but while hers was pointed at him, his was pointed at me.

"Put down the phone and the gun," Senior ordered her.

Lydia couldn't play the same game; Junior had moved fast away from the wall, was already behind his father.

Slowly, Lydia placed the phone in its cradle and the gun on the desk.

Under her breath, I heard her mutter, "Dumb."

Without moving, Senior demanded, "Daniel, what the hell is going on here?"

They know all about it, Dad, the materials and the murders and everything. We have to kill them and bury the bodies. That's what I expected to hear from Junior, what I waited for.

But Junior just looked stricken and confused. His mouth opened, closed again; he made no sound.

"Daniel!"

Still nothing from Junior; well, hell, then, let me try it.

"It's over, Crowell," I said, in a voice that sounded weak to me but got everyone's attention. "The materials scam and everything that grew out of it. Pelligrini, Romeo, Hamilton. Falco's part in it. We know. DeMattis knows. Give it up."

A lot of that was wild fabrication. I wasn't sure how the murders tied in and I still had no idea how Falco did. But all

I was selling here was the thought that there was no percentage in killing Lydia and me.

Senior said, "What the hell are you talking about?" He peered intently at me. "You're that mason, one of Lozano's men, came in that day to look at the drawings. What's going on?" He gestured at Lydia with the gun, to move over and stand next to me; easier to cover us both that way. Then he half turned, to face Junior.

"Daniel? What in goddamn blazes is this about?"

Again, Junior didn't answer, so again, I did.

"The scam kind of got out of hand, didn't it?" I said softly, calmly. Keep things even, bring the temperature down, get everyone's adrenaline level back to normal. Especially the guy with the gun. "It wasn't supposed to last long, just bring in a few bucks until times got better. But Reg Phillips found out about it by accident, right? And something had to be done about him. And Pelligrini? That's what happened to him, too? There isn't—"

"Pelligrini didn't know shit about that!" Dan Junior raised a tight fist. "You shut the fuck up!" He rushed across the room toward me. I scrambled to rise, to meet him, although I doubted I had the strength to handle even Dan Crowell, Jr.; but I didn't have to. Lydia took a quick side step, yanked him hard in the direction he was going. He crashed into the file cabinet I was leaning on, shaking my world with nausea and pain. With a moan, he slipped to the floor.

"Hold it!" Senior roared. Everyone stopped moving, everyone turned to him.

"You two," he said, coldly and deliberately, "shut up. Don't move, don't talk." We didn't need the wave of the gun to tell us which two he meant. "Daniel! Get the hell up and explain to me what's going on here. What are these people doing here? What scam is he talking about? What the hell do you know about what happened to Phillips and Pelligrini?"

Lydia and I exchanged looks. Her eyes were confused. Mine probably were, too. What did Senior mean, "What scam"? Why was he asking Junior what Junior knew?

Junior stood slowly, holding a hand to his head. The bandaged gash he'd gotten in the coalition fight had opened, started to bleed again.

He looked at his father's red, furious face, at his glowering eyes and tight mouth. Junior lowered his hand, straightened his back, and spoke.

"Joe Romeo hit Phillips over the head with a brick. I shot Pelligrini and buried him in the pit. Some son of a bitch I paid five thousand dollars to, threw Romeo off the scaffold, and then I shot that son of a bitch. That's what happened to them."

twenty-one

loud air-conditioner rumbling and soft breathing, and the pounding of my own heart; that was everything I could hear in Dan Crowell, Sr.'s office, as Lydia, Senior, and I stared at the man who'd just admitted to three murders.

He stood, soft body straight, facing his father, seeing no one else. The set of his shoulders and the line of his jaw showed me a Dan Crowell, Jr. I hadn't seen before, not even from the man standing over me with a gun, threatening to kill me.

"What?" Senior choked out finally, still red, still unmoving.

"What the hell else was I going to do?"

"Do? About what? Daniel, what do you mean?"

"Oh, Christ, Dad! Someone had to keep this damn business afloat. Someone had to run around cleaning up after you."

"Cleaning . . ." Senior frowned, showed a confusion that might have had as much to do with the tone of Junior's words as with their meaning. He spoke slowly to his son. "What the hell are you talking about? What did you do?"

"What I had to do. You're coming on like a Mack truck, like always, promising this, sure about that, but there's no goddamn money and the business is going down the tubes."

"No." Senior shook his head in bafflement. "What are you talking about? There was enough."

"Enough? Partial payments to the subs? Invoices six months behind to every goddamn supplier we have?"

"The subs know I'm good for it. In times like this they won't walk, where are they gonna go? And suppliers can wait. They always do."

"They were calling every three days! They hired collection agencies!"

"And I told you, when that happened, to give the calls to me! I can handle them. This is the way I've always done business, Daniel."

"No. You used to do business smart. There was always a cushion, something for the future. You were always spread around. Now all our eggs are in this one damn basket. You underfigured the fucking job, so you could look like a hero to Mrs. Armstrong, and even the price you gave her, she doesn't have. Mrs. Armstrong's sinking, broke, and you're bound and determined we're gonna go down with her!"

Senior was silent, his angry eyes boring into his son. Junior met that look without flinching. I wondered, suddenly, how many times in his life he'd been able to do that before.

"This was for the future, Daniel," Senior said. "Your future."

"The way you're going, there won't be a future."

"Mrs. Armstrong's not broke."

"The bank—"

Senior shook his head dismissively. "The new bank loan'll come through when we're fifty percent closed in. She has what she needs to take her through till then."

"Bullshit she does. Where'd she get it?"

"What's the difference where she got it? It's there. Things are tight, but we'll make it."

"She'll make it, you mean."

"We'll make it, Daniel. Crowell Construction has a partnership agreement with Armstrong Properties. Contingent on this project being successful."

Junior took a moment to answer. "Partnership? What the hell are you doing, setting up a partnership?"

Senior hesitated a moment, then demanded, "You mean, because I'm dying?" He spoke as though the hostility of his words could hide the pain behind them.

Junior's face reddened, but he answered. "Yeah. Yeah, that's what I mean. You've got to face facts, Dad. What makes you think you'll be around to carry out any partnership?"

"I won't. But you will."

"I—"

"You will, and you need this, Daniel. She's good. Smart, tough, ballsy. If this project's a success, people will be lining up to finance whatever she wants to do next. The contractor hooked up with her will be set up for life."

"Set up for life?" Junior repeated. He sounded like a man who was sure he was missing something, as though he thought that—looked at in a different light—what he was saying and what was being said to him would connect in some different, reasonable way.

"*If* this one's a success," Senior said. "That's the key. That's why I was cutting this so close. I had to show her, Daniel, show her that Crowell could do it. I knew it would make things tight now, but it was an investment. It was for your future."

Junior said nothing, but I thought I saw the steel in his spine start to give way, saw the softness in his body start to drag his shoulders down.

"It was under control, Daniel," Senior told his son. "I don't know what you thought, but it was under control."

Beside me, Lydia moved just slightly, touched my shoulder. Could I stand? she was asking. Could I be part of it, if this was the time to make our move?

I wasn't good for much, right now, but whatever Lydia started, whatever she needed, I'd try. I nodded, a movement so small and brief that Dan Senior never should have caught it.

But he did. The gun, which had never wavered, rose slightly, its meaning clear. His eyes met mine; he didn't have to speak. He looked for a moment at Lydia, then back at his son. "Why are they here?" he said. "Daniel, what did you do?"

I could imagine those words in that tone being spoken to a young boy standing in front of a broken window, a crumpled fender.

"I—" Junior started, and then again: "I— Why the hell didn't you tell me?"

"Tell you what?"

"About the partnership! About why you were cutting things so goddamn close, why you lowballed the price, why there wasn't any money! Why didn't you tell me?"

Senior looked genuinely puzzled. "I would have," he said, "if I'd thought you needed to know."

Junior looked into his father's eyes. He didn't speak.

Then something happened in his own eyes, a slow dulling, an extinguishing. Rust on once-bright metal; dust and ashes smothering the mirrored surface of polished stone. He let out a breath, a long, soft exhalation. Looking at no one, speaking in a monotone, he began once more, and laid out the materials scam, the subs' part and his own. Senior listened silently, nothing showing on his face.

"Phillips," Junior said, stared down at his hands. "Phillips found out. He was doing some school project. He asked could he look at the drawings and the spec. You told him yes."

He stopped, looked at his father, looked for something.

Senior nodded, and said, "You said you didn't think it was a good idea, laborers in the trailer. You said the same thing when this guy here came in. I couldn't figure out what your problem was."

"Yeah," Junior said. I might have expected bitterness; all I heard was defeat. "He's an honest guy, Phillips," Junior went on. "He came to me, when he saw it. It wasn't part of his school thing, the materials we were substituting, but he was working with the shit we were giving him every day, and he had his face buried in the drawings for a week. He saw it, and he came to me because he thought it was the subs. He thought it wasn't right. I told him thanks, and I'd take care of it. That bought me a little time, but he would have figured it out when he realized no one was getting fired and the shit the men were working with never changed."

"So you had Joe Romeo try to kill him?" Senior's voice was unbelieving.

"No. I told Romeo to buy him off. He couldn't, they argued, and what happened, happened."

"And then—"

"And then I was in!" A spark, more desperation than anger, ignited in Junior's eyes. "Jesus, I was up to my ass! On one side I had Romeo squeezing me; on the other side I had these fucking private eyes you goddamn had to hire, looking for some way to squeeze Romeo. I had to get rid of him."

Senior moved his eyes slowly then, to Lydia and me. His face was unreadable, hard, and the look he gave us was long. He turned back to his son.

"The coalition riot—?"

"It was a good idea," Junior said, raising his chin. "In fact, it was a great one."

The room was silent then, for a long time. Behind the pounding in my head I heard the echo of Joe Romeo's scream.

"You were the man who paid Chester Hamilton," I said, surprised to hear my own voice.

"How the hell do you know—"

"I was there."

Junior paled. "Where? When?"

"When you shot him," I said. "I was there."

He faltered, seemed unsure where to look. "What did he—?"

"Tell me? Just about everything, except your name; but what he was paid to do, where he met you, what you looked like. I put it all in my report to DeMattis."

More fabrication, and Lydia knew it, but standing quiet by my side, she showed nothing. Let him think the game was really up.

I said, "You shot him because you were afraid we'd find him. You didn't know I already had. The same as you killed Romeo because you thought if he were gone, we'd go away."

Senior stared at his son, spoke slowly. "That's what you said. The day Joe died, you said, 'Well, at least one good thing, we can get rid of those private eyes now.' You never wanted DeMattis here in the first place."

"I couldn't afford it! When you came back from that dinner with DeMattis's card in your pocket, saying you talked to him, you liked him, he suggested maybe we bring him in to look into the equipment that walked—Jesus, you don't know what that did to me!"

"And you talked me out of it."

"Until Pelligrini disappeared, and you got this asshole idea that it was Joe! And all of a sudden, we got DeMattis on board, and you don't even make him tell you what the hell he's doing. Did you know he had a guy on the scaffold?"

Senior looked over at me, shook his head slowly.

"Pelligrini," I said. The pain in my head was exhausting me, and the soft blackness, the sleepiness, was closing toward me from the edges of my vision again. I knew I had to fight it, though I wasn't sure, anymore, why. But talking seemed to keep it at bay, so I spoke again. "Pelligrini knew, too? He was shaking you down?"

"Not until after he disappeared. Before that, he was in, he was solid."

"After he disappeared? He was still alive?"

"Damn right. Alive and wanted to do business. For a shit-load of money, he'd keep quiet. Quiet! So we met, here, in the fucking basement. After that, he kept quiet." He looked at his father. "You should have told me," he said softly. "About the pump. I didn't know."

Senior met his son's eyes, then looked away, without an answer.

"In," Lydia said suddenly, beside me. "But not in the materials scam. You said he didn't know about that. The equipment that was stolen, then, that Pelligrini was fencing—that was you too, wasn't it?"

"Daniel?" Senior's voice wavered, as though he were standing on ground that was no longer solid. "Our equipment? You stole that?"

"Yeah, sure." Junior's words carried exasperation and disgust, but who it was for, I didn't know. "I set it up, Pelligrini stole it and fenced it. That was going pretty well, until you had to bring on another guard, tighten things up around here. Shit." He shook his head.

"Falco," I said, although speech was getting harder. "That's where Falco comes in. That's his connection, the stolen equipment. He must have been your receiver, the guy behind the fence."

Dan Junior said, "Who?"

"Oh, Jesus, come on," I said. "How much worse can it be? One way or another you killed three men, but you won't admit to doing business with a wiseguy?"

Senior said, "Daniel? Is this true, too?"

Junior said, "No. I'm not that dumb. Maybe someone like that was way back behind the guys I was dealing with, but I never heard of him."

"No," I said. The darkness was creeping in now, softening the pain, softening everything, and I knew I couldn't stop it. "No. He was closer than that. Something going *on this site.* Falco had something going *on this site.*"

Junior looked at Lydia. "What the hell is he talking about?"

Images came to me: Falco leaning on the railing in the evening breeze on the Staten Island Ferry; Elena Pelligrini, wearing black, sitting in her darkened living room; Chuck walking into the night beyond the smoked-glass windows of a noisy bar.

"It doesn't matter," I heard her say. "He needs a doctor."

"No." That was Dan Crowell, Sr. "No. I have to think."

"Don't make this worse," she warned him.

"I said no!"

Lydia had started to move; beside me, I felt her stop. That must have something to do with the gun. I realized my eyes had shut; I forced them open again.

"Daniel," Senior said, "why did you do all this? Just to keep the business going? Kill those men, plan all these elaborate schemes? What was it for?"

Junior met his father's eyes, but hesitated, as though, with everything he'd just told us, what he was about to say was the hardest admission of all. When he spoke, his voice was calm, with a clarity I hadn't heard before.

"For you," he said. "It was for you."

"Me?" Senior's voice was hesitant. That may have been an

answer he hadn't expected, maybe one he'd never heard before. "What does that mean?"

"Just until . . ." Junior appeared to gather strength, went on. "Another six months," he said. "Maybe a year. That's what the doctor said."

"For me?" Senior repeated. "Another six months?"

He said the words vaguely, sounding like he didn't know what they meant. He seemed to sag for a second, almost to go out of focus; then he sharpened, came back. "That's how long I'm going to live, Daniel. I know that. Then what? What were you going to do then?"

"I didn't care. It wasn't going to matter after that."

"What wasn't?"

"This business!" The sharp contempt in Junior's voice was a shock to me, chasing back the soft blackness like a sudden breeze. "Crowell Construction. The hell with it. I'd close it, or go bankrupt, or who gives a shit? I just needed to keep it going as long as you were around. As long as you cared."

"Why?"

Why. A simple question, the hardest of all to answer.

"Because I've been watching you," Junior said quietly. "Seeing your face every time you sent me out on the scaffold because you couldn't go yourself, every time you had to leave early because you were too tired to stay. When you asked me to come into the business, I knew you were really in trouble. Me, here? Jesus. But that's why I came. Because you wouldn't have wanted me here if you'd had a choice."

Senior seemed about to protest; Junior didn't give him a chance.

"And then," he said, "then, sometimes you'd screw up. That time you came back after chemo and called the steel guy to yell at him about where the hell was his delivery, and he'd delivered the week before. Shit like that. You were losing it."

He said that, soft chin jutting forward, and then paused, waiting for a response. Senior looked at him, but didn't seem able to speak.

Junior closed his eyes, maybe in relief, maybe in exhaustion. Opening them, he went on. "So when I saw how bad things were with the money, I thought it was the same thing. You screwing up, because you were sick. All I was trying to do was keep Crowell Construction going as long as you were around."

Senior stared, an expression of disbelief covering his features. He regarded his son as though he'd never seen him before.

"And all I was doing," Senior said slowly, "was trying to make sure it would keep going after that."

The black fog that surrounded me was thicker now, too dense to see or move through. I wasn't even sure whether people were still speaking, whether the silence that seemed to fill the room was real or was part of the fog. I tried to look around, to see.

Lydia spoke, calm, direct, controlled. "I'm going to the phone," she said. "I'm going to call a doctor."

"No."

That was Dan Crowell, Sr., as calm and controlled as she was.

"Don't make this worse, Mr. Crowell," Lydia said. "Mr. DeMattis has Bill's report. No matter what happens to us, this is over."

"Maybe not," Senior said, and his voice sounded sad to me. "There's nothing in that report but theories; if you had any real proof DeMattis and the cops would be here by now."

"And besides," Junior threw in eagerly, "Smith said before, he was in here looking for something for a shakedown. I don't think he actually told DeMattis anything. Maybe there's not even really any report." I saw him reach onto the desk for the gun Lydia had taken from him.

Oh, Christ, you idiot, I thought, partly for Dan Junior, partly for myself.

"I'm sorry, Lydia." Senior's voice came floating through the fog, and he truly did sound sorry. "I liked you from the beginning."

"Your son killed three men," Lydia said. "He stole from this building and from you."

There was the briefest of pauses before Senior said, "He's my son."

I couldn't move; the blackness was a weight now, bearing down on my arms and my body, making them heavy and slow. *Lydia,* I thought, trying to tell her silently, to make her understand, *take your chance when it comes, make your move.* I knew I couldn't help, couldn't be part of it; but I didn't want her holding herself back, keeping herself down because I was down, getting buried under the weight that was crushing me.

I willed her to move, to do something that would save her, that would end the chilling stillness, the old, deep silence that was filling the room.

Nothing; then soft words from Dan Crowell, Sr. in a tone I didn't like; unhurried movement, Dan Junior walking toward Lydia. I looked at her through the thickening blackness, tried to tell her something with my eyes. She stood still, met my look, turned to Junior.

And she didn't move; but a crash, a yell, a blur of motion erupted across the room. Dan Senior grunted, stumbled forward, someone's short arms snared around him from behind, crushing his own arms to his chest.

Then Lydia flew ahead, spun a kick that sent Senior's gun rocketing into the far wall. Junior swung, gun arm stiff, looking for a target. I heard the soft pop of a silenced shot and the metallic ring as a bullet hit steel. Junior yelled, moved, trained the gun on Lydia, but before he could shoot, the bulk of his father was shoved forward, into him. The Crowells, tangled together, off balance, crashed to the floor near me. Lydia and the other blur swooped down on top of them, Lydia wrestling the gun from Junior while the blur held Senior down.

Lydia straightened, held the gun out, said, "Hold this on them while I call the cops."

"What are you, crazy?" the blur panted, in Mike DiMaio's voice. "I'll call the cops. You hold that. I don't know shit about guns. I'm just a bricklayer."

twenty-two

Cops came, and paramedics, and so did the soft blackness I'd fought against. A complicated dance of people and equipment was played out to the accompaniment of soft questions and loud orders. I did nothing but what I was told, ended up on a stretcher with a needle in my arm and a bandage on my head. The last thing I knew about was the stretcher rolling through the shadows of the unfinished building, toward the ramp; the last things I saw were the lines and patterns of steel and pipe and wire emerging rhythmically, then disappearing again, in the darkness overhead.

In the morning, things were different. I was in St. Luke's, I had a mild concussion, I had a different needle in my other arm and drugs in me, and I woke up with Lydia sitting by the side of my bed and one question in my mind.

"Hi," Lydia smiled when she saw my eyes were open.

"DiMaio," I croaked. "What—?"

Lydia blinked. " 'Oh, Lydia, so nice to see you're alive too,' " she said airily.

"You're beautiful," I said, my voice hoarse, my throat scratchy. "I'm mad about you. I'm glad you're alive. I wouldn't want you any other way. DiMaio—"

"Who, me?"

That came from the chair beside Lydia, which, squinting, I realized was occupied too. I tried to move so I could see better, was reminded that movement ought to be slow for a while. I let the pain pass, grunted, "Yeah. You."

DiMaio grinned. That made everyone in the room smiling except me.

"Where—?" I said, swallowed to ease the dryness. "What—?"

"You mean, how come I popped up out of nowhere last night just in time to save your ass?"

"Yeah," I said. "I mean that."

"Well," he said, still grinning, resettling himself in his chair, "I was up here visiting Reg last night, you know, telling him what you were gonna do. And it's funny, but when a guy doesn't answer, you have to kind of do his part of the thinking, too."

"Sort of like what I have to do," Lydia remarked parenthetically, with a sweet smile at me.

I growled at her, "You think just because I'm lying here—"

"Oh, no," she protested. "I think that's *why* you're lying there."

"Mike," I sighed, "go on."

With a grin from her to me, DiMaio continued. "So, anyway, I thought to myself, if you screwed up—uh, I mean, if anything happened to you—maybe there wasn't anyone else who knew what you knew. See, I didn't know about Lydia then." They smiled at each other. My head hurt.

DiMaio went on. "So I thought, maybe these bastards'll get away with all the shit they've been pulling, if Smith screws up. Maybe no one'll ever pay for what happened to Reg. And I said that out loud to Reg, that I was worried about that. And you know what?"

"What?"

"He woke up. He looked at me. He didn't say anything, but he looked at me. Like he knew how it was when you and me was laying bricks together. You know?"

"Uh-huh." I knew.

"So when he did that, I knew what I was supposed to do. I was supposed to get my ass back to that trailer and make sure everything went all right."

"Christ," I mumbled. "A babysitter."

"One you needed," Lydia said.

"*We* needed," I pointed out.

"True. And I already thanked him."

I looked at DiMaio, met his clear blue eyes. I was searching for the words, the right ones, but he stood, stuck his hands in his pockets, grinned again. He said, "Nah. Wouldn't be like you, Smith. Say something nice, I might pass out or something."

"My job," I said. "Passing out. Hey."

"Hey what?"

"Speaking of jobs. Why aren't you at work?"

DiMaio looked away. "Site's closed down today."

"Shit," I breathed. "Just today?"

He shrugged. "For a while. Mrs. Armstrong's there, Crowell's bonding company's there. Cops, auditors, Christ knows what."

"Jesus," I said. "I'm sorry."

"Oh, I don't know." The grin came back suddenly. "My money's on Mrs. Armstrong. Word is, she made it clear she'll be goddamned if she's gonna stop this building. When the men showed up this morning, they told us call tomorrow. Seems like some trades could be back to work in a day or two."

"That's good news."

DiMaio, hands still in his pockets, looked down at the floor, pushed at something with the toe of his workboot. "Lozano was there. I saw him."

"What did he say?"

"Nothing. He had nothing to say to me, I had nothing to say to him. Just looked at each other. Shit." He shook his head. "I liked that guy."

"I know. So did I."

Lydia rose from her chair, stood next to DiMaio. "Now that you're conscious," she said to me, "go back to sleep. The police will come by later, to talk to you. I already spoke to Bzomowski and Mackey."

"They know about Hamilton?" I asked. "About me being there?"

She nodded. DiMaio glanced from me to her, seemed about to ask something. Lydia stopped him with a look, the kind that says, *I'll tell you later.*

"They're pissed?" I asked her.

"Angry but ready to talk. Depending on what you have to offer, it will probably turn out all right. You want me to stay, for when they come?"

"No," I said, closing my eyes, inviting the soft darkness back. It didn't come, just regular tiredness, and relief. "No, I'll deal with them. You kids run along."

I opened my eyes briefly when I heard DiMaio snort, smiled and closed them again as Lydia leaned forward and brushed her soft lips on my cheek.

Chuck came to see me later that day, moving through the door hesitantly, with a worried smile. Whether the worry was for how I was, or for how things were between us, wasn't clear.

"Hey," he said, looking down at me from the side of the bed. "You still speaking to me?"

"Why not?" I asked.

He shrugged. "Oh, I don't know. I lied to you. I sent you into what turned out to be a den of God-knows-what. You came this close to getting killed and it wasn't me had anything to do with pulling you out. Other than that, I guess, no reason."

"Hell," I said, "every friendship has its problems."

He relaxed then, but after that, I didn't have much to say to him, though I wasn't sure why. Something I'd heard, something I knew, kept me from hearing him, from saying to him anything he didn't know. I was waiting, until I could think more clearly, remember better.

He seemed to take it as a symptom, the sleepiness and distraction of a man with a concussion. I let him think that, didn't tell him about Falco and the ferry, didn't ask him anything. Finally, he left.

The cops were easier. Bzomowski and Mackey turned out to be okay guys, one tall, one shorter, one light, one dark, one younger, one about my age. They were pissed off at me because I was there when Hamilton was shot and never told them; they were pissed off because I'd been investigating and hadn't given them anything I'd found; they were pissed off because I was a P.I. and they were cops. I couldn't blame them for any of that.

Given all that, though, the interview went smoothly, only two or three threats to pull my license, only one—from Bzomowski—to throw me in jail the minute I got out of the hospital. It was a chess game and we all knew it. I would give them everything I had, except some sources—in this case, Maggio—that they would half-heartedly try to squeeze out of me. I would testify if the case came to court, though the way it looked, it wouldn't: Dan Junior's lawyer, at the request of his client, was already working on a plea bargain, all charges against the old man to be dropped in return for Junior-tells-all. And I would keep my license with the provisional warning that I wouldn't be this lucky if I ever crossed their paths again.

Then—five years from now in Bzomowski's case, ten in Mackey's—I'd be drinking in some cop watering hole and some cop I knew would tell me that a detective buddy of his had put in his twenty years, resigned, and gotten himself a private license, guy was pretty good, did I have any business I didn't want I could throw his way, get him started off? And I'd say sure, no problem; I'd finish my beer and leave my card. In between that and this it wasn't likely I'd see these guys again.

So when Bzomowski and Mackey decided we were through, and my hospital room was empty again, my mind went back to Chuck. I tried to loosen the reins, let my thoughts wander, see if whatever it was I was uneasy about would surface. I knew who'd killed Pelligrini, Romeo, Hamilton; I knew who'd attacked Reg Phillips. I knew about Falco, as far as he went with Chuck; I knew that was what Chuck hadn't been telling me. Chuck had admitted it, even apologized for it.

So what was my problem?

Falco's connection, that was one of the things still bothering me. I let it rise to the top, watched it and considered it, but didn't try to pin it down. Like working on a piece of music I didn't understand, I made myself stop trying to get it to be what I wanted, and just look and work with it and see what it was.

Chuck had told me Falco was connected on that site. That's why he'd been so eager to take this job on when it came, because it might be his way to shut down Falco at last.

But Dan Crowell, Jr. said he didn't know him. No point in lying about that. He would have been better off saying, *Yeah, the Mafia made me do it.* Bzomowski and Mackey would have eaten it up; that's the kind of stuff that can make a cop's career, if he can bring it home.

So what then? Falco behind someone smaller, Lozano maybe, or one of the other subs? I didn't see it. Not enough money to be made. Behind the guy buying the stolen equipment? Not close enough. Not on the site.

Maybe Chuck was wrong.

I let that idea float around for a while, a new variation, a disharmony that changed the nature of the piece completely.

Chuck had said Falco was tied in here, but he'd gotten that from someone he referred to as "street scum." Maybe he was just wrong. Maybe there was no connection. It wasn't as though you needed one to explain any of these things, anything that had happened.

I followed the new idea, to see what would happen if it were true, if Falco were out of the picture. What I found out was that I was still uneasy, that something else was still eating at me. I tried some more to figure out what it was, but I got nowhere. I'd just decided to forget it, to let the question stay where it was, moving vaguely in the shadows in my head, maybe see if sleep would make a difference in my outlook, when the bedside phone rang.

"Hi," I said, figuring it was Lydia, wanting her to think I was feeling good.

"For a man who's just caused an enormous amount of disruption which he almost didn't survive himself, you're remarkably cheerful," a woman's voice told me drily.

"Mrs. Armstrong. How are you?"

"Probably better than you, though it's likely I've had less sleep," she answered.

"Every cloud has a silver lining. To what do I owe the honor?"

"Damage control," she said bluntly.

"Are you at the site?"

"Yes," she said. "I have been since the police called me last night, about the same time the EMS took you out of here. This is the first chance I've had to be alone, and I don't know how long it will last."

"And you're calling me? I'm flattered."

"Don't be. The amount of trouble you've caused here will take me months to undo."

"I didn't cause it," I pointed out, though probably uselessly. "I just uncovered it."

"In as public and dramatic a way as possible."

"Is that why you're calling? To complain? Because if it is, call tomorrow, okay? Or maybe next month."

"It's not. I'm calling, as I said, for damage control. I want to know what you told the police."

"Everything. Did you expect me not to?"

Blowing right past my question, she said, "Specifically, did you tell them it was I who led you to Chester Hamilton?"

"Specifically," I said, "no, I didn't."

She seemed to breathe a sigh of relief. "May I ask why not?"

"It didn't seem necessary. I don't like to confuse cops with more facts than they need."

"Well, in any case, thank you," she said, making it clear by her tone that she didn't believe my answer. "I appreciate your discretion."

"It's my alter ego," I said. "When I'm not being public and dramatic. Now may I ask you why you care? Even if it got out, the public-relations problem you'd have if the world knew you could find your way to a guy like Chester Hamilton couldn't possibly hold a candle to the problems you have right now."

"No. But it would create problems of its own."

"Your source," I said, guessing. "He doesn't want his cover blown."

"Can you blame him?"

"No," I said. "He could probably get himself killed if something like that got out. Very altruistic of you, very protective. To spend your brief time alone calling me to look after your source."

"Am I hearing sarcasm from you, Mr. Smith?"

"Or is it that you're not through with him? Is it that you need him for something else, this source?"

"In fact I do. He's indispensible to me in other ways. You know, Mr. Smith, I almost regret the relationship you and I have established."

"You mean the fact that we ever met?"

"No, I mean the way we dislike each other. Under other circumstances I think we might have worked well together."

"Maybe. If you ever want to try it out, give me a call."

I hung up and closed my eyes into a drugged sleep with the thought in mind that there was one prospective client I didn't ever have to worry about taking on. In a cushioned, slightly hazy state that I knew was hiding a hell of a headache, I drifted off without being able to think of a single circumstance under which Denise Armstrong would call me.

And she didn't. I called her.

Toward evening, nurses and doctors came and went, orderlies did the same, then the nurses came back with something to stick in my arm and something they told me was dinner. I was hungry, which was good, they said. I was also desperate for a cigarette, which I didn't mention, because they wouldn't have said it was good. They were pretty sour, those nurses. If they'd had a cigarette, they probably wouldn't have given it to me anyway, I mused dreamily as I ate. Not generous. Not like Louie Falco, offering me a Cuban cigar on the Staten Island Ferry, even though the breeze would make it burn faster than a cigar that good should. Not that I was a cigar aficionado. I could take them or leave them, though if Falco were here right now offering me that cigar, I'd take it. I'd—

If Louie Falco were here right now, offering me that cigar. That legit Cuban cigar.

A small electric jolt ran up my spine as the rest of the pieces fell into place.

I swallowed the dregs of my coffee—decaf, this was a hospital—and grabbed for the phone. I called Denise Armstrong's office.

She was there, late in the workday though it was. I asked her. She told me.

I put the phone down, lay back on the pillow. I closed my eyes to shut out the drab brightness of the hospital walls. In my head, the Scriabin études began to play, effortlessly, clearly, their crystal notes and dark chords leading inevitably from one to another, back again, around. Listening, I went with it, felt the rightness of it, the completeness and the truth. I marvelled at how something so obvious and so right could have remained hidden for so long. I ached to get back to my piano, to try it for myself.

I wanted a cigarette more desperately than ever. I wondered if there was any way I could get out of the hospital tonight.

I decided there probably wasn't, so I settled for calling Lydia. She'd called me late in the afternoon, to see how I was. I'd been better and told her so, we'd talked for a while, and that had been pretty much that. She'd offered to come back up here to visit, but she was all the way down in Chinatown, I could hear her mother in the background, probably complaining about me, and I was sleepy anyway. I'd told her not to bother.

"Even though the sight of your gorgeous face would act as a balm on my wounds, a salve to my injuries, a tonic to my system—"

"I don't know that I want to be a tonic to your system," she'd told me. "I'll come collect you in the morning, if they let you go."

"They will," I'd said, even then aching for a smoke. "If they know what's good for them."

"I think they're supposed to worry about what's good for *you*."

"And who worries about what's good for you?"

"My mother. She'd doing it right now. See you in the morning."

That's how that had gone, but that was before the puzzle was complete, all the connections made, the links and variations and reverberations clear to me. I didn't like it, but I believed it, and I called Lydia to talk it over with her.

She wasn't there.

Out, about, somewhere. Probably having a good time. Maybe with DiMaio. Certainly none of my business.

All right, then. Deal with it all in the morning. Nothing to be done now, Smith. Nothing except sleep.

So I tried to sleep.

To my surprise, I succeeded.

twenty-three

In the morning, Lydia came to take me home.

"Not home," I said, as we stepped out onto the sidewalk in the shadow of St. Luke's. The air was clear, the day starting out hot but dry. The perfect blue of the cloudless sky was the color Lydia's eyes would be, if she had blue eyes.

"In your condition, where else do you expect to go?" she asked me.

"I'm in great condition," I told her. "Fit as a fiddle, strong as a bull, happy as a clam—"

"And dumb as a post. You need to go home and rest."

"Will that make me smarter?"

"Unlikely."

"Then let's not bother."

"You know," she said, "I'm getting a little tired of this."

"Of what?"

"This macho, stand-aside-ma'am, Bill-Smith-is-a-tough-guy stuff. This is something new with you, since you started being a construction worker."

I drew a cigarette from my pocket. "I don't—"

"You do so. I had to come running twice in the last few days to save you from some stupid situation you wouldn't have gotten into if you'd made me part of it in the first place!"

She said all that on one breath, eyes flashing. Thrown, I took out a match, put it to my cigarette.

"And don't think I don't know what you're doing with that

cigarette," she snapped. "You're buying time to try to think up some wise-guy answer, some dumb joke that'll make me not mad anymore. Well, forget it."

I took the cigarette from my mouth, squashed the dumb joke I'd been about to make. "You really are mad, aren't you?"

"Mad? Bill, I could have been killed in that trailer last night! And so could you have! Not to mention how much more time you'd have spent in a hospital if I hadn't been there on the ferry."

She stood in the building's massive shadow, feet planted, shoulders squared, jaw set angrily, and she was right. I didn't have any answer for her except the truth. I knew she wouldn't want to hear it, but I said it anyway.

"I didn't want you to get hurt."

At that she turned away. I saw her draw in a breath, shake her head; then she turned back.

"No," she said. "It can't work like that. If I'm your partner, I'm your partner, Bill. If I'm not, then . . . then this isn't working."

"I—"

"The Crowells," she said suddenly. "What you're doing to me, it's exactly what the Crowells did to each other. Each one did all the thinking to make things turn out well for the other one. And look how that ended up. You don't want us to end up like the Crowells, do you?"

"Hmm. Which one do I get to be?"

"Don't be funny!"

"I'm sorry," I said quickly. "I'm . . ." I lifted my hands, dropped them helplessly. We stood facing each other, wordless, as people walked in and out of the building, as traffic passed and stopped.

Then she smiled, an unexpected smile that seemed to bring a blessedly cool mountain breeze to stir the city air between us. "I don't believe I'm standing here on the sidewalk yelling at a sick man," she said. "Let's go. I said what I wanted to say; you know how it has to be."

"I'll try," I said.

She held my eyes a moment longer. Then she stepped into the street and raised an arm to hail a cab.

"Where is it you want to go?" she asked.

"Chuck's."

She looked over her shoulder at me as a cab swerved across three lanes of traffic and bounced to a halt at our feet. "We're going to see Mr. DeMattis?"

The cab stopped, we got in, I gave the cabbie Chuck's East Side address, and I told her why.

As the cab charged downtown and across, and I finished, Lydia turned to peer out the grimy window at the sweaty pedestrians and short-tempered July drivers all around us.

"Are you sure?" she asked me.

"Just about. Maybe Chuck can explain it differently. I want to give him a chance."

He couldn't. I knew he couldn't. It had taken me too long to catch on, but when I finally had, I'd gotten it right.

The cavelike, tomb-still coolness of Chuck's granite lobby drew us in, earned my gratitude after the lurching cab's smell of curry, the hospital's sharp antiseptic scent and never-ending stream of offstage noises, and the melted-asphalt aroma and honking horns in between. Neither Lydia nor I spoke on the swift elevator ride up to Chuck's skybox office.

Chuck was in. He kept us waiting no time at all, not even long enough to sit and leaf through a copy of *Security Industry Report* in the leather seats in his client waiting area.

"What the hell are you doing here?" he asked me as he ushered us through into his glass-walled office. "You should be at home, lying around flat on your back. You feel okay?" he inquired anxiously.

"I feel lousy, but I'll be all right in a few days. I wanted to talk to you, Chuck. This couldn't wait."

"What couldn't wait? On this case?"

I nodded, lit a cigarette—my third since the hospital—and reached for the marble-slab ashtray. Lydia and I sat in leather-and-chrome chairs facing Chuck's mile-wide glass desk. Chuck busied himself at the espresso machine by the stainless-steel sink.

"Lydia? You want coffee? No? Smith, I know you do. Jesus, what about that Dan Crowell, Junior, huh? Some surprise that was."

The machine hissed steam as I answered. "It sure was. Especially to you, I'll bet."

Chuck raised his eyebrows as he brought two thimble-sized espressos over, placed one in its saucer in front of me, sat with the other in the swiveling desk chair.

"Me, you, everybody," he said. "The cops, the old man. Anybody wasn't surprised?"

"I guess not. But he's not what you were looking for, was he?"

"No," Chuck said, sipping his espresso. "I was looking for Louie Falco, behind Joe Romeo. You know that." He shook his head. "I gotta say it again, buddy, I'm sorry about that. I was so sure he was there. I was so damn sure."

"Because you knew he was on that site," I said.

He nodded. "I thought I did. I keep track of that son of a bitch—excuse my French, Lydia—and that's what I heard: Falco has something going on the Armstrong site, connected up there. I was so damn sure it was true."

"So sure," I said, "that you set it up so you could get at him." I drank some espresso, put the cup back on the glass desktop. After two days of hospital decaf, Chuck's rich, bitter espresso tasted like the nectar of the gods.

"I don't get you," Chuck answered, with a look from Lydia to me.

"Yes, you do." Behind Chuck, out over Queens, a silent helicopter drifted through the clear sky like a lazy fly. I said, "Here's how it went. You heard Falco had something going up there. That made your mouth water. Then you met Dan Senior at some dinner, and you took the opportunity to casually ask him how it was going, get to know the guy. Just making small talk, am I right?"

Chuck didn't answer, just took another sip of his espresso.

"So he told you," I went on. "It wasn't going so well. Equipment walking, that sort of thing. You heard that, I bet you could hardly stand it. You gave him your card, even suggested he bring you in to look into it. But he didn't, did he?"

"Not right away," Chuck agreed, putting his cup down, folding his hands across his belly. "Not until later."

"Later," I said. "After Lenny Pelligrini disappeared."

Chuck nodded slowly.

"See, something's been eating at me," I said, "but it took me a little time to figure out what it was. Something I heard in the trailer the other night. But a lot went on in there, and I wasn't in such great shape, so remembering wasn't all that easy. Now I have it."

Chuck just waited. I think he knew that I had it, too.

"It was Pelligrini," I said. "Dan Junior said that after he disappeared, he tried to shake Junior down. That's why Junior killed him. Okay, but then why did he disappear? Once they dug him up, I figured, like everyone else, that he'd been dead since he was first missing. But it turns out he wasn't. So why did he disappear?"

Chuck said nothing. He could have given me some lie, some plausible explanation, something to deflect what I was thinking. What I was thinking couldn't be proved anyway, so he could have tried to make me doubt it. But Chuck had been an honest cop. He didn't even try.

"He disappeared because you told him to, Chuck."

Chuck didn't answer me. He didn't look away. In the carpeted, insulated quiet of his bright, cool office, he waited for me to tell him what all three of us already knew.

"His mother asked you to talk to him," I said, "and you did. But he wasn't interested. Your side of the law's not as attractive to a young kid as the other side, the side where you get to swagger and have pretty girls hanging off your arm. Louie's side. The kid wasn't interested in your advice, but he didn't mind disappearing for a little while, for a few bucks. You paid him, didn't you, Chuck?"

For a few moments, Chuck said nothing. Between Lydia's chair and mine was about six feet of carpeted office; still I could feel her beside me, soft and calm, reassuring. I waited for Chuck to speak.

"Two thousand," he said softly. "Lot of money, but a small price, if it would lead me to Louie."

"You didn't know about the stolen equipment, all the things the kid was involved in then, did you?" I asked.

"No."

"What was the story you gave him, why he should disappear?"

Chuck regarded me steadily. "I told him something was about to go down, something his mother didn't want him caught up in. The money was to carry him until he got something else, once he resurfaced."

"But he wasn't supposed to do that for a while."

"No."

"Because you knew what Crowell's reaction would be, once he was gone."

"How could I know?" Chuck shrugged. "But I hoped. I knew about the kid and Romeo, they had a couple of run-ins."

"About what?"

"Seems the kid was trying to get Romeo to take him on, use him in whatever he had going, but Romeo wasn't interested."

"Same as the kid wanted from Falco."

"Yeah. Yeah, the same." Chuck sighed with a gravelly sound. "Anyway, I knew the Crowells were looking at Romeo—or the old man was; turns out Junior wasn't looking at anything but how to save his own ass. But I figured, the kid disappears, Crowell's got my card in his pocket, just maybe it's the last straw. It worked, too," he added, a soft, sad note in his voice. "Kid disappeared, Crowell's on the phone to me next day."

"It worked, except the kid tried to get something out of it besides your two thousand bucks."

Chuck kept his eyes on me for a few moments longer. Then he pushed his chair back, stood. He turned to the window, put his hands in his pockets and watched a tug shoulder its way upriver.

"That's what must've happened," he finally said. "The kid must've figured he lucked out, that I took him out of it just before his golden goose got its head whacked off, without me knowing it was him. I was making that crap up, about something going down. I didn't know. . . . But he couldn't resist trying to put the squeeze on Dan Junior for a few more bucks, before things blew up."

"So Junior killed him," I said. Chuck's broad back was a dark interruption of the bright and peaceful scene behind the glass. "And then Senior brought you in. Brought us in. And so Junior had Hamilton kill Romeo, to make us go away. And then Junior killed Hamilton."

Chuck nodded, said, "Yeah," so softly I almost couldn't hear him.

"Because of how badly you wanted Louie Falco."

Chuck still didn't turn. "Because of how bad I wanted Louie," he said. "Elena Pelligrini. She asked me to help." He shook his head. "That kid," he said. "So stupid. It would've happened like this, sooner or later." Chuck's voice was asking me for something, but I didn't have what he wanted.

"Maybe," I said. "Maybe."

Chuck went on as if he hadn't heard me. "Three men dead," he said. "One lucky he's not. Because of how bad I wanted Louie." He stared in silence out the window, then said, his voice low, "And I wasn't even right. The word I had was bad. That S.O.B. hasn't got his filthy fingers in anything going on on that site. Not a goddamned thing."

I lit another cigarette, inhaled deeply. The brightness of the window was making my head ache, or maybe it wasn't that. The cigarette helped some. I spoke again.

"Yes, he does, Chuck."

Chuck looked over his shoulder at me. "What are you talking about?"

I knocked some ash from my cigarette. "He's the money," I said. "He's what's carrying Denise Armstrong from one bank loan to the next."

Chuck turned to face me. "What?" The single word was almost lost.

"I spoke to her. The rate's high, but not much higher than your Visa card. She thinks she can handle it, because it won't be for long. I think she's crazy. I told her that. She asked me where I thought a black woman should have gone for an interim construction loan when the banks have turned her down." I took in some more smoke, rubbed at my temple to ease the dull pain there. "I asked if she knew what kind of money she was laundering, doing this."

"What'd she say?"

"As far as she's concerned, she's always laundering some white man's blood money. She doesn't see much difference, borrowing from Louie Falco or from Citibank."

One side of Chuck's mouth rose in a small, joyless smile. "She couldn't come up with a black loan shark?"

"She tried. Falco's rates were better."

"Jesus," Chuck said. "Jesus fucking goddamned Christ." He ran his hand over the smooth skin of his head. "Don't she know what that can turn into? Bloodsucker like Falco? First payment she misses, rates'll double, next thing she knows it'll take everything she's got just to cover the vig. Jesus—"

"This is a little different," I told him. "They have lawyers. They have a contract."

"What are you talking about, lawyers? For a loan-shark deal?"

"Not a loan-shark deal," I said. "He's an investor."

"Bullshit." Automatically Chuck glanced at Lydia, but she didn't react and he didn't apologize.

"He's getting out of the life," I said, watched Chuck's face. "He's made his pile the dirty way, now he's going legit. Import-export, investing, whatever. He told me that."

Chuck stared at me. "You talked to Louie?"

"My case," I said.

He shook his head slowly, came back to his chair and sat. "That legit stuff is a pile of crap," he said.

"He said you knew it, too," I answered. "That he was going straight."

"Straight." Chuck curled his lip as though there was a bad smell in the air.

"That's why you were so hot to get him now," I said. "When you heard he had something going on the Armstrong site. You were afraid he'd cover his tracks, wash the money, get so squeaky-clean no one would ever be able to get to him again. That's why you started this whole thing."

Chuck's hands rested on his desktop, palms down, fingers spread. He looked up from them, said to me, "I thought it was all Louie. All that shit going on up there, I thought it was Louie. I didn't know about Junior. But it was my last chance. I had to nail him now, before it was too late."

I said, "It's already too late."

"It was my chance," he said.

"You passed up your chances, Chuck. Years ago. When you looked the other way, when you walked away from it. When you could have brought him in, and you didn't. Setting up the Pelligrini kid, and me, and the Crowells, to do it for you now—it doesn't work like that."

I stood, slowly. My head was pounding. Everything I'd said was true; we all knew it. But nothing Chuck had done was illegal, and nothing Chuck had done could be proved.

Chuck and I found each other's eyes, he at his grand glass desk in his high-rent office, New York spread out behind him, me on my way downtown to my walk-up over Shorty's, to my open windows and my piano.

I thought about a darkened living room, about Elena Pelligrini, who'd lost her son, who didn't blame Chuck, who was grateful that he had tried to help and was waiting for his help now, to bring Louie Falco down.

I could see in Chuck's eyes that he was thinking about her too.

Chuck said nothing. In the brightness of the July morning light streaming into the office, I found I had to turn away from what I saw in his face.

Lydia stood also, with a long look at Chuck. She turned to leave with me. She had said nothing the whole time we'd been here. She didn't speak now, either, just walked beside me past the plaques and framed photos in the waiting area and out through the big glass entry door; but the soft, cool touch of her hand on mine told me everything I needed to know.

twenty-four

It was another week before I was up near the Armstrong site again. The late afternoon was hot and sticky, the air over New York cloudless but layered with haze. I stood outside the fence, watched the boom of the crane move majestically against the sky. I heard the whine of saw blades on steel, the thud of hammers, the shouts of men.

Crews had begun going back to work the day before. The bonding company that covered the Crowells was acting as general contractor. The weeklong shutdown had been costly, and getting back up to speed would be, too, but Denise Armstrong had held a press conference the day after the story hit the papers and the eleven o'clock news. She announced that this building, which was the start of a neighborhood renewal long overdue, would not be stopped, that construction would shortly resume, following the original, high-quality details laid out in the documents. She assured the press and the public that any shoddy construction already in place would be ripped out and rebuilt, and any residue of bad feeling or mistrust would be overcome by the forward motion and energy generated by the continuing work.

Privately I gave odds of two to one against brickwork coming out—just too damn expensive, and since it had been caught before it went above six stories, it might still be low enough, as Lozano had said, not to matter—but I gave fifty-fifty on the drywall, the plumbing connections. Lawsuits were multiplying like rabbits, and the criminal investigations were in full force, but the site seemed normal as I stood and watched the work. The controlled chaos of construction appeared, as always, both balletlike and random, the movement of men and materials at once self-explanatory and inexplicable.

I had my eyes focused on the brickwork on the north side, trying to make out progress through the scaffold netting, when a voice beside me spoke.

"Looks okay to you?"

"Looks great." I turned to DiMaio, standing in a sweat-soaked T-shirt, mason's bag in one hand, hard hat in the other, grin beneath his sandy mustache. "Miss me?" I asked.

"Oh, yeah," he said. "Every time I look over where Ray's working and he's half a course ahead of me instead of two courses behind, I think how much I miss you."

"Yeah, but does he do good work?"

"As good as you, Smith, I guarantee it." He wiped beads of sweat from his forehead with the back of his hand. "Didn't someone say something about a beer?"

"I thought I heard that, too," I agreed, and we headed for the Liffy, on Ninety-sixth Street, where DiMaio liked to drink.

"How's Phillips?" I asked as we walked.

"Better." DiMaio nodded. "He can talk pretty good now, and he got out of bed yesterday. They're thinking he may be all right."

"That's good, Mike. Does he remember what happened?"

"Nah. They say he still might, but maybe not. He knows it was you saved his ass, though, because I told him. He says thanks."

We waited for the light to change, felt heat radiate up from concrete and asphalt. "So Lydia's your partner, huh?" DiMaio said as a cab pulled up, disgorged three passengers onto the sidewalk, then sped away looking for the next buck to make.

"Sort of," I said, starting forward again. "I'm sorry we couldn't tell you that from the beginning."

"Shit, why should you? You didn't know me from a hole in

the ground." His grin widened. "Must've been tough for you when I took her out."

I shrugged. "Not my business."

"Oh, yeah, right."

"No, it's true."

He gave me a sharp look. "What is it, you guys keeping it a secret or something?"

"A secret? You mean me and Lydia?" I shook my head. "No, you're wrong. It's not like that."

"What's not like what? I'm not supposed to know? Christ, Smith, I'm the guy who saved both your butts the other day. Give me a break."

"No, it's just there's nothing going on between me and Lydia."

DiMaio snorted. "Yeah, okay, have it your way. Just, if a girl went charging into a roomful of guns to save *my* ass, I'd think maybe . . . But hell, what do I know?"

We reached Ninety-sixth Street, turned up the block. The steamy afternoon seemed to have gotten hotter, but the cars' honking horns were sounding more harmonious notes than I'd ever heard them play before, and the fume-laden air suddenly smelled sweet to me.

"Anyway," DiMaio was saying, "that's your problem. All's I want is a beer. Christ, I'm melting here. You know how when you start a job you can go inside the building and it's so damn cold in there it cools you down, even in shit like this? I don't know, maybe you didn't do enough of this kind of work to know what I'm talking about."

"No," I said. "I do."

He nodded, went on. "And then one day, the building's halfway built and you try that and it don't work anymore. Gotta be something to do with the mass of the concrete or something, I don't know. Reg could explain it. Anyway, that's what it's like up there now. Since we come back on the job yesterday, you go inside, it's just kind of warm, you know? Normal. Like anyplace else."

He pulled open the door to the Liffy Tavern. As the cool air and the quiet talk of working men at the end of the day rolled out to greet us, I thought about the Armstrong building, the great steel skeleton and thick concrete slabs, the miles of wire and pipe and the complicated brick skin. I thought about the couple of days' worth of bricks on the sixth floor, north side, that I'd put there, that would be part of this building now as long as the building stood.

As he moved through the room, I heard Mike DiMaio's voice raised in greeting to the men he knew, from this job, from ones before. I let the door to the tavern close behind me and headed with him for the bar, to sit and have a beer at the end of the working day.

In all of New York's Chinatown, there is no one like P.I. Lydia Chin, who has a nose for trouble, a disapproving Chinese mother, and a partner named Bill Smith who's been living above a bar for sixteen years.

Hired to find some precious stolen porcelain, Lydia follows a trail of clues from highbrow art dealers into a world of Chinese gangs. Suddenly, this case has become as complex as her community itself—and as deadly as a killer on the loose...

China Trade

S. J. Rozan